STARVE

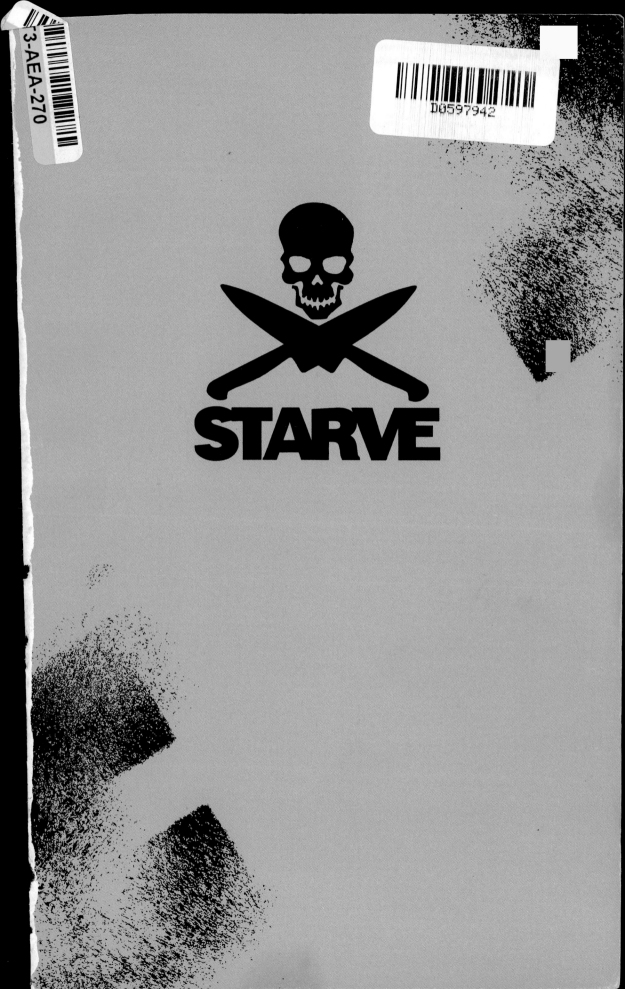

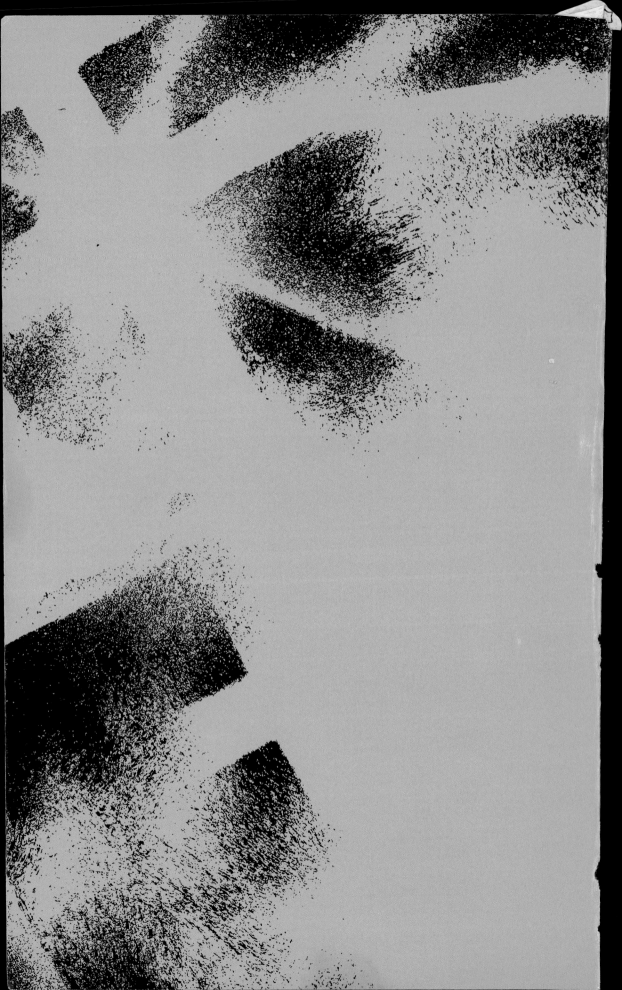

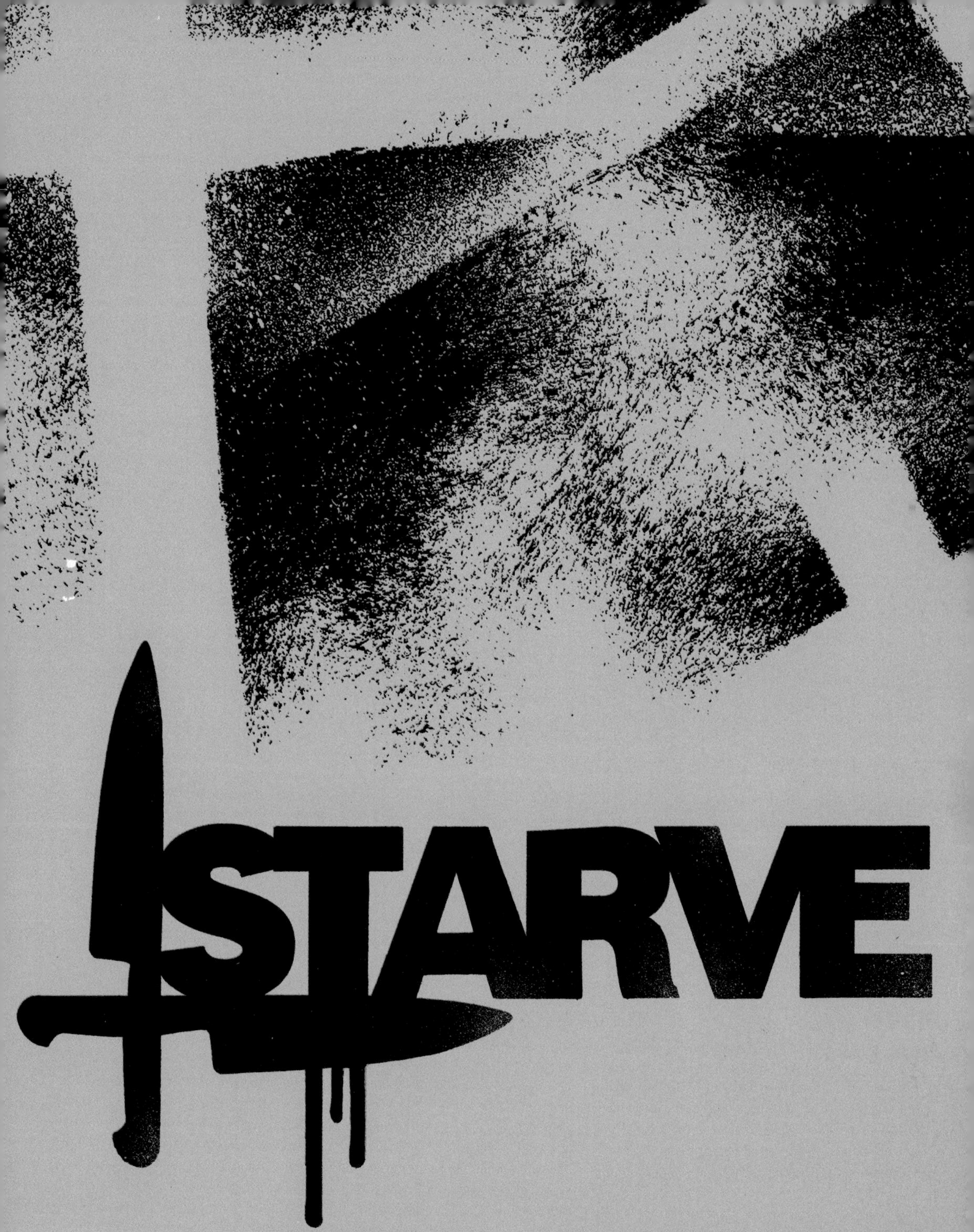

STARVE

CREATED BY BRIAN WOOD, DANIJEL ZEZELJ, AND DAVE STEWART

LETTERING BY STEVE WANDS

DESIGN BY BRENNAN THOME

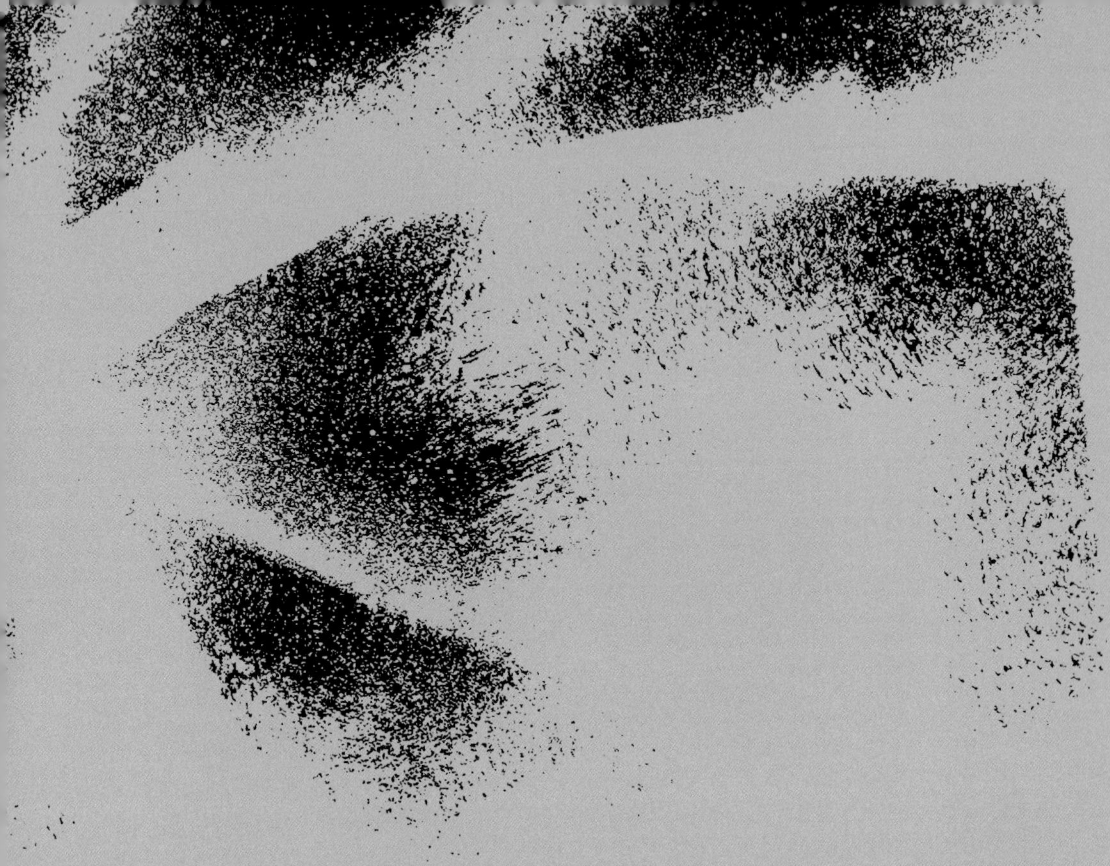

STARVE, VOL 2. First Printing. August 2016. Published by Image Comics, Inc. Office of publication: 2001 Center Street, 6th Floor, Berkeley, CA 94704. Copyright © 2016 Brian Wood, Danijel Zezelj, and Dave Stewart. All rights reserved. Originally published in single magazine form as STARVE #6-10. STARVE™ (including all prominent characters featured herein), its logo and all character likenesses are trademarks of Brian Wood, Danijel Zezelj, and Dave Stewart, unless otherwise noted. Image Comics® and its logos are registered trademarks of Image Comics, Inc. No part of this publication may be reproduced or transmitted, in any form or by any means (except for short excerpts for review purposes) without the express written permission of Image Comics, Inc. All names, characters, events and locales in this publication are entirely fictional. Any resemblance to actual persons (living or dead), events or places, without satiric intent, is coincidental. PRINTED IN THE U.S.A. For information regarding the CPSIA on this printed material call: 203-595-3636 and provide reference # RICH – 696512. ISBN: 978-1-63215-832-1. For international rights, contact: foreignlicensing@imagecomics.com.

TABLE OF CONTENTS

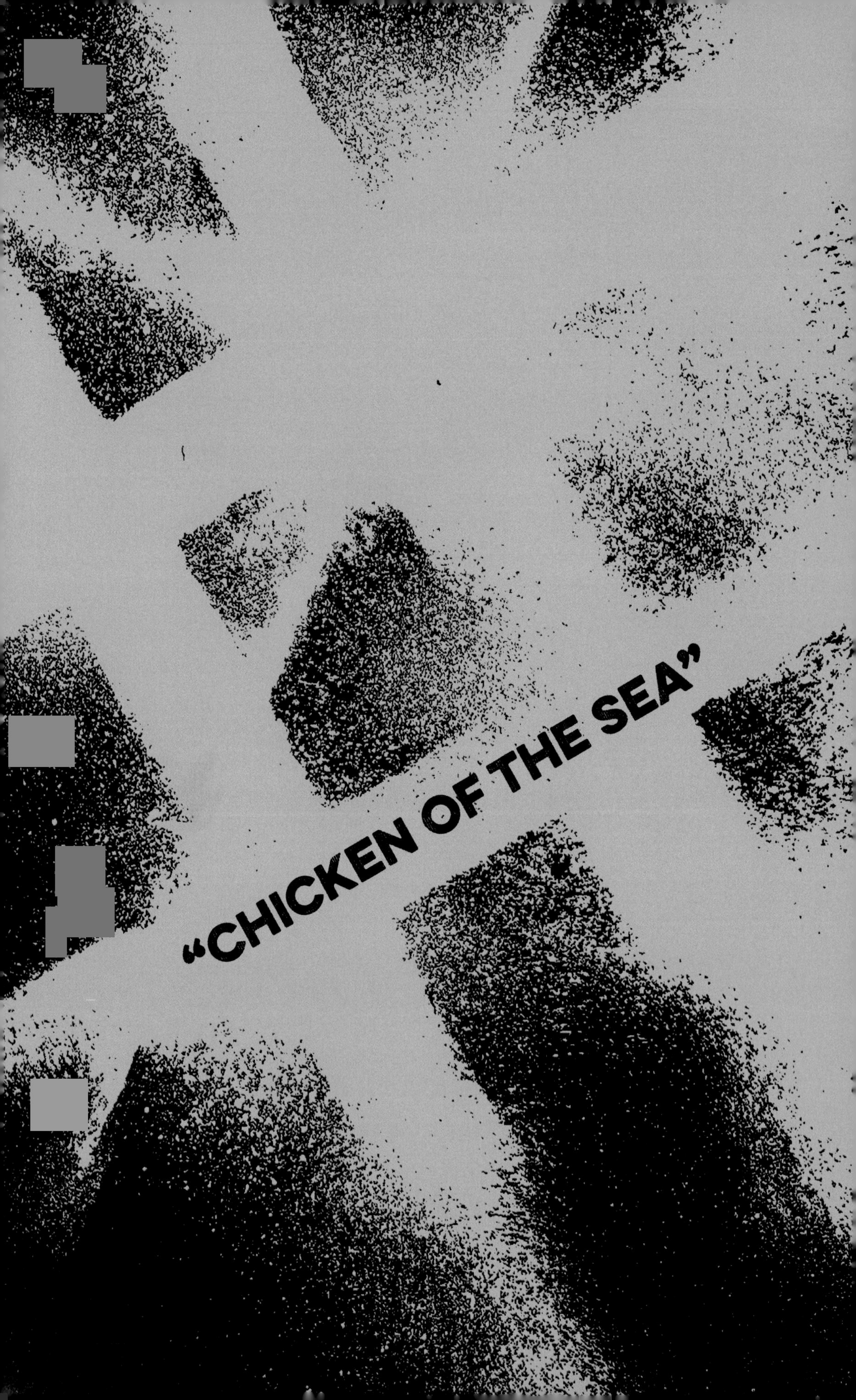
"CHICKEN OF THE SEA"

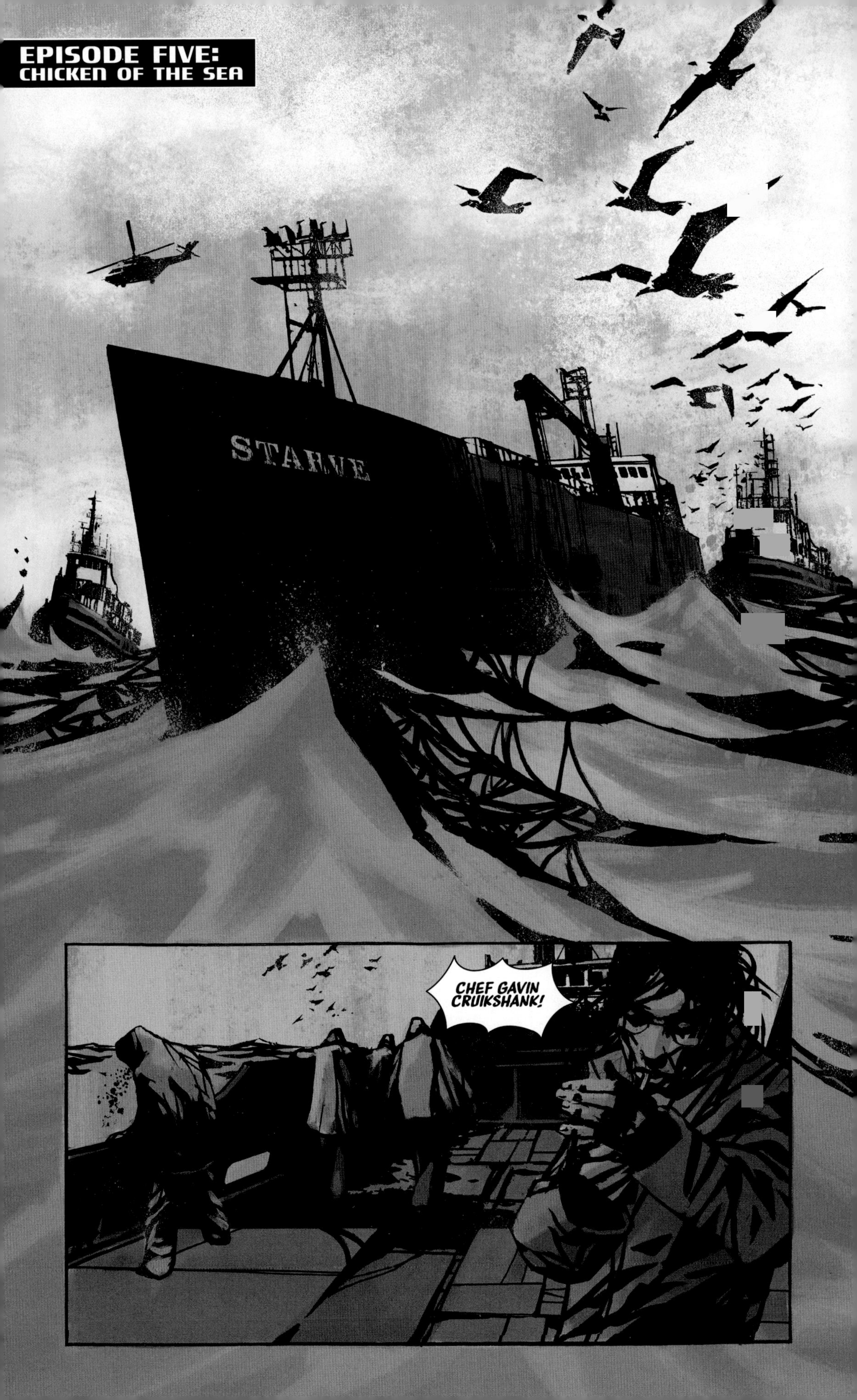
EPISODE FIVE:
CHICKEN OF THE SEA
STARVE
CHEF GAVIN CRUIKSHANK!

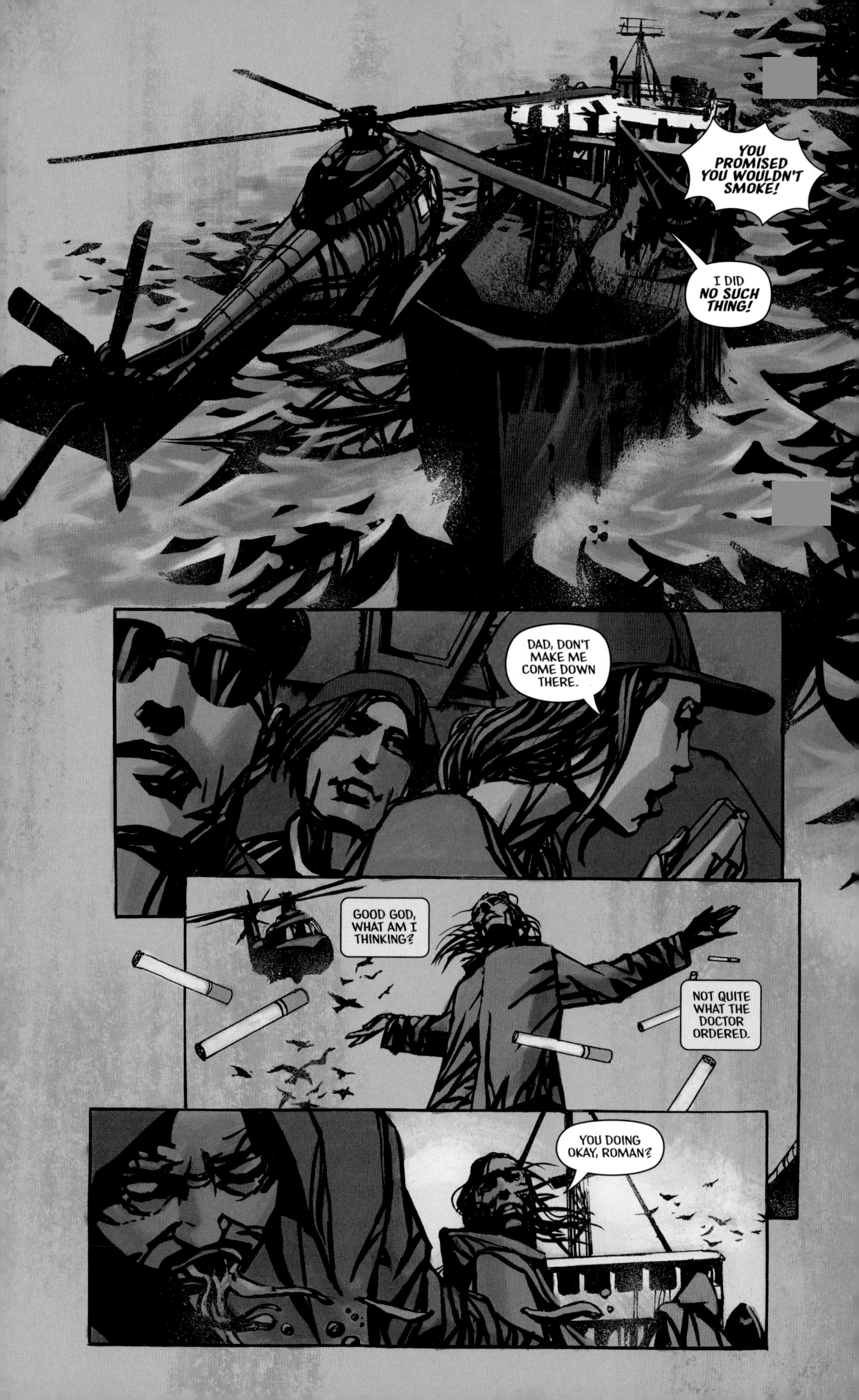
YOU PROMISED YOU WOULDN'T SMOKE!
I DID NO SUCH THING!
DAD, DON'T MAKE ME COME DOWN THERE.
GOOD GOD, WHAT AM I THINKING?
NOT QUITE WHAT THE DOCTOR ORDERED.
YOU DOING OKAY, ROMAN?

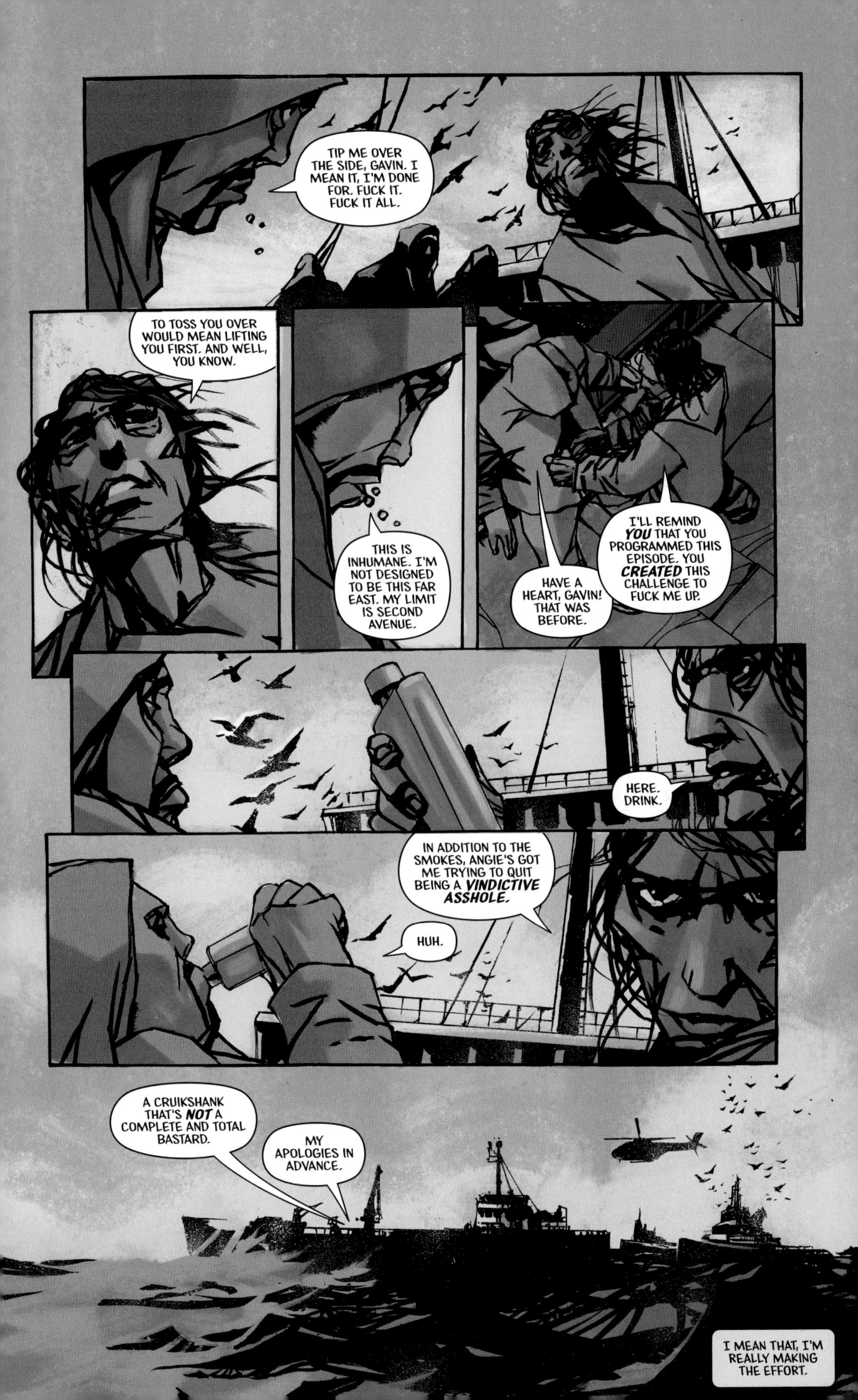
TIP ME OVER THE SIDE, GAVIN. I MEAN IT, I'M DONE FOR. FUCK IT. FUCK IT ALL.
TO TOSS YOU OVER WOULD MEAN LIFTING YOU FIRST. AND WELL, YOU KNOW.
THIS IS INHUMANE. I'M NOT DESIGNED TO BE THIS FAR EAST. MY LIMIT IS SECOND AVENUE.
I'LL REMIND *YOU* THAT YOU PROGRAMMED THIS EPISODE. YOU *CREATED* THIS CHALLENGE TO FUCK ME UP.
HAVE A HEART, GAVIN! THAT WAS BEFORE.
HERE. DRINK.
IN ADDITION TO THE SMOKES, ANGIE'S GOT ME TRYING TO QUIT BEING A *VINDICTIVE ASSHOLE.*
HUH.
A CRUIKSHANK THAT'S *NOT* A COMPLETE AND TOTAL BASTARD.
MY APOLOGIES IN ADVANCE.
I MEAN THAT, I'M REALLY MAKING THE EFFORT.

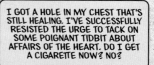
I GOT A HOLE IN MY CHEST THAT'S STILL HEALING. I'VE SUCCESSFULLY RESISTED THE URGE TO TACK ON SOME POIGNANT TIDBIT ABOUT AFFAIRS OF THE HEART. DO I GET A CIGARETTE NOW? NO?

THIS CHALLENGE IS A GOOD ONE. I SUSPECT IT WAS DESIGNED TO GIVE THESE OLD BONES A SHOCK I COULDN'T HANDLE, BUT I LOVE BEING OUT ON THE WATER, AND *RED CRAB*, FOR SOME REASON, SEEM TO BE SUFFERING OUR ENVIRONMENTAL SINS JUST FINE.

GORGEOUS THINGS, THE RED CRAB. WE'LL CATCH 'EM, STASH 'EM, AND COOK THEM FOR OUR ADORING AUDIENCE HERE AND AT HOME.

I'M HAVING A PRETTY DECENT DAY.

ALMOST MAKES ME FORGET ABOUT GREER.

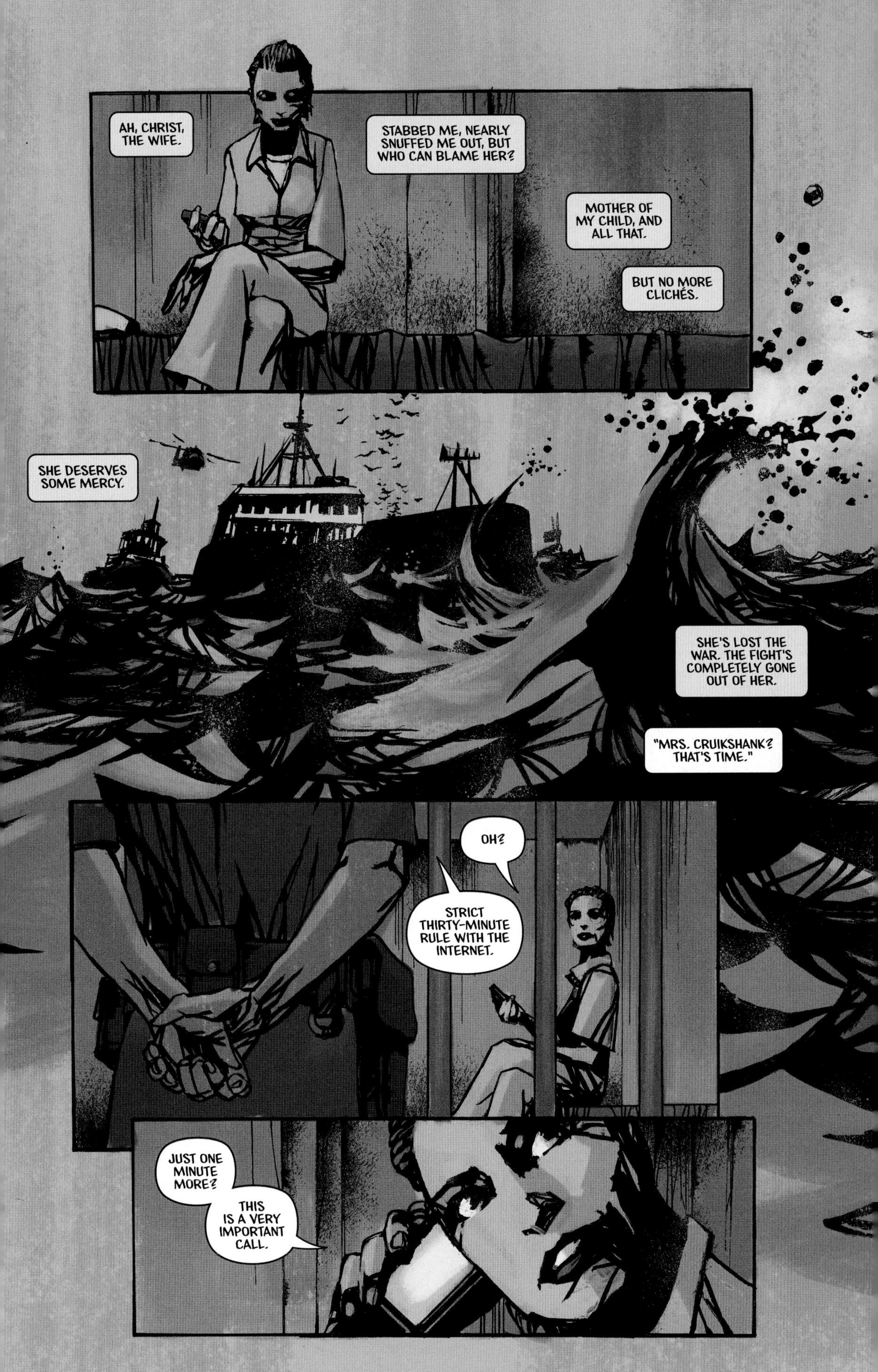
AH, CHRIST, THE WIFE.
STABBED ME, NEARLY SNUFFED ME OUT, BUT WHO CAN BLAME HER?
MOTHER OF MY CHILD, AND ALL THAT.
BUT NO MORE CLICHÉS.
SHE DESERVES SOME MERCY.
SHE'S LOST THE WAR. THE FIGHT'S COMPLETELY GONE OUT OF HER.
"MRS. CRUIKSHANK? THAT'S TIME."
OH?
STRICT THIRTY-MINUTE RULE WITH THE INTERNET.
JUST ONE MINUTE MORE?
THIS IS A VERY IMPORTANT CALL.

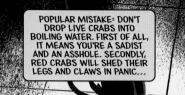

POPULAR MISTAKE: DON'T DROP LIVE CRABS INTO BOILING WATER. FIRST OF ALL, IT MEANS YOU'RE A SADIST AND AN ASSHOLE. SECONDLY, RED CRABS WILL SHED THEIR LEGS AND CLAWS IN PANIC...

...THE PANIC AT BEING BOILED ALIVE. BECAUSE YOU'RE A *SADIST* AND AN *ASSHOLE*.

THERE'S A SPOT, ON THE BOTTOM NEAR THE BACK, UNDER A FLAP OF FLESH.

KRAK

DEAD, IMMEDIATE AND PAINLESS. I WON'T SAY THE POOR FUCKERS DIDN'T HAVE A RATHER UNPLEASANT LAST COUPLE HOURS, BUT THEN AGAIN, NEITHER DID I.

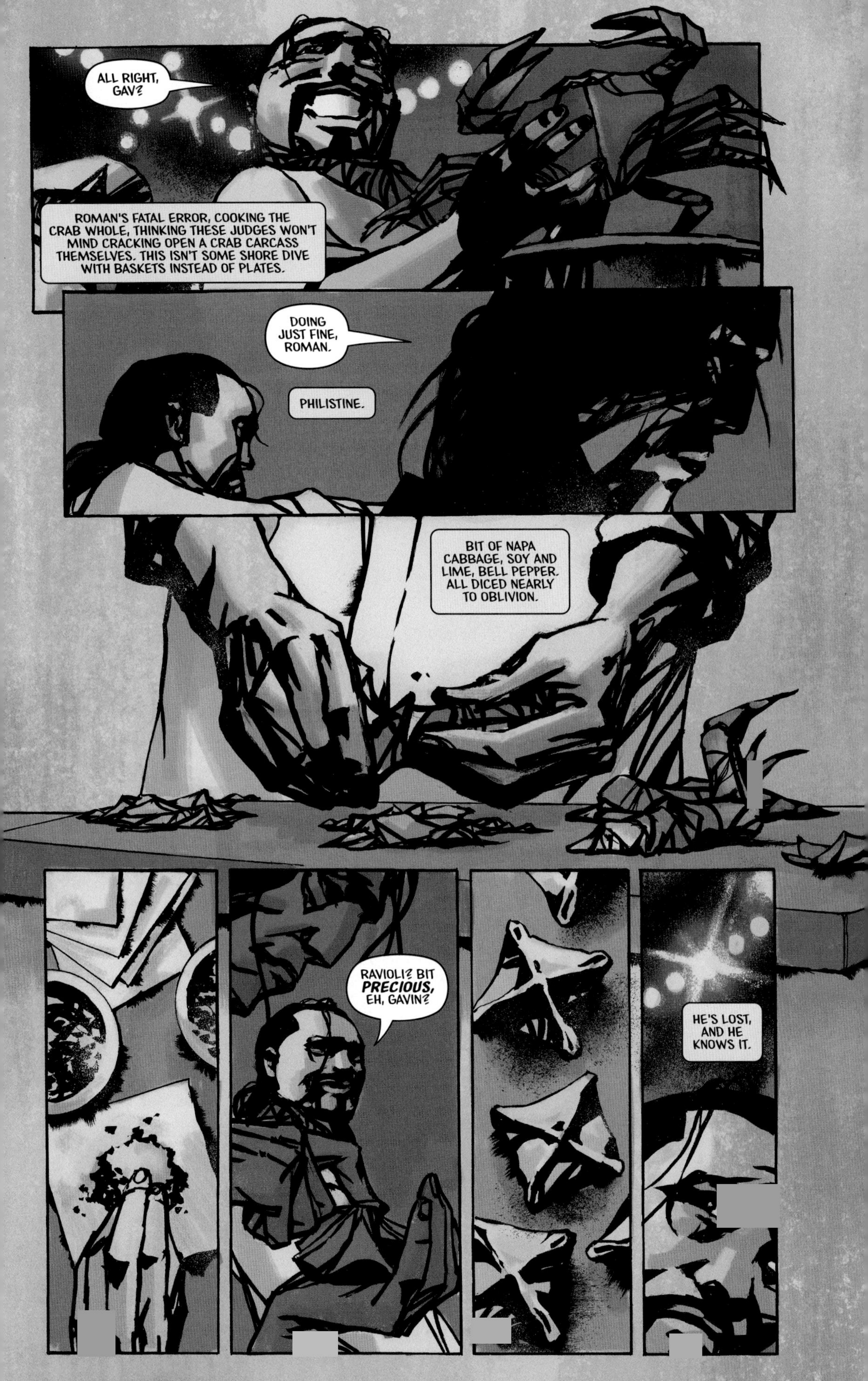
ALL RIGHT, GAV?
ROMAN'S FATAL ERROR, COOKING THE CRAB WHOLE, THINKING THESE JUDGES WON'T MIND CRACKING OPEN A CRAB CARCASS THEMSELVES. THIS ISN'T SOME SHORE DIVE WITH BASKETS INSTEAD OF PLATES.
DOING JUST FINE, ROMAN.
PHILISTINE.
BIT OF NAPA CABBAGE, SOY AND LIME, BELL PEPPER. ALL DICED NEARLY TO OBLIVION.
RAVIOLI? BIT *PRECIOUS,* EH, GAVIN?
HE'S LOST, AND HE KNOWS IT.

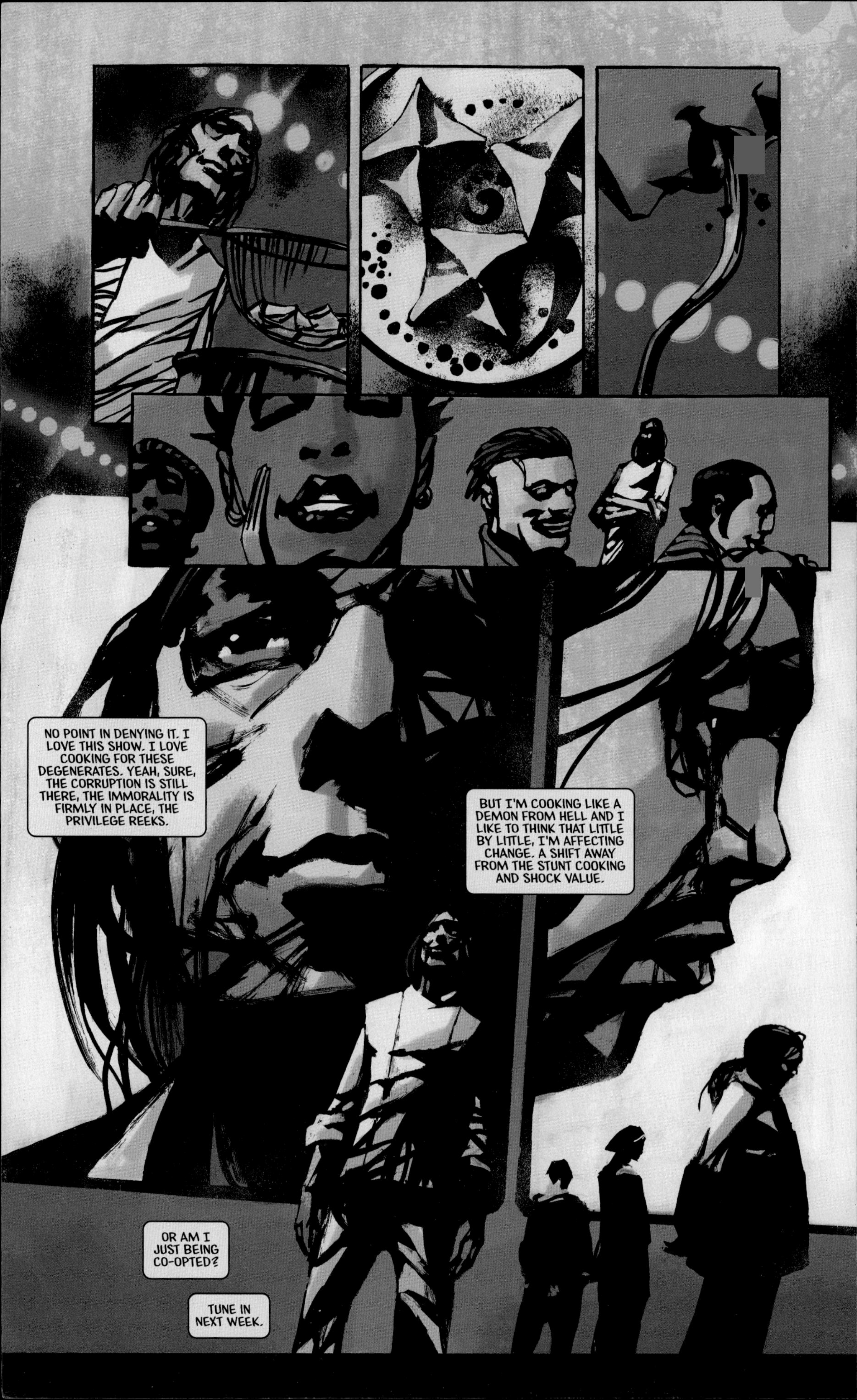
NO POINT IN DENYING IT. I LOVE THIS SHOW. I LOVE COOKING FOR THESE DEGENERATES. YEAH, SURE, THE CORRUPTION IS STILL THERE, THE IMMORALITY IS FIRMLY IN PLACE, THE PRIVILEGE REEKS.
BUT I'M COOKING LIKE A DEMON FROM HELL AND I LIKE TO THINK THAT LITTLE BY LITTLE, I'M AFFECTING CHANGE. A SHIFT AWAY FROM THE STUNT COOKING AND SHOCK VALUE.
OR AM I JUST BEING CO-OPTED?
TUNE IN NEXT WEEK.

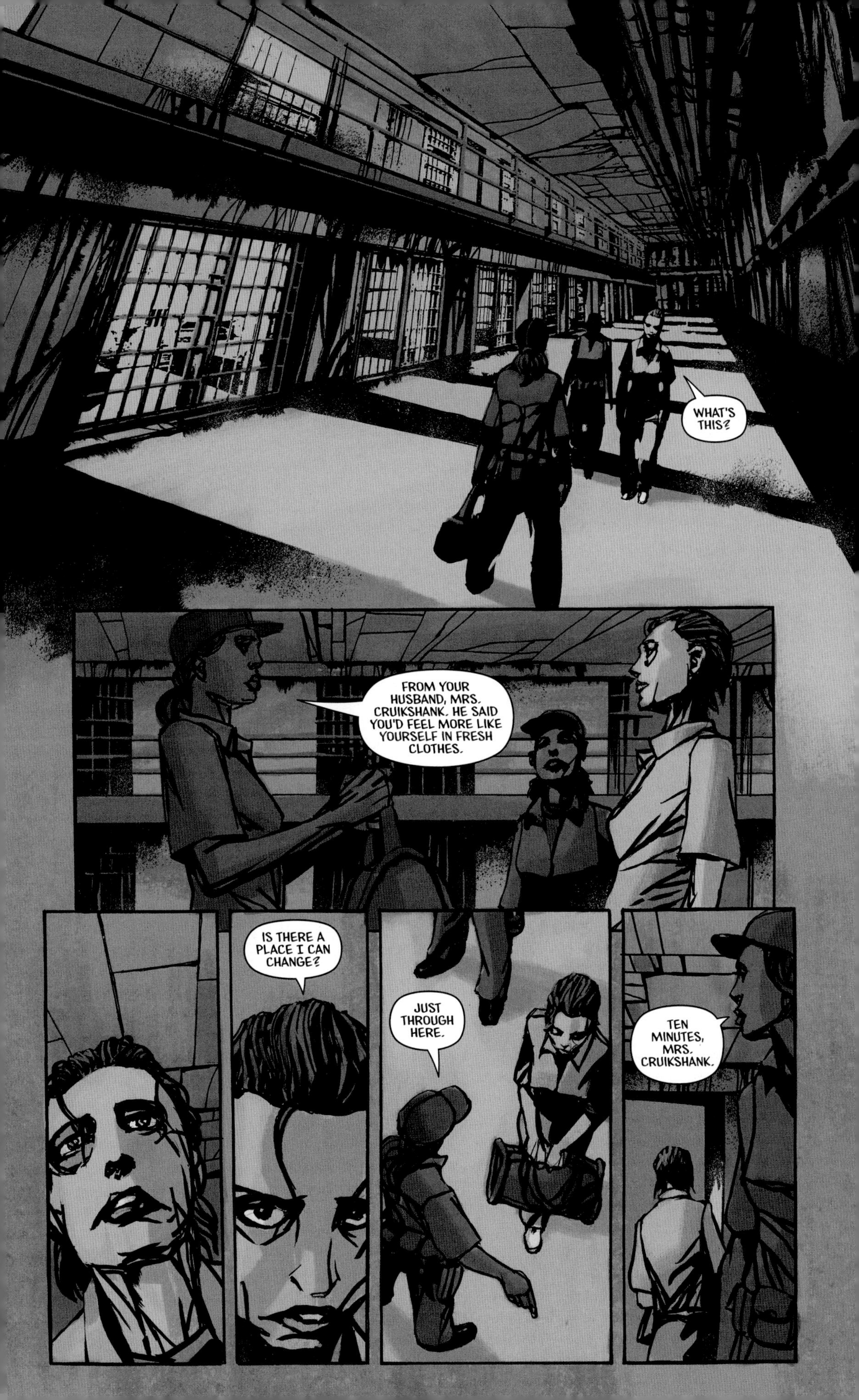
WHAT'S THIS?
FROM YOUR HUSBAND, MRS. CRUIKSHANK. HE SAID YOU'D FEEL MORE LIKE YOURSELF IN FRESH CLOTHES.
IS THERE A PLACE I CAN CHANGE?
JUST THROUGH HERE.
TEN MINUTES, MRS. CRUIKSHANK.

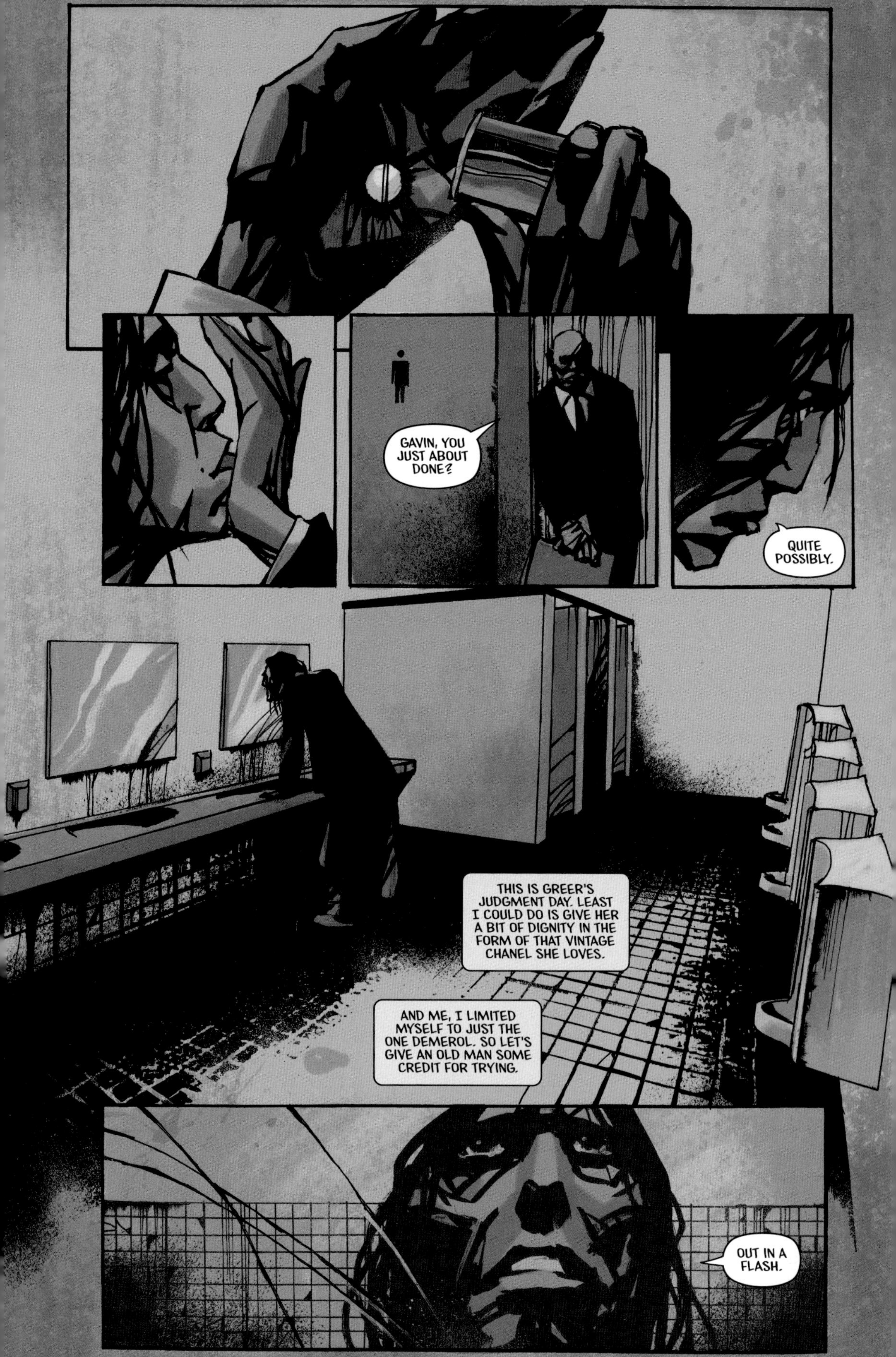
GAVIN, YOU JUST ABOUT DONE?
QUITE POSSIBLY.
THIS IS GREER'S JUDGMENT DAY. LEAST I COULD DO IS GIVE HER A BIT OF DIGNITY IN THE FORM OF THAT VINTAGE CHANEL SHE LOVES.
AND ME, I LIMITED MYSELF TO JUST THE ONE DEMEROL. SO LET'S GIVE AN OLD MAN SOME CREDIT FOR TRYING.
OUT IN A FLASH.

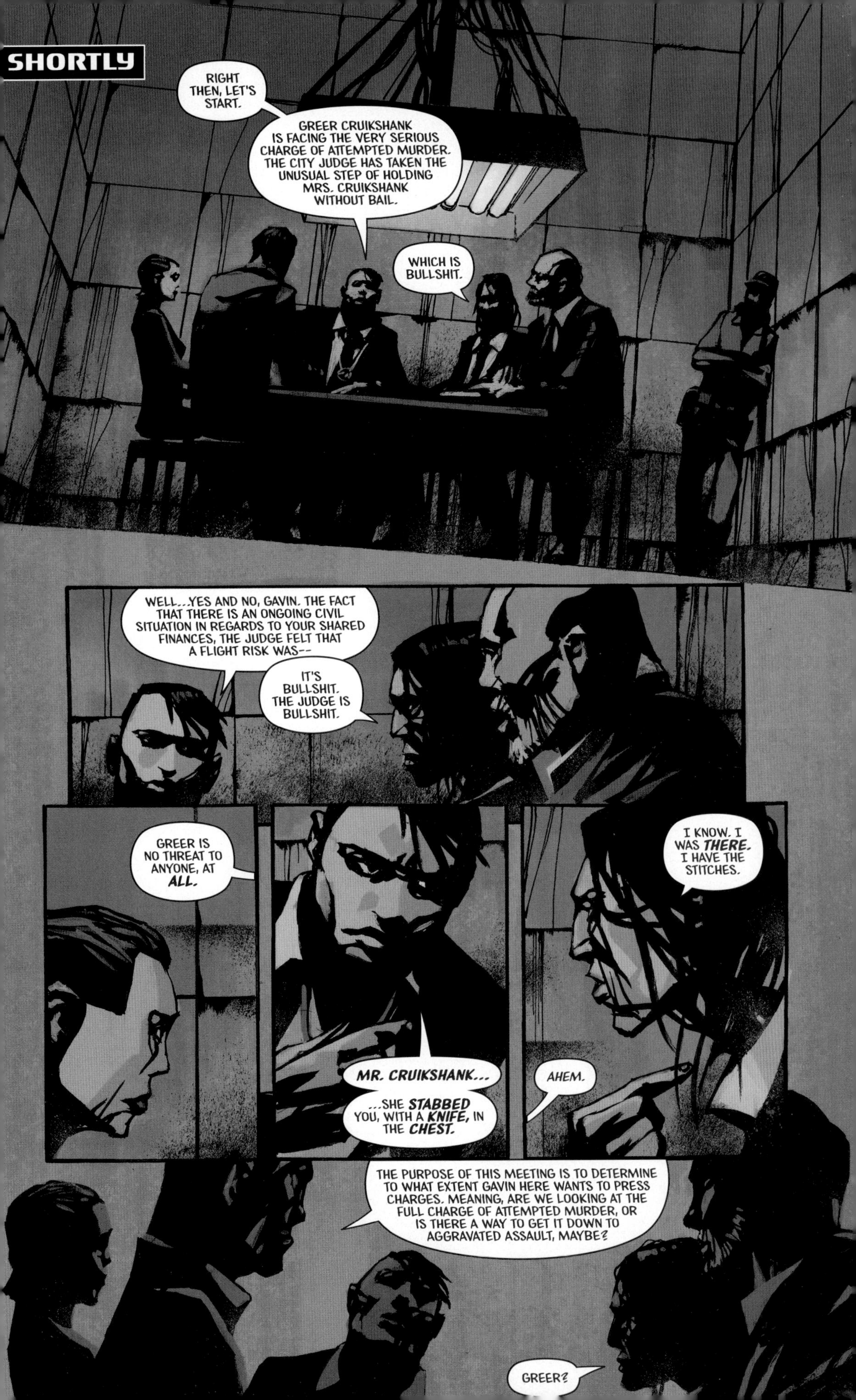
SHORTLY
RIGHT THEN, LET'S START.
GREER CRUIKSHANK IS FACING THE VERY SERIOUS CHARGE OF ATTEMPTED MURDER. THE CITY JUDGE HAS TAKEN THE UNUSUAL STEP OF HOLDING MRS. CRUIKSHANK WITHOUT BAIL.
WHICH IS BULLSHIT.
WELL...YES AND NO, GAVIN. THE FACT THAT THERE IS AN ONGOING CIVIL SITUATION IN REGARDS TO YOUR SHARED FINANCES, THE JUDGE FELT THAT A FLIGHT RISK WAS--
IT'S BULLSHIT. THE JUDGE IS BULLSHIT.
GREER IS NO THREAT TO ANYONE, AT ALL.
MR. CRUIKSHANK...
...SHE STABBED YOU, WITH A KNIFE, IN THE CHEST.
I KNOW. I WAS THERE. I HAVE THE STITCHES.
AHEM.
THE PURPOSE OF THIS MEETING IS TO DETERMINE TO WHAT EXTENT GAVIN HERE WANTS TO PRESS CHARGES. MEANING, ARE WE LOOKING AT THE FULL CHARGE OF ATTEMPTED MURDER, OR IS THERE A WAY TO GET IT DOWN TO AGGRAVATED ASSAULT, MAYBE?
GREER?

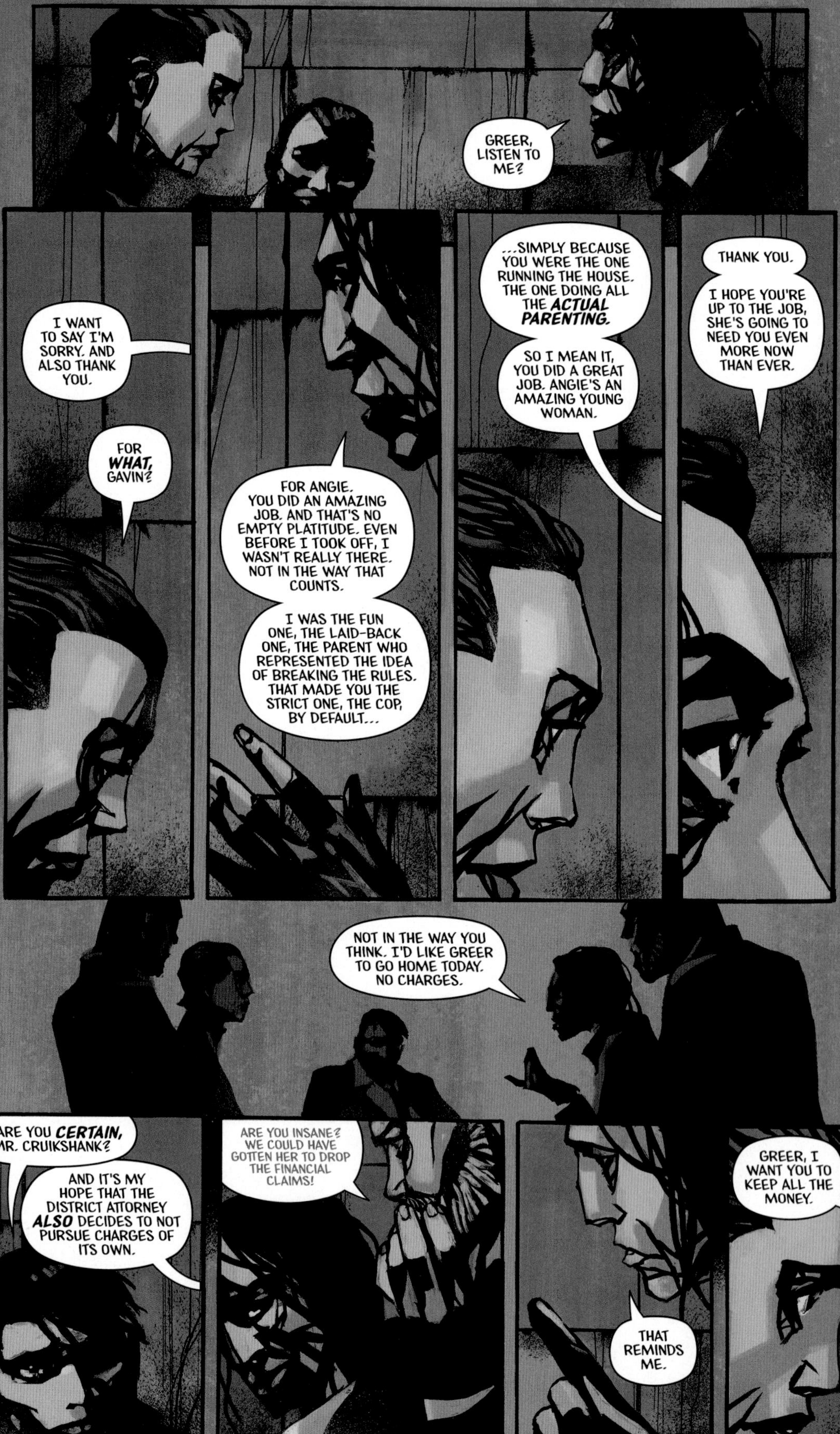
GREER, LISTEN TO ME?
I WANT TO SAY I'M SORRY. AND ALSO THANK YOU.
FOR WHAT, GAVIN?
FOR ANGIE. YOU DID AN AMAZING JOB. AND THAT'S NO EMPTY PLATITUDE. EVEN BEFORE I TOOK OFF, I WASN'T REALLY THERE. NOT IN THE WAY THAT COUNTS.
I WAS THE FUN ONE, THE LAID-BACK ONE, THE PARENT WHO REPRESENTED THE IDEA OF BREAKING THE RULES. THAT MADE YOU THE STRICT ONE, THE COP, BY DEFAULT...
...SIMPLY BECAUSE YOU WERE THE ONE RUNNING THE HOUSE. THE ONE DOING ALL THE ACTUAL PARENTING.
SO I MEAN IT, YOU DID A GREAT JOB. ANGIE'S AN AMAZING YOUNG WOMAN.
THANK YOU.
I HOPE YOU'RE UP TO THE JOB, SHE'S GOING TO NEED YOU EVEN MORE NOW THAN EVER.
NOT IN THE WAY YOU THINK. I'D LIKE GREER TO GO HOME TODAY. NO CHARGES.
...ARE YOU CERTAIN, MR. CRUIKSHANK?
AND IT'S MY HOPE THAT THE DISTRICT ATTORNEY ALSO DECIDES TO NOT PURSUE CHARGES OF ITS OWN.
ARE YOU INSANE? WE COULD HAVE GOTTEN HER TO DROP THE FINANCIAL CLAIMS!
THAT REMINDS ME.
GREER, I WANT YOU TO KEEP ALL THE MONEY.

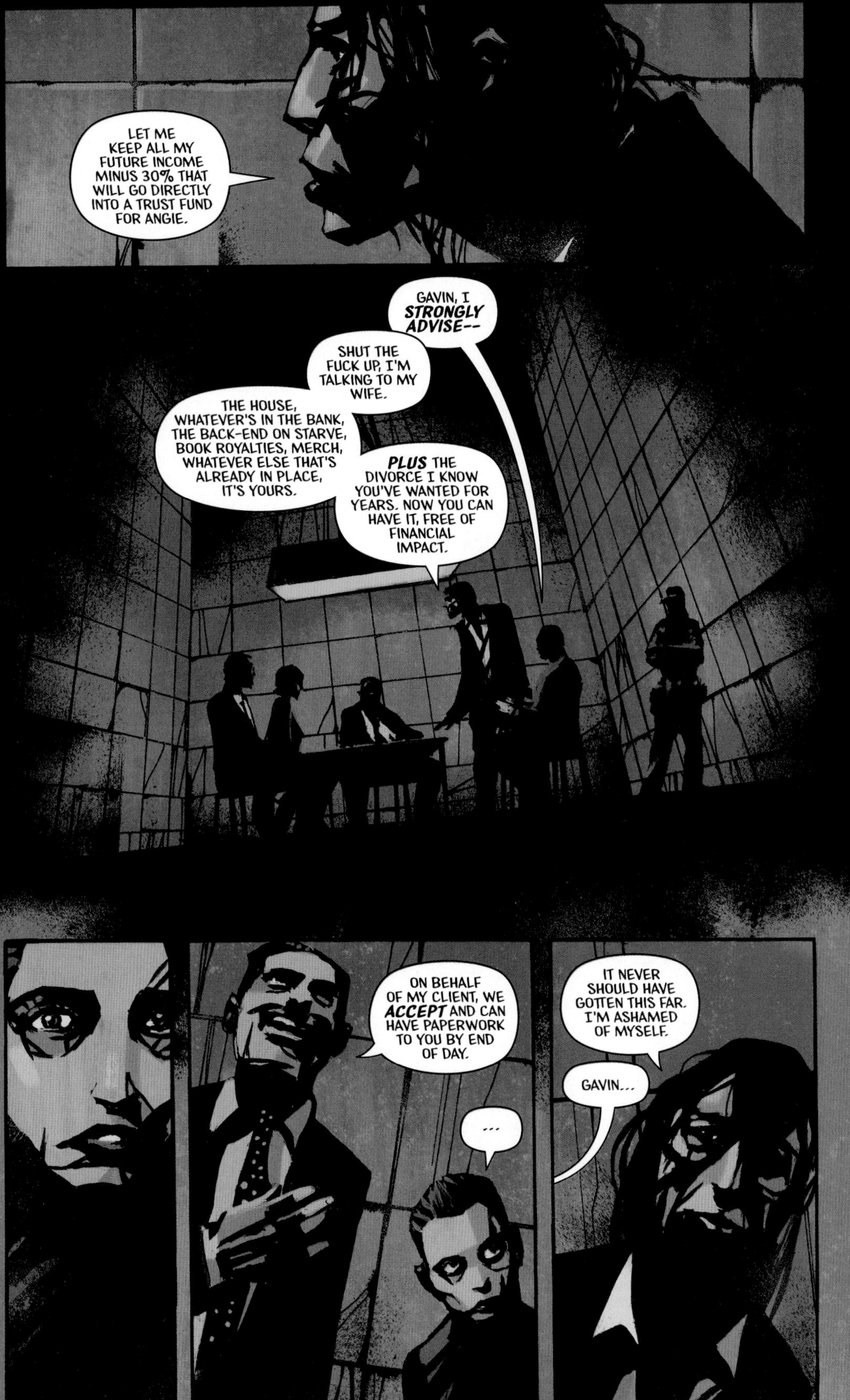
LET ME KEEP ALL MY FUTURE INCOME MINUS 30% THAT WILL GO DIRECTLY INTO A TRUST FUND FOR ANGIE.
GAVIN, I STRONGLY ADVISE--
SHUT THE FUCK UP, I'M TALKING TO MY WIFE.
THE HOUSE, WHATEVER'S IN THE BANK, THE BACK-END ON STARVE, BOOK ROYALTIES, MERCH, WHATEVER ELSE THAT'S ALREADY IN PLACE, IT'S YOURS.
PLUS THE DIVORCE I KNOW YOU'VE WANTED FOR YEARS. NOW YOU CAN HAVE IT, FREE OF FINANCIAL IMPACT.
ON BEHALF OF MY CLIENT, WE ACCEPT AND CAN HAVE PAPERWORK TO YOU BY END OF DAY.
...
IT NEVER SHOULD HAVE GOTTEN THIS FAR. I'M ASHAMED OF MYSELF.
GAVIN...

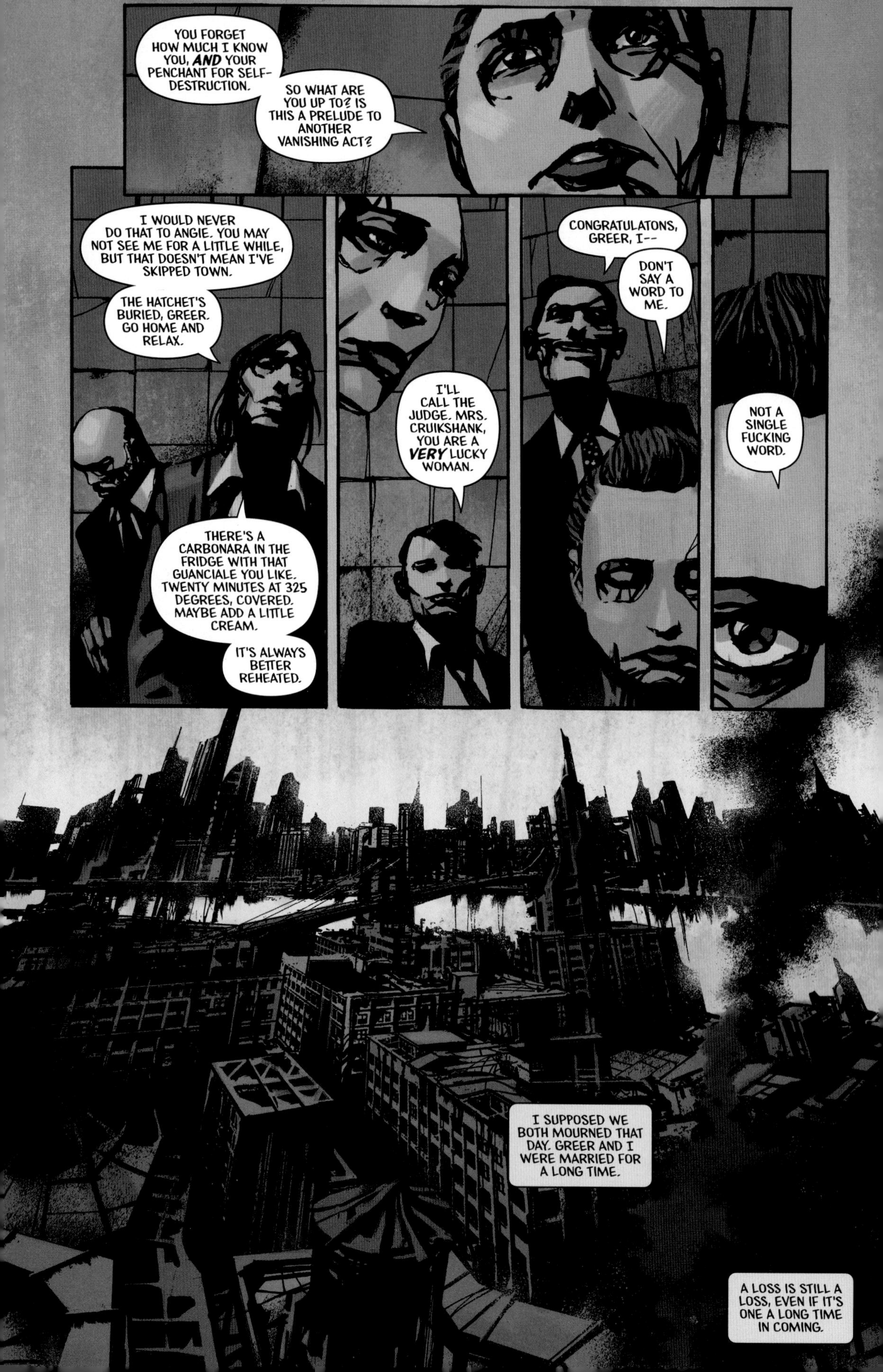
YOU FORGET HOW MUCH I KNOW YOU, AND YOUR PENCHANT FOR SELF-DESTRUCTION.
SO WHAT ARE YOU UP TO? IS THIS A PRELUDE TO ANOTHER VANISHING ACT?
I WOULD NEVER DO THAT TO ANGIE. YOU MAY NOT SEE ME FOR A LITTLE WHILE, BUT THAT DOESN'T MEAN I'VE SKIPPED TOWN.
THE HATCHET'S BURIED, GREER. GO HOME AND RELAX.
THERE'S A CARBONARA IN THE FRIDGE WITH THAT GUANCIALE YOU LIKE. TWENTY MINUTES AT 325 DEGREES, COVERED. MAYBE ADD A LITTLE CREAM.
IT'S ALWAYS BETTER REHEATED.
I'LL CALL THE JUDGE. MRS. CRUIKSHANK, YOU ARE A VERY LUCKY WOMAN.
CONGRATULATONS, GREER, I--
DON'T SAY A WORD TO ME.
NOT A SINGLE FUCKING WORD.
I SUPPOSED WE BOTH MOURNED THAT DAY. GREER AND I WERE MARRIED FOR A LONG TIME.
A LOSS IS STILL A LOSS, EVEN IF IT'S ONE A LONG TIME IN COMING.

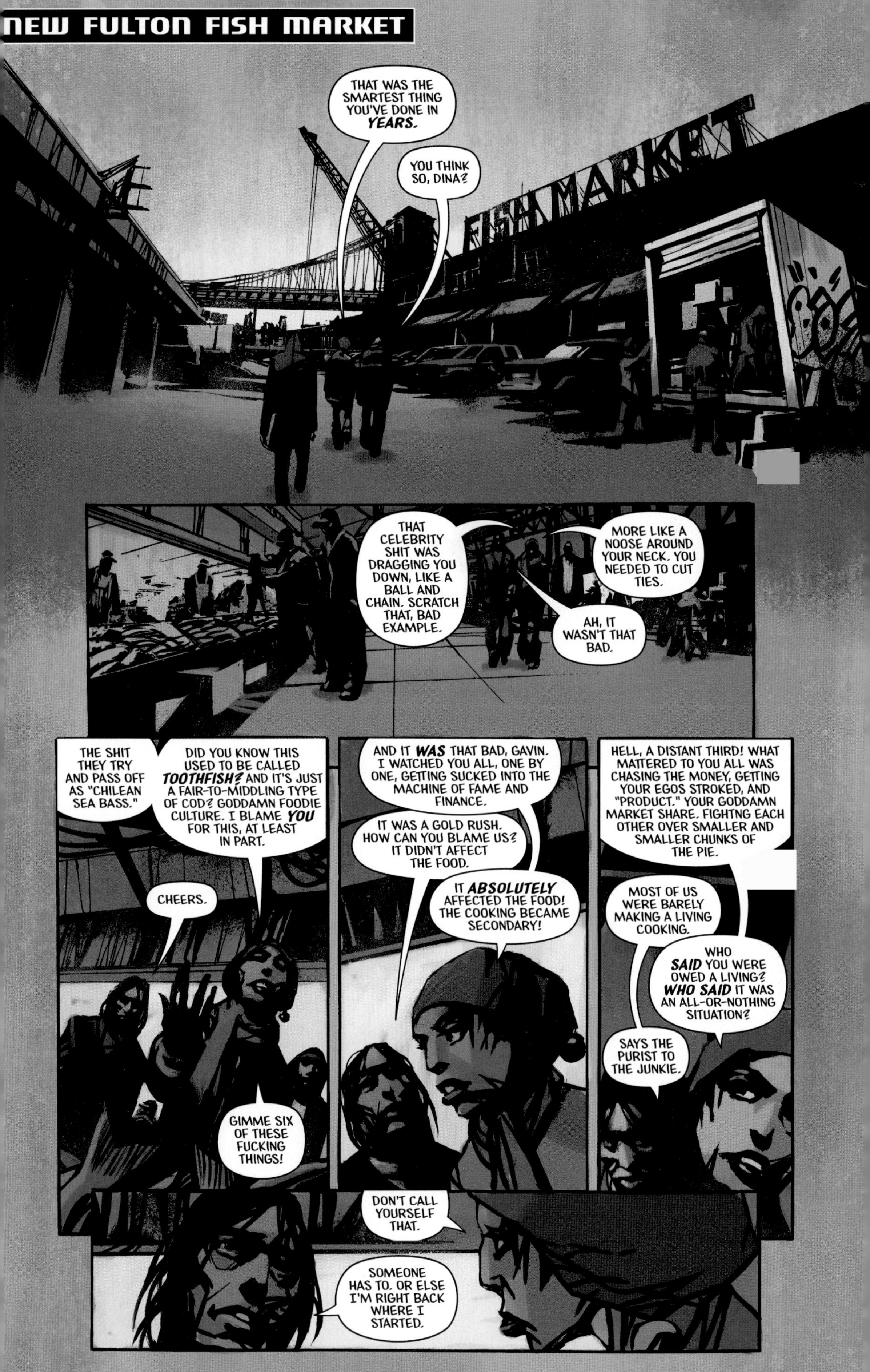
NEW FULTON FISH MARKET
THAT WAS THE SMARTEST THING YOU'VE DONE IN YEARS.
YOU THINK SO, DINA?
FISH MARKET
THAT CELEBRITY SHIT WAS DRAGGING YOU DOWN, LIKE A BALL AND CHAIN. SCRATCH THAT, BAD EXAMPLE.
MORE LIKE A NOOSE AROUND YOUR NECK. YOU NEEDED TO CUT TIES.
AH, IT WASN'T THAT BAD.
THE SHIT THEY TRY AND PASS OFF AS "CHILEAN SEA BASS."
DID YOU KNOW THIS USED TO BE CALLED TOOTHFISH? AND IT'S JUST A FAIR-TO-MIDDLING TYPE OF COD? GODDAMN FOODIE CULTURE. I BLAME YOU FOR THIS, AT LEAST IN PART.
CHEERS.
GIMME SIX OF THESE FUCKING THINGS!
AND IT WAS THAT BAD, GAVIN. I WATCHED YOU ALL, ONE BY ONE, GETTING SUCKED INTO THE MACHINE OF FAME AND FINANCE.
IT WAS A GOLD RUSH. HOW CAN YOU BLAME US? IT DIDN'T AFFECT THE FOOD.
IT ABSOLUTELY AFFECTED THE FOOD! THE COOKING BECAME SECONDARY!
HELL, A DISTANT THIRD! WHAT MATTERED TO YOU ALL WAS CHASING THE MONEY, GETTING YOUR EGOS STROKED, AND "PRODUCT." YOUR GODDAMN MARKET SHARE. FIGHTNG EACH OTHER OVER SMALLER AND SMALLER CHUNKS OF THE PIE.
MOST OF US WERE BARELY MAKING A LIVING COOKING.
WHO SAID YOU WERE OWED A LIVING? WHO SAID IT WAS AN ALL-OR-NOTHING SITUATION?
SAYS THE PURIST TO THE JUNKIE.
DON'T CALL YOURSELF THAT.
SOMEONE HAS TO. OR ELSE I'M RIGHT BACK WHERE I STARTED.

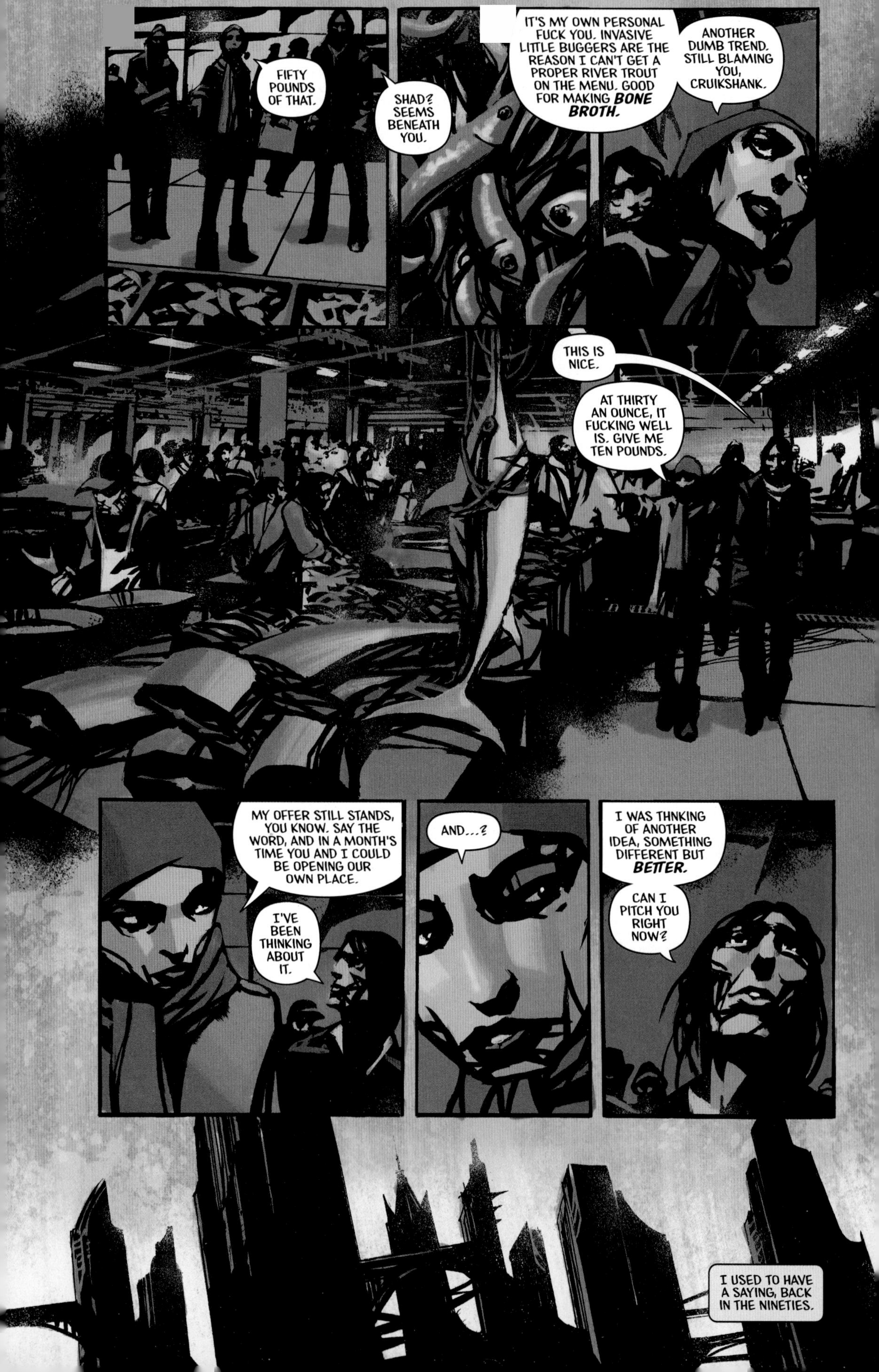
FIFTY POUNDS OF THAT.
SHAD? SEEMS BENEATH YOU.
IT'S MY OWN PERSONAL FUCK YOU. INVASIVE LITTLE BUGGERS ARE THE REASON I CAN'T GET A PROPER RIVER TROUT ON THE MENU. GOOD FOR MAKING BONE BROTH.
ANOTHER DUMB TREND. STILL BLAMING YOU, CRUIKSHANK.
THIS IS NICE.
AT THIRTY AN OUNCE, IT FUCKING WELL IS. GIVE ME TEN POUNDS.
MY OFFER STILL STANDS, YOU KNOW. SAY THE WORD, AND IN A MONTH'S TIME YOU AND I COULD BE OPENING OUR OWN PLACE.
I'VE BEEN THINKING ABOUT IT.
AND...?
I WAS THNKING OF ANOTHER IDEA, SOMETHING DIFFERENT BUT BETTER.
CAN I PITCH YOU RIGHT NOW?
I USED TO HAVE A SAYING, BACK IN THE NINETIES.

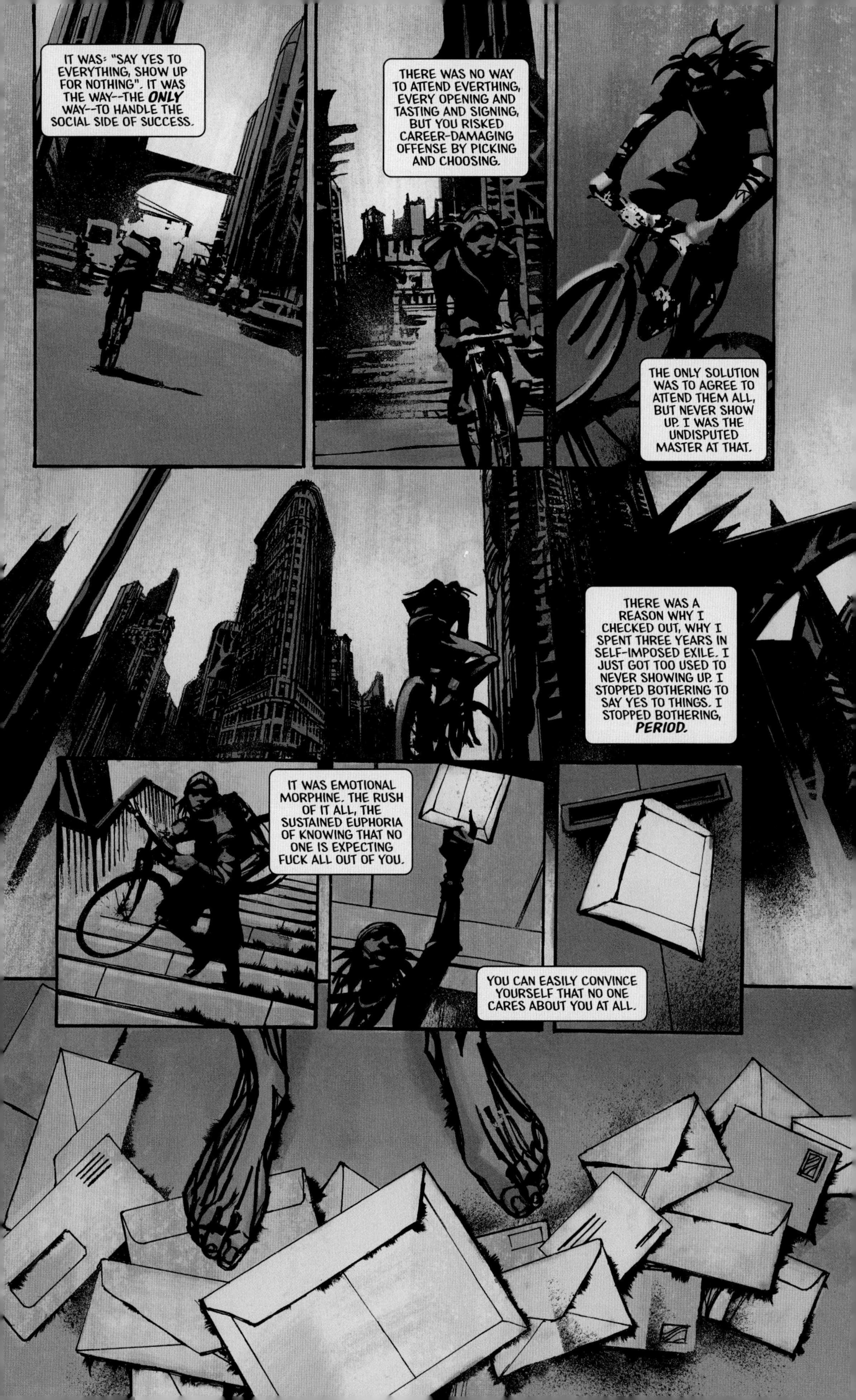
IT WAS: "SAY YES TO EVERYTHING, SHOW UP FOR NOTHING". IT WAS THE WAY--THE ONLY WAY--TO HANDLE THE SOCIAL SIDE OF SUCCESS.
THERE WAS NO WAY TO ATTEND EVERTHING, EVERY OPENING AND TASTING AND SIGNING, BUT YOU RISKED CAREER-DAMAGING OFFENSE BY PICKING AND CHOOSING.
THE ONLY SOLUTION WAS TO AGREE TO ATTEND THEM ALL, BUT NEVER SHOW UP. I WAS THE UNDISPUTED MASTER AT THAT.
THERE WAS A REASON WHY I CHECKED OUT, WHY I SPENT THREE YEARS IN SELF-IMPOSED EXILE. I JUST GOT TOO USED TO NEVER SHOWING UP. I STOPPED BOTHERING TO SAY YES TO THINGS. I STOPPED BOTHERING, PERIOD.
IT WAS EMOTIONAL MORPHINE. THE RUSH OF IT ALL, THE SUSTAINED EUPHORIA OF KNOWING THAT NO ONE IS EXPECTING FUCK ALL OUT OF YOU.
YOU CAN EASILY CONVINCE YOURSELF THAT NO ONE CARES ABOUT YOU AT ALL.

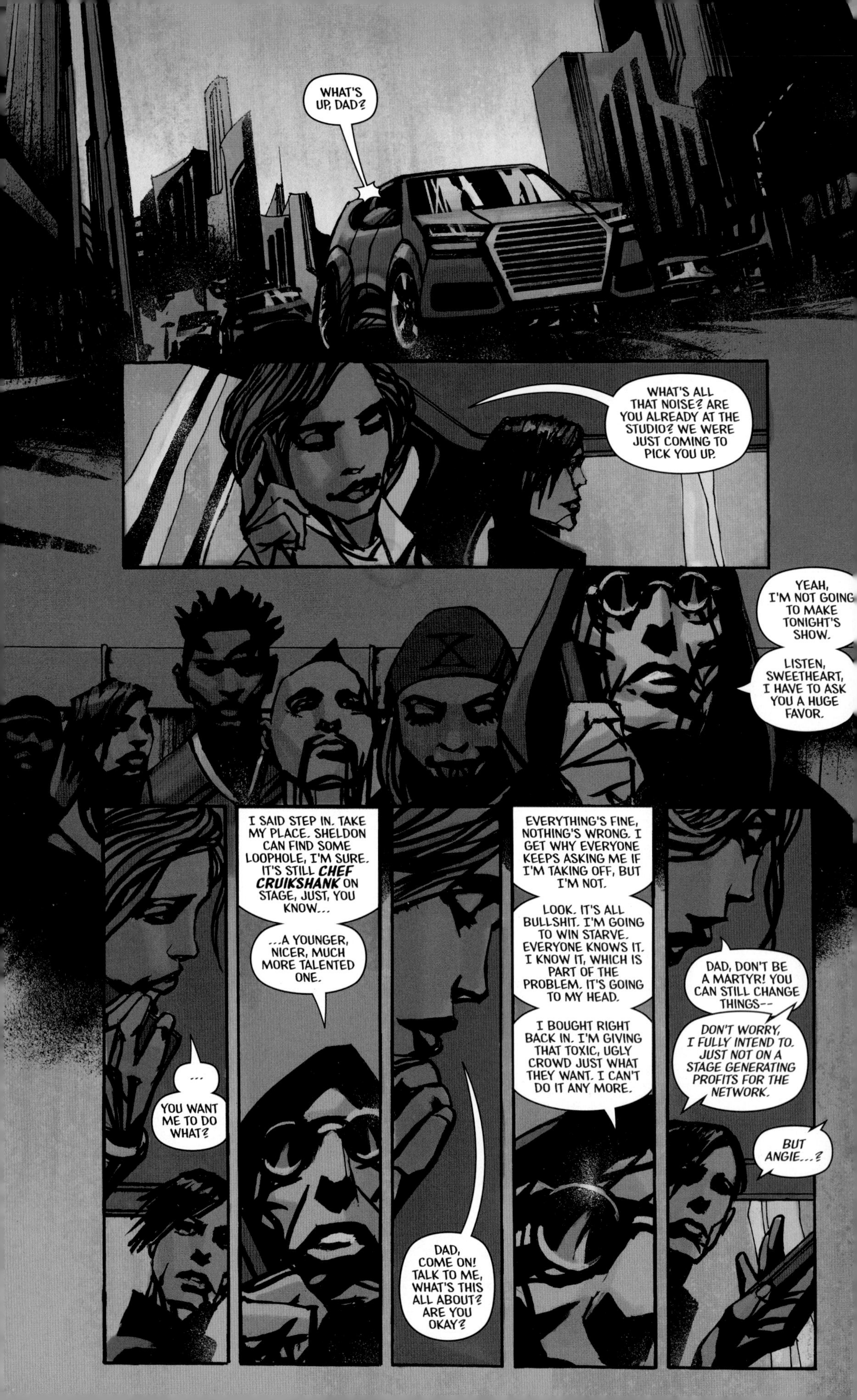

WHAT'S UP, DAD?
WHAT'S ALL THAT NOISE? ARE YOU ALREADY AT THE STUDIO? WE WERE JUST COMING TO PICK YOU UP.
YEAH, I'M NOT GOING TO MAKE TONIGHT'S SHOW.
LISTEN, SWEETHEART, I HAVE TO ASK YOU A HUGE FAVOR.
...
YOU WANT ME TO DO WHAT?
I SAID STEP IN. TAKE MY PLACE. SHELDON CAN FIND SOME LOOPHOLE, I'M SURE. IT'S STILL ***CHEF CRUIKSHANK*** ON STAGE, JUST, YOU KNOW...
...A YOUNGER, NICER, MUCH MORE TALENTED ONE.
DAD, COME ON! TALK TO ME, WHAT'S THIS ALL ABOUT? ARE YOU OKAY?
EVERYTHING'S FINE, NOTHING'S WRONG. I GET WHY EVERYONE KEEPS ASKING ME IF I'M TAKING OFF, BUT I'M NOT.
LOOK. IT'S ALL BULLSHIT. I'M GOING TO WIN STARVE. EVERYONE KNOWS IT. I KNOW IT, WHICH IS PART OF THE PROBLEM. IT'S GOING TO MY HEAD.
I BOUGHT RIGHT BACK IN. I'M GIVING THAT TOXIC, UGLY CROWD JUST WHAT THEY WANT. I CAN'T DO IT ANY MORE.
DAD, DON'T BE A MARTYR! YOU CAN STILL CHANGE THINGS--
DON'T WORRY, I FULLY INTEND TO. JUST NOT ON A STAGE GENERATING PROFITS FOR THE NETWORK.
BUT ANGIE...?

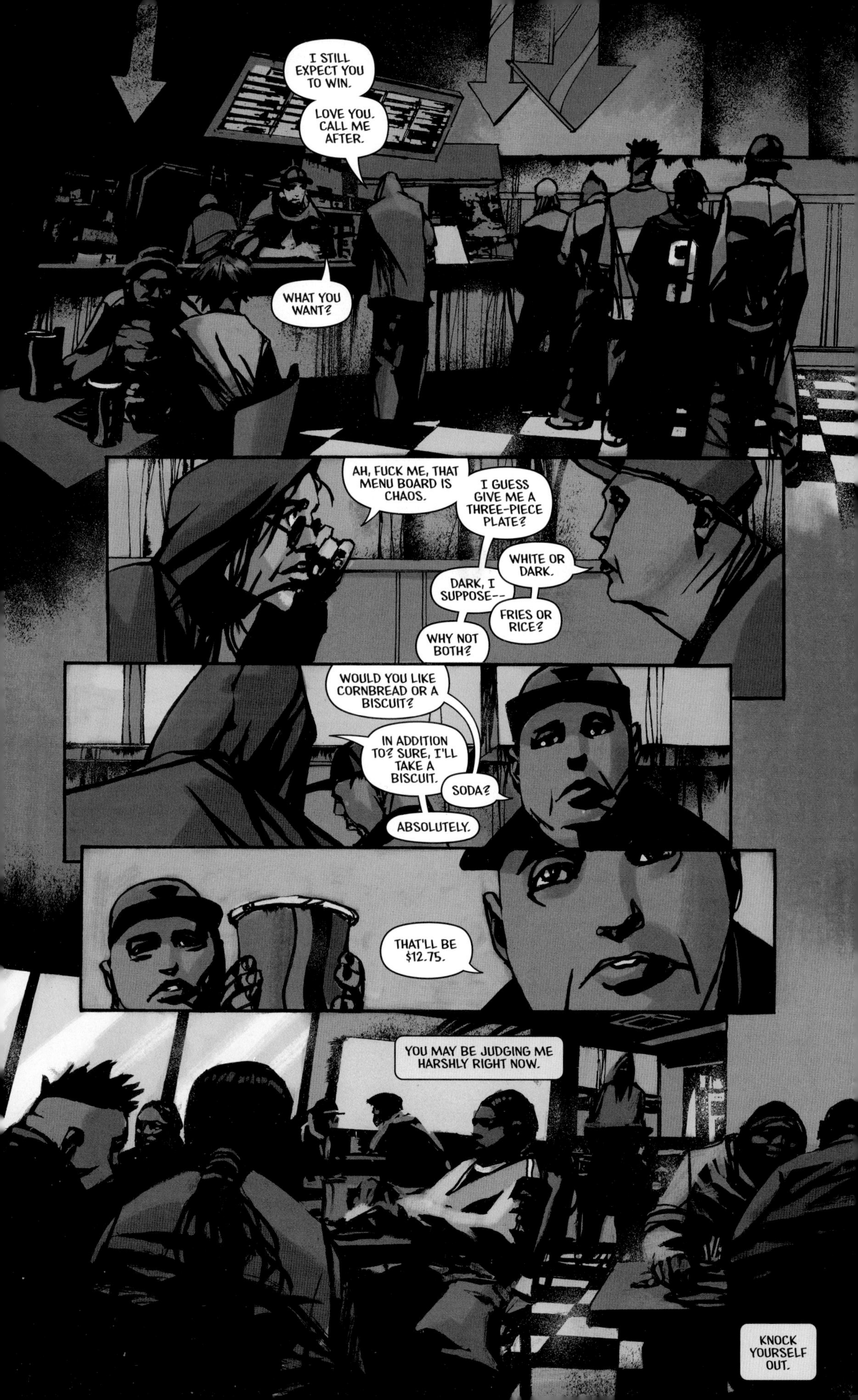
I STILL EXPECT YOU TO WIN.
LOVE YOU. CALL ME AFTER.
WHAT YOU WANT?
AH, FUCK ME, THAT MENU BOARD IS CHAOS.
I GUESS GIVE ME A THREE-PIECE PLATE?
WHITE OR DARK.
DARK, I SUPPOSE--
FRIES OR RICE?
WHY NOT BOTH?
WOULD YOU LIKE CORNBREAD OR A BISCUIT?
IN ADDITION TO? SURE, I'LL TAKE A BISCUIT.
SODA?
ABSOLUTELY.
THAT'LL BE $12.75.
YOU MAY BE JUDGING ME HARSHLY RIGHT NOW.
KNOCK YOURSELF OUT.

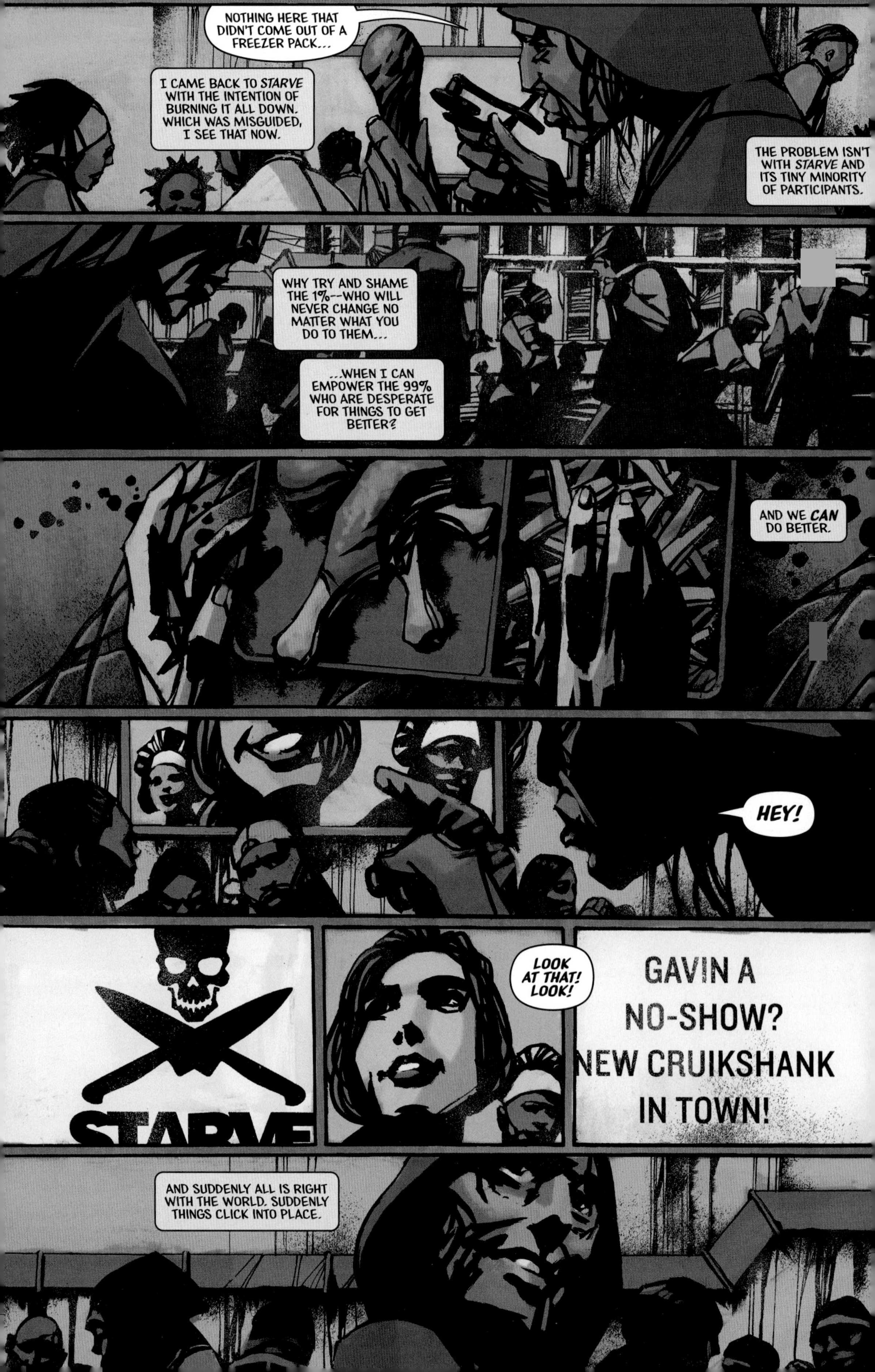
NOTHING HERE THAT DIDN'T COME OUT OF A FREEZER PACK...
I CAME BACK TO STARVE WITH THE INTENTION OF BURNING IT ALL DOWN. WHICH WAS MISGUIDED, I SEE THAT NOW.
THE PROBLEM ISN'T WITH STARVE AND ITS TINY MINORITY OF PARTICIPANTS.
WHY TRY AND SHAME THE 1%--WHO WILL NEVER CHANGE NO MATTER WHAT YOU DO TO THEM...
...WHEN I CAN EMPOWER THE 99% WHO ARE DESPERATE FOR THINGS TO GET BETTER?
AND WE CAN DO BETTER.
HEY!
STARVE
LOOK AT THAT! LOOK!
GAVIN A NO-SHOW? NEW CRUIKSHANK IN TOWN!
AND SUDDENLY ALL IS RIGHT WITH THE WORLD. SUDDENLY THINGS CLICK INTO PLACE.

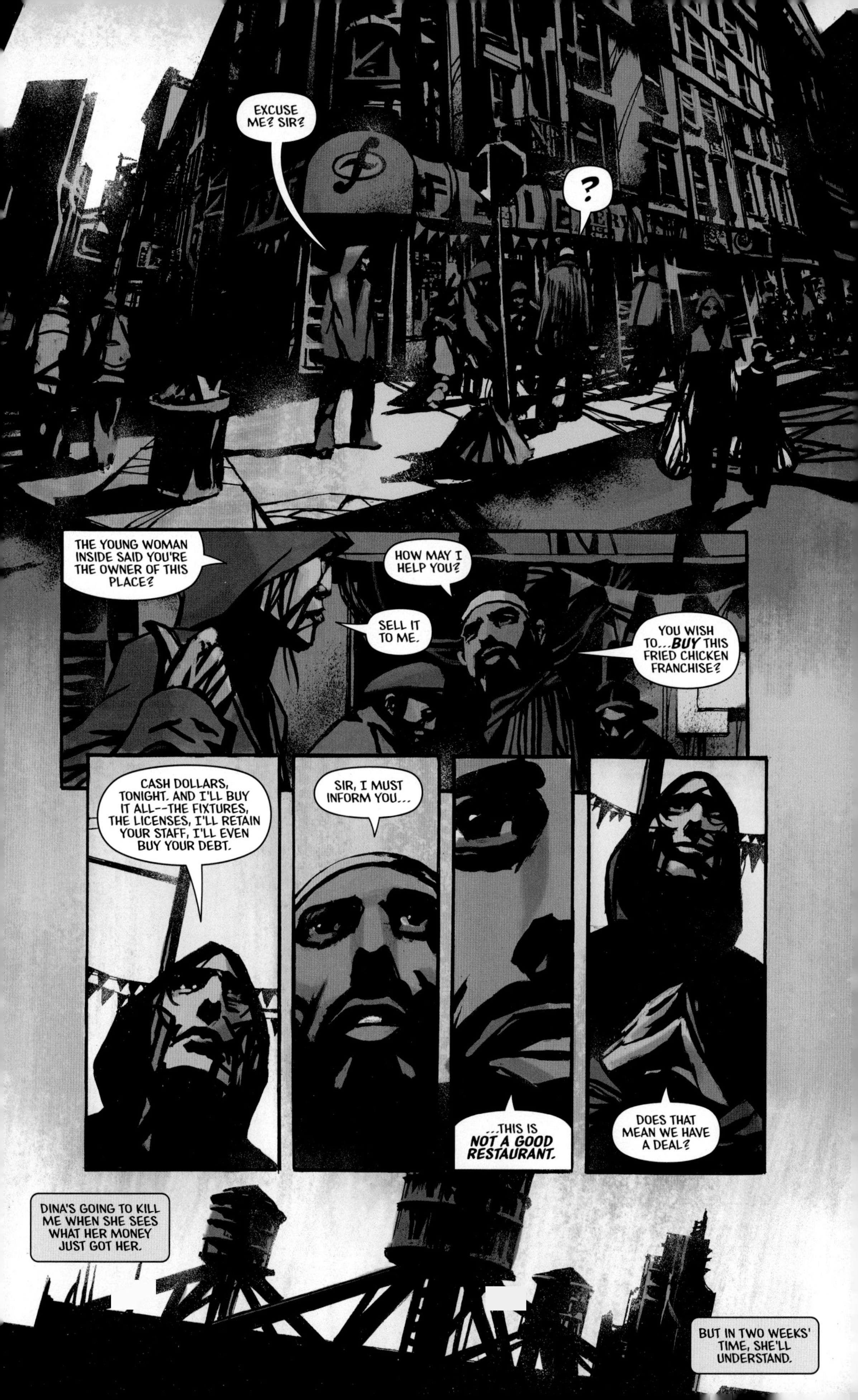
EXCUSE ME? SIR?
?
THE YOUNG WOMAN INSIDE SAID YOU'RE THE OWNER OF THIS PLACE?
HOW MAY I HELP YOU?
SELL IT TO ME.
YOU WISH TO...BUY THIS FRIED CHICKEN FRANCHISE?
CASH DOLLARS, TONIGHT. AND I'LL BUY IT ALL--THE FIXTURES, THE LICENSES, I'LL RETAIN YOUR STAFF, I'LL EVEN BUY YOUR DEBT.
SIR, I MUST INFORM YOU...
...THIS IS NOT A GOOD RESTAURANT.
DOES THAT MEAN WE HAVE A DEAL?
DINA'S GOING TO KILL ME WHEN SHE SEES WHAT HER MONEY JUST GOT HER.
BUT IN TWO WEEKS' TIME, SHE'LL UNDERSTAND.

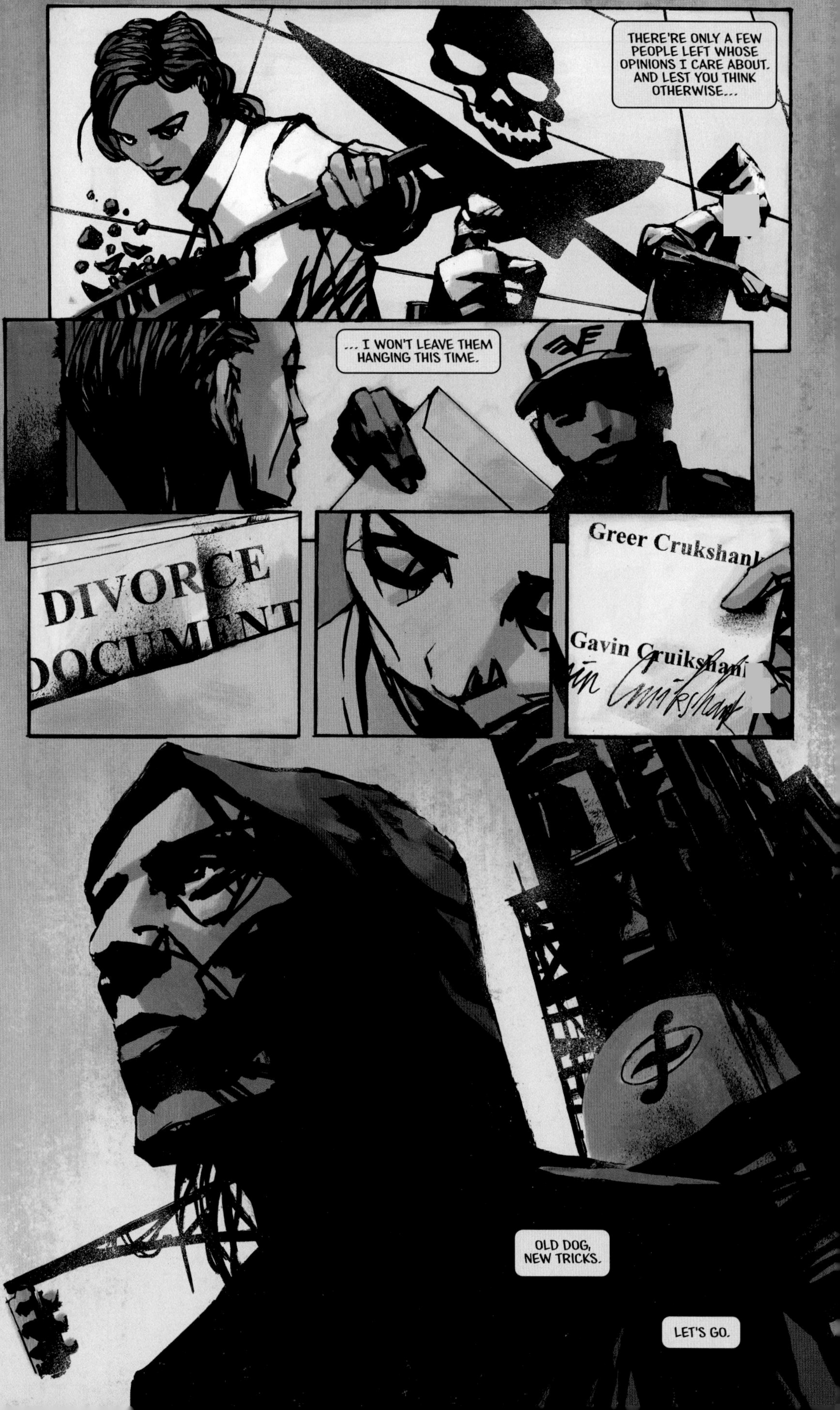
THERE'RE ONLY A FEW PEOPLE LEFT WHOSE OPINIONS I CARE ABOUT. AND LEST YOU THINK OTHERWISE...
... I WON'T LEAVE THEM HANGING THIS TIME.
DIVORCE
Greer Crukshan
Gavin Cruikshan
OLD DOG, NEW TRICKS.
LET'S GO.

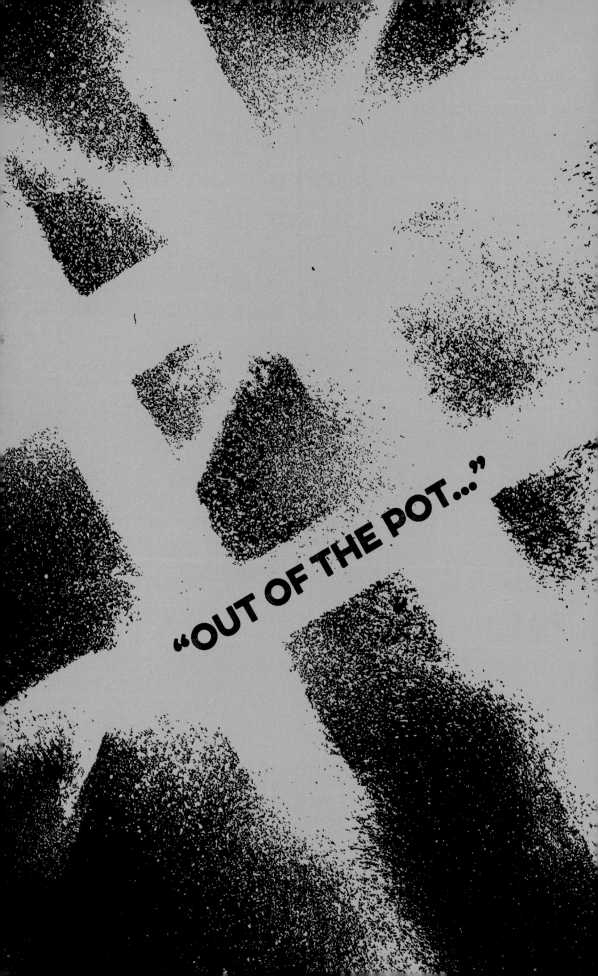

"OUT OF THE POT..."

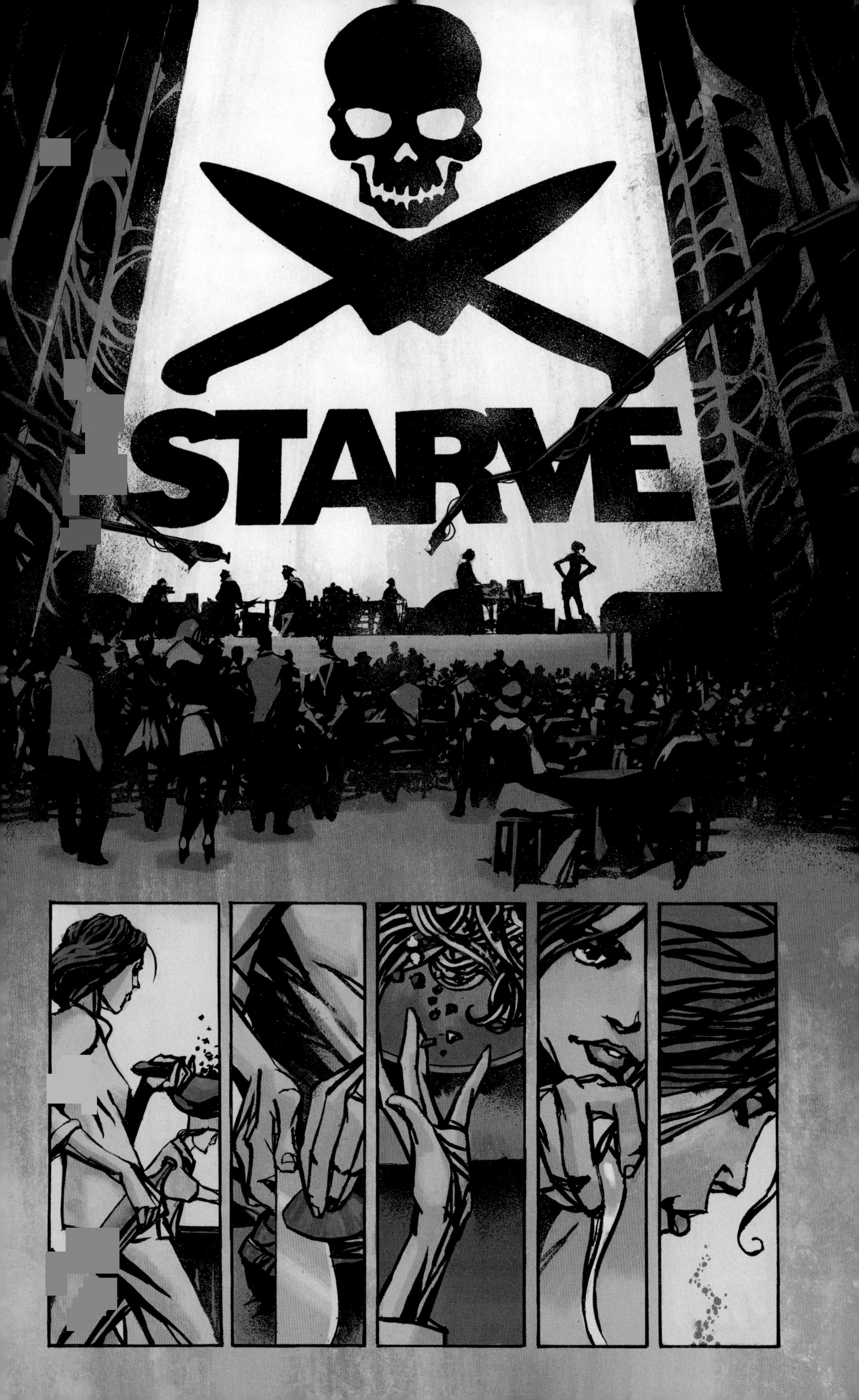
STARVE

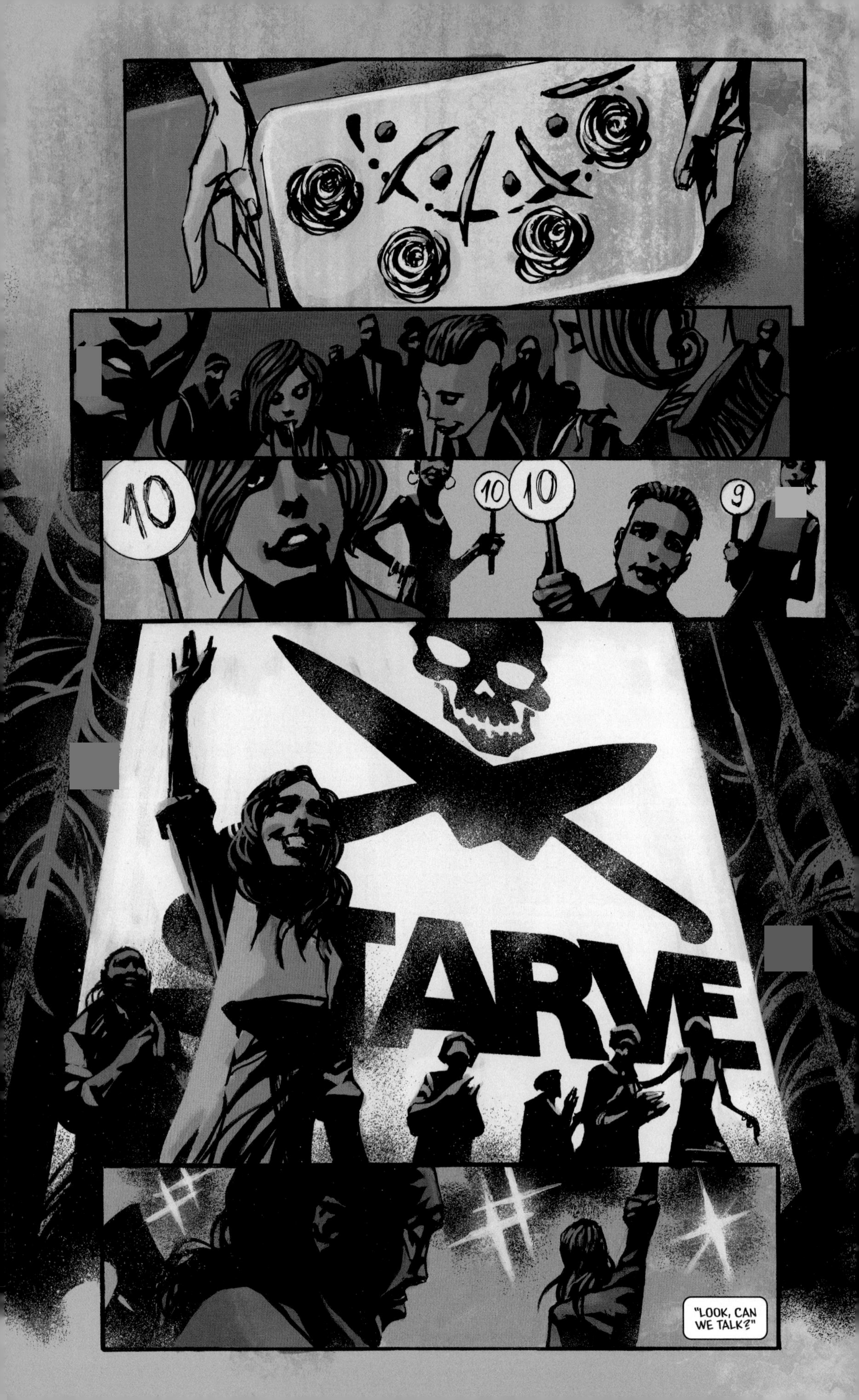
10
10
10
9
TARVE
"LOOK, CAN WE TALK?"

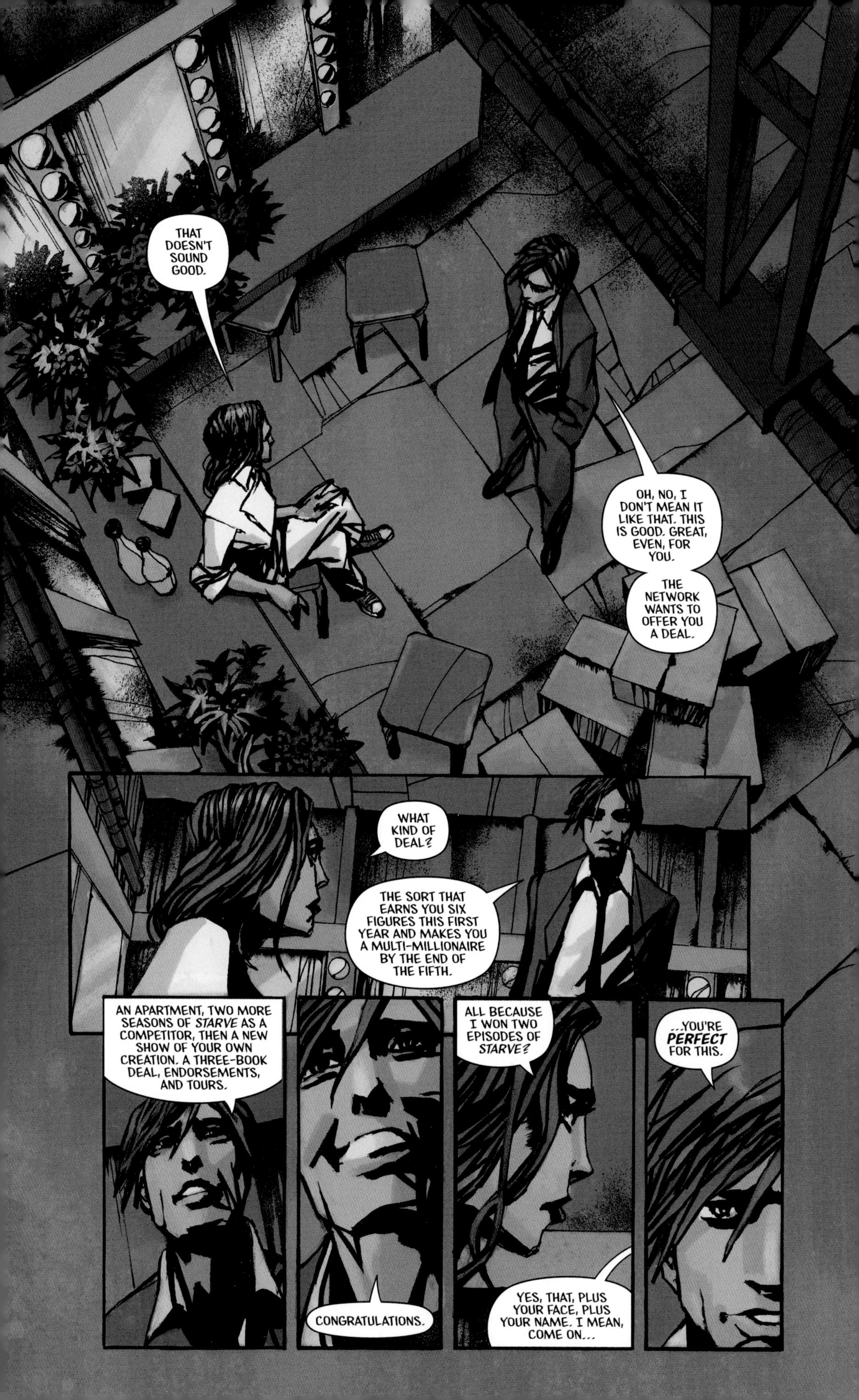
THAT DOESN'T SOUND GOOD.
OH, NO, I DON'T MEAN IT LIKE THAT. THIS IS GOOD. GREAT, EVEN, FOR YOU.
THE NETWORK WANTS TO OFFER YOU A DEAL.
WHAT KIND OF DEAL?
THE SORT THAT EARNS YOU SIX FIGURES THIS FIRST YEAR AND MAKES YOU A MULTI-MILLIONAIRE BY THE END OF THE FIFTH.
AN APARTMENT, TWO MORE SEASONS OF *STARVE* AS A COMPETITOR, THEN A NEW SHOW OF YOUR OWN CREATION. A THREE-BOOK DEAL, ENDORSEMENTS, AND TOURS.
CONGRATULATIONS.
ALL BECAUSE I WON TWO EPISODES OF *STARVE*?
YES, THAT, PLUS YOUR FACE, PLUS YOUR NAME. I MEAN, COME ON...
...YOU'RE **PERFECT** FOR THIS.

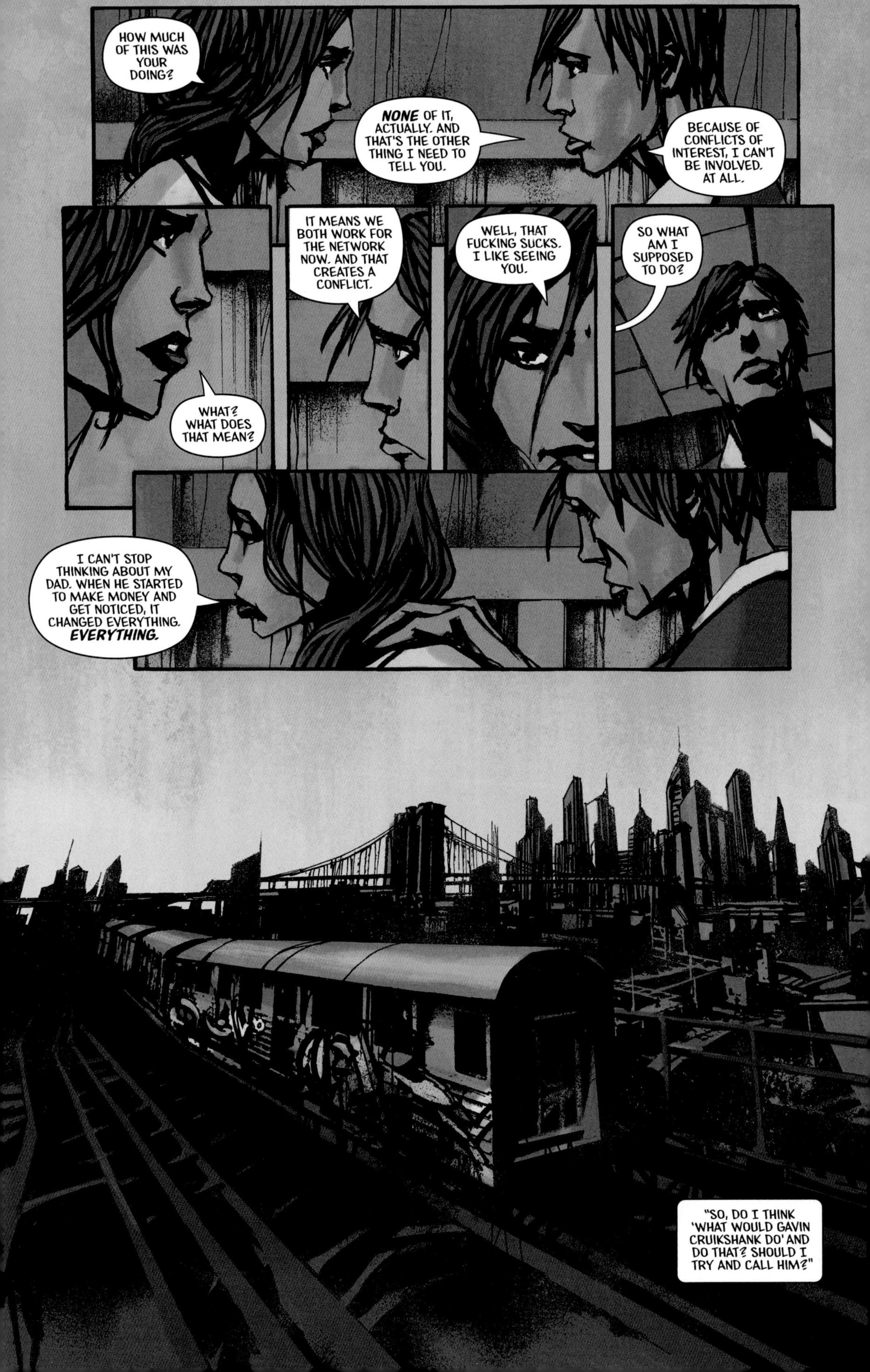
HOW MUCH OF THIS WAS YOUR DOING?
NONE OF IT, ACTUALLY. AND THAT'S THE OTHER THING I NEED TO TELL YOU.
BECAUSE OF CONFLICTS OF INTEREST, I CAN'T BE INVOLVED. AT ALL.
WHAT? WHAT DOES THAT MEAN?
IT MEANS WE BOTH WORK FOR THE NETWORK NOW. AND THAT CREATES A CONFLICT.
WELL, THAT FUCKING SUCKS. I LIKE SEEING YOU.
SO WHAT AM I SUPPOSED TO DO?
I CAN'T STOP THINKING ABOUT MY DAD. WHEN HE STARTED TO MAKE MONEY AND GET NOTICED, IT CHANGED EVERYTHING. EVERYTHING.
"SO, DO I THINK 'WHAT WOULD GAVIN CRUIKSHANK DO' AND DO THAT? SHOULD I TRY AND CALL HIM?"

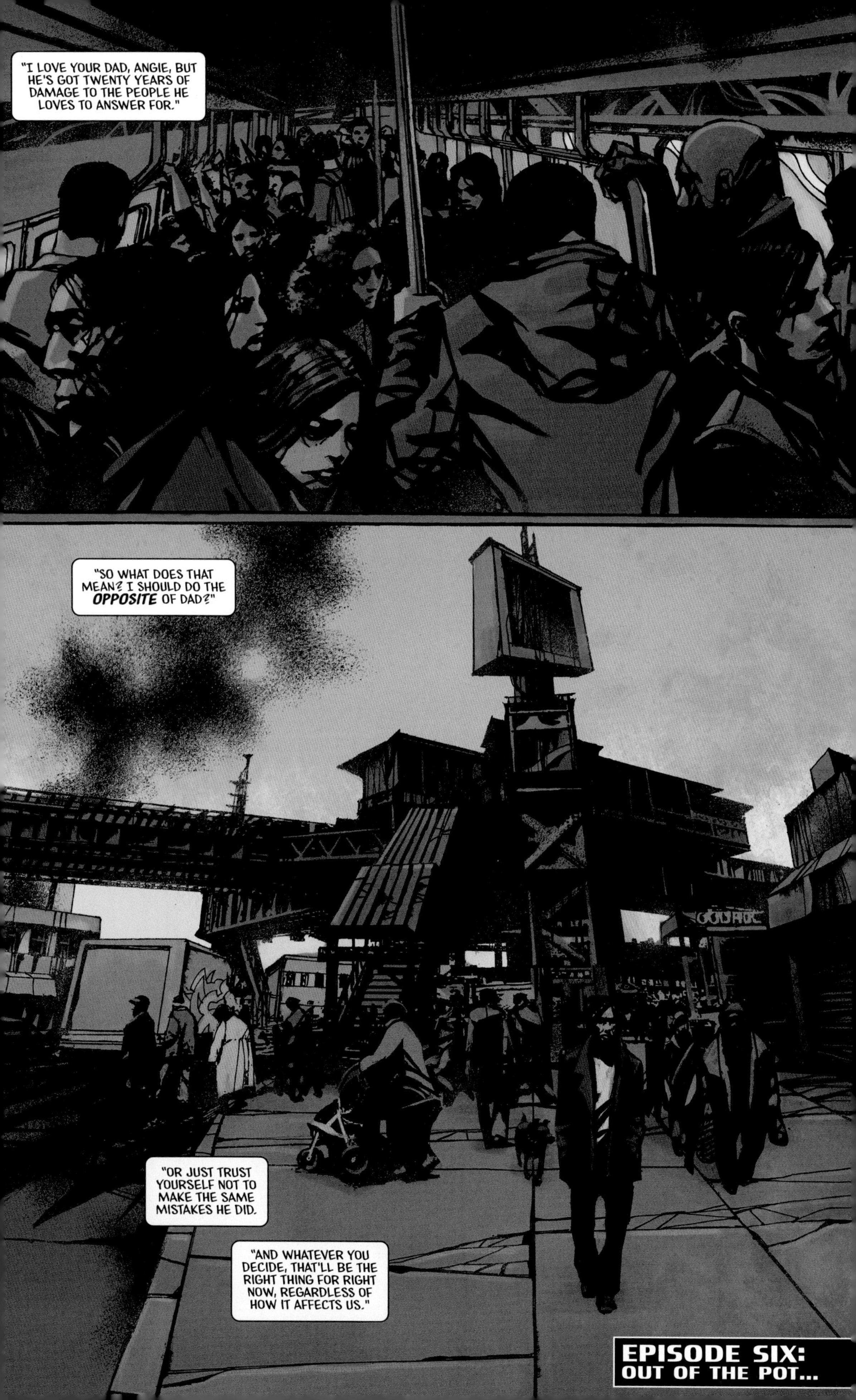
"I LOVE YOUR DAD, ANGIE, BUT HE'S GOT TWENTY YEARS OF DAMAGE TO THE PEOPLE HE LOVES TO ANSWER FOR."
"SO WHAT DOES THAT MEAN? I SHOULD DO THE *OPPOSITE* OF DAD?"
"OR JUST TRUST YOURSELF NOT TO MAKE THE SAME MISTAKES HE DID.
"AND WHATEVER YOU DECIDE, THAT'LL BE THE RIGHT THING FOR RIGHT NOW, REGARDLESS OF HOW IT AFFECTS US."
EPISODE SIX: OUT OF THE POT...

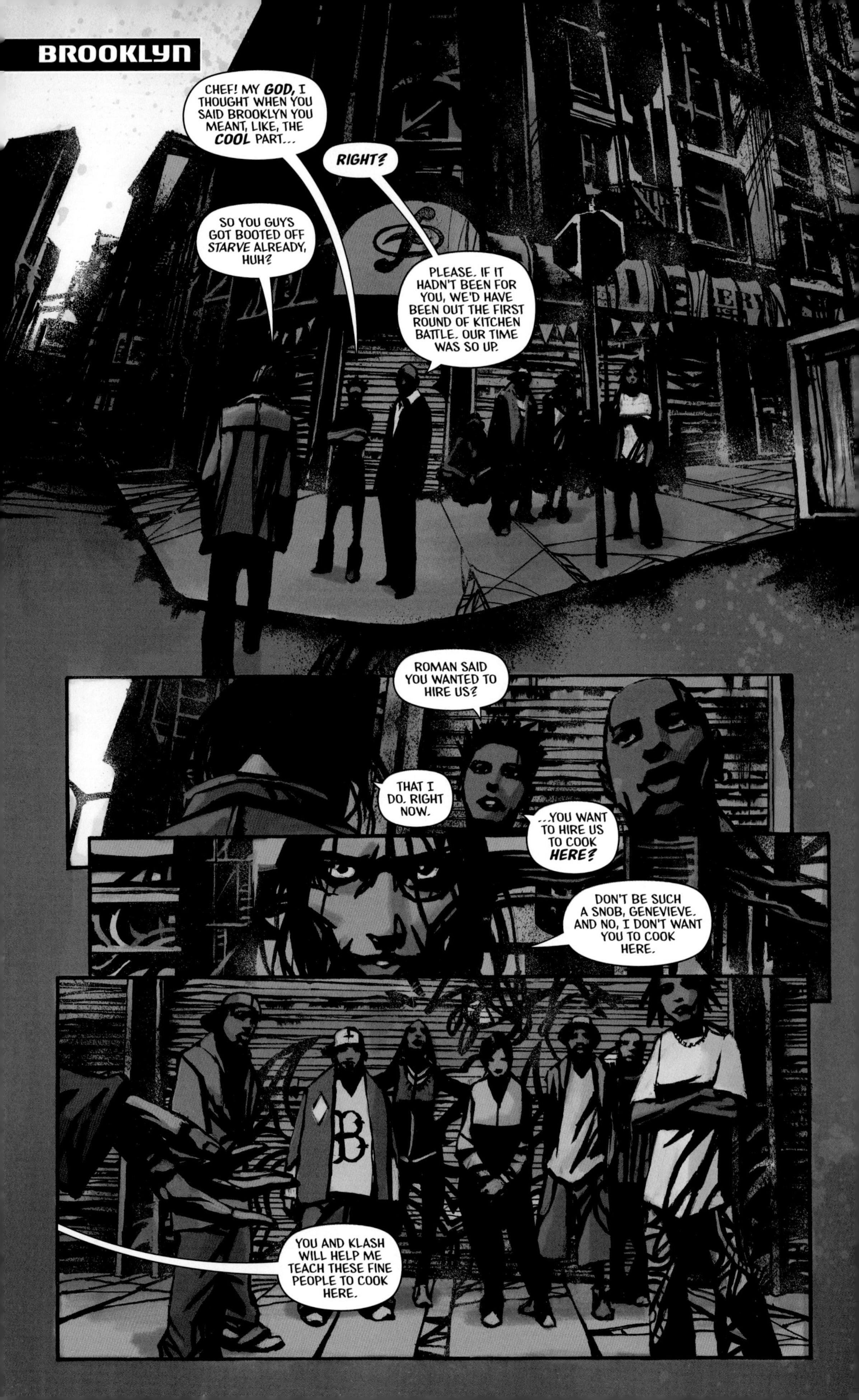
BROOKLYN
CHEF! MY GOD, I THOUGHT WHEN YOU SAID BROOKLYN YOU MEANT, LIKE, THE COOL PART...
RIGHT?
SO YOU GUYS GOT BOOTED OFF STARVE ALREADY, HUH?
PLEASE. IF IT HADN'T BEEN FOR YOU, WE'D HAVE BEEN OUT THE FIRST ROUND OF KITCHEN BATTLE. OUR TIME WAS SO UP.
ROMAN SAID YOU WANTED TO HIRE US?
THAT I DO. RIGHT NOW.
...YOU WANT TO HIRE US TO COOK HERE?
DON'T BE SUCH A SNOB, GENEVIEVE. AND NO, I DON'T WANT YOU TO COOK HERE.
YOU AND KLASH WILL HELP ME TEACH THESE FINE PEOPLE TO COOK HERE.

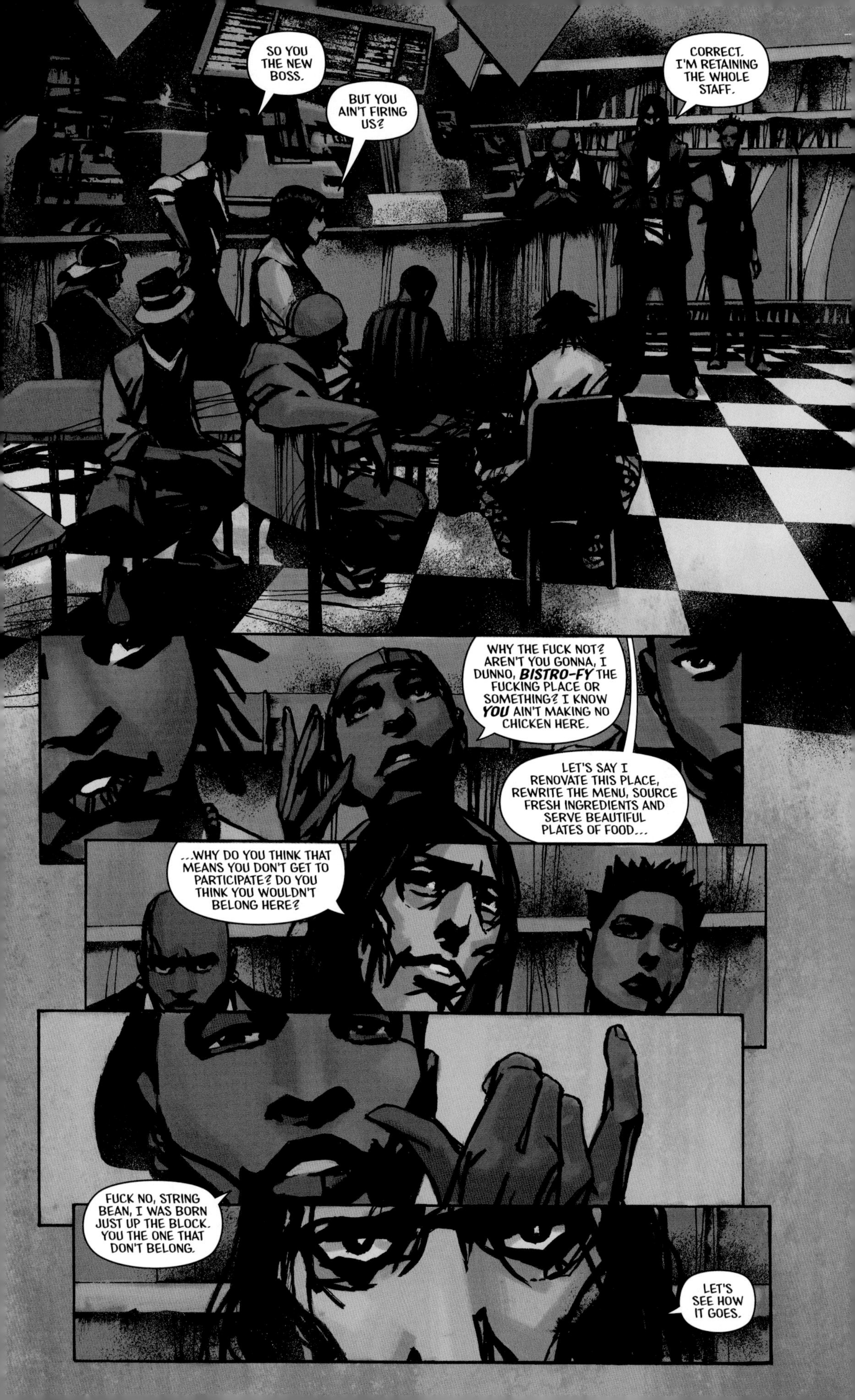
SO YOU THE NEW BOSS.
BUT YOU AIN'T FIRING US?
CORRECT. I'M RETAINING THE WHOLE STAFF.
WHY THE FUCK NOT? AREN'T YOU GONNA, I DUNNO, BISTRO-FY THE FUCKING PLACE OR SOMETHING? I KNOW YOU AIN'T MAKING NO CHICKEN HERE.
LET'S SAY I RENOVATE THIS PLACE, REWRITE THE MENU, SOURCE FRESH INGREDIENTS AND SERVE BEAUTIFUL PLATES OF FOOD...
...WHY DO YOU THINK THAT MEANS YOU DON'T GET TO PARTICIPATE? DO YOU THINK YOU WOULDN'T BELONG HERE?
FUCK NO, STRING BEAN, I WAS BORN JUST UP THE BLOCK. YOU THE ONE THAT DON'T BELONG.
LET'S SEE HOW IT GOES.

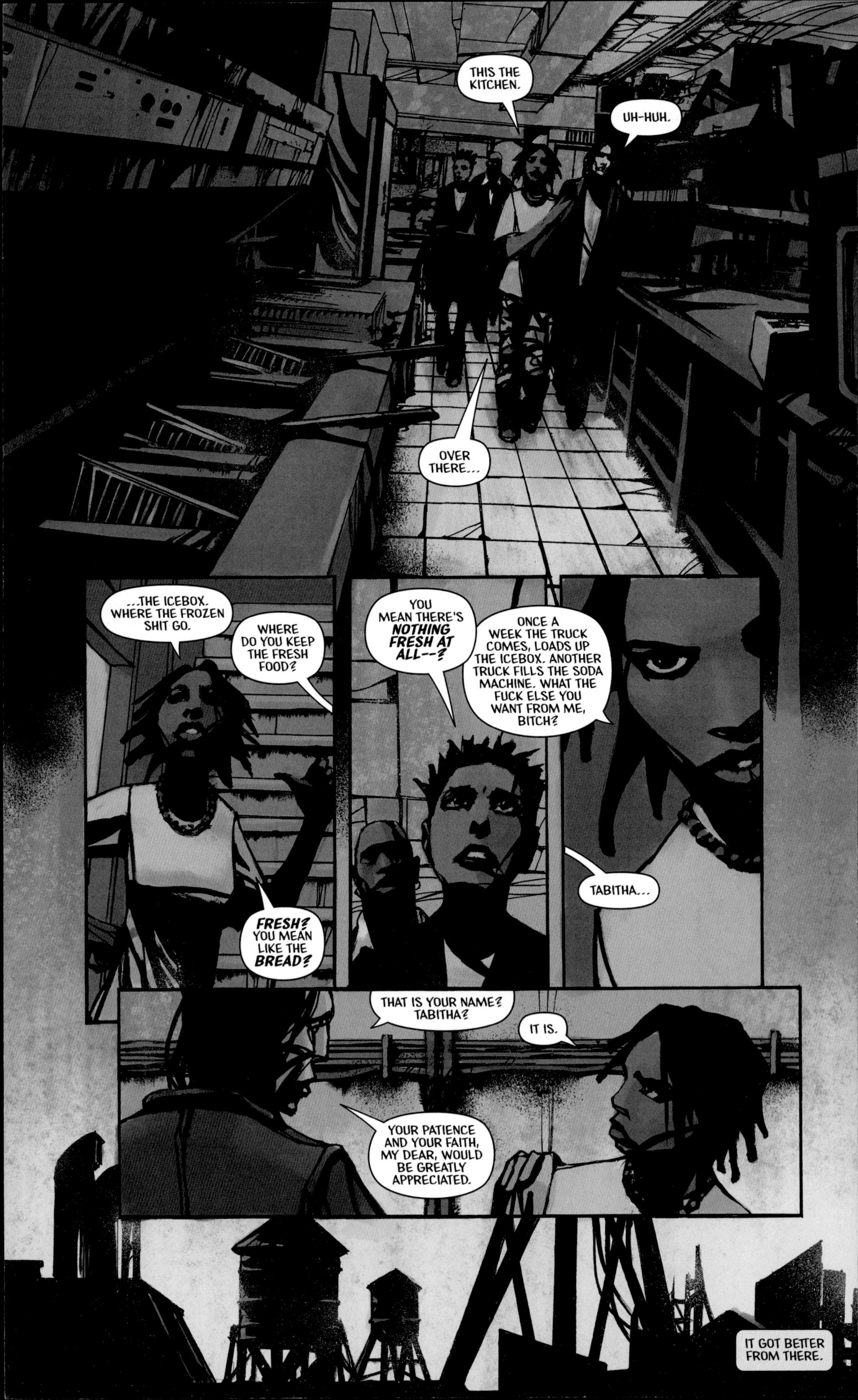
THIS THE KITCHEN.
UH-HUH.
OVER THERE...
...THE ICEBOX. WHERE THE FROZEN SHIT GO.
WHERE DO YOU KEEP THE FRESH FOOD?
FRESH? YOU MEAN LIKE THE BREAD?
YOU MEAN THERE'S NOTHING FRESH AT ALL--?
ONCE A WEEK THE TRUCK COMES, LOADS UP THE ICEBOX. ANOTHER TRUCK FILLS THE SODA MACHINE. WHAT THE FUCK ELSE YOU WANT FROM ME, BITCH?
TABITHA...
THAT IS YOUR NAME? TABITHA?
IT IS.
YOUR PATIENCE AND YOUR FAITH, MY DEAR, WOULD BE GREATLY APPRECIATED.
IT GOT BETTER FROM THERE.

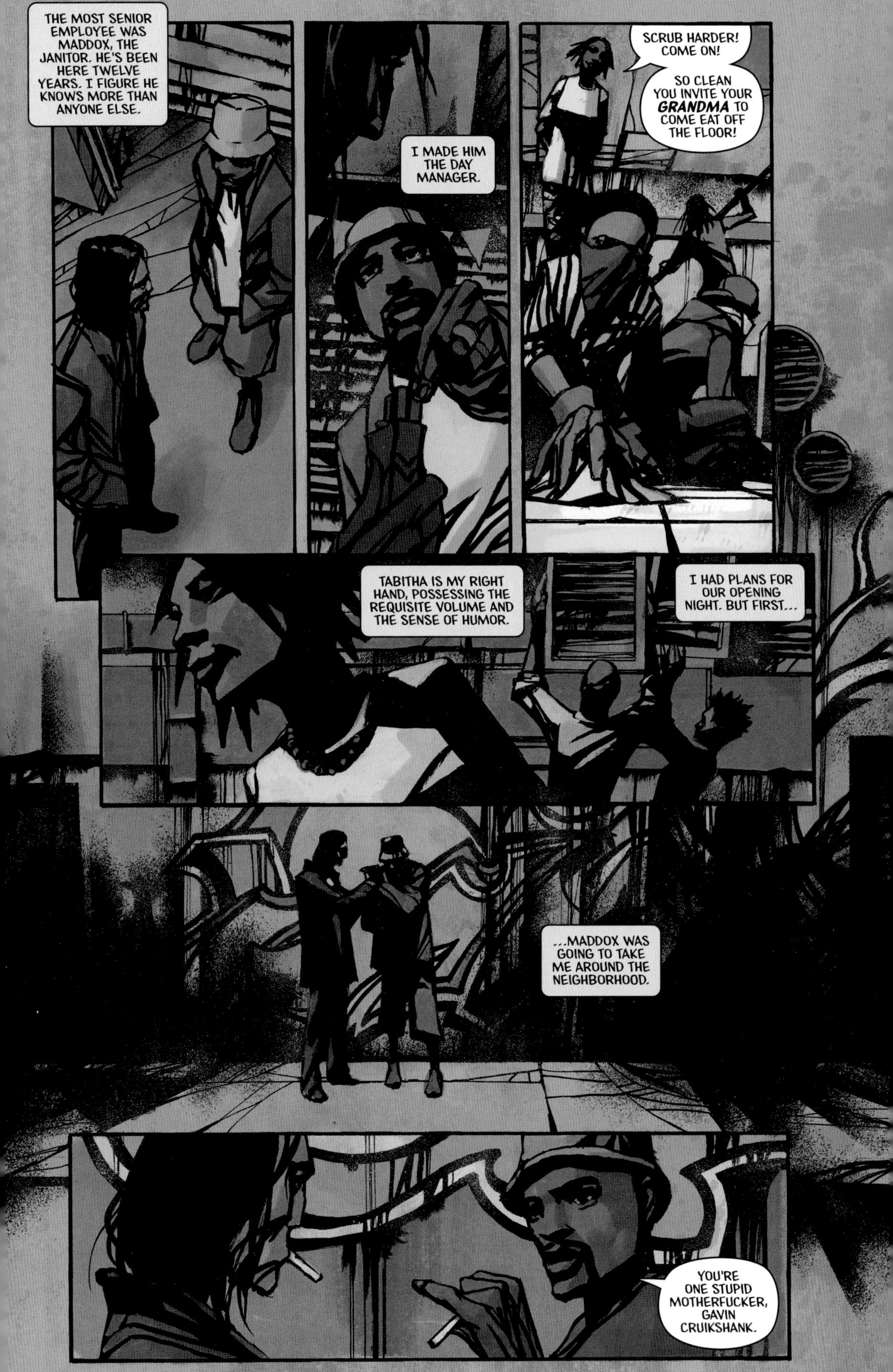
THE MOST SENIOR EMPLOYEE WAS MADDOX, THE JANITOR. HE'S BEEN HERE TWELVE YEARS. I FIGURE HE KNOWS MORE THAN ANYONE ELSE.
I MADE HIM THE DAY MANAGER.
SCRUB HARDER! COME ON!
SO CLEAN YOU INVITE YOUR GRANDMA TO COME EAT OFF THE FLOOR!
TABITHA IS MY RIGHT HAND, POSSESSING THE REQUISITE VOLUME AND THE SENSE OF HUMOR.
I HAD PLANS FOR OUR OPENING NIGHT. BUT FIRST...
...MADDOX WAS GOING TO TAKE ME AROUND THE NEIGHBORHOOD.
YOU'RE ONE STUPID MOTHERFUCKER, GAVIN CRUIKSHANK.

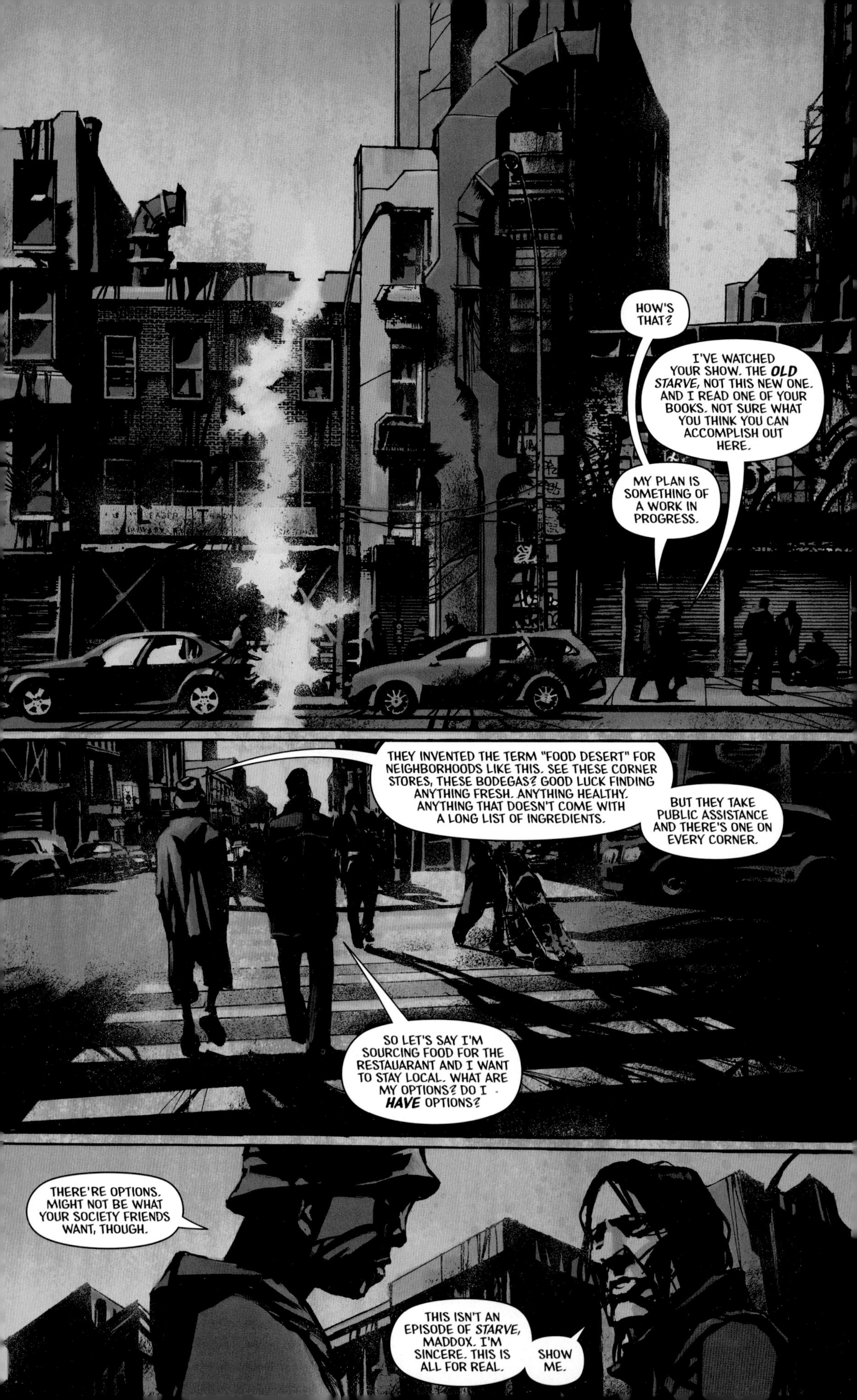

HOW'S THAT?
I'VE WATCHED YOUR SHOW. THE OLD STARVE, NOT THIS NEW ONE. AND I READ ONE OF YOUR BOOKS. NOT SURE WHAT YOU THINK YOU CAN ACCOMPLISH OUT HERE.
MY PLAN IS SOMETHING OF A WORK IN PROGRESS.
THEY INVENTED THE TERM "FOOD DESERT" FOR NEIGHBORHOODS LIKE THIS. SEE THESE CORNER STORES, THESE BODEGAS? GOOD LUCK FINDING ANYTHING FRESH. ANYTHING HEALTHY. ANYTHING THAT DOESN'T COME WITH A LONG LIST OF INGREDIENTS.
BUT THEY TAKE PUBLIC ASSISTANCE AND THERE'S ONE ON EVERY CORNER.
SO LET'S SAY I'M SOURCING FOOD FOR THE RESTAURANT AND I WANT TO STAY LOCAL. WHAT ARE MY OPTIONS? DO I HAVE OPTIONS?
THERE'RE OPTIONS. MIGHT NOT BE WHAT YOUR SOCIETY FRIENDS WANT, THOUGH.
THIS ISN'T AN EPISODE OF STARVE, MADDOX. I'M SINCERE. THIS IS ALL FOR REAL.
SHOW ME.

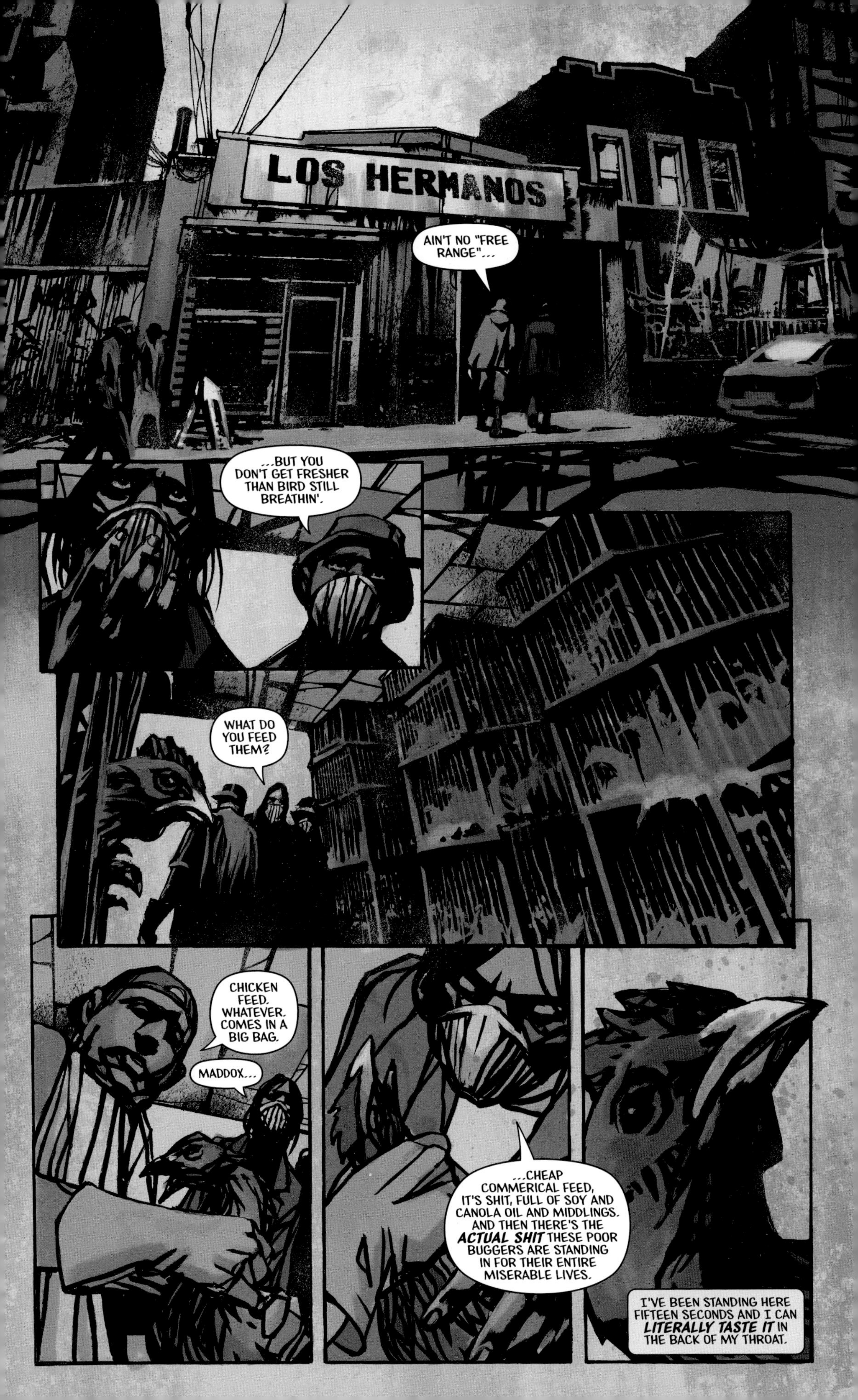
LOS HERMANOS
AIN'T NO "FREE RANGE"...
...BUT YOU DON'T GET FRESHER THAN BIRD STILL BREATHIN'.
WHAT DO YOU FEED THEM?
CHICKEN FEED. WHATEVER. COMES IN A BIG BAG.
MADDOX...
...CHEAP COMMERICAL FEED, IT'S SHIT, FULL OF SOY AND CANOLA OIL AND MIDDLINGS. AND THEN THERE'S THE ACTUAL SHIT THESE POOR BUGGERS ARE STANDING IN FOR THEIR ENTIRE MISERABLE LIVES.
I'VE BEEN STANDING HERE FIFTEEN SECONDS AND I CAN LITERALLY TASTE IT IN THE BACK OF MY THROAT.

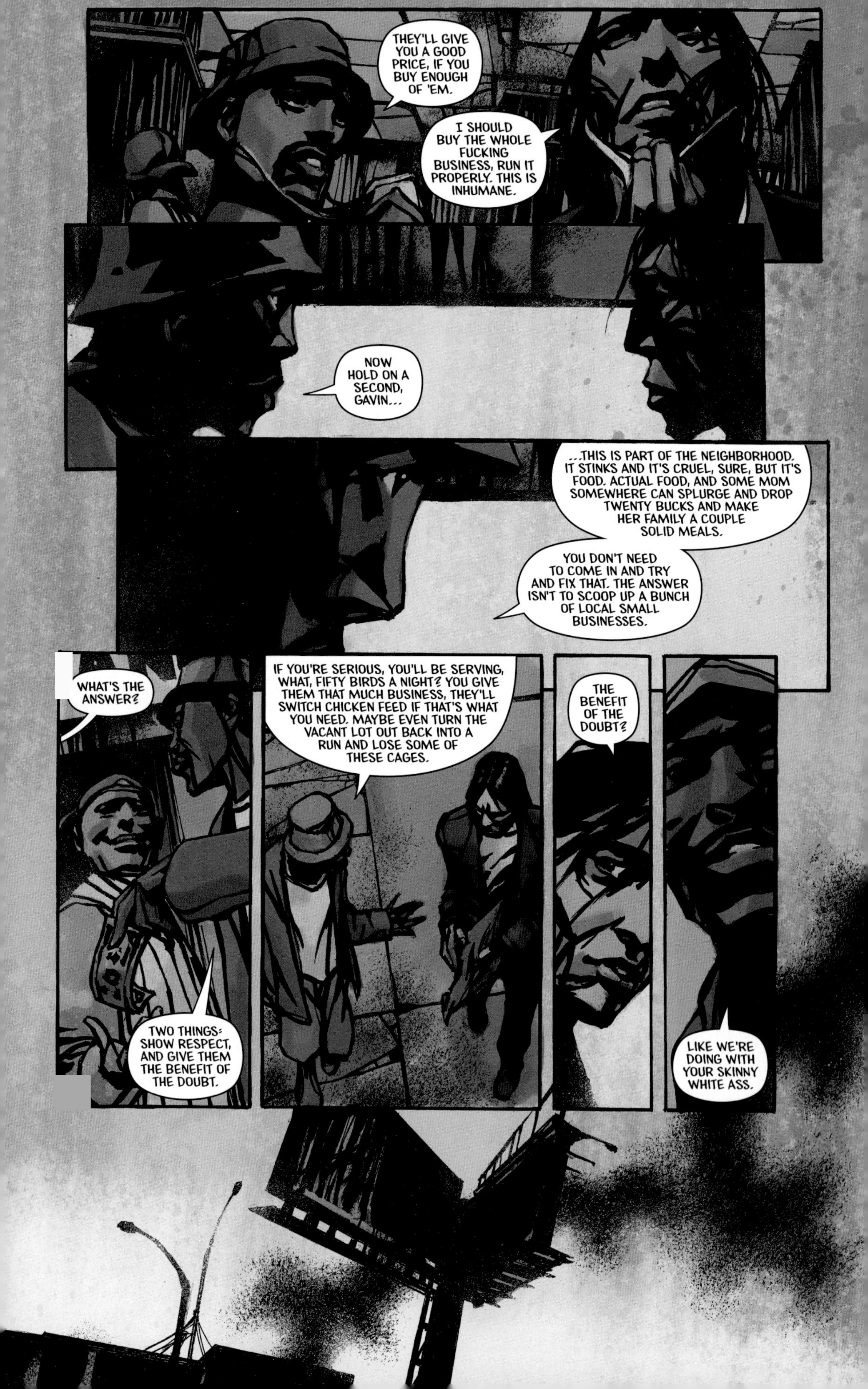
THEY'LL GIVE YOU A GOOD PRICE, IF YOU BUY ENOUGH OF 'EM.
I SHOULD BUY THE WHOLE FUCKING BUSINESS, RUN IT PROPERLY. THIS IS INHUMANE.
NOW HOLD ON A SECOND, GAVIN...
...THIS IS PART OF THE NEIGHBORHOOD. IT STINKS AND IT'S CRUEL, SURE, BUT IT'S FOOD. ACTUAL FOOD, AND SOME MOM SOMEWHERE CAN SPLURGE AND DROP TWENTY BUCKS AND MAKE HER FAMILY A COUPLE SOLID MEALS.
YOU DON'T NEED TO COME IN AND TRY AND FIX THAT. THE ANSWER ISN'T TO SCOOP UP A BUNCH OF LOCAL SMALL BUSINESSES.
WHAT'S THE ANSWER?
TWO THINGS: SHOW RESPECT, AND GIVE THEM THE BENEFIT OF THE DOUBT.
IF YOU'RE SERIOUS, YOU'LL BE SERVING, WHAT, FIFTY BIRDS A NIGHT? YOU GIVE THEM THAT MUCH BUSINESS, THEY'LL SWITCH CHICKEN FEED IF THAT'S WHAT YOU NEED. MAYBE EVEN TURN THE VACANT LOT OUT BACK INTO A RUN AND LOSE SOME OF THESE CAGES.
THE BENEFIT OF THE DOUBT?
LIKE WE'RE DOING WITH YOUR SKINNY WHITE ASS.

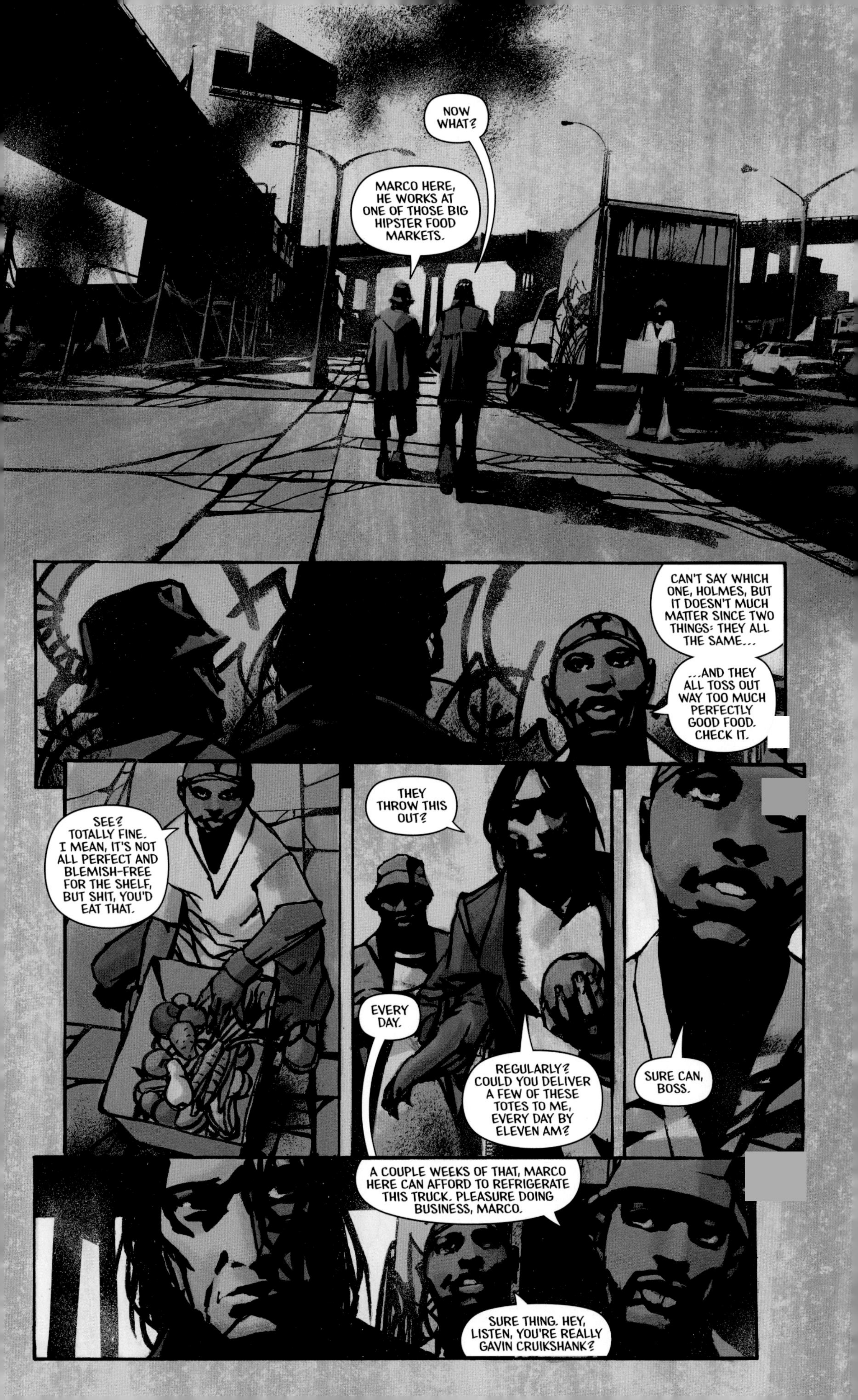
MARCO HERE, HE WORKS AT ONE OF THOSE BIG HIPSTER FOOD MARKETS.
NOW WHAT?
CAN'T SAY WHICH ONE, HOLMES, BUT IT DOESN'T MUCH MATTER SINCE TWO THINGS: THEY ALL THE SAME...
...AND THEY ALL TOSS OUT WAY TOO MUCH PERFECTLY GOOD FOOD. CHECK IT.
SEE? TOTALLY FINE. I MEAN, IT'S NOT ALL PERFECT AND BLEMISH-FREE FOR THE SHELF, BUT SHIT, YOU'D EAT THAT.
THEY THROW THIS OUT?
EVERY DAY.
REGULARLY? COULD YOU DELIVER A FEW OF THESE TOTES TO ME, EVERY DAY BY ELEVEN AM?
SURE CAN, BOSS.
A COUPLE WEEKS OF THAT, MARCO HERE CAN AFFORD TO REFRIGERATE THIS TRUCK. PLEASURE DOING BUSINESS, MARCO.
SURE THING. HEY, LISTEN, YOU'RE REALLY GAVIN CRUIKSHANK?

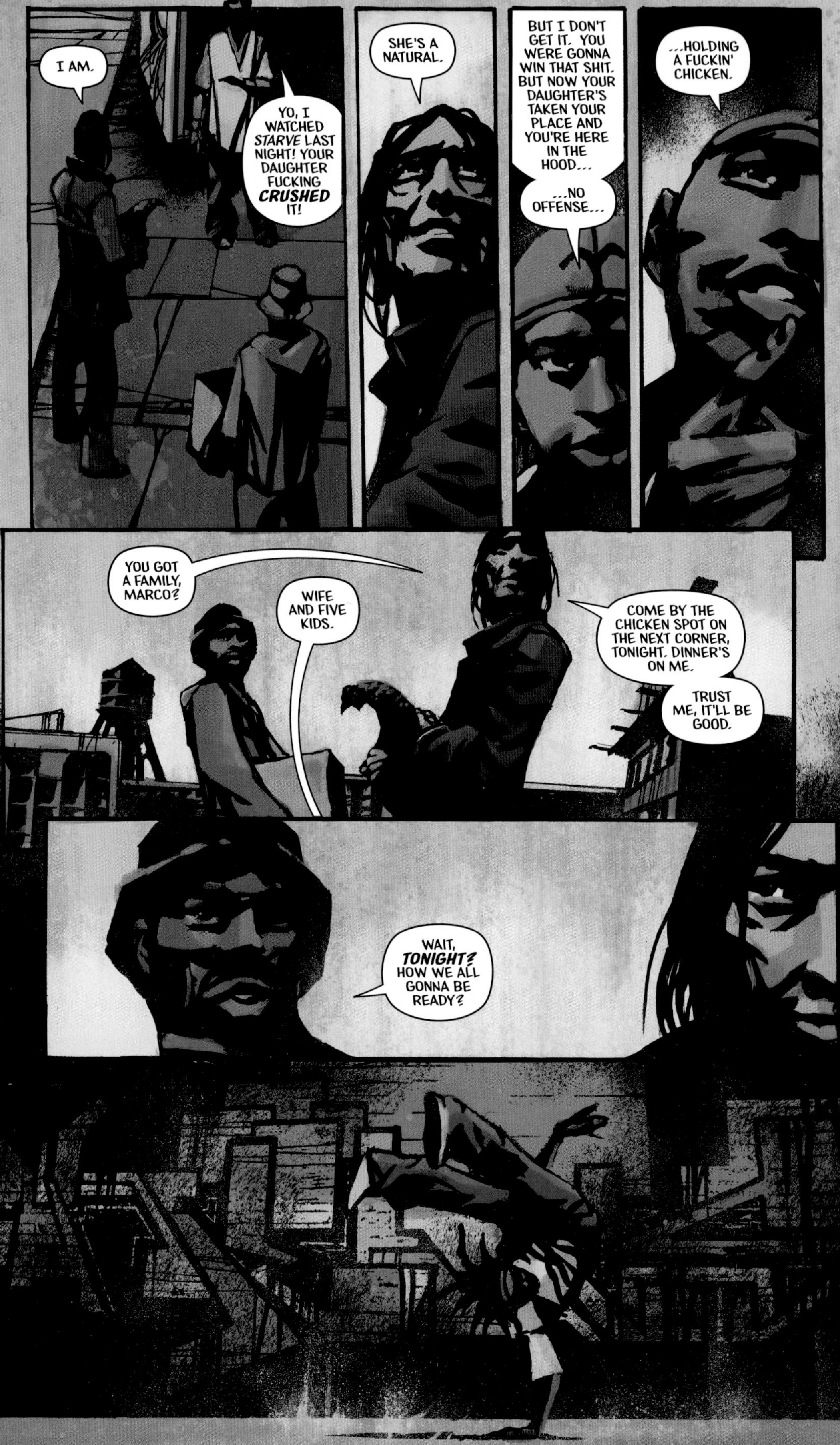
I AM.
YO, I WATCHED STARVE LAST NIGHT! YOUR DAUGHTER FUCKING CRUSHED IT!
SHE'S A NATURAL.
BUT I DON'T GET IT. YOU WERE GONNA WIN THAT SHIT. BUT NOW YOUR DAUGHTER'S TAKEN YOUR PLACE AND YOU'RE HERE IN THE HOOD...
...NO OFFENSE...
...HOLDING A FUCKIN' CHICKEN.
YOU GOT A FAMILY, MARCO?
WIFE AND FIVE KIDS.
COME BY THE CHICKEN SPOT ON THE NEXT CORNER, TONIGHT. DINNER'S ON ME.
TRUST ME, IT'LL BE GOOD.
WAIT, TONIGHT? HOW WE ALL GONNA BE READY?

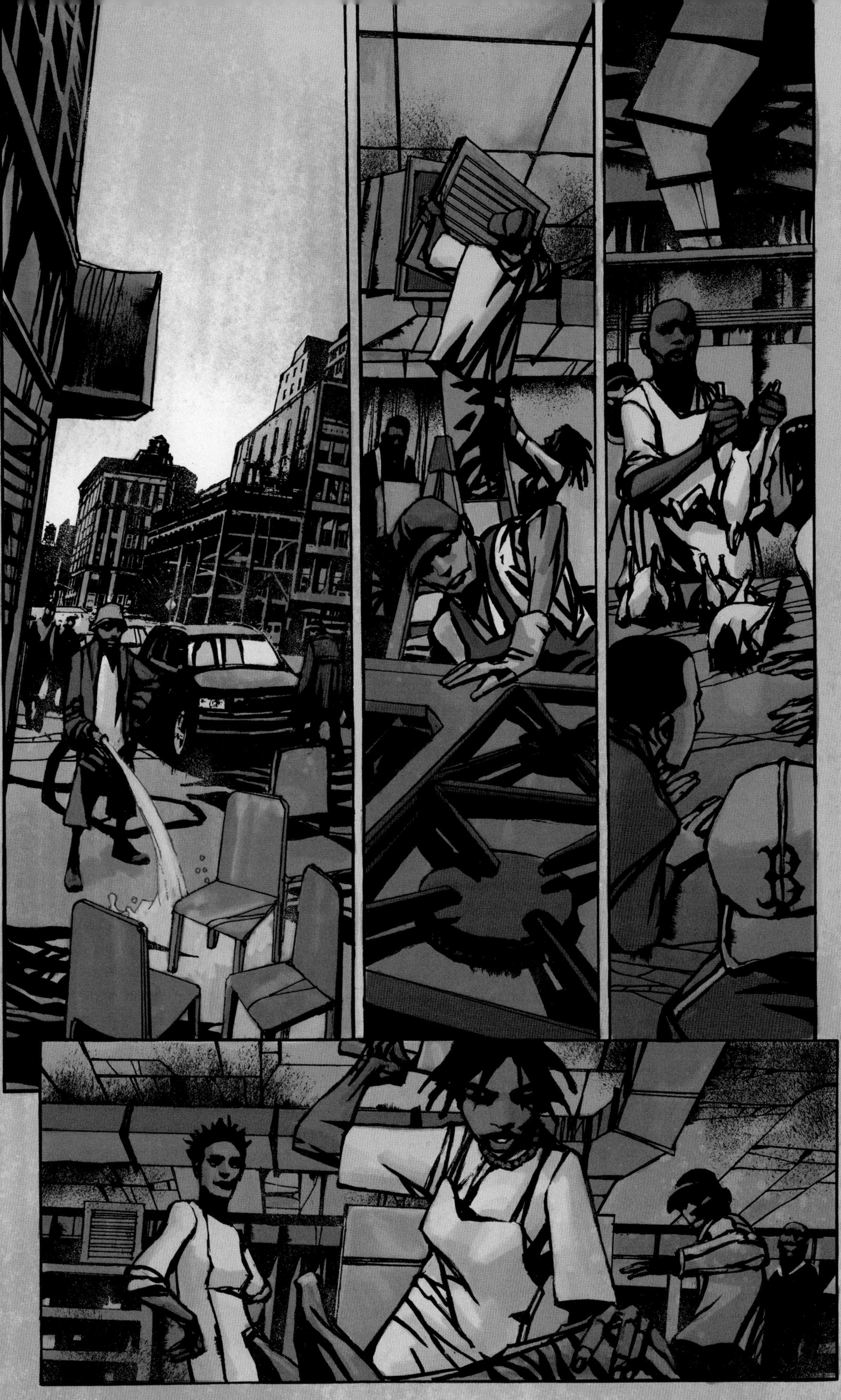

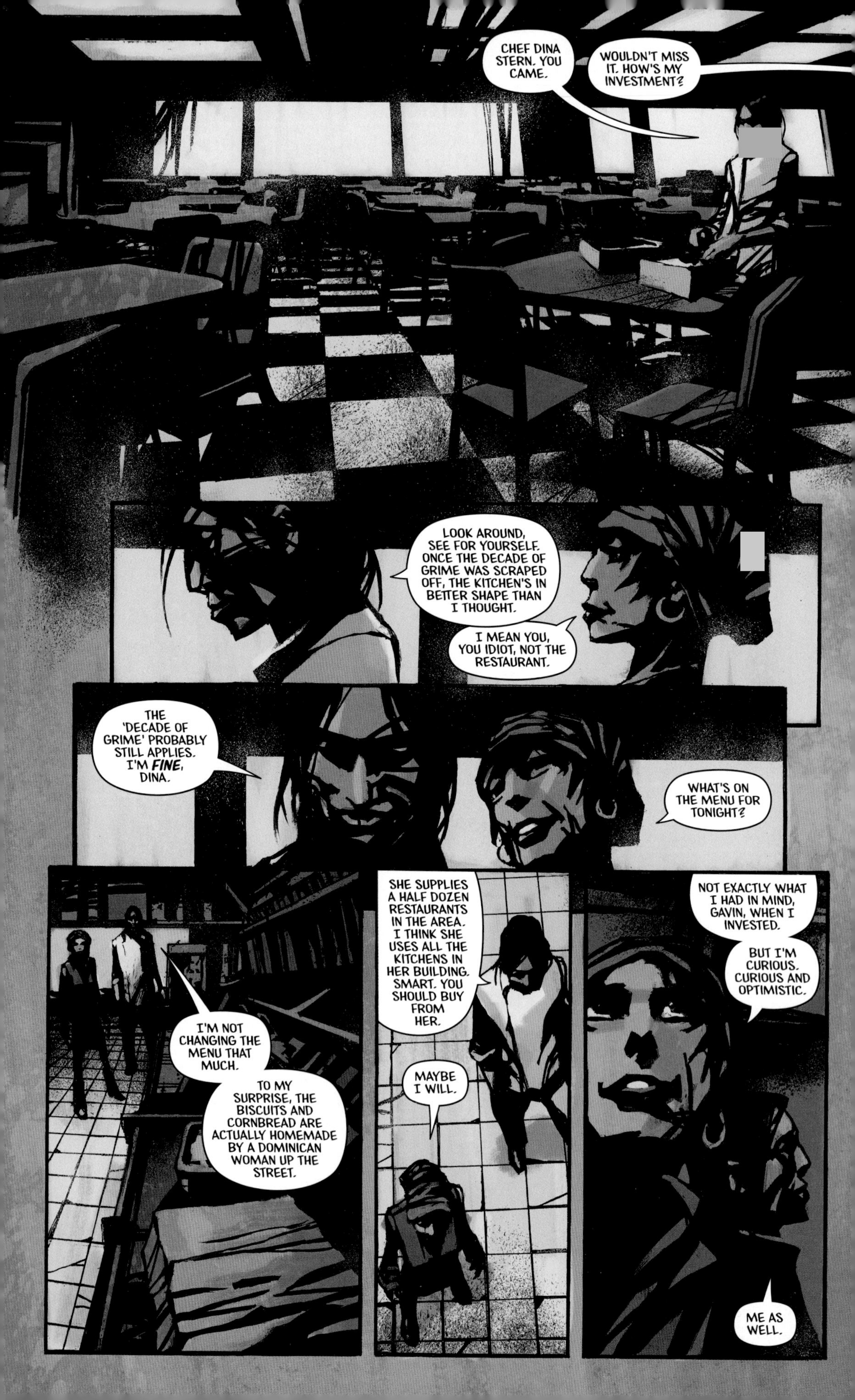
CHEF DINA STERN. YOU CAME.
WOULDN'T MISS IT. HOW'S MY INVESTMENT?
LOOK AROUND, SEE FOR YOURSELF. ONCE THE DECADE OF GRIME WAS SCRAPED OFF, THE KITCHEN'S IN BETTER SHAPE THAN I THOUGHT.
I MEAN YOU, YOU IDIOT, NOT THE RESTAURANT.
THE 'DECADE OF GRIME' PROBABLY STILL APPLIES. I'M FINE, DINA.
WHAT'S ON THE MENU FOR TONIGHT?
I'M NOT CHANGING THE MENU THAT MUCH.
TO MY SURPRISE, THE BISCUITS AND CORNBREAD ARE ACTUALLY HOMEMADE BY A DOMINICAN WOMAN UP THE STREET.
SHE SUPPLIES A HALF DOZEN RESTAURANTS IN THE AREA. I THINK SHE USES ALL THE KITCHENS IN HER BUILDING. SMART. YOU SHOULD BUY FROM HER.
MAYBE I WILL.
NOT EXACTLY WHAT I HAD IN MIND, GAVIN, WHEN I INVESTED.
BUT I'M CURIOUS. CURIOUS AND OPTIMISTIC.
ME AS WELL.

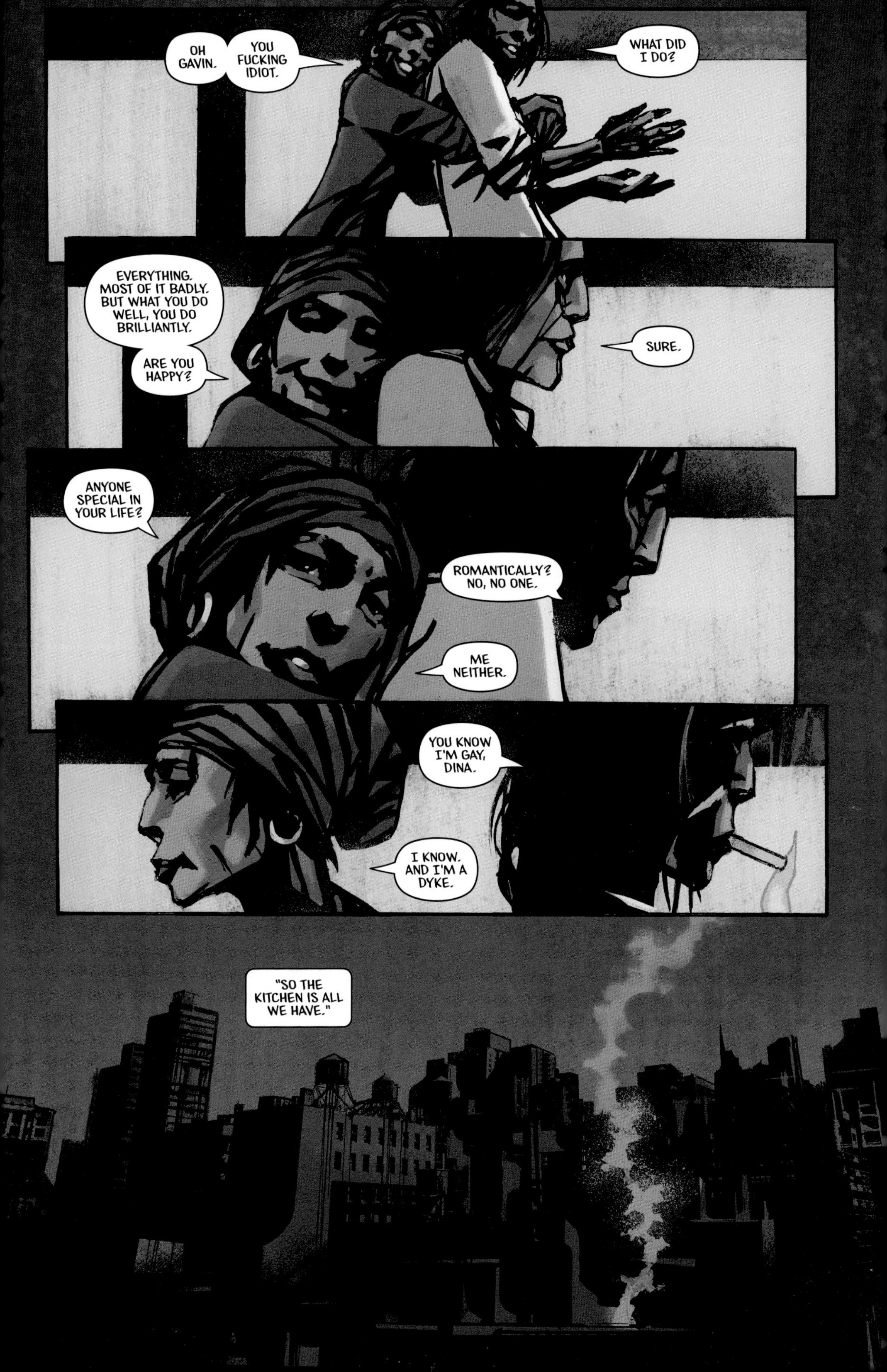
OH GAVIN.
YOU FUCKING IDIOT.
WHAT DID I DO?
EVERYTHING. MOST OF IT BADLY. BUT WHAT YOU DO WELL, YOU DO BRILLIANTLY.
ARE YOU HAPPY?
SURE.
ANYONE SPECIAL IN YOUR LIFE?
ROMANTICALLY? NO, NO ONE.
ME NEITHER.
YOU KNOW I'M GAY, DINA.
I KNOW. AND I'M A DYKE.
"SO THE KITCHEN IS ALL WE HAVE."

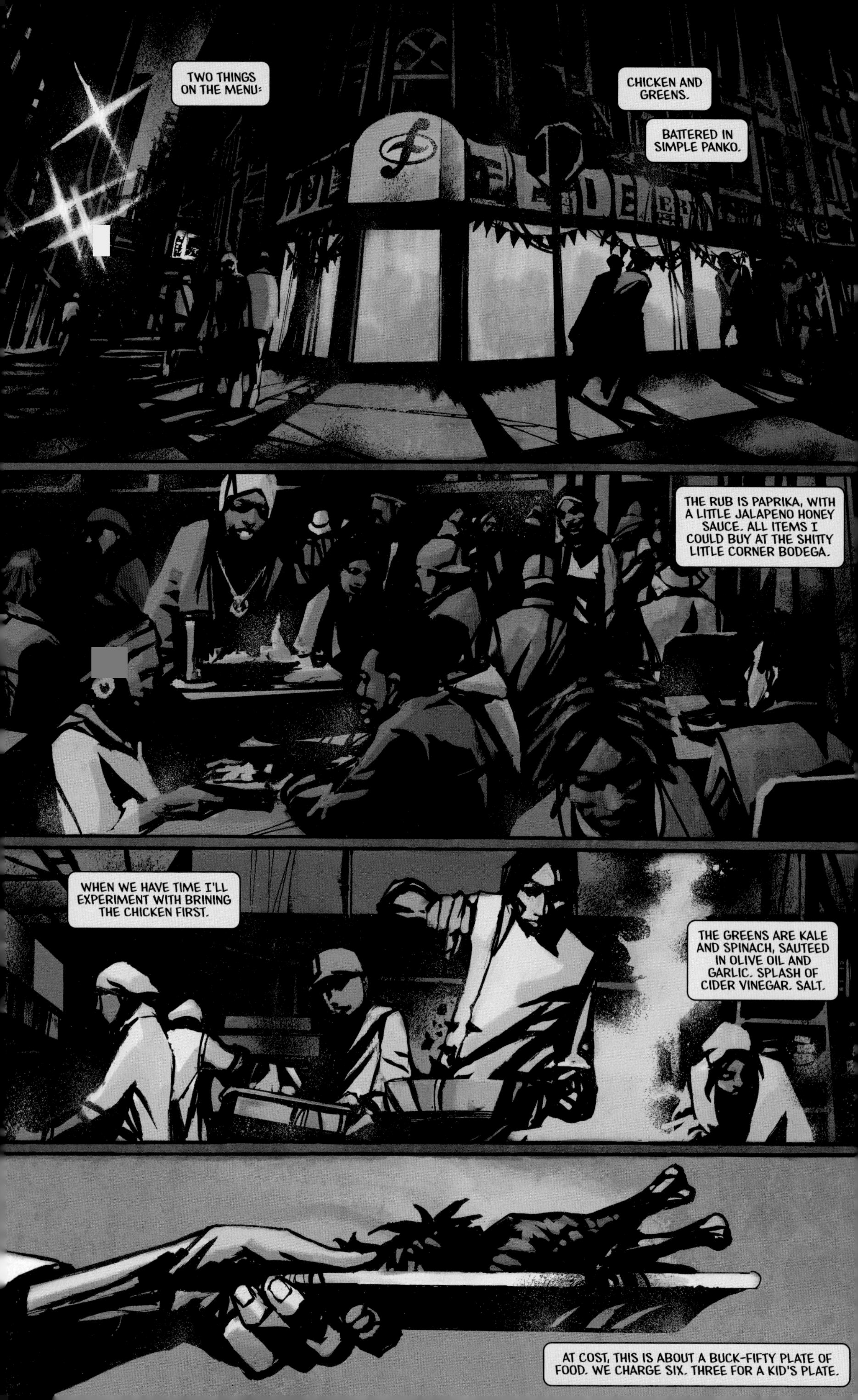
TWO THINGS ON THE MENU:
CHICKEN AND GREENS.
BATTERED IN SIMPLE PANKO.
THE RUB IS PAPRIKA, WITH A LITTLE JALAPENO HONEY SAUCE. ALL ITEMS I COULD BUY AT THE SHITTY LITTLE CORNER BODEGA.
WHEN WE HAVE TIME I'LL EXPERIMENT WITH BRINING THE CHICKEN FIRST.
THE GREENS ARE KALE AND SPINACH, SAUTEED IN OLIVE OIL AND GARLIC. SPLASH OF CIDER VINEGAR. SALT.
AT COST, THIS IS ABOUT A BUCK-FIFTY PLATE OF FOOD. WE CHARGE SIX. THREE FOR A KID'S PLATE.

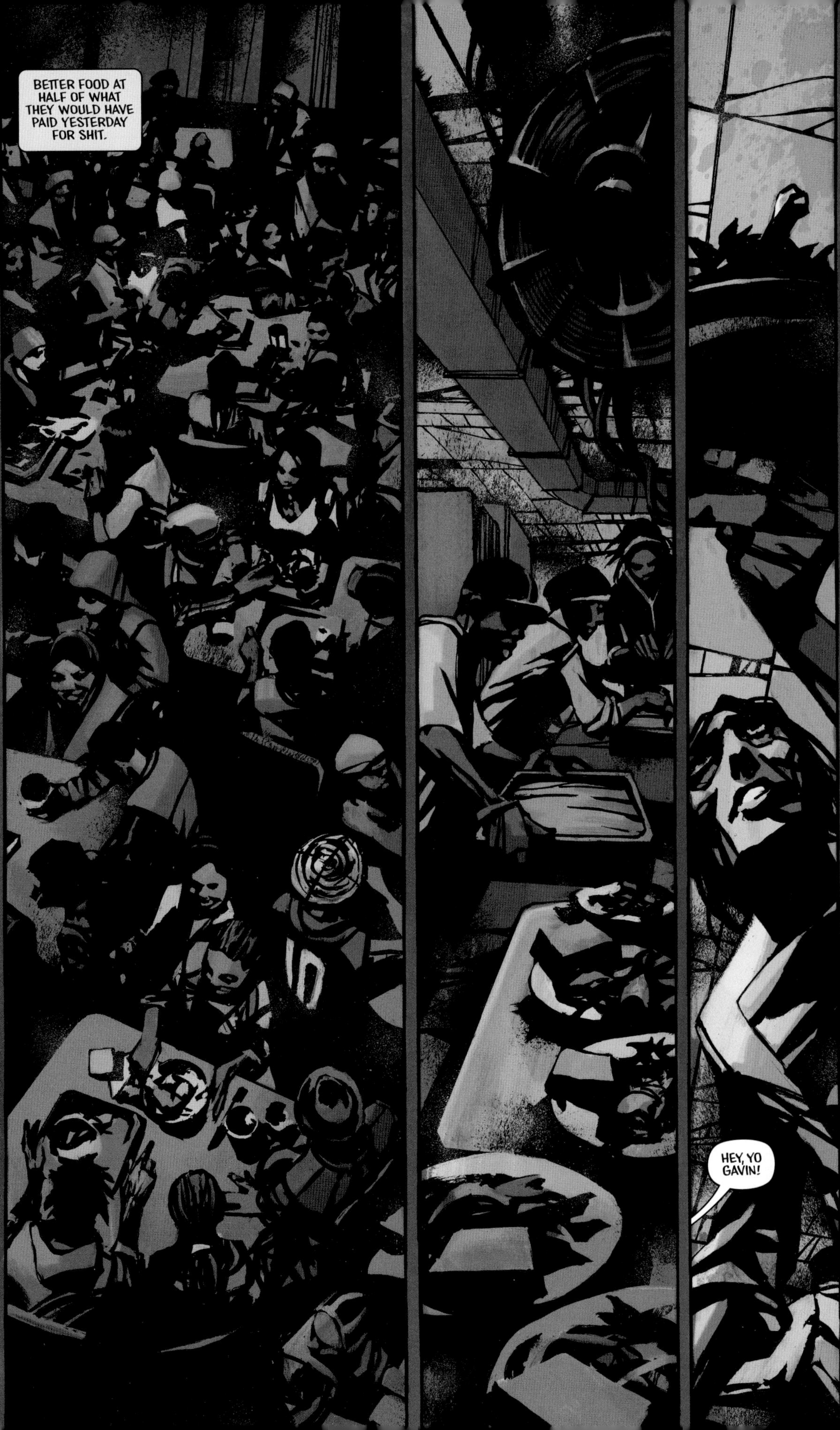
BETTER FOOD AT HALF OF WHAT THEY WOULD HAVE PAID YESTERDAY FOR SHIT.
HEY, YO GAVIN!

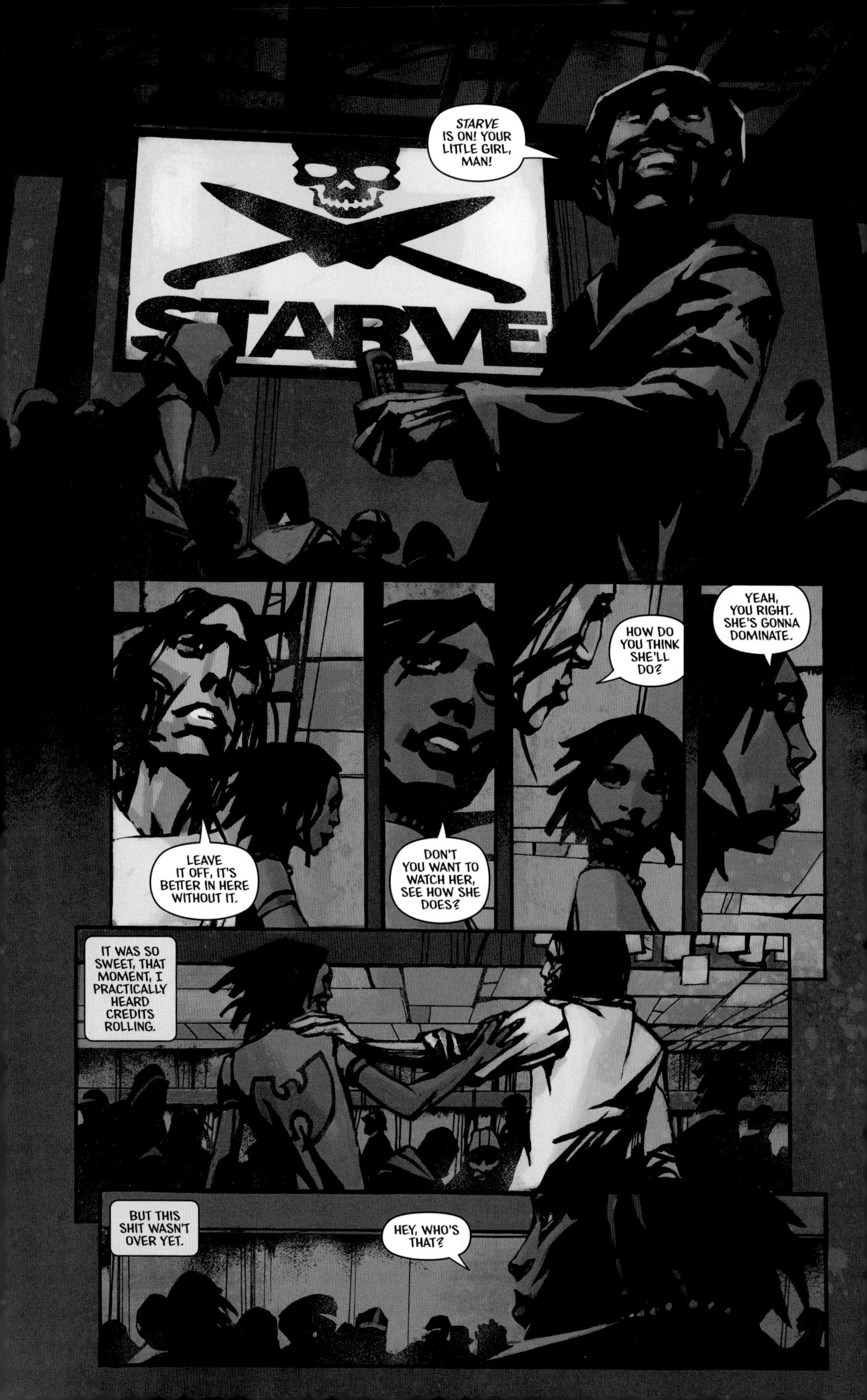
STARVE
STARVE IS ON! YOUR LITTLE GIRL, MAN!
LEAVE IT OFF, IT'S BETTER IN HERE WITHOUT IT.
DON'T YOU WANT TO WATCH HER, SEE HOW SHE DOES?
HOW DO YOU THINK SHE'LL DO?
YEAH, YOU RIGHT. SHE'S GONNA DOMINATE.
IT WAS SO SWEET, THAT MOMENT, I PRACTICALLY HEARD CREDITS ROLLING.
BUT THIS SHIT WASN'T OVER YET.
HEY, WHO'S THAT?

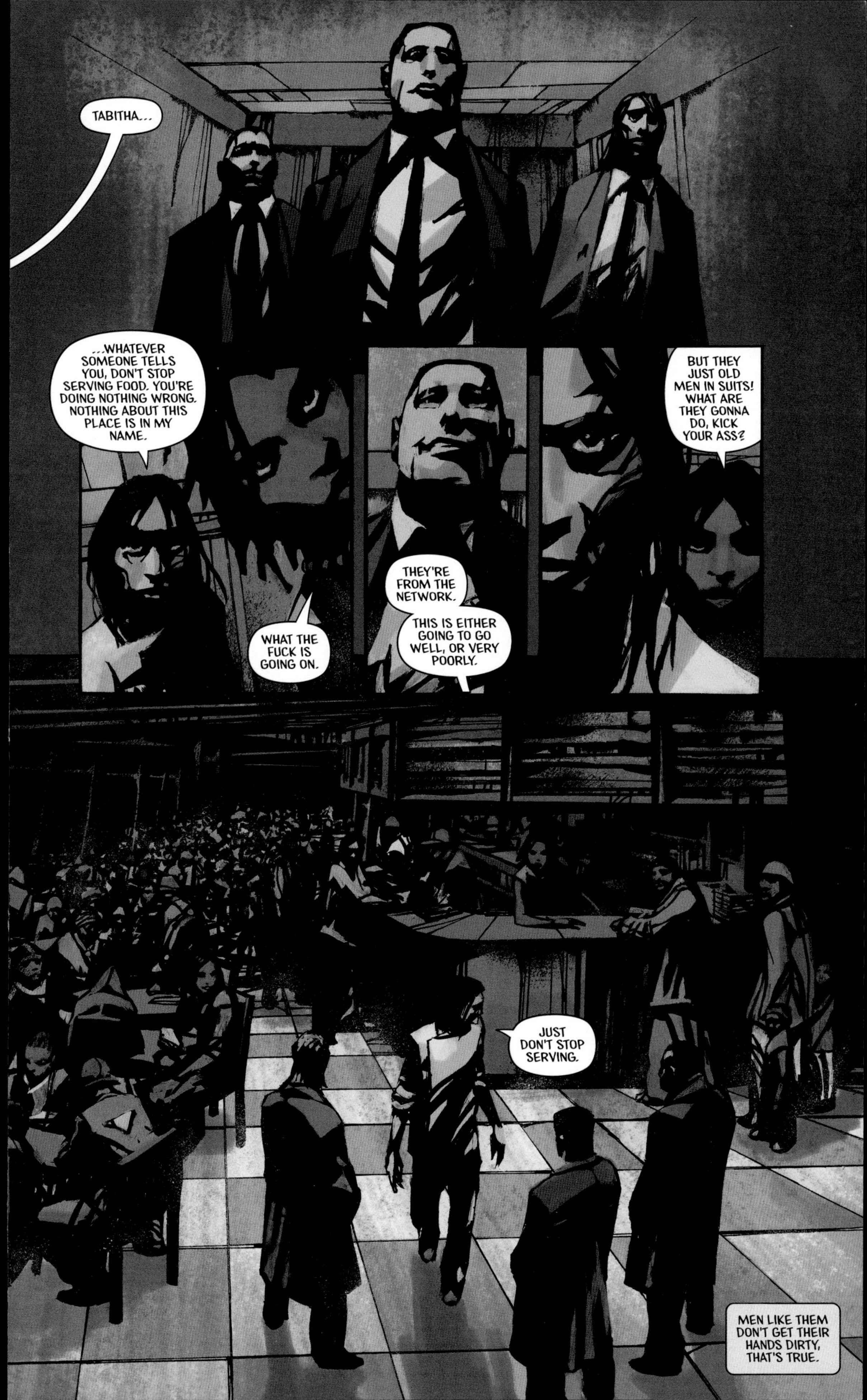
TABITHA...
...WHATEVER SOMEONE TELLS YOU, DON'T STOP SERVING FOOD. YOU'RE DOING NOTHING WRONG. NOTHING ABOUT THIS PLACE IS IN MY NAME.
WHAT THE FUCK IS GOING ON.
THEY'RE FROM THE NETWORK.
THIS IS EITHER GOING TO GO WELL, OR VERY POORLY.
BUT THEY JUST OLD MEN IN SUITS! WHAT ARE THEY GONNA DO, KICK YOUR ASS?
JUST DON'T STOP SERVING.
MEN LIKE THEM DON'T GET THEIR HANDS DIRTY, THAT'S TRUE.

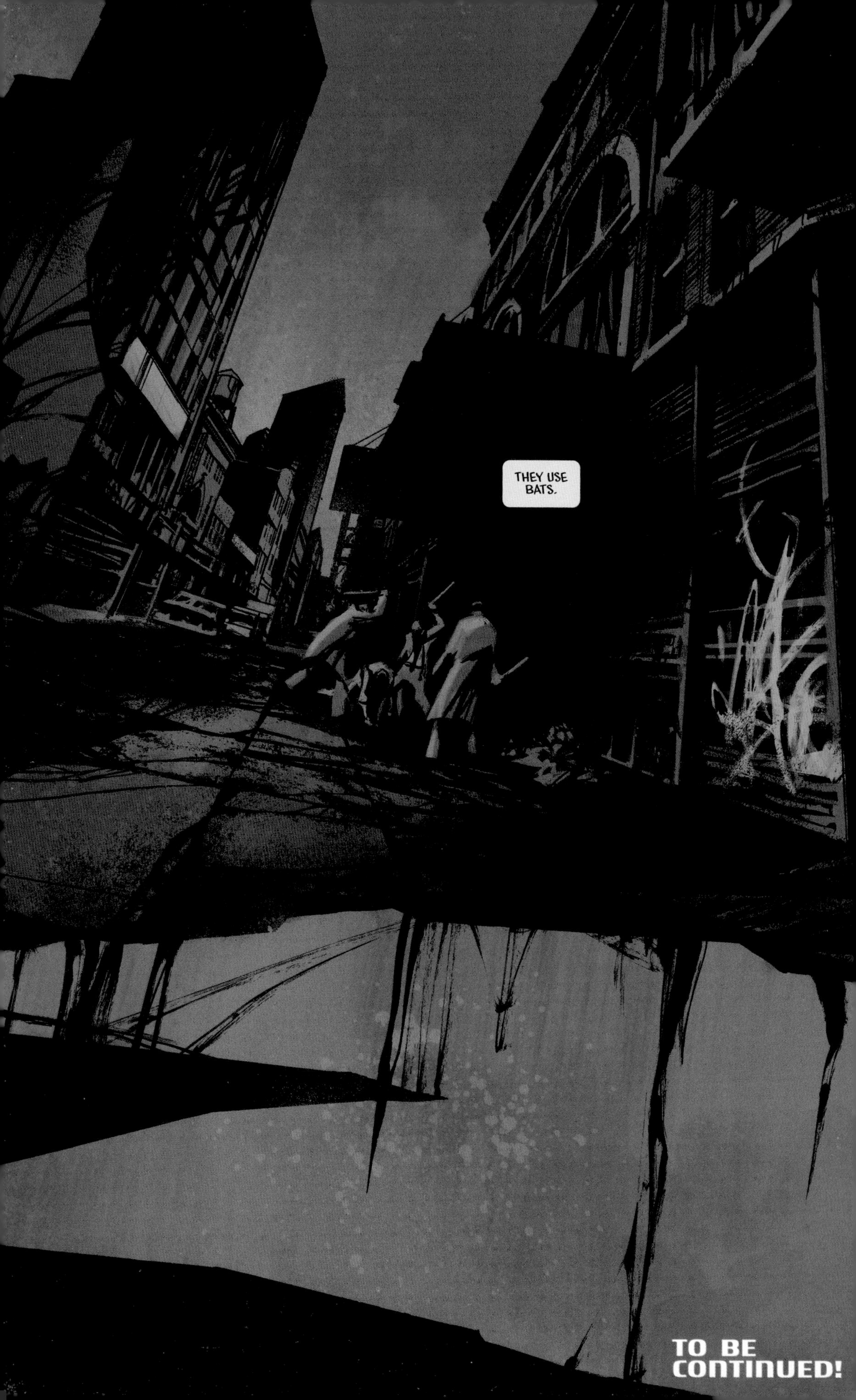
THEY USE BATS.
TO BE CONTINUED!

"...AND INTO THE FIRE"

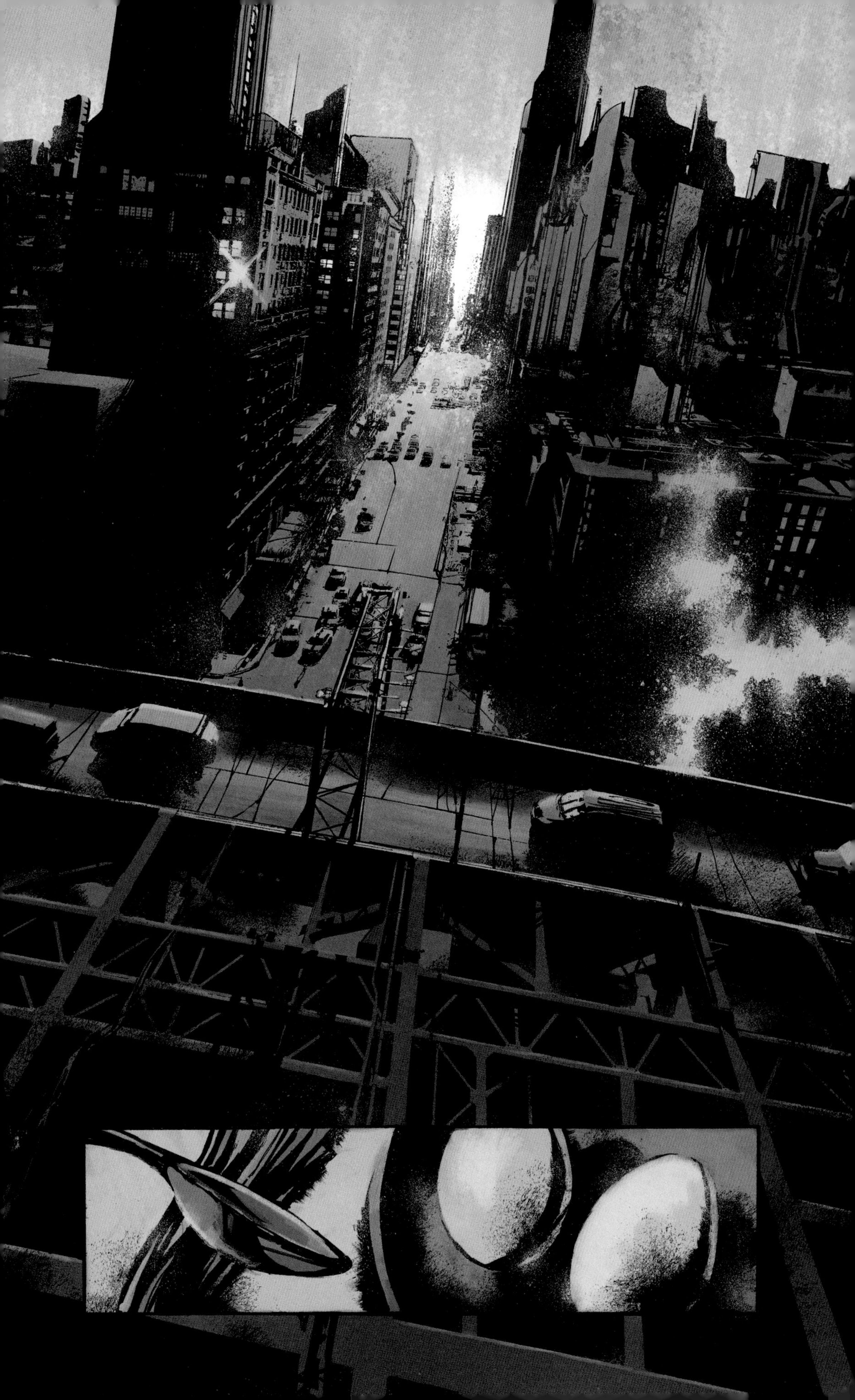

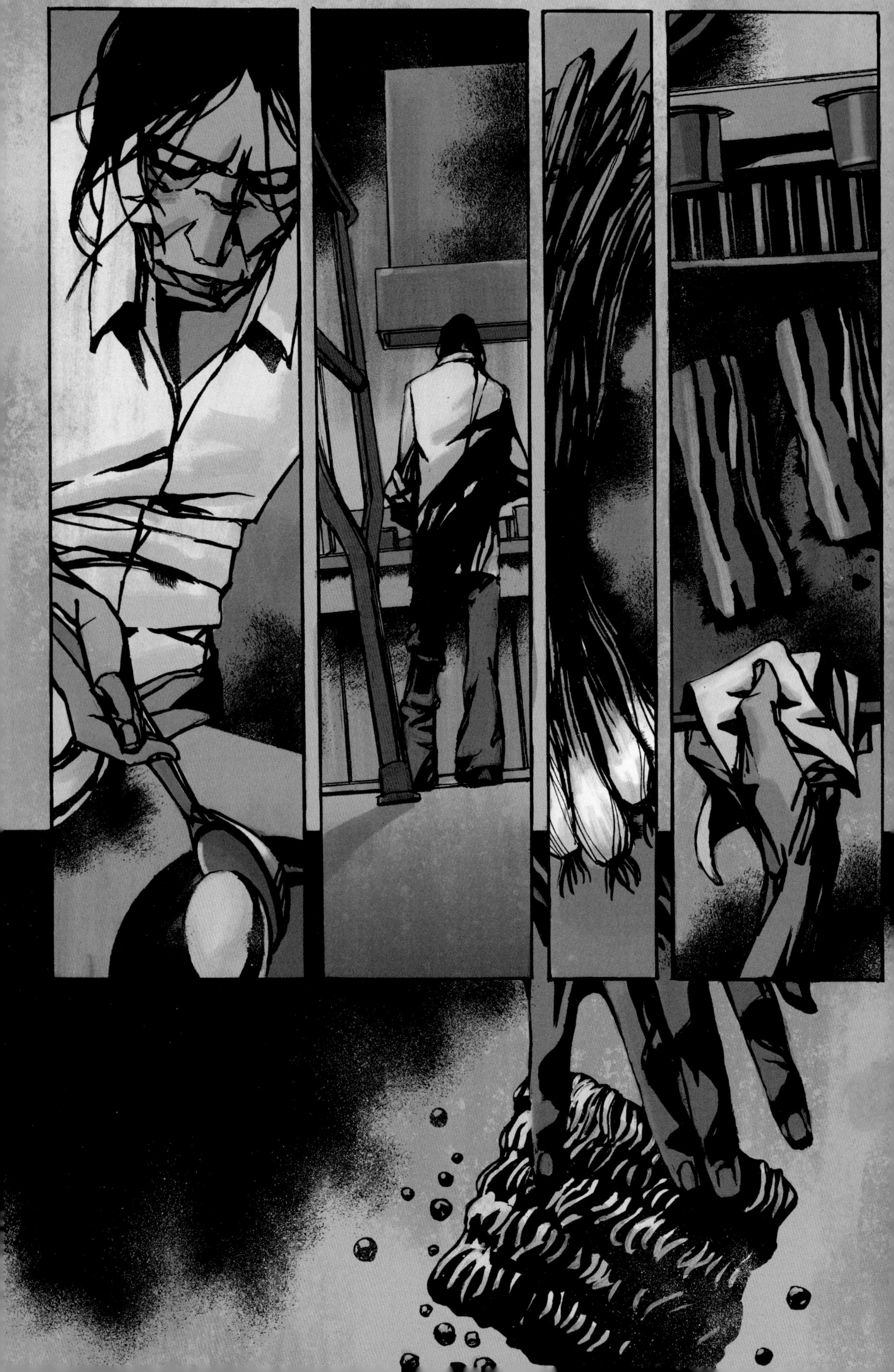

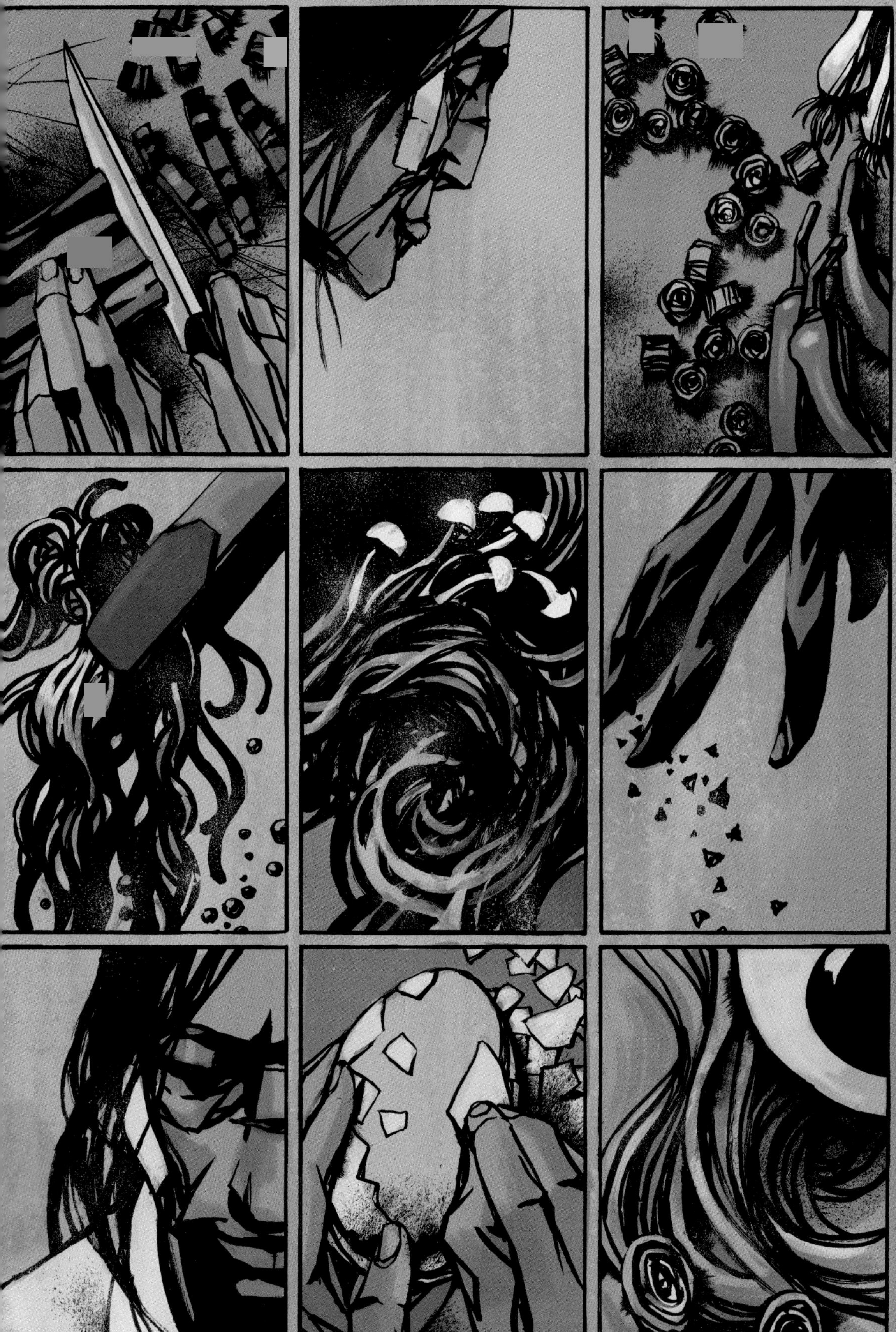

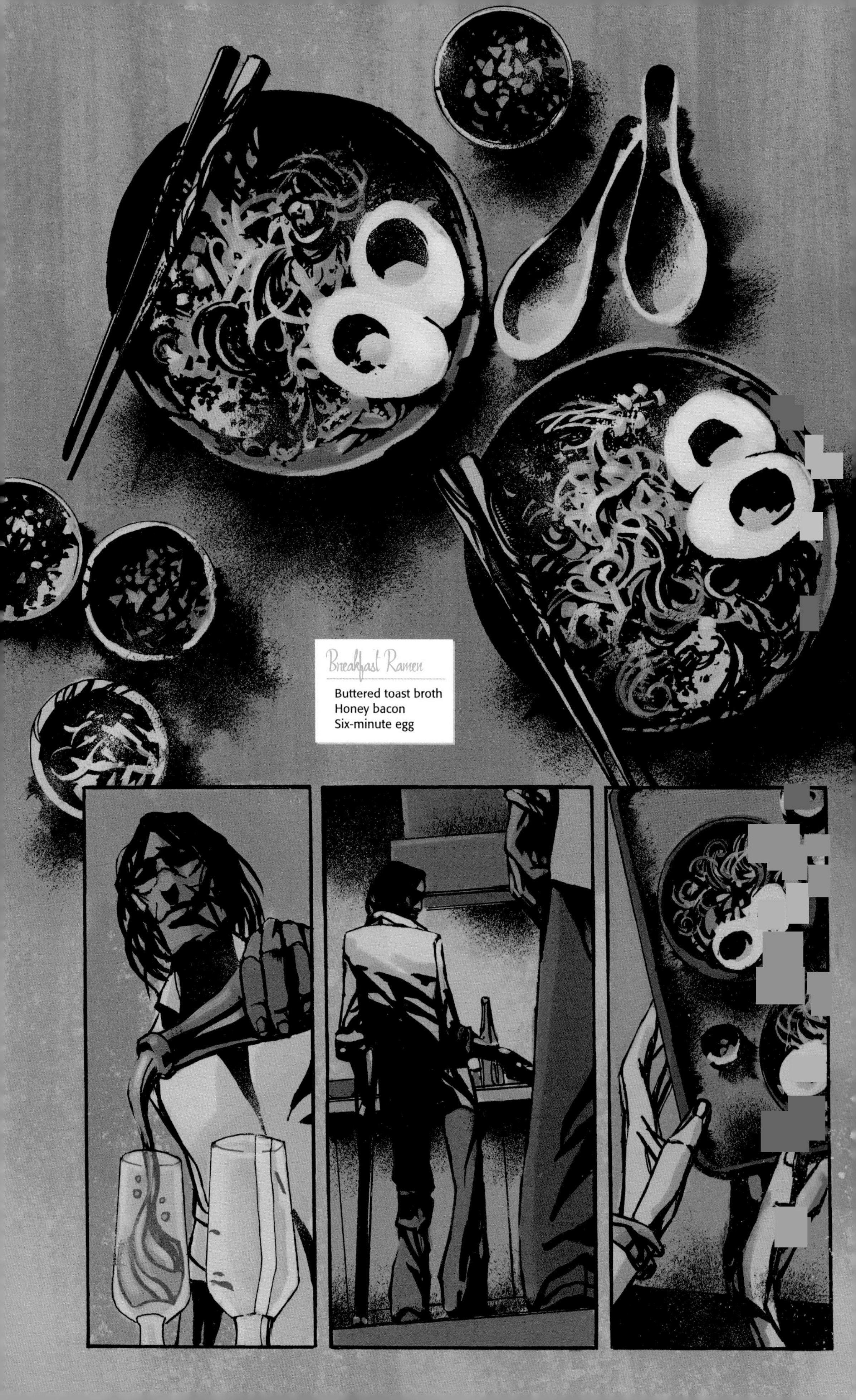
Breakfast Ramen
Buttered toast broth
Honey bacon
Six-minute egg

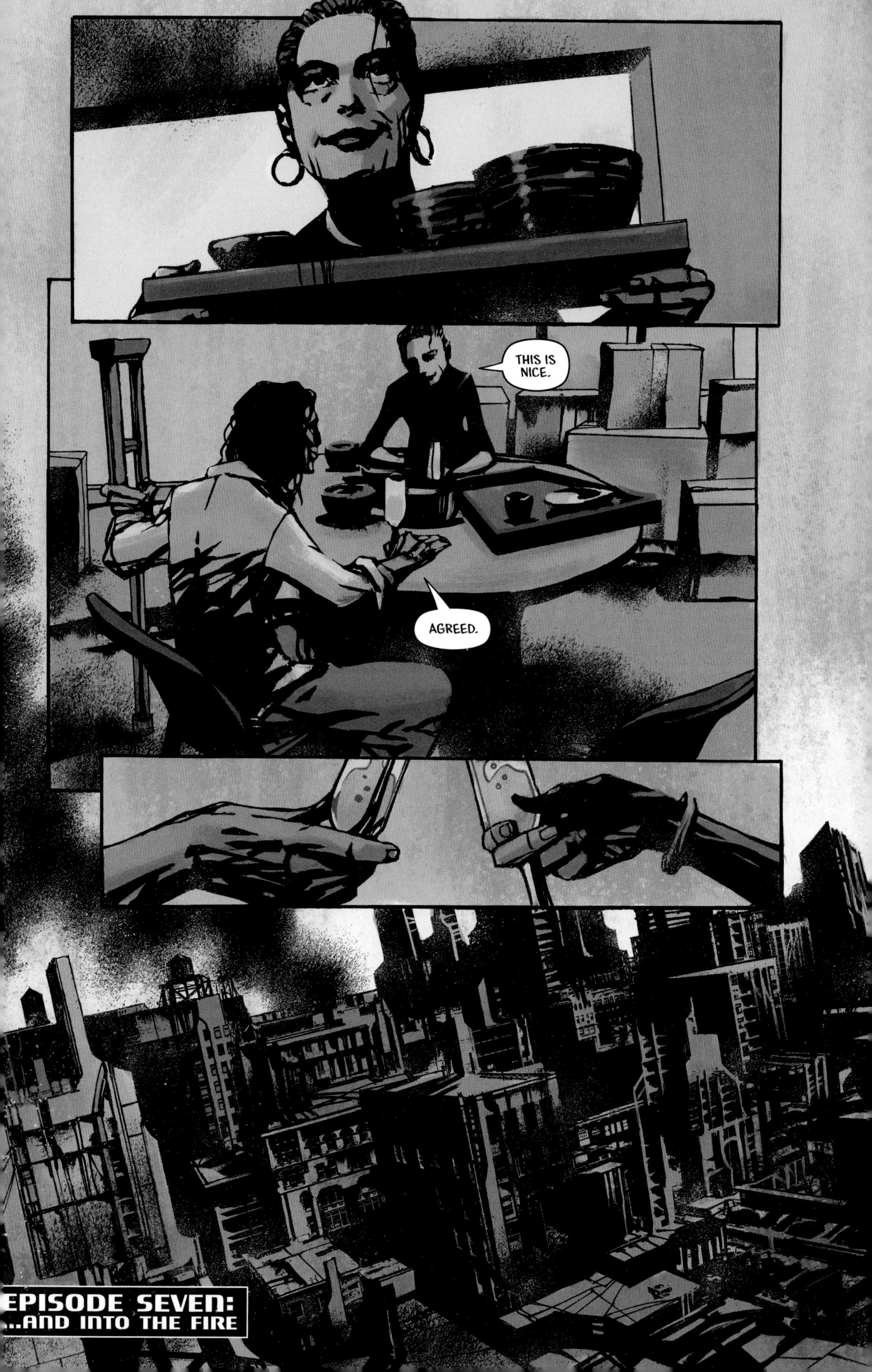
THIS IS NICE.
AGREED.
EPISODE SEVEN:
...AND INTO THE FIRE

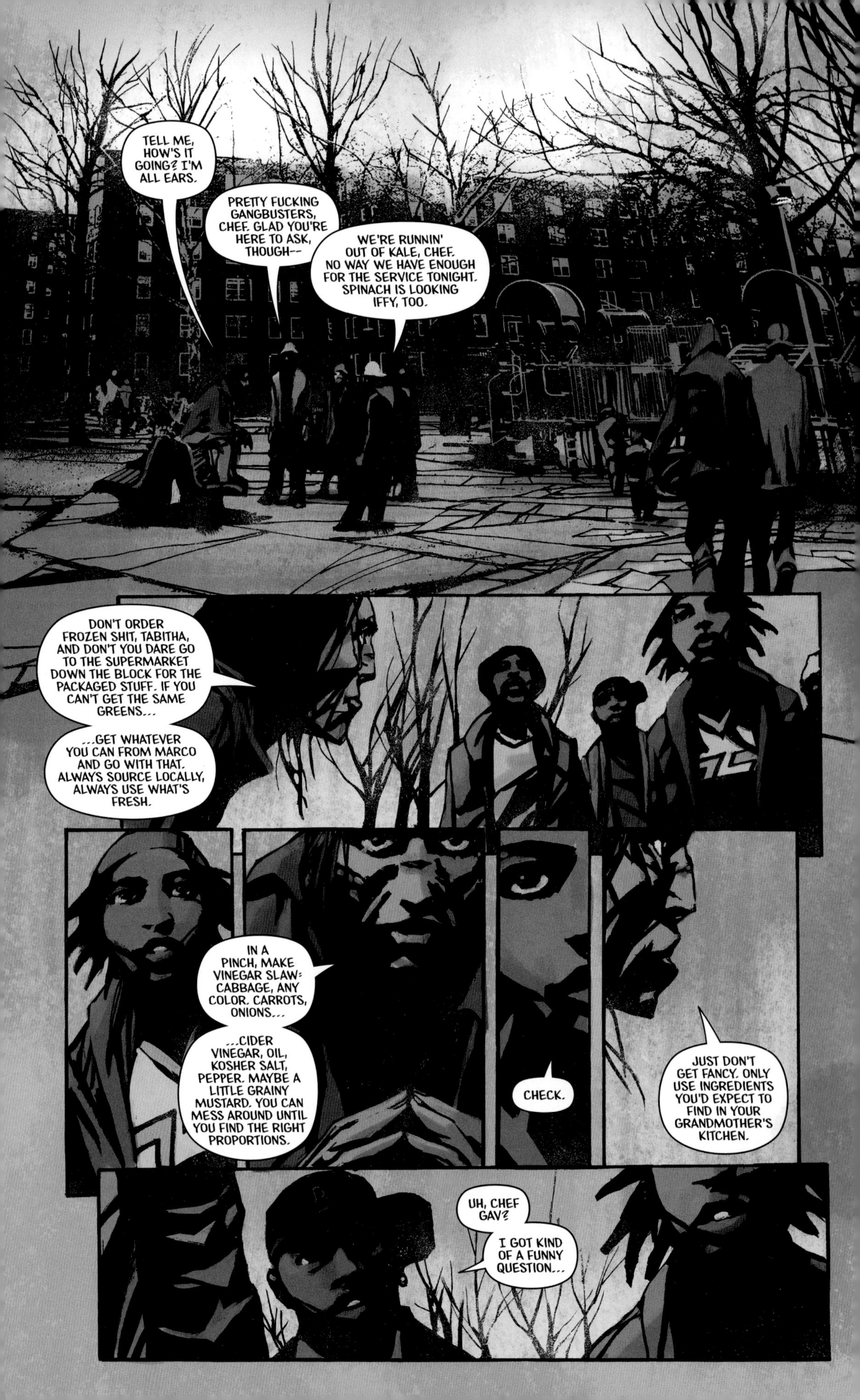
TELL ME, HOW'S IT GOING? I'M ALL EARS.
PRETTY FUCKING GANGBUSTERS, CHEF. GLAD YOU'RE HERE TO ASK, THOUGH--
WE'RE RUNNIN' OUT OF KALE, CHEF. NO WAY WE HAVE ENOUGH FOR THE SERVICE TONIGHT. SPINACH IS LOOKING IFFY, TOO.
DON'T ORDER FROZEN SHIT, TABITHA, AND DON'T YOU DARE GO TO THE SUPERMARKET DOWN THE BLOCK FOR THE PACKAGED STUFF. IF YOU CAN'T GET THE SAME GREENS...
...GET WHATEVER YOU CAN FROM MARCO AND GO WITH THAT. ALWAYS SOURCE LOCALLY, ALWAYS USE WHAT'S FRESH.
IN A PINCH, MAKE VINEGAR SLAW: CABBAGE, ANY COLOR. CARROTS, ONIONS...
...CIDER VINEGAR, OIL, KOSHER SALT, PEPPER. MAYBE A LITTLE GRAINY MUSTARD. YOU CAN MESS AROUND UNTIL YOU FIND THE RIGHT PROPORTIONS.
CHECK.
JUST DON'T GET FANCY. ONLY USE INGREDIENTS YOU'D EXPECT TO FIND IN YOUR GRANDMOTHER'S KITCHEN.
UH, CHEF GAV?
I GOT KIND OF A FUNNY QUESTION...

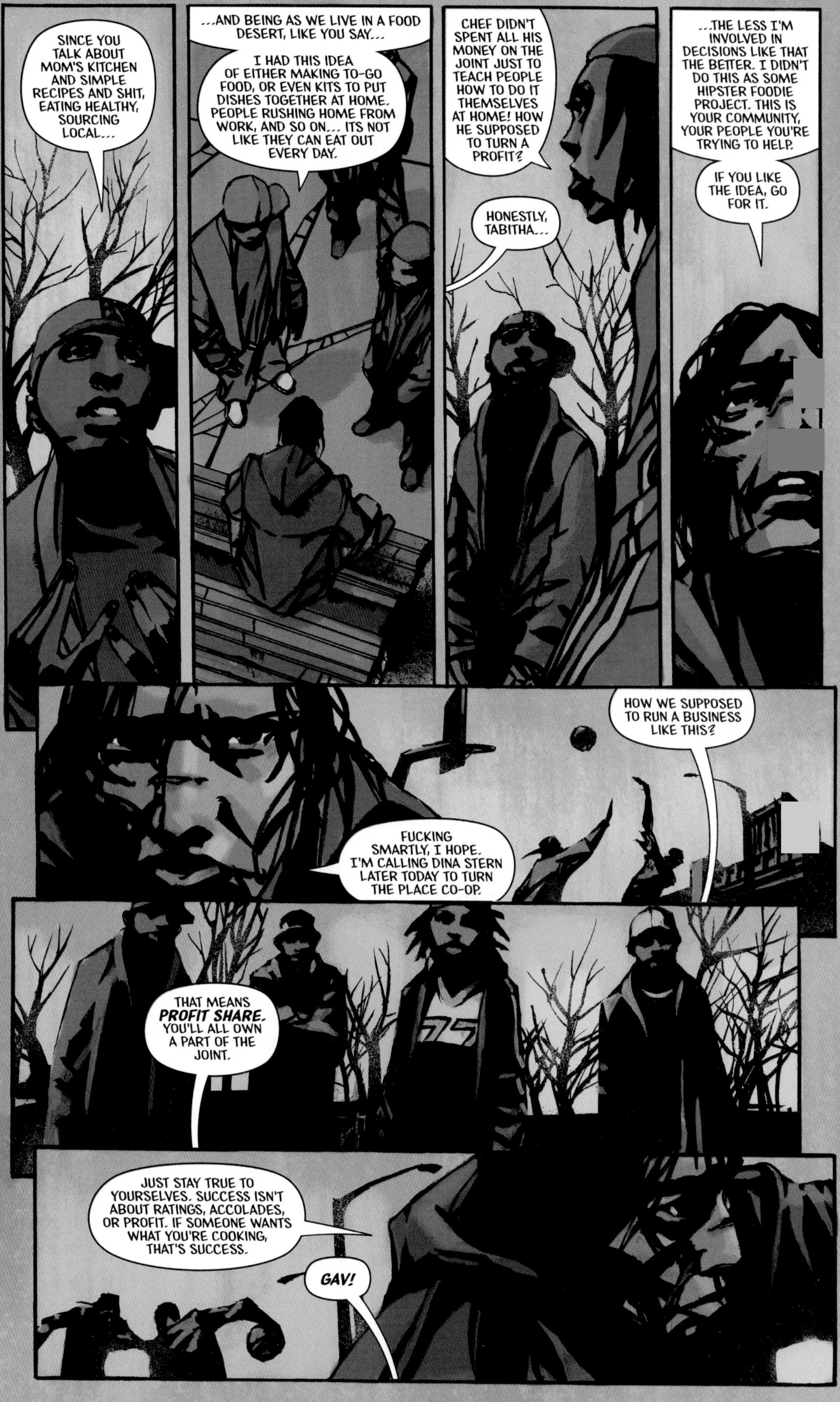
SINCE YOU TALK ABOUT MOM'S KITCHEN AND SIMPLE RECIPES AND SHIT, EATING HEALTHY, SOURCING LOCAL...
...AND BEING AS WE LIVE IN A FOOD DESERT, LIKE YOU SAY...
I HAD THIS IDEA OF EITHER MAKING TO-GO FOOD, OR EVEN KITS TO PUT DISHES TOGETHER AT HOME. PEOPLE RUSHING HOME FROM WORK, AND SO ON... ITS NOT LIKE THEY CAN EAT OUT EVERY DAY.
CHEF DIDN'T SPENT ALL HIS MONEY ON THE JOINT JUST TO TEACH PEOPLE HOW TO DO IT THEMSELVES AT HOME! HOW HE SUPPOSED TO TURN A PROFIT?
HONESTLY, TABITHA...
...THE LESS I'M INVOLVED IN DECISIONS LIKE THAT THE BETTER. I DIDN'T DO THIS AS SOME HIPSTER FOODIE PROJECT. THIS IS YOUR COMMUNITY, YOUR PEOPLE YOU'RE TRYING TO HELP.
IF YOU LIKE THE IDEA, GO FOR IT.
HOW WE SUPPOSED TO RUN A BUSINESS LIKE THIS?
FUCKING SMARTLY, I HOPE. I'M CALLING DINA STERN LATER TODAY TO TURN THE PLACE CO-OP.
THAT MEANS ***PROFIT SHARE.*** YOU'LL ALL OWN A PART OF THE JOINT.
JUST STAY TRUE TO YOURSELVES. SUCCESS ISN'T ABOUT RATINGS, ACCOLADES, OR PROFIT. IF SOMEONE WANTS WHAT YOU'RE COOKING, THAT'S SUCCESS.
GAV!

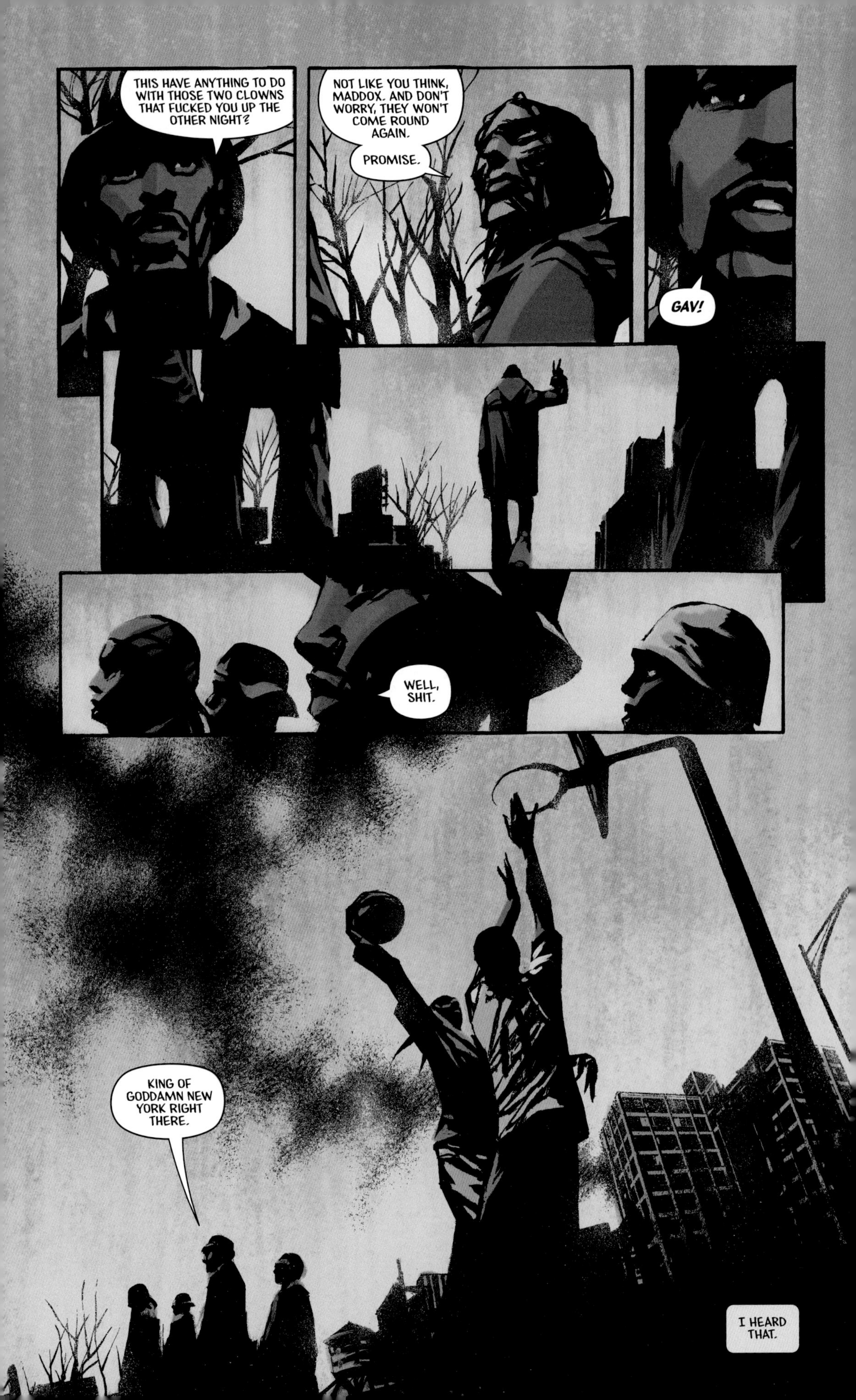
THIS HAVE ANYTHING TO DO WITH THOSE TWO CLOWNS THAT FUCKED YOU UP THE OTHER NIGHT?
NOT LIKE YOU THINK, MADDOX. AND DON'T WORRY, THEY WON'T COME ROUND AGAIN.
PROMISE.
GAV!
WELL, SHIT.
KING OF GODDAMN NEW YORK RIGHT THERE.
I HEARD THAT.

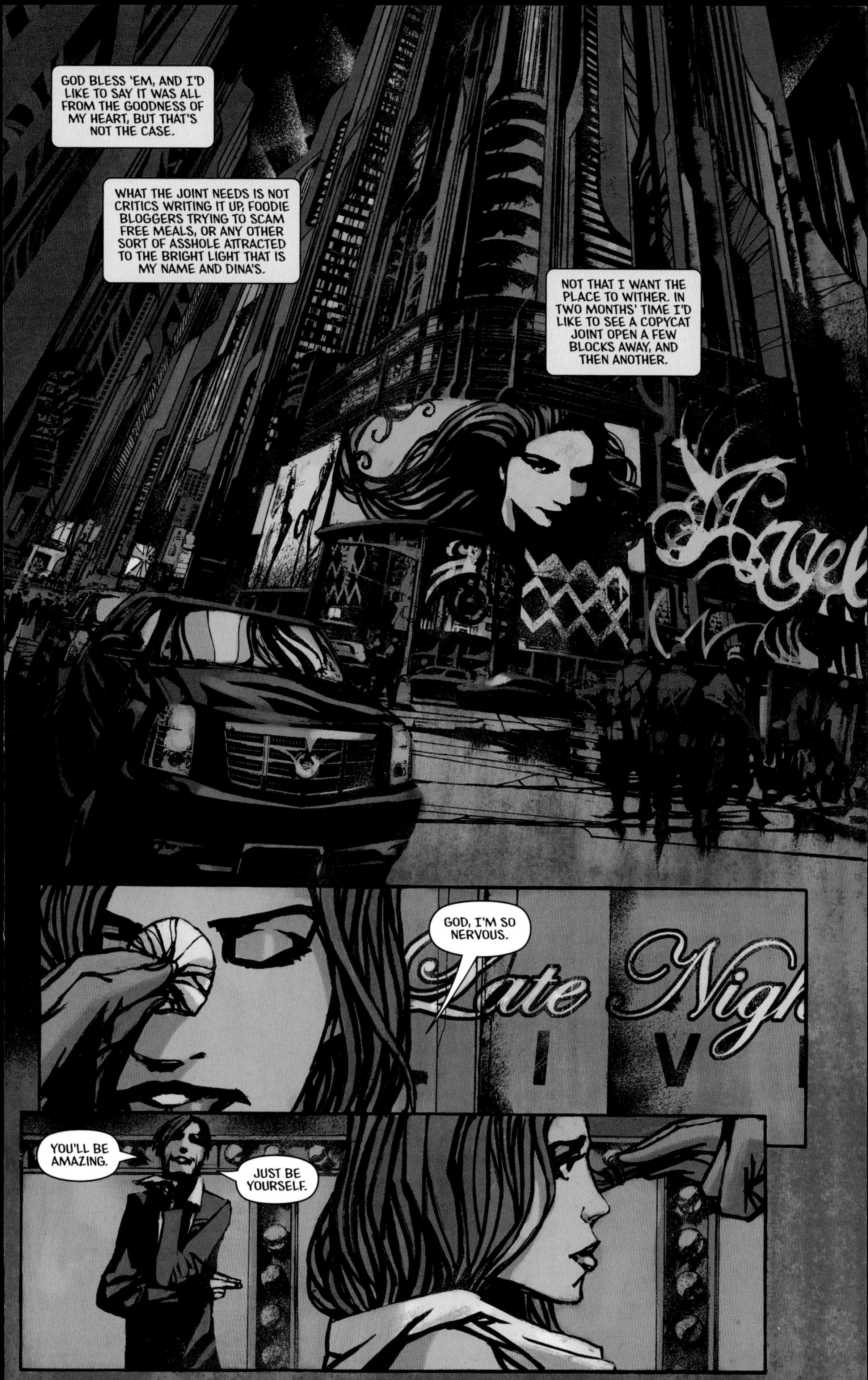
GOD BLESS 'EM, AND I'D LIKE TO SAY IT WAS ALL FROM THE GOODNESS OF MY HEART, BUT THAT'S NOT THE CASE.
WHAT THE JOINT NEEDS IS NOT CRITICS WRITING IT UP, FOODIE BLOGGERS TRYING TO SCAM FREE MEALS, OR ANY OTHER SORT OF ASSHOLE ATTRACTED TO THE BRIGHT LIGHT THAT IS MY NAME AND DINA'S.
NOT THAT I WANT THE PLACE TO WITHER. IN TWO MONTHS' TIME I'D LIKE TO SEE A COPYCAT JOINT OPEN A FEW BLOCKS AWAY, AND THEN ANOTHER.
GOD, I'M SO NERVOUS.
YOU'LL BE AMAZING.
JUST BE YOURSELF.

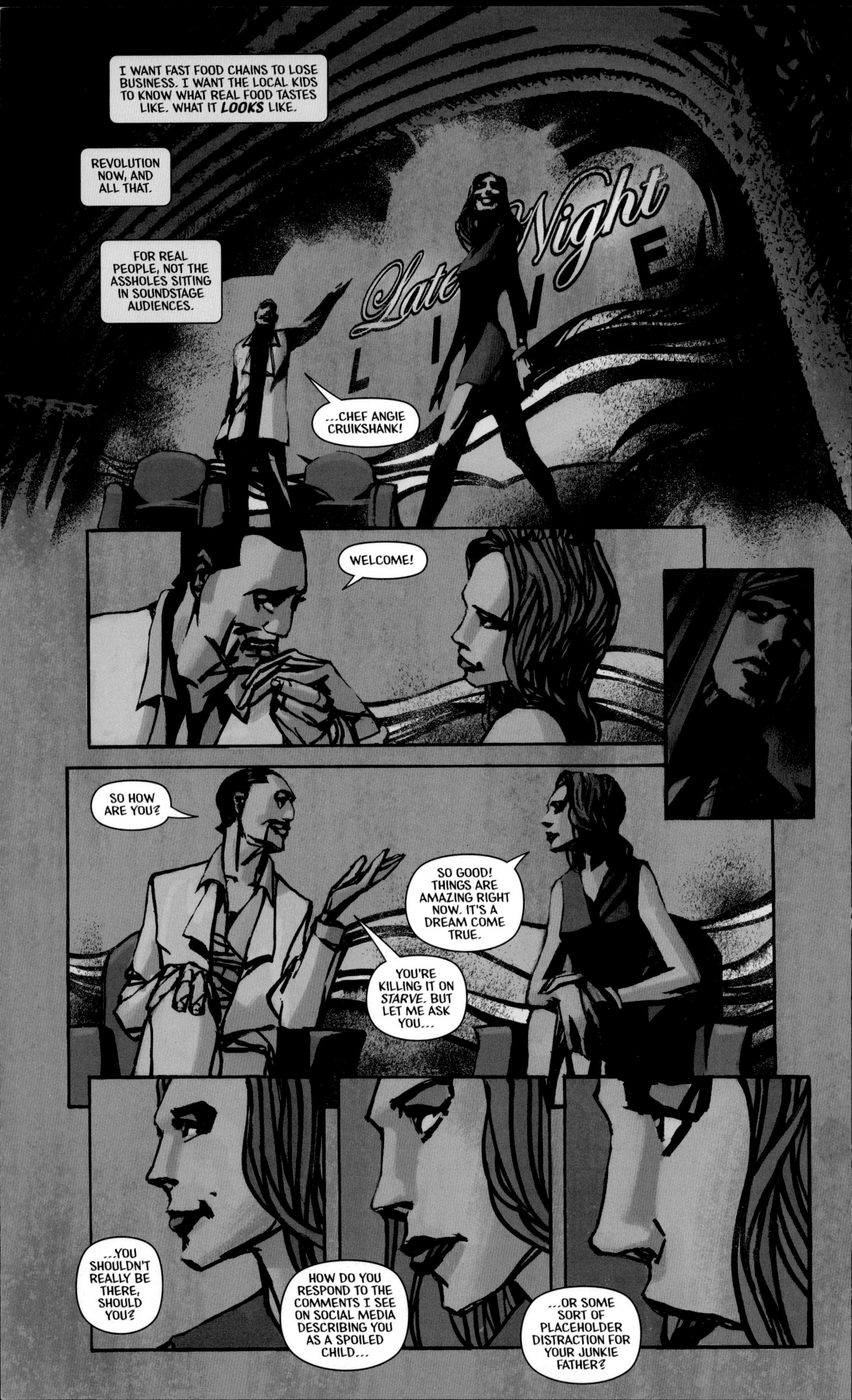
I WANT FAST FOOD CHAINS TO LOSE BUSINESS. I WANT THE LOCAL KIDS TO KNOW WHAT REAL FOOD TASTES LIKE. WHAT IT *LOOKS* LIKE.
REVOLUTION NOW, AND ALL THAT.
FOR REAL PEOPLE, NOT THE ASSHOLES SITTING IN SOUNDSTAGE AUDIENCES.
Late Night
LIVE
...CHEF ANGIE CRUIKSHANK!
WELCOME!
SO HOW ARE YOU?
SO GOOD! THINGS ARE AMAZING RIGHT NOW. IT'S A DREAM COME TRUE.
YOU'RE KILLING IT ON *STARVE*. BUT LET ME ASK YOU...
...YOU SHOULDN'T REALLY BE THERE, SHOULD YOU?
HOW DO YOU RESPOND TO THE COMMENTS I SEE ON SOCIAL MEDIA DESCRIBING YOU AS A SPOILED CHILD...
...OR SOME SORT OF PLACEHOLDER DISTRACTION FOR YOUR JUNKIE FATHER?

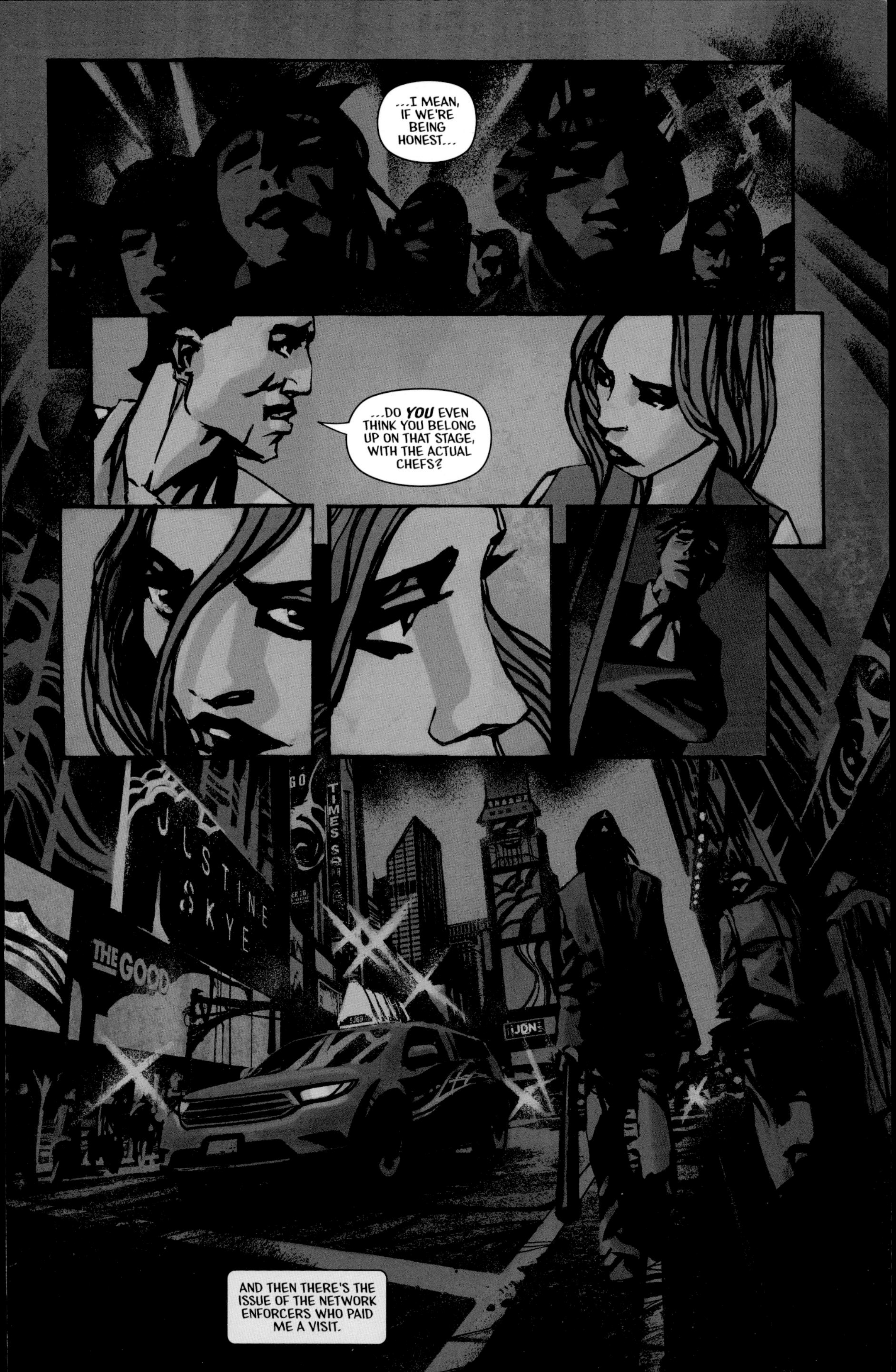
...I MEAN, IF WE'RE BEING HONEST...
...DO YOU EVEN THINK YOU BELONG UP ON THAT STAGE, WITH THE ACTUAL CHEFS?
JUSTINE SKYE
THE GOOD
TIMES SQ
AND THEN THERE'S THE ISSUE OF THE NETWORK ENFORCERS WHO PAID ME A VISIT.

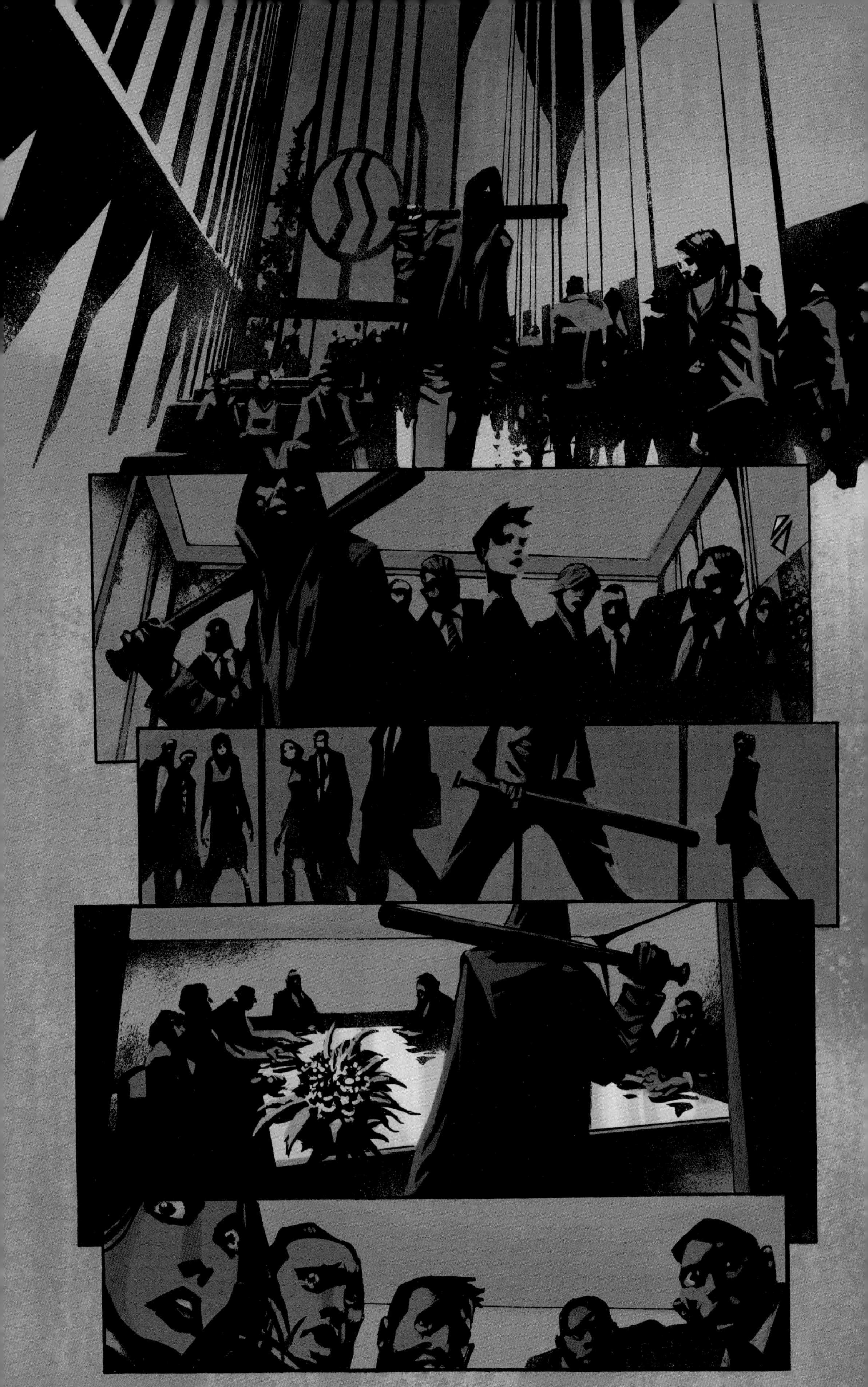

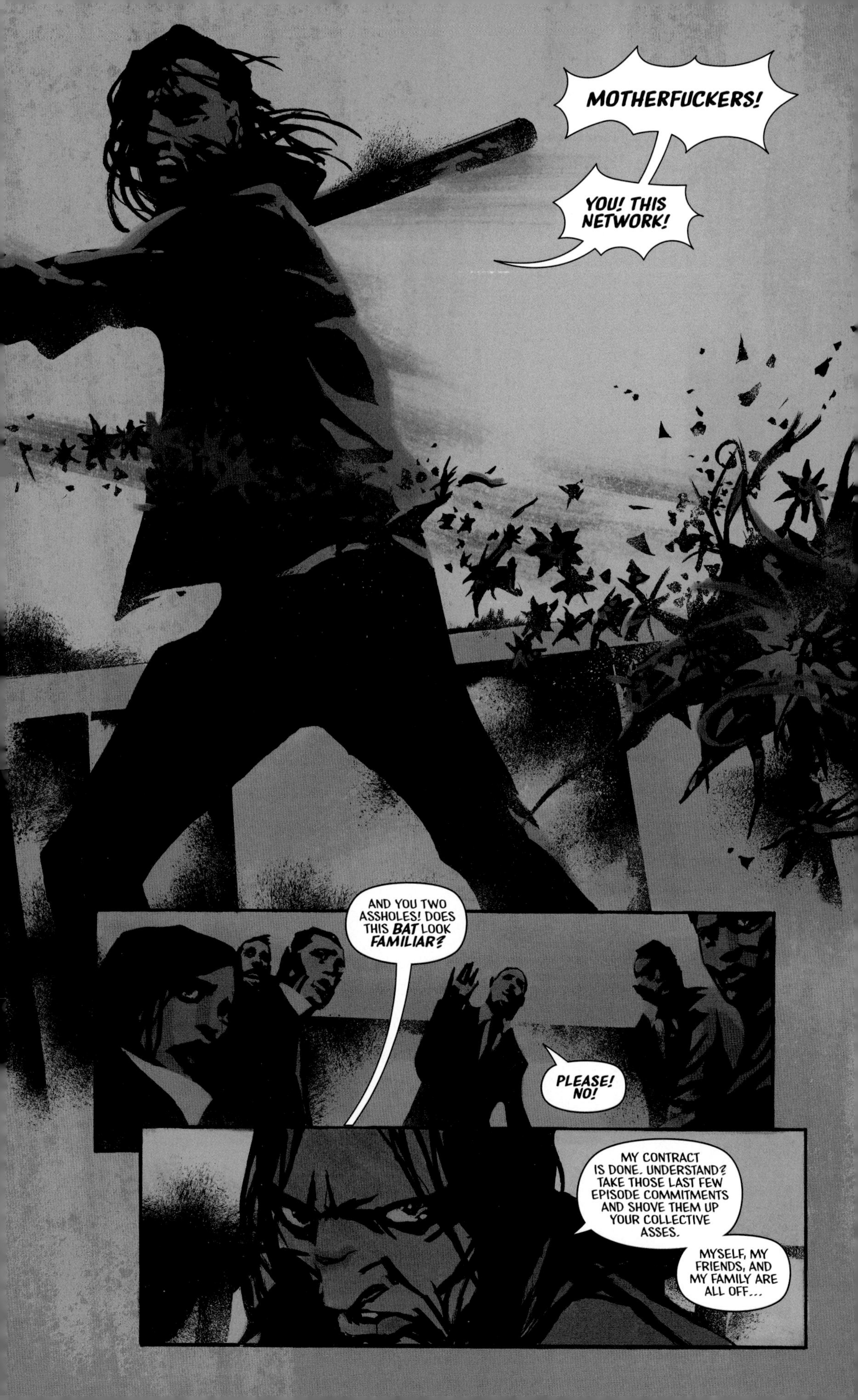
MOTHERFUCKERS!
YOU! THIS NETWORK!
AND YOU TWO ASSHOLES! DOES THIS BAT LOOK FAMILIAR?
PLEASE! NO!
MY CONTRACT IS DONE. UNDERSTAND? TAKE THOSE LAST FEW EPISODE COMMITMENTS AND SHOVE THEM UP YOUR COLLECTIVE ASSES.
MYSELF, MY FRIENDS, AND MY FAMILY ARE ALL OFF...

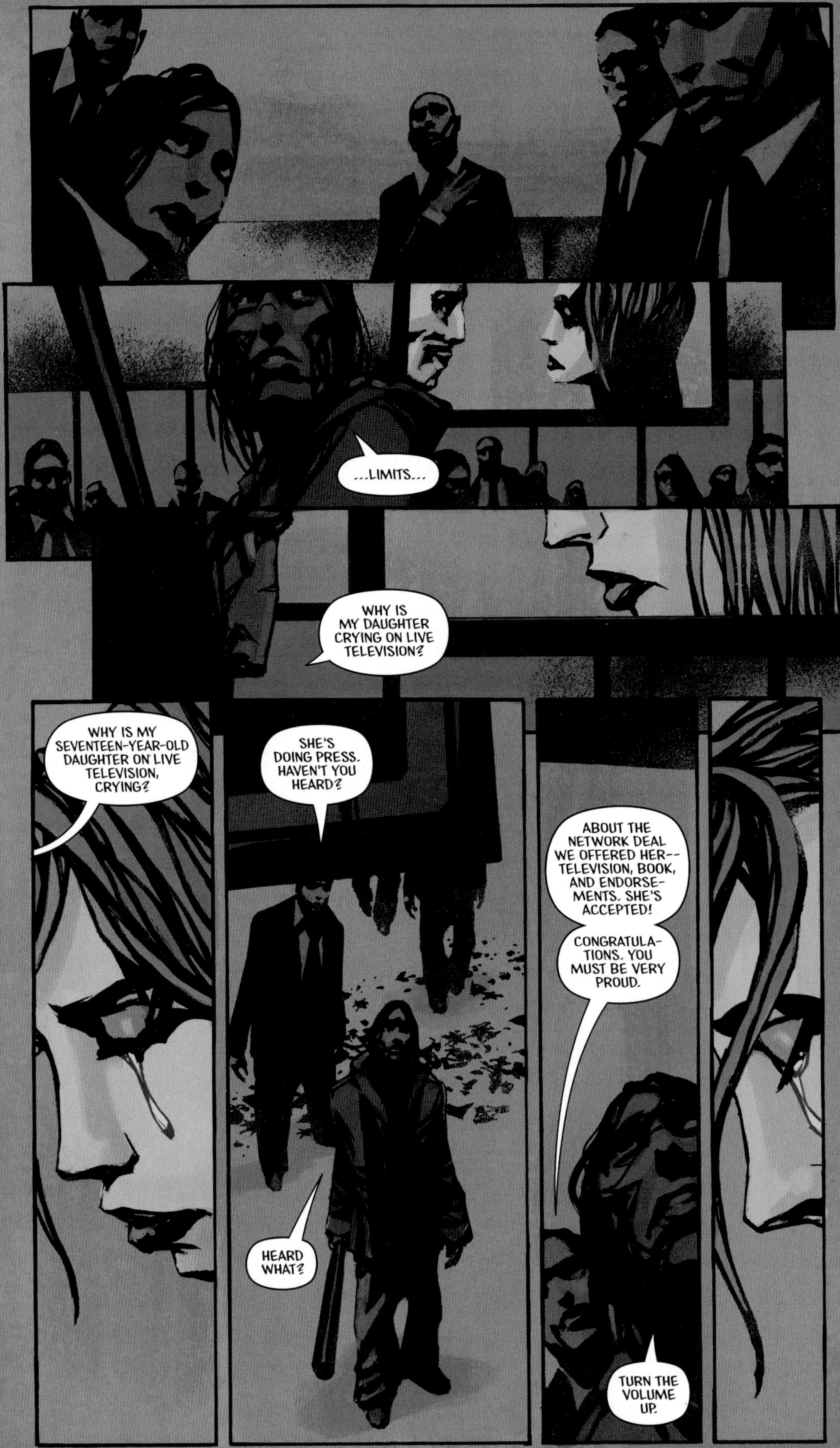
...LIMITS...
WHY IS MY DAUGHTER CRYING ON LIVE TELEVISION?
WHY IS MY SEVENTEEN-YEAR-OLD DAUGHTER ON LIVE TELEVISION, CRYING?
SHE'S DOING PRESS. HAVEN'T YOU HEARD?
HEARD WHAT?
ABOUT THE NETWORK DEAL WE OFFERED HER-- TELEVISION, BOOK, AND ENDORSE-MENTS. SHE'S ACCEPTED!
CONGRATULA-TIONS. YOU MUST BE VERY PROUD.
TURN THE VOLUME UP.

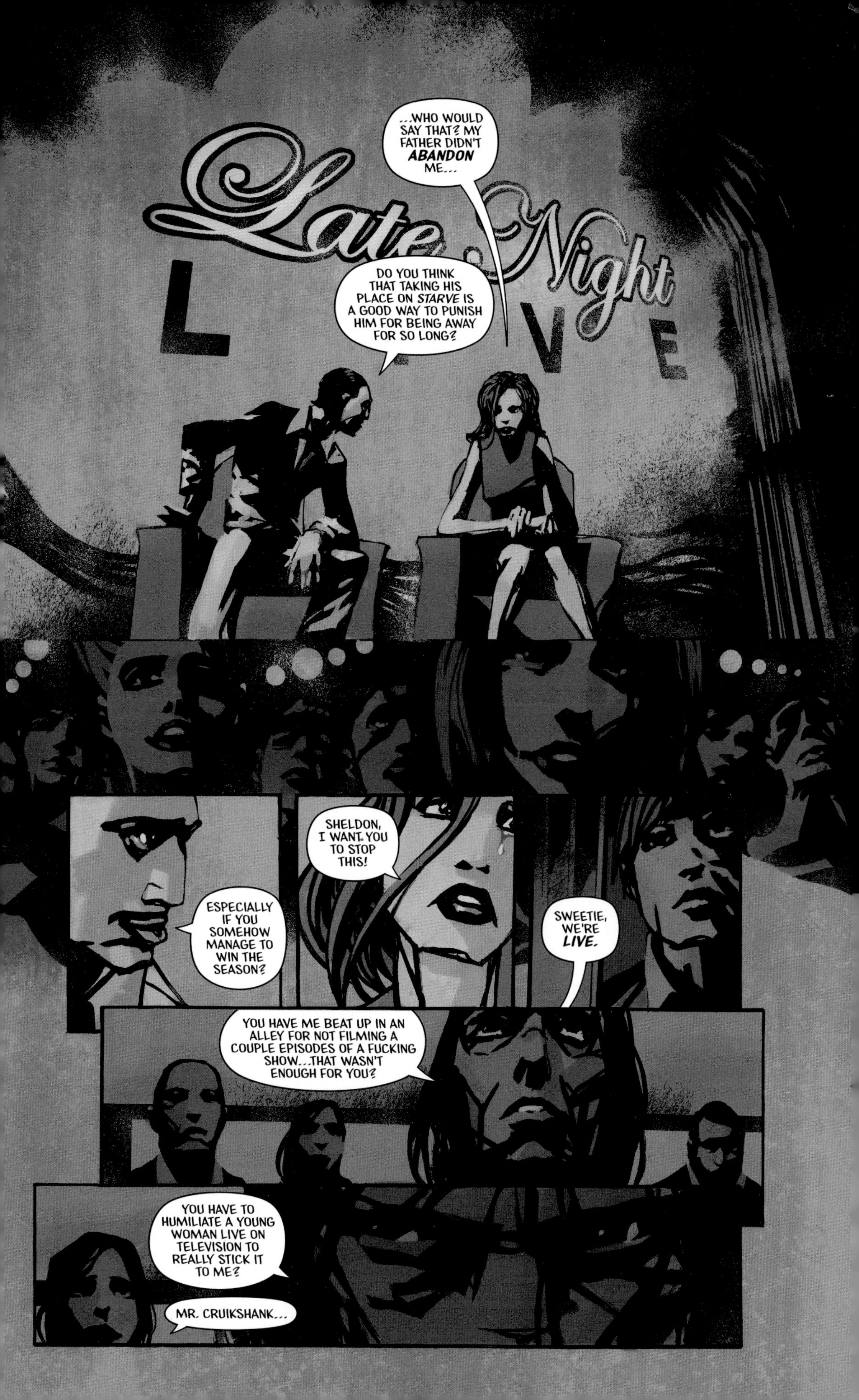
Late Night
L VE
...WHO WOULD SAY THAT? MY FATHER DIDN'T ABANDON ME...
DO YOU THINK THAT TAKING HIS PLACE ON STARVE IS A GOOD WAY TO PUNISH HIM FOR BEING AWAY FOR SO LONG?
ESPECIALLY IF YOU SOMEHOW MANAGE TO WIN THE SEASON?
SHELDON, I WANT YOU TO STOP THIS!
SWEETIE, WE'RE LIVE.
YOU HAVE ME BEAT UP IN AN ALLEY FOR NOT FILMING A COUPLE EPISODES OF A FUCKING SHOW...THAT WASN'T ENOUGH FOR YOU?
YOU HAVE TO HUMILIATE A YOUNG WOMAN LIVE ON TELEVISION TO REALLY STICK IT TO ME?
MR. CRUIKSHANK...

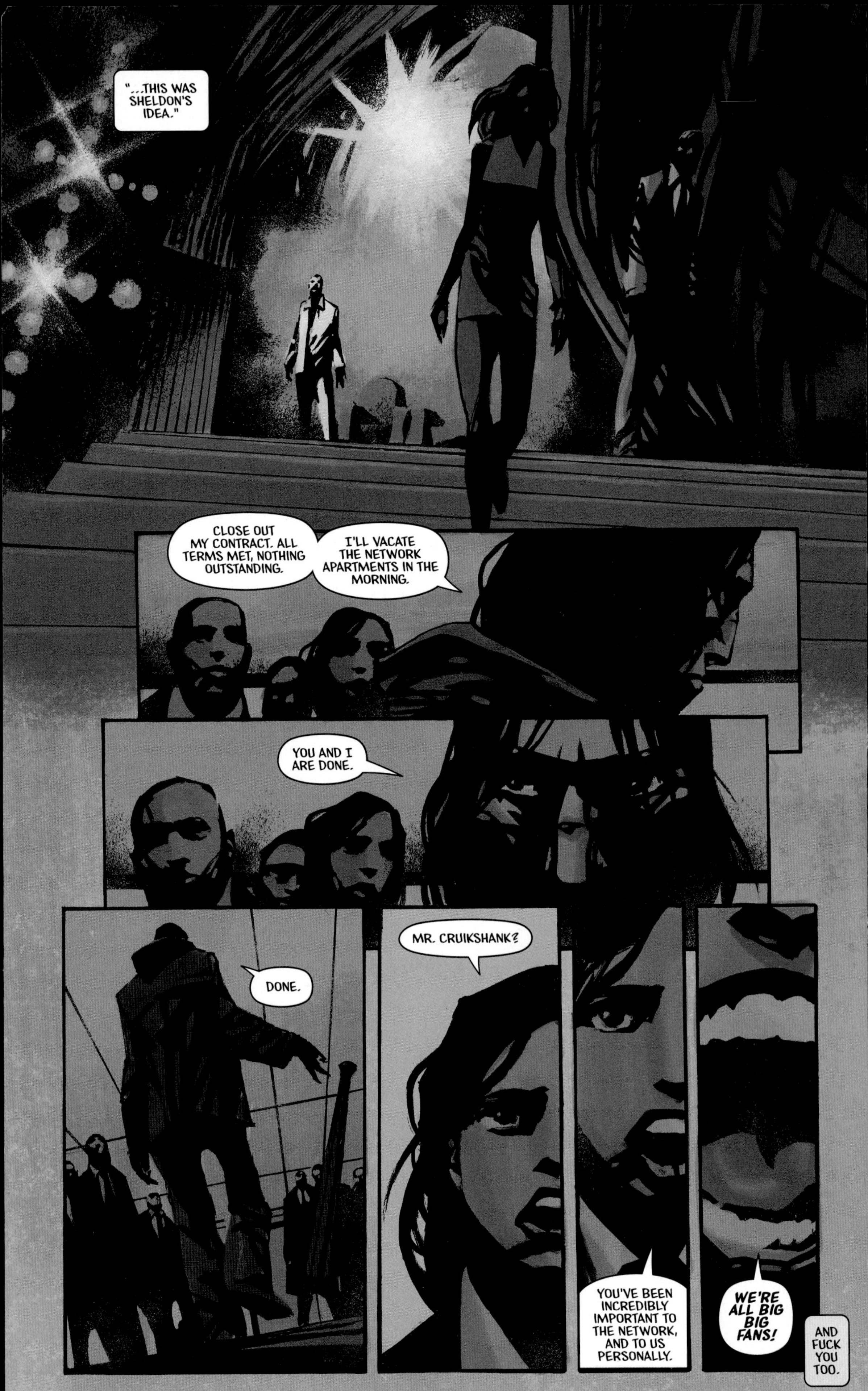
"...THIS WAS SHELDON'S IDEA."
CLOSE OUT MY CONTRACT. ALL TERMS MET, NOTHING OUTSTANDING.
I'LL VACATE THE NETWORK APARTMENTS IN THE MORNING.
YOU AND I ARE DONE.
DONE.
MR. CRUIKSHANK?
YOU'VE BEEN INCREDIBLY IMPORTANT TO THE NETWORK, AND TO US PERSONALLY.
WE'RE ALL BIG BIG FANS!
AND FUCK YOU TOO.

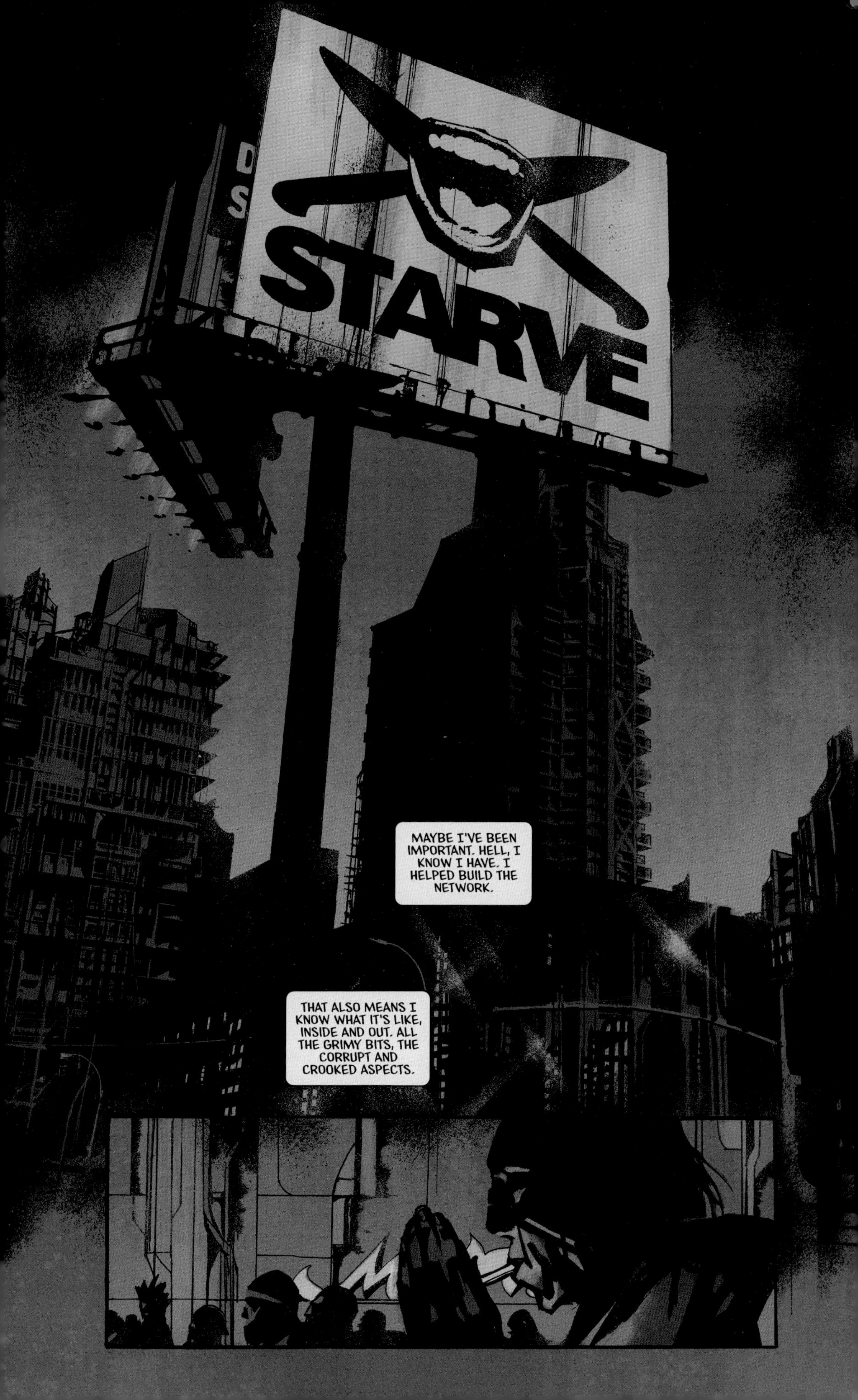
STARVE
MAYBE I'VE BEEN IMPORTANT. HELL, I KNOW I HAVE. I HELPED BUILD THE NETWORK.
THAT ALSO MEANS I KNOW WHAT IT'S LIKE, INSIDE AND OUT. ALL THE GRIMY BITS, THE CORRUPT AND CROOKED ASPECTS.

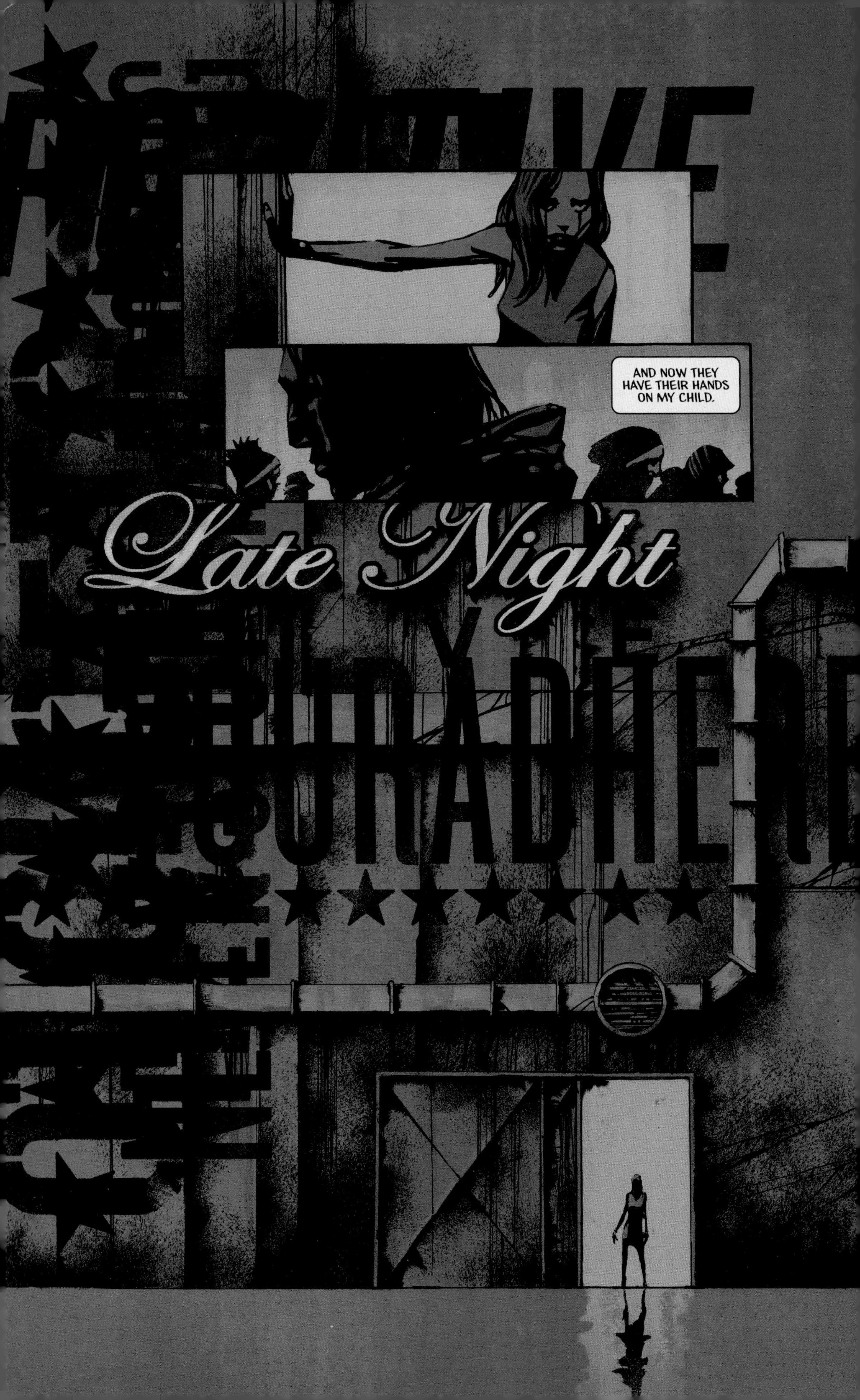
AND NOW THEY HAVE THEIR HANDS ON MY CHILD.
Late Night

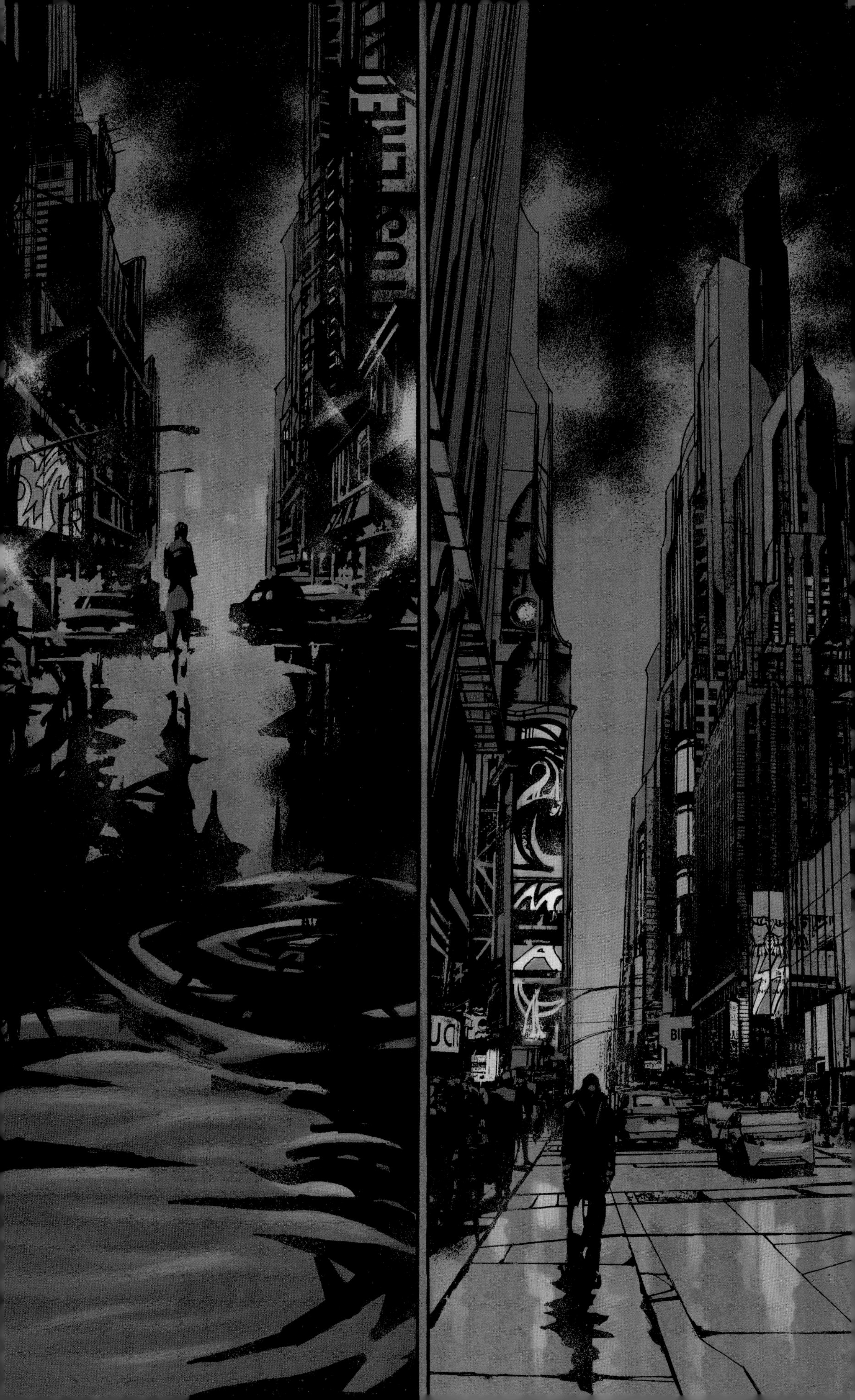

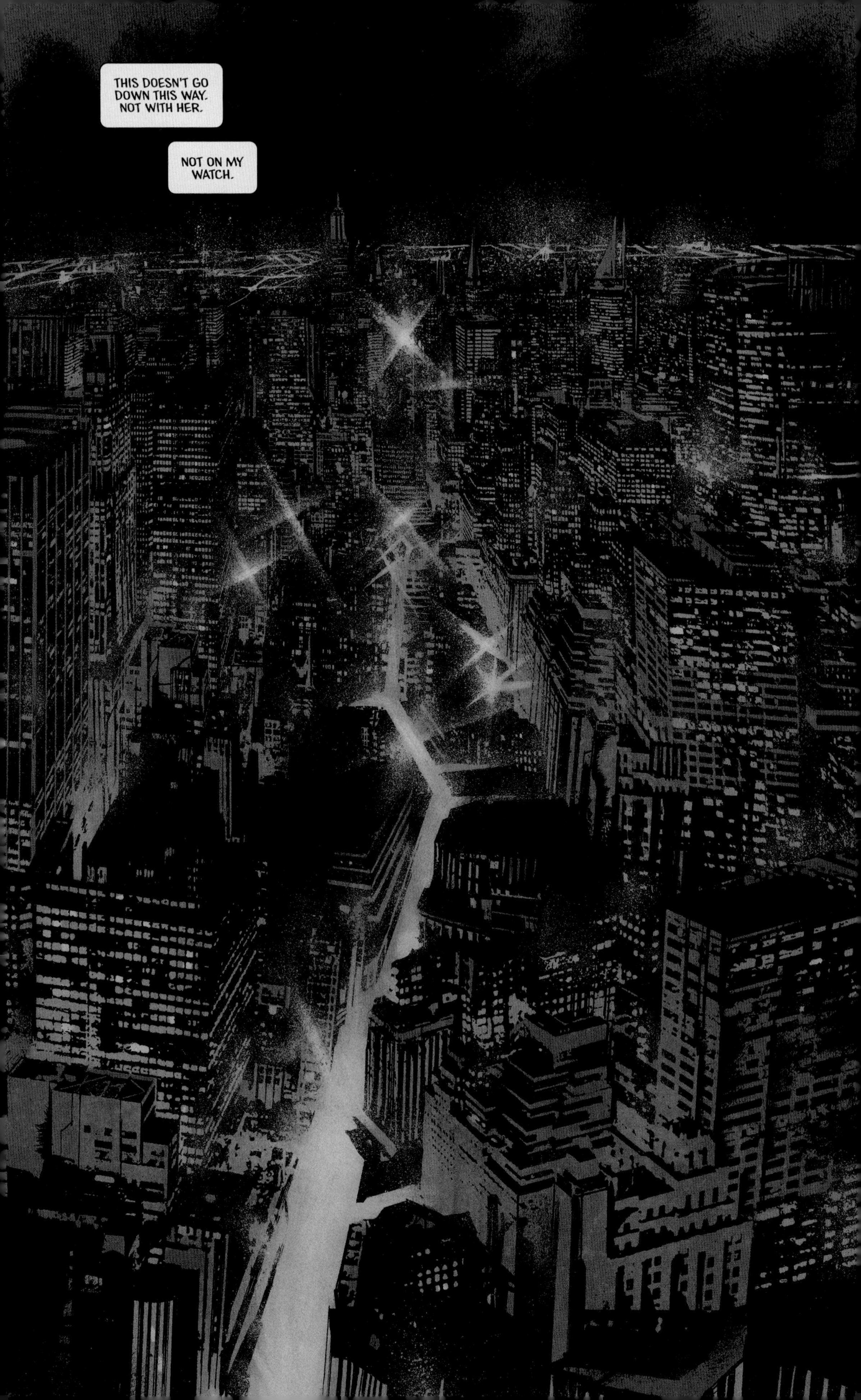
THIS DOESN'T GO DOWN THIS WAY. NOT WITH HER.
NOT ON MY WATCH.

"I FOUGHT THE LAW"

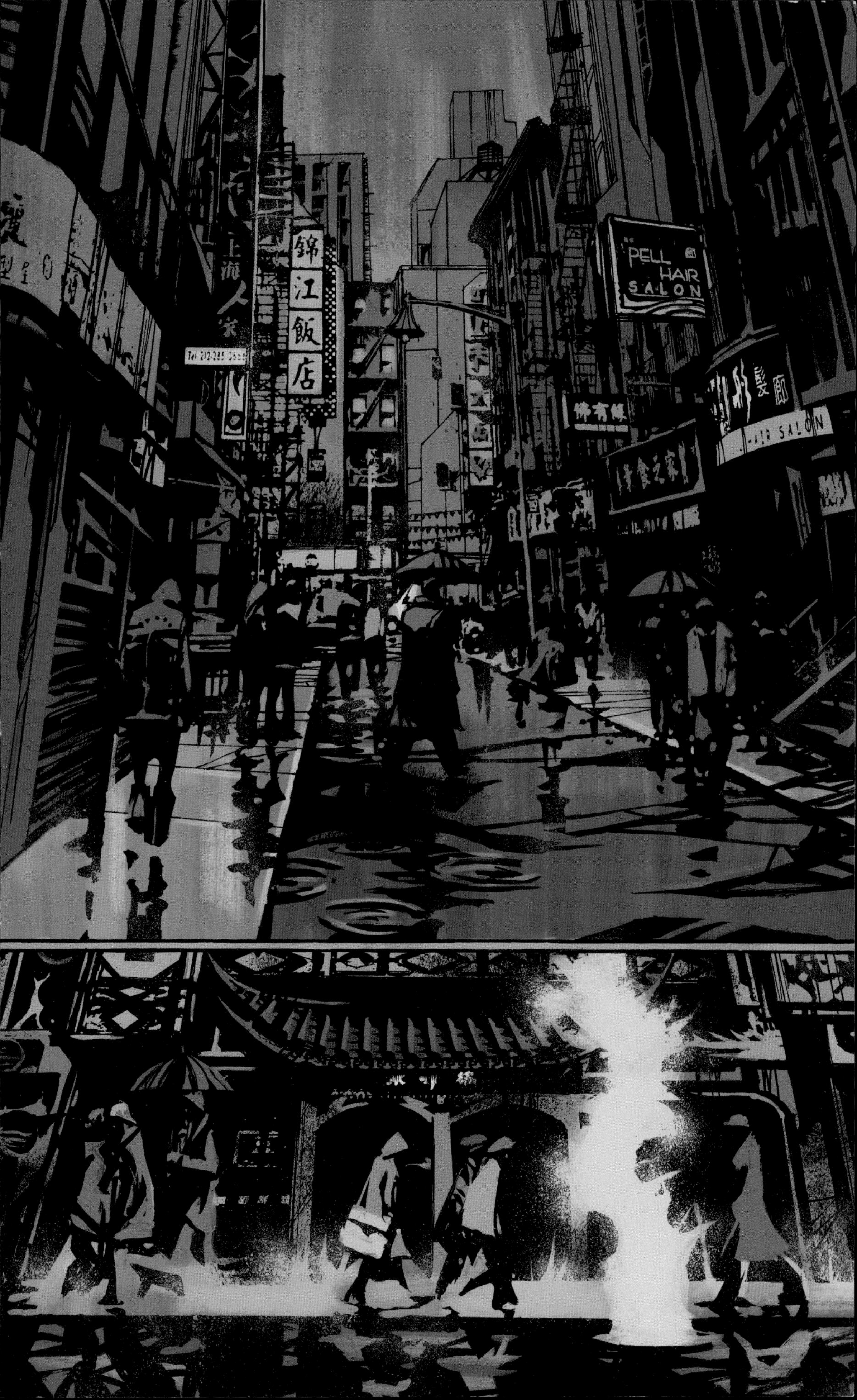
錦江飯店
PELL HAIR SALON

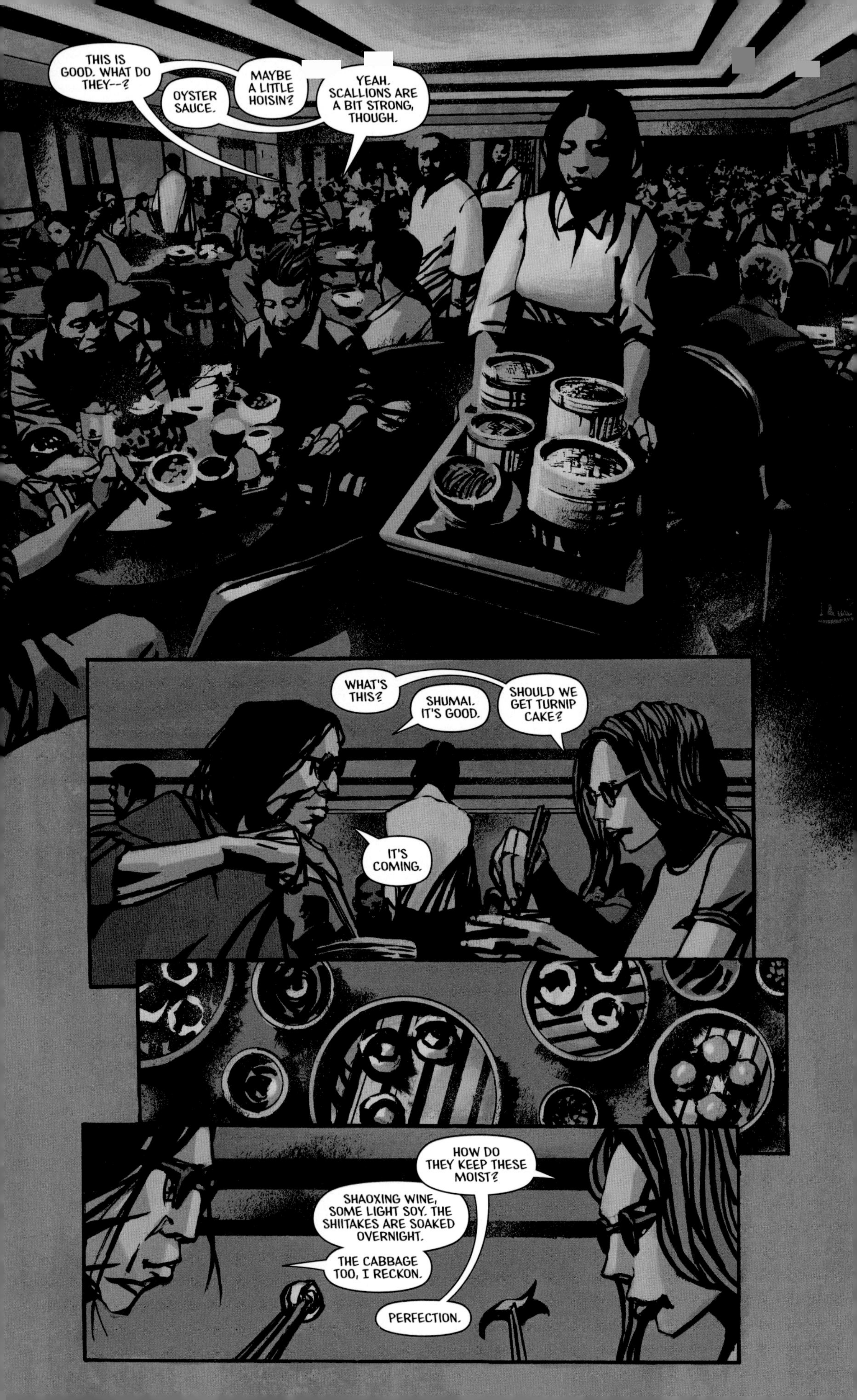

THIS IS GOOD. WHAT DO THEY--?
OYSTER SAUCE.
MAYBE A LITTLE HOISIN?
YEAH. SCALLIONS ARE A BIT STRONG, THOUGH.
WHAT'S THIS?
SHUMAI. IT'S GOOD.
SHOULD WE GET TURNIP CAKE?
IT'S COMING.
HOW DO THEY KEEP THESE MOIST?
SHAOXING WINE, SOME LIGHT SOY. THE SHIITAKES ARE SOAKED OVERNIGHT.
THE CABBAGE TOO, I RECKON.
PERFECTION.

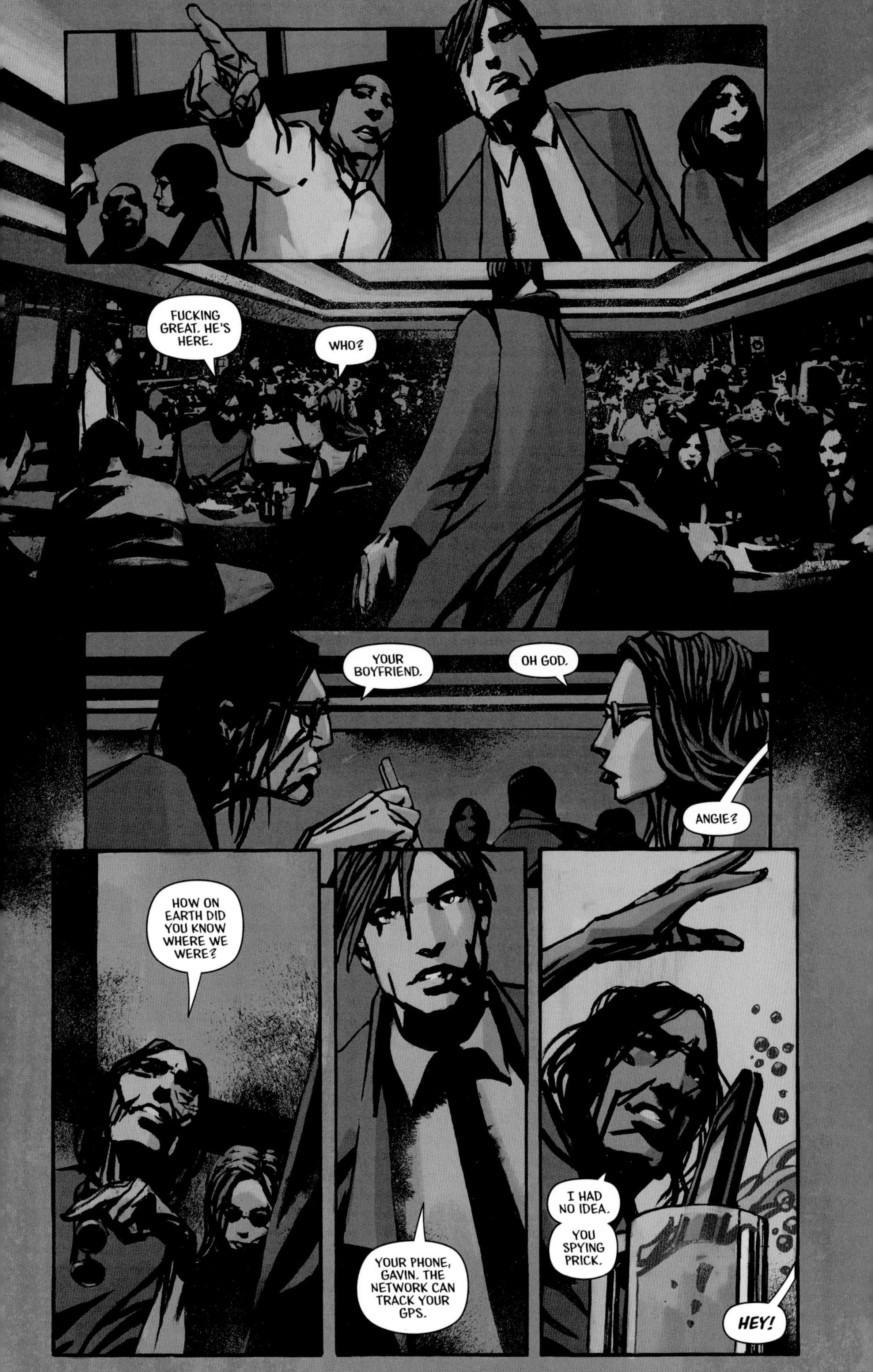
FUCKING GREAT. HE'S HERE.
WHO?
YOUR BOYFRIEND.
OH GOD.
ANGIE?
HOW ON EARTH DID YOU KNOW WHERE WE WERE?
YOUR PHONE, GAVIN. THE NETWORK CAN TRACK YOUR GPS.
I HAD NO IDEA.
YOU SPYING PRICK.
HEY!

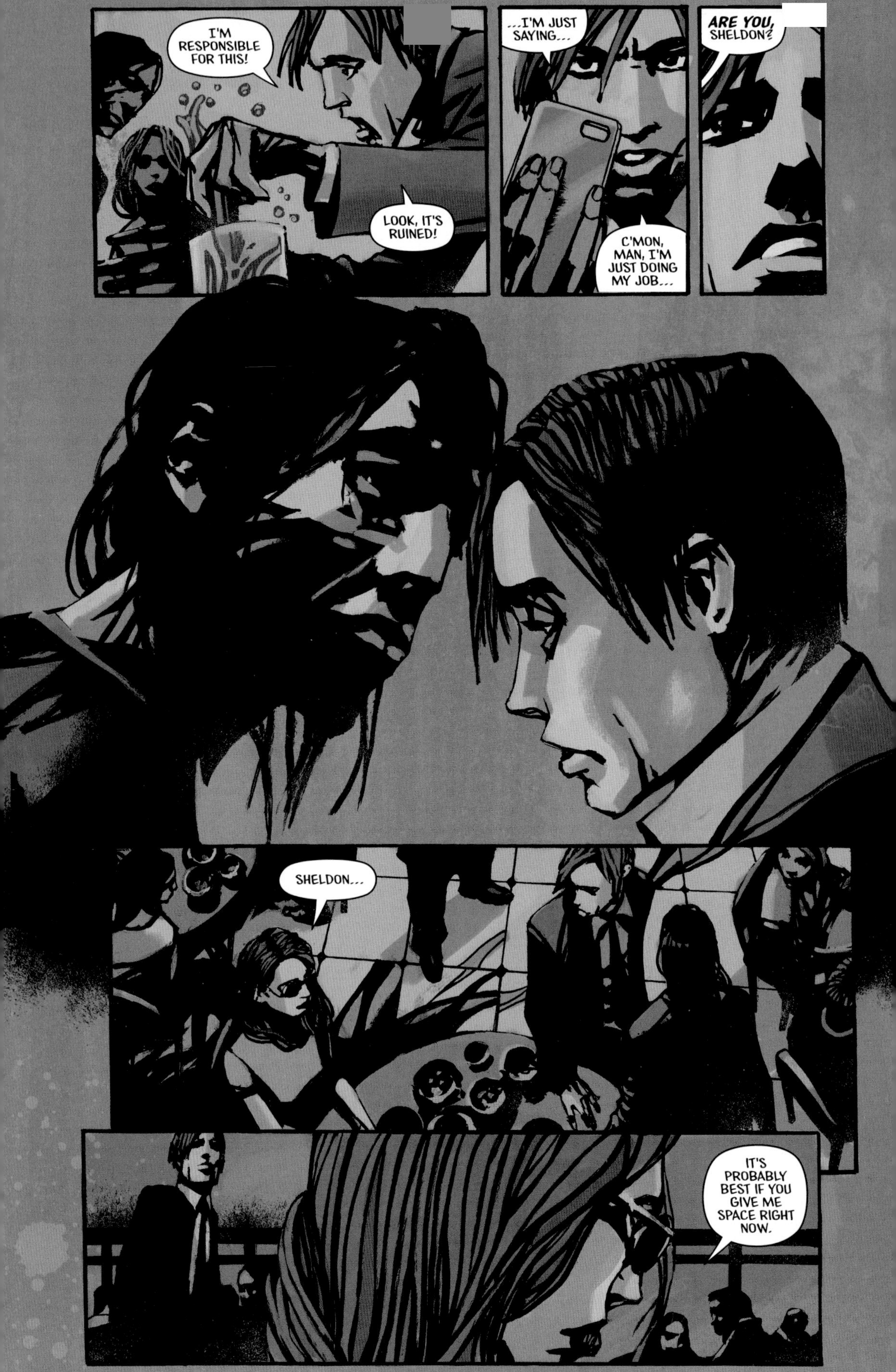

I'M RESPONSIBLE FOR THIS!
LOOK, IT'S RUINED!
...I'M JUST SAYING...
C'MON, MAN, I'M JUST DOING MY JOB...
ARE YOU, SHELDON?
SHELDON...
IT'S PROBABLY BEST IF YOU GIVE ME SPACE RIGHT NOW.

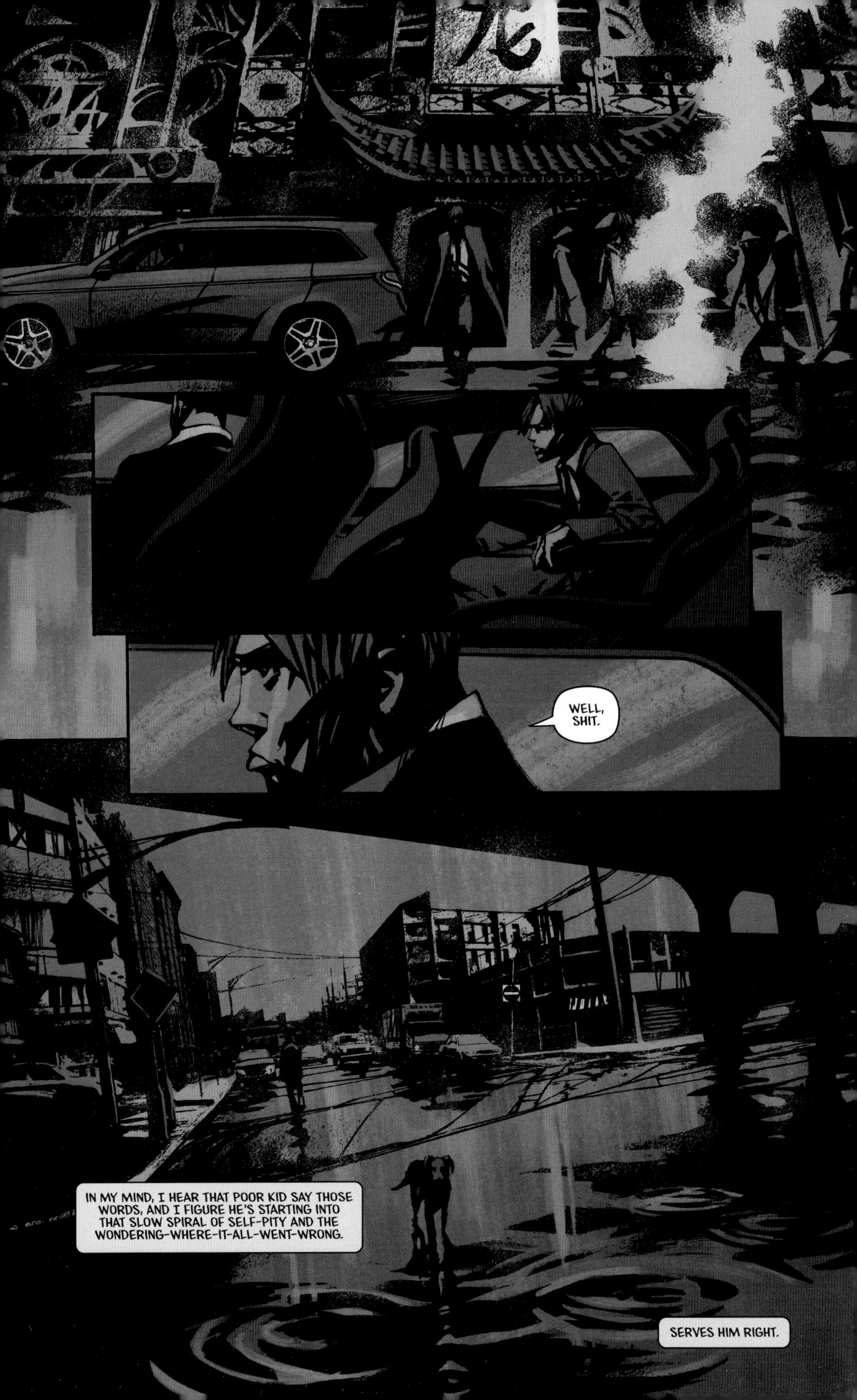
WELL, SHIT.
IN MY MIND, I HEAR THAT POOR KID SAY THOSE WORDS, AND I FIGURE HE'S STARTING INTO THAT SLOW SPIRAL OF SELF-PITY AND THE WONDERING-WHERE-IT-ALL-WENT-WRONG.
SERVES HIM RIGHT.

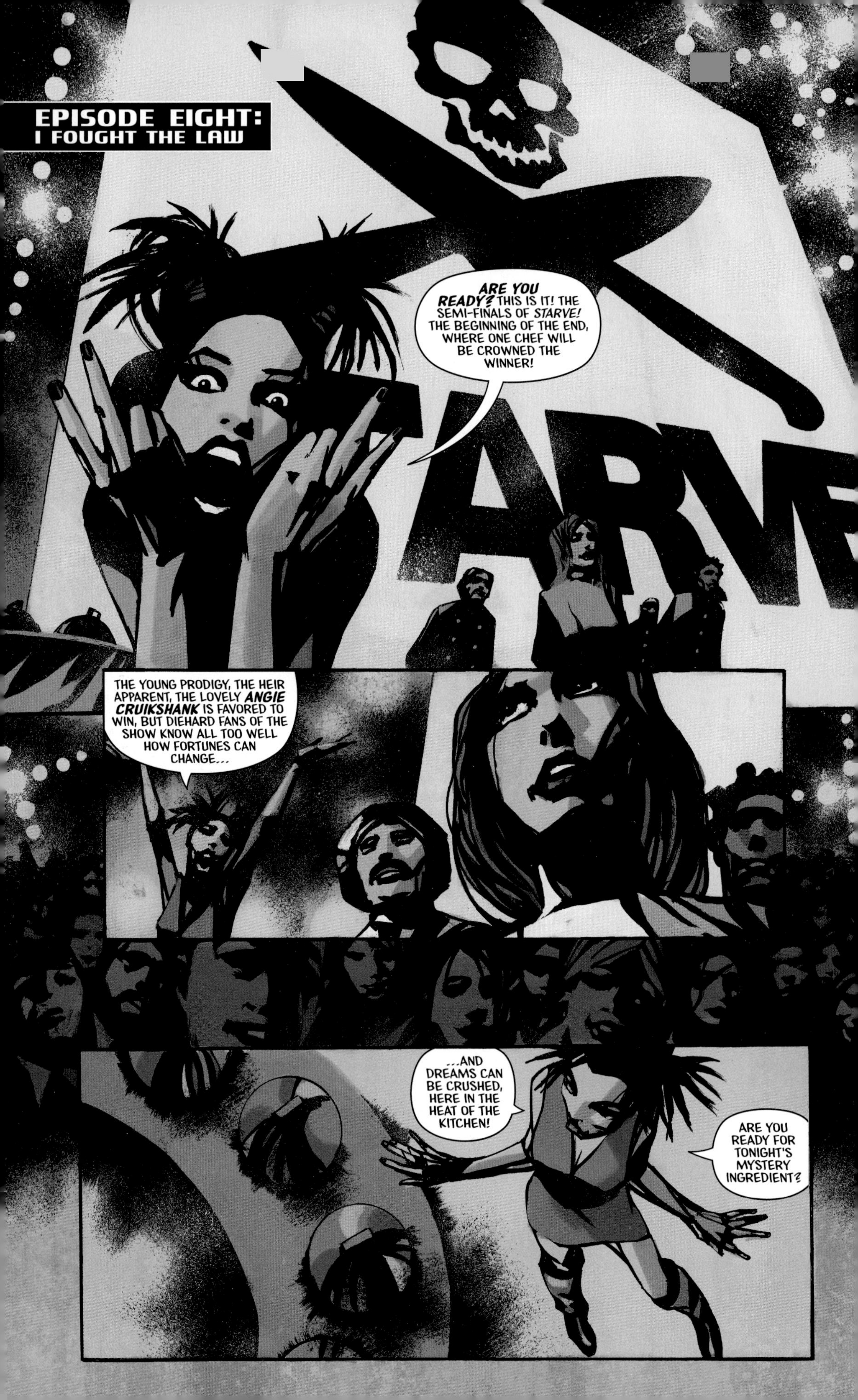

EPISODE EIGHT:
I FOUGHT THE LAW
ARE YOU READY? THIS IS IT! THE SEMI-FINALS OF STARVE! THE BEGINNING OF THE END, WHERE ONE CHEF WILL BE CROWNED THE WINNER!
THE YOUNG PRODIGY, THE HEIR APPARENT, THE LOVELY ANGIE CRUIKSHANK IS FAVORED TO WIN, BUT DIEHARD FANS OF THE SHOW KNOW ALL TOO WELL HOW FORTUNES CAN CHANGE...
...AND DREAMS CAN BE CRUSHED, HERE IN THE HEAT OF THE KITCHEN!
ARE YOU READY FOR TONIGHT'S MYSTERY INGREDIENT?

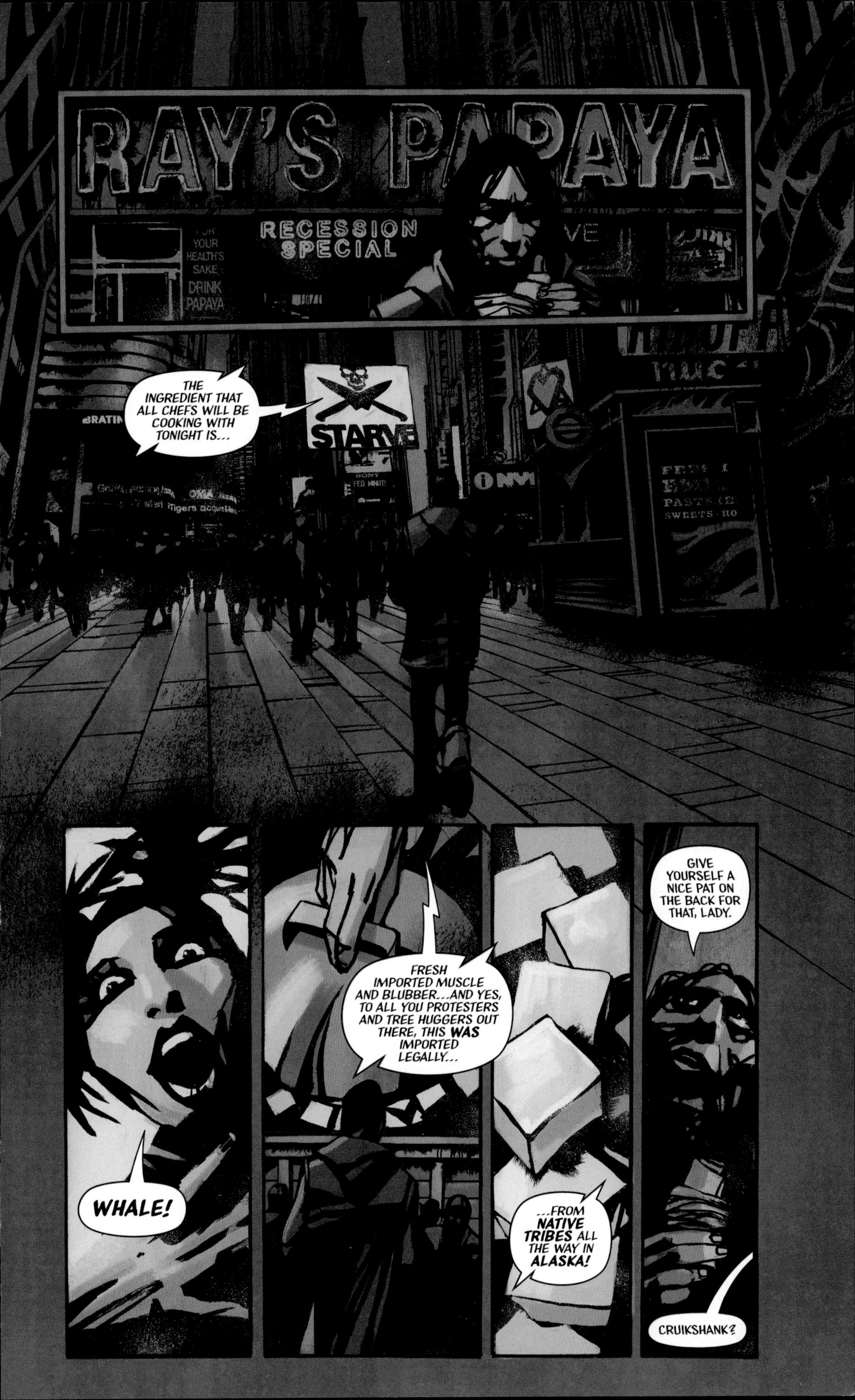
RAY'S PAPAYA
RECESSION SPECIAL
FOR YOUR HEALTH'S SAKE DRINK PAPAYA
THE INGREDIENT THAT ALL CHEFS WILL BE COOKING WITH TONIGHT IS...
STARVE
WHALE!
FRESH IMPORTED MUSCLE AND BLUBBER...AND YES, TO ALL YOU PROTESTERS AND TREE HUGGERS OUT THERE, THIS WAS IMPORTED LEGALLY...
...FROM NATIVE TRIBES ALL THE WAY IN ALASKA!
GIVE YOURSELF A NICE PAT ON THE BACK FOR THAT, LADY.
CRUIKSHANK?

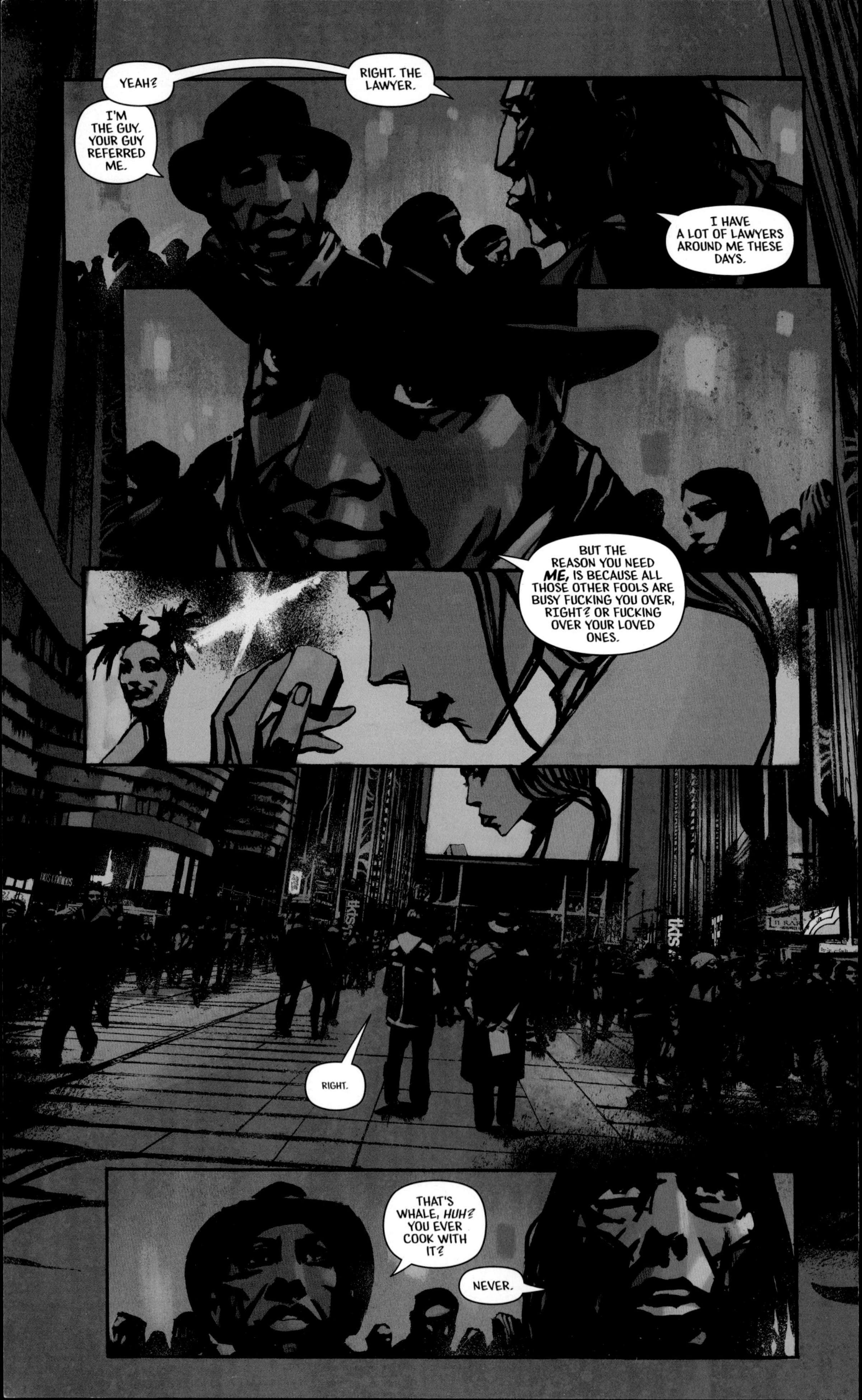
YEAH?
I'M THE GUY. YOUR GUY REFERRED ME.
RIGHT. THE LAWYER.
I HAVE A LOT OF LAWYERS AROUND ME THESE DAYS.
BUT THE REASON YOU NEED ME, IS BECAUSE ALL THOSE OTHER FOOLS ARE BUSY FUCKING YOU OVER, RIGHT? OR FUCKING OVER YOUR LOVED ONES.
RIGHT.
THAT'S WHALE, HUH? YOU EVER COOK WITH IT?
NEVER.

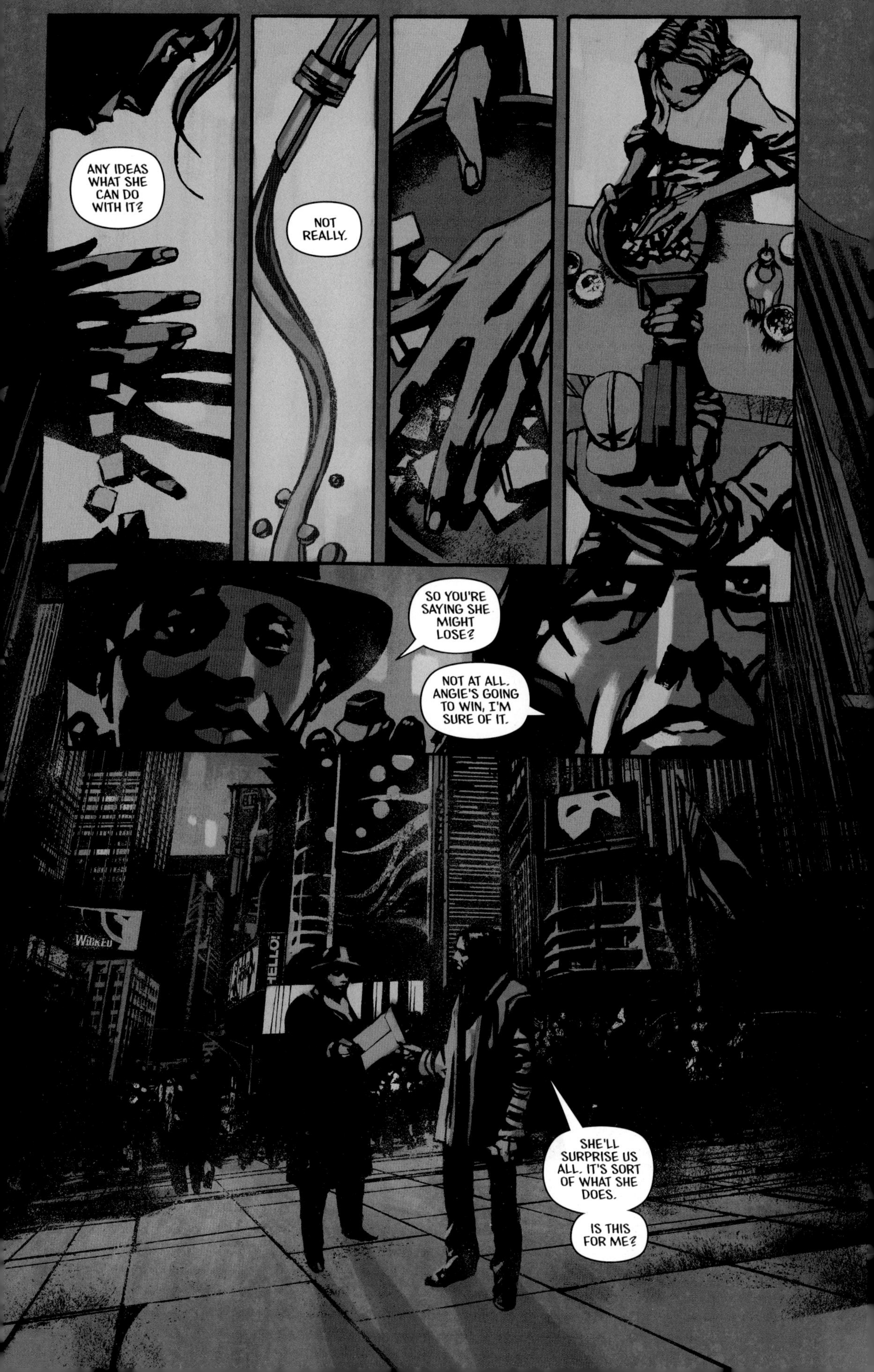
ANY IDEAS WHAT SHE CAN DO WITH IT?
NOT REALLY.
SO YOU'RE SAYING SHE MIGHT LOSE?
NOT AT ALL. ANGIE'S GOING TO WIN, I'M SURE OF IT.
WICKED
HELLO!
SHE'LL SURPRISE US ALL. IT'S SORT OF WHAT SHE DOES.
IS THIS FOR ME?

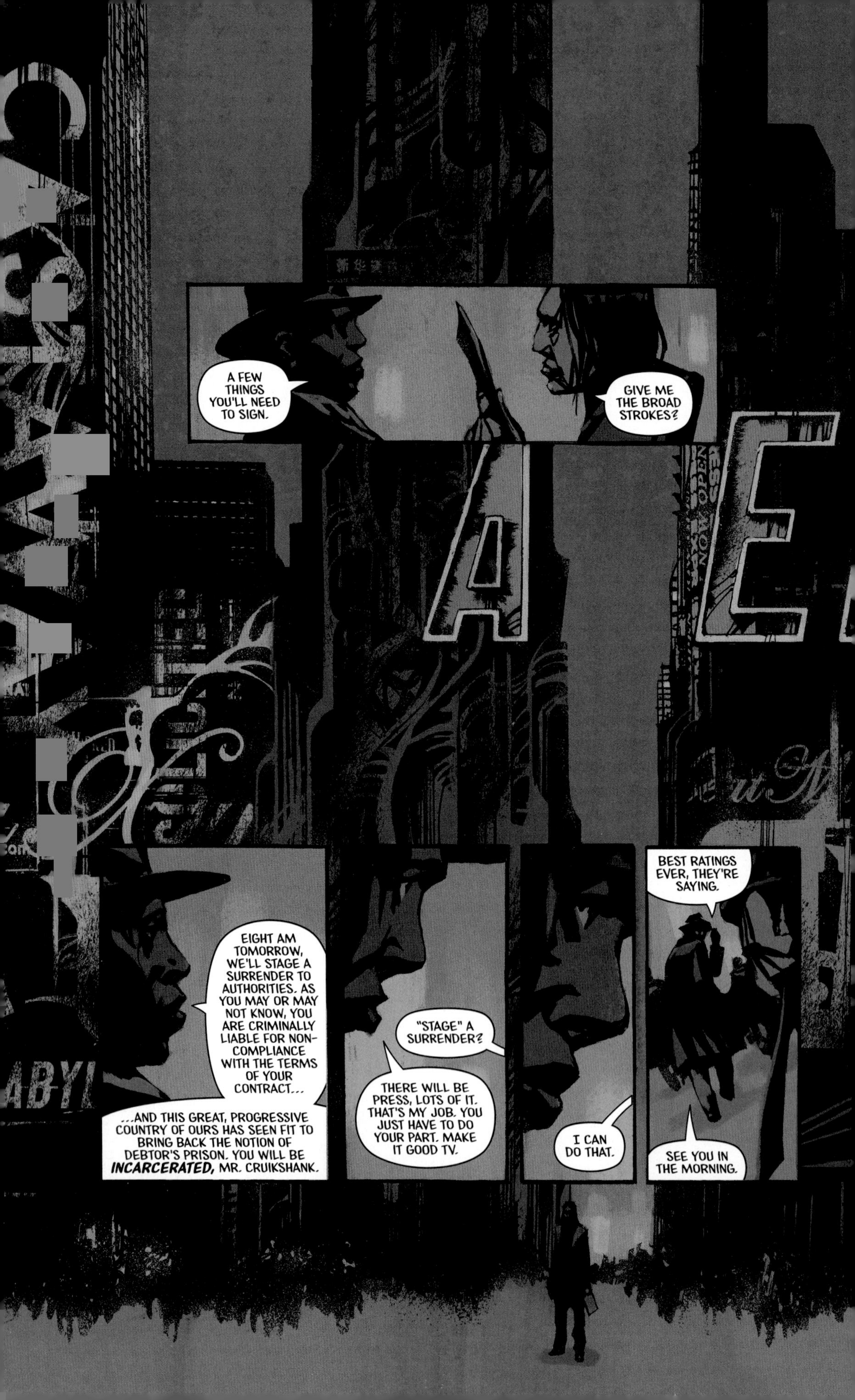

A FEW THINGS YOU'LL NEED TO SIGN.
GIVE ME THE BROAD STROKES?
EIGHT AM TOMORROW, WE'LL STAGE A SURRENDER TO AUTHORITIES. AS YOU MAY OR MAY NOT KNOW, YOU ARE CRIMINALLY LIABLE FOR NON-COMPLIANCE WITH THE TERMS OF YOUR CONTRACT...
...AND THIS GREAT, PROGRESSIVE COUNTRY OF OURS HAS SEEN FIT TO BRING BACK THE NOTION OF DEBTOR'S PRISON. YOU WILL BE ***INCARCERATED,*** MR. CRUIKSHANK.
"STAGE" A SURRENDER?
THERE WILL BE PRESS, LOTS OF IT. THAT'S MY JOB. YOU JUST HAVE TO DO YOUR PART. MAKE IT GOOD TV.
I CAN DO THAT.
BEST RATINGS EVER, THEY'RE SAYING.
SEE YOU IN THE MORNING.

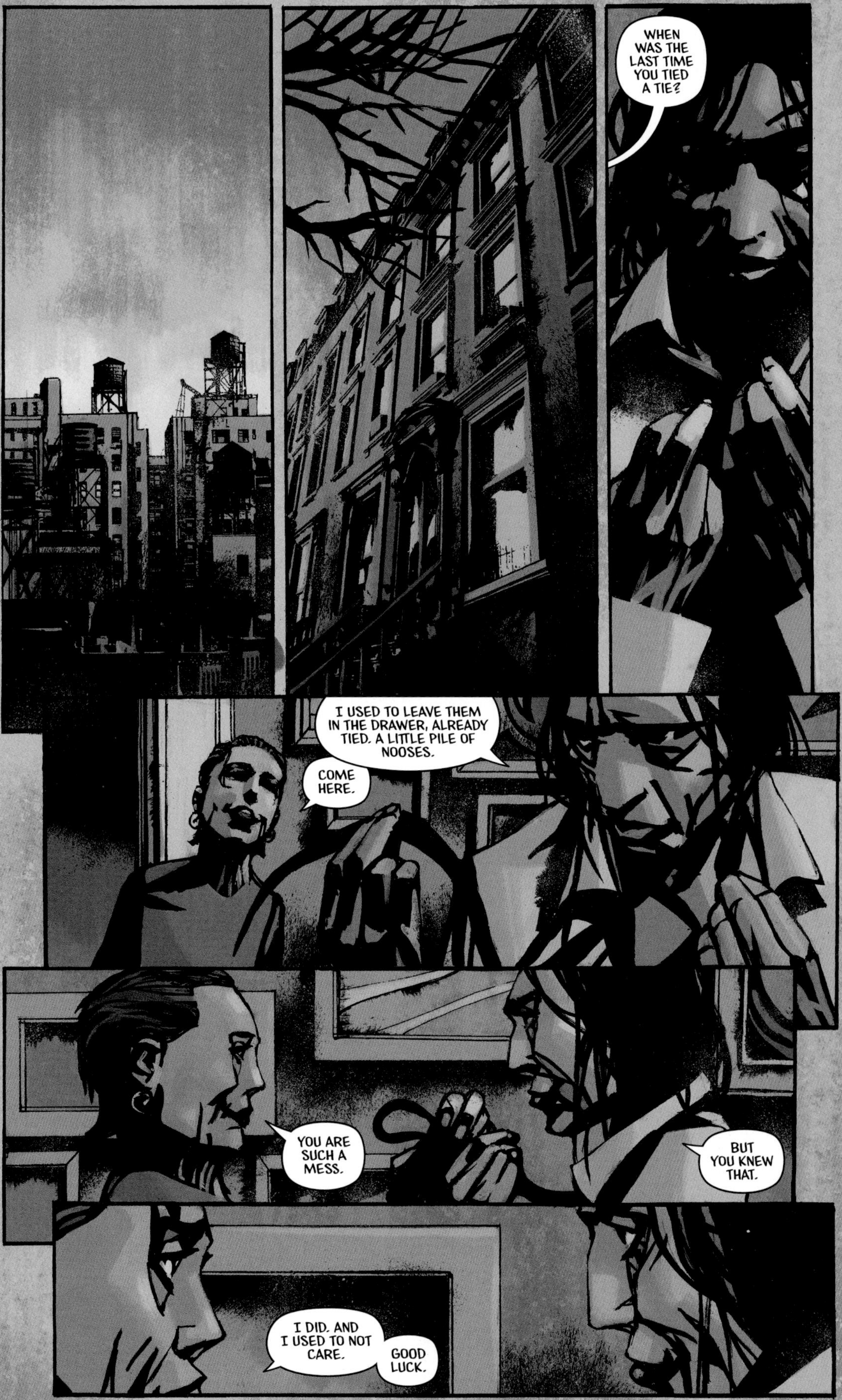
WHEN WAS THE LAST TIME YOU TIED A TIE?
I USED TO LEAVE THEM IN THE DRAWER, ALREADY TIED. A LITTLE PILE OF NOOSES.
COME HERE.
YOU ARE SUCH A MESS.
BUT YOU KNEW THAT.
I DID. AND I USED TO NOT CARE.
GOOD LUCK.

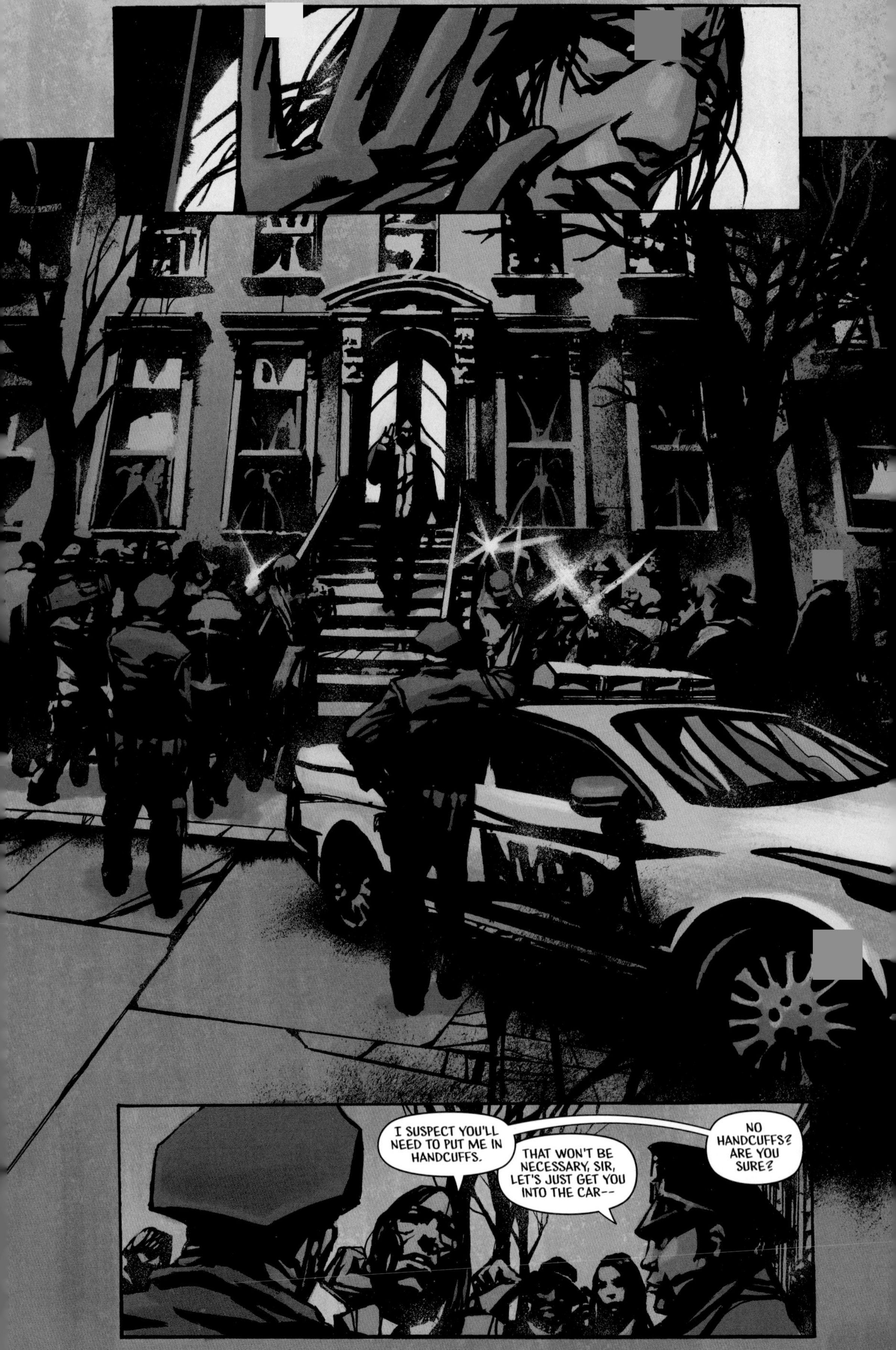

NYPD
I SUSPECT YOU'LL NEED TO PUT ME IN HANDCUFFS.
THAT WON'T BE NECESSARY, SIR, LET'S JUST GET YOU INTO THE CAR--
NO HANDCUFFS? ARE YOU SURE?

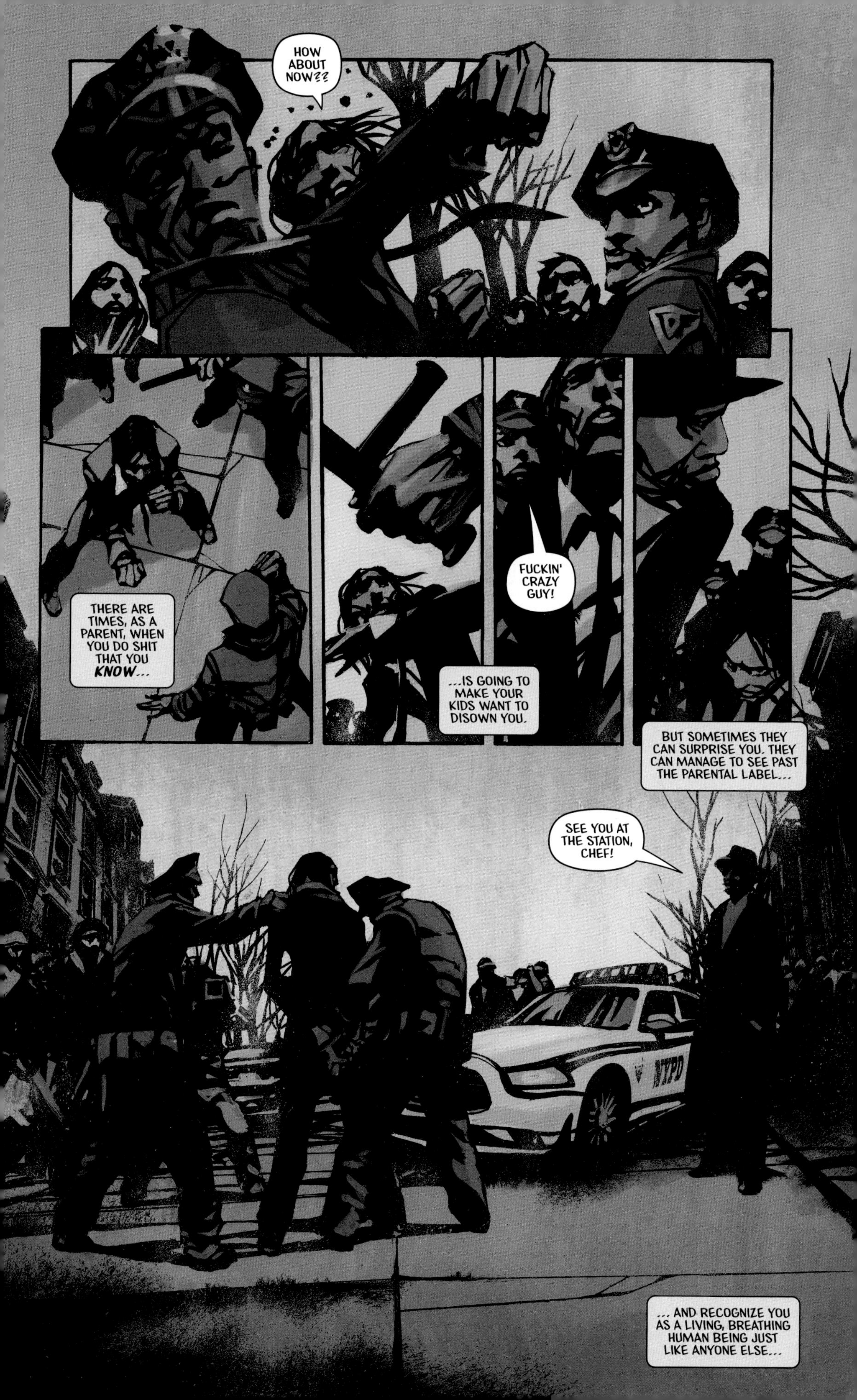
HOW ABOUT NOW??
THERE ARE TIMES, AS A PARENT, WHEN YOU DO SHIT THAT YOU KNOW...
...IS GOING TO MAKE YOUR KIDS WANT TO DISOWN YOU.
FUCKIN' CRAZY GUY!
BUT SOMETIMES THEY CAN SURPRISE YOU. THEY CAN MANAGE TO SEE PAST THE PARENTAL LABEL...
SEE YOU AT THE STATION, CHEF!
NYPD
... AND RECOGNIZE YOU AS A LIVING, BREATHING HUMAN BEING JUST LIKE ANYONE ELSE...

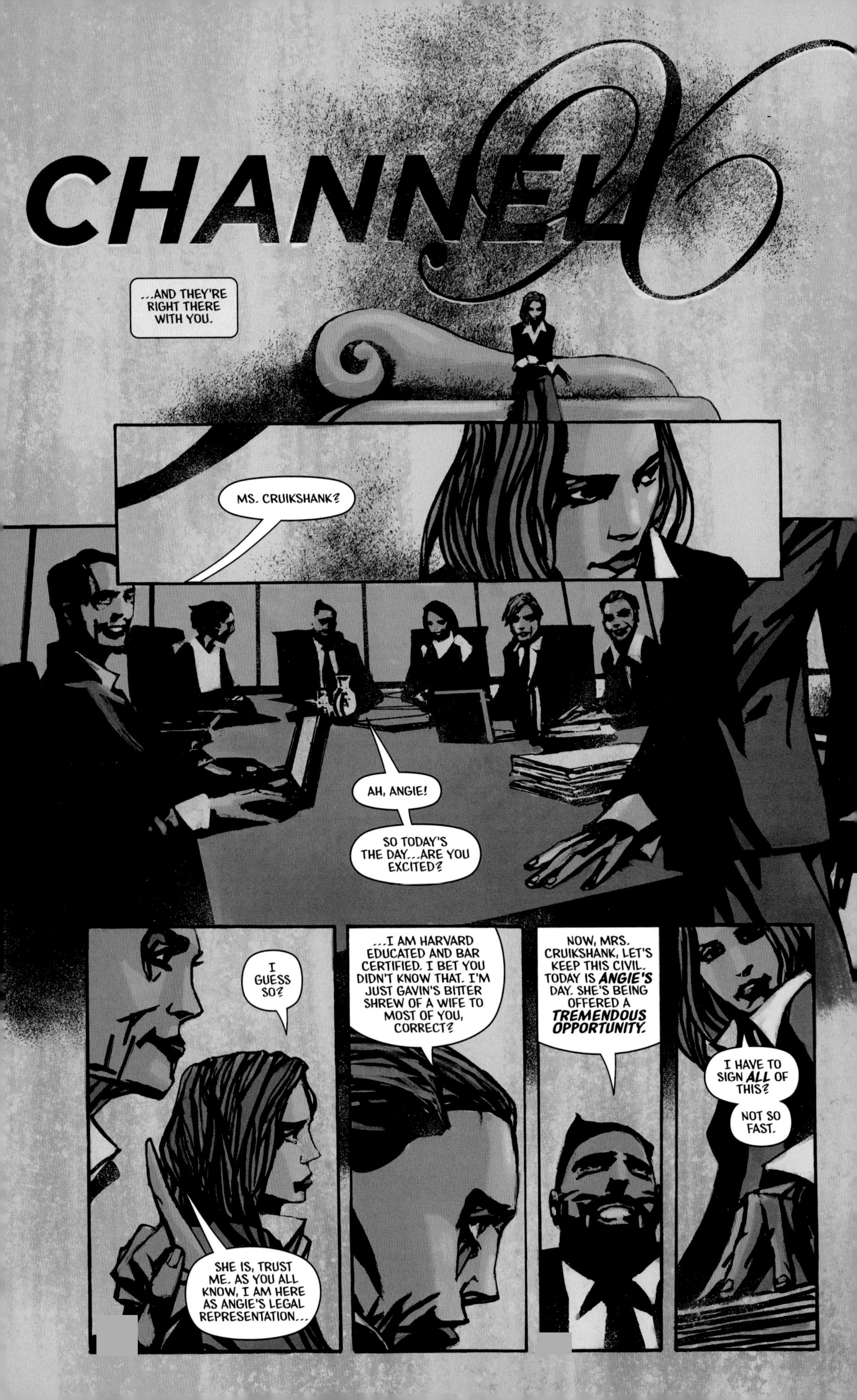

CHANNEL
...AND THEY'RE RIGHT THERE WITH YOU.
MS. CRUIKSHANK?
AH, ANGIE!
SO TODAY'S THE DAY...ARE YOU EXCITED?
I GUESS SO?
SHE IS, TRUST ME. AS YOU ALL KNOW, I AM HERE AS ANGIE'S LEGAL REPRESENTATION...
...I AM HARVARD EDUCATED AND BAR CERTIFIED. I BET YOU DIDN'T KNOW THAT. I'M JUST GAVIN'S BITTER SHREW OF A WIFE TO MOST OF YOU, CORRECT?
NOW, MRS. CRUIKSHANK, LET'S KEEP THIS CIVIL. TODAY IS ***ANGIE'S*** DAY. SHE'S BEING OFFERED A ***TREMENDOUS OPPORTUNITY.***
I HAVE TO SIGN ***ALL*** OF THIS?
NOT SO FAST.

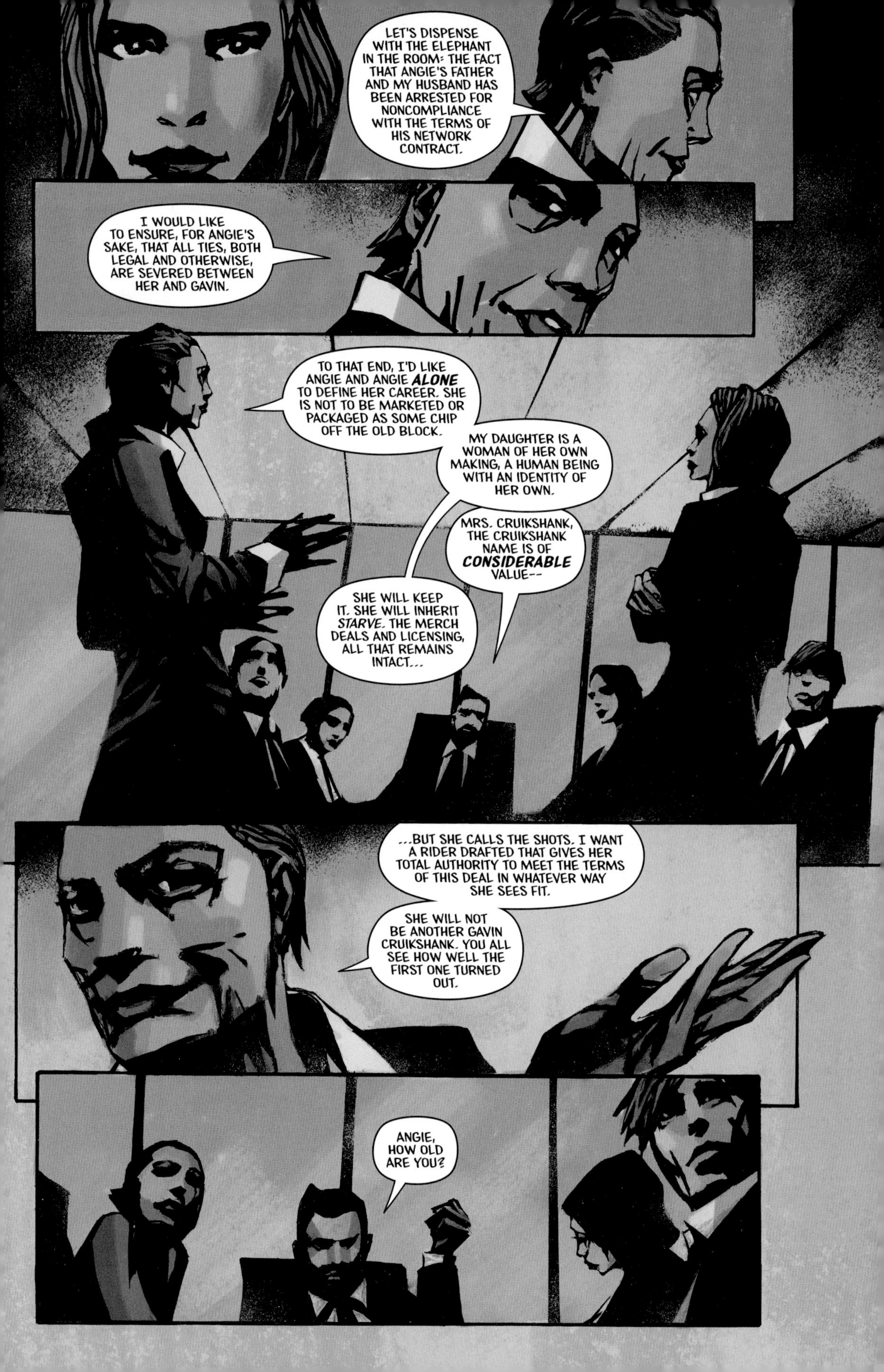
LET'S DISPENSE WITH THE ELEPHANT IN THE ROOM: THE FACT THAT ANGIE'S FATHER AND MY HUSBAND HAS BEEN ARRESTED FOR NONCOMPLIANCE WITH THE TERMS OF HIS NETWORK CONTRACT.
I WOULD LIKE TO ENSURE, FOR ANGIE'S SAKE, THAT ALL TIES, BOTH LEGAL AND OTHERWISE, ARE SEVERED BETWEEN HER AND GAVIN.
TO THAT END, I'D LIKE ANGIE AND ANGIE ***ALONE*** TO DEFINE HER CAREER. SHE IS NOT TO BE MARKETED OR PACKAGED AS SOME CHIP OFF THE OLD BLOCK.
MY DAUGHTER IS A WOMAN OF HER OWN MAKING, A HUMAN BEING WITH AN IDENTITY OF HER OWN.
MRS. CRUIKSHANK, THE CRUIKSHANK NAME IS OF ***CONSIDERABLE*** VALUE--
SHE WILL KEEP IT. SHE WILL INHERIT *STARVE*. THE MERCH DEALS AND LICENSING, ALL THAT REMAINS INTACT...
...BUT SHE CALLS THE SHOTS. I WANT A RIDER DRAFTED THAT GIVES HER TOTAL AUTHORITY TO MEET THE TERMS OF THIS DEAL IN WHATEVER WAY SHE SEES FIT.
SHE WILL NOT BE ANOTHER GAVIN CRUIKSHANK. YOU ALL SEE HOW WELL THE FIRST ONE TURNED OUT.
ANGIE, HOW OLD ARE YOU?

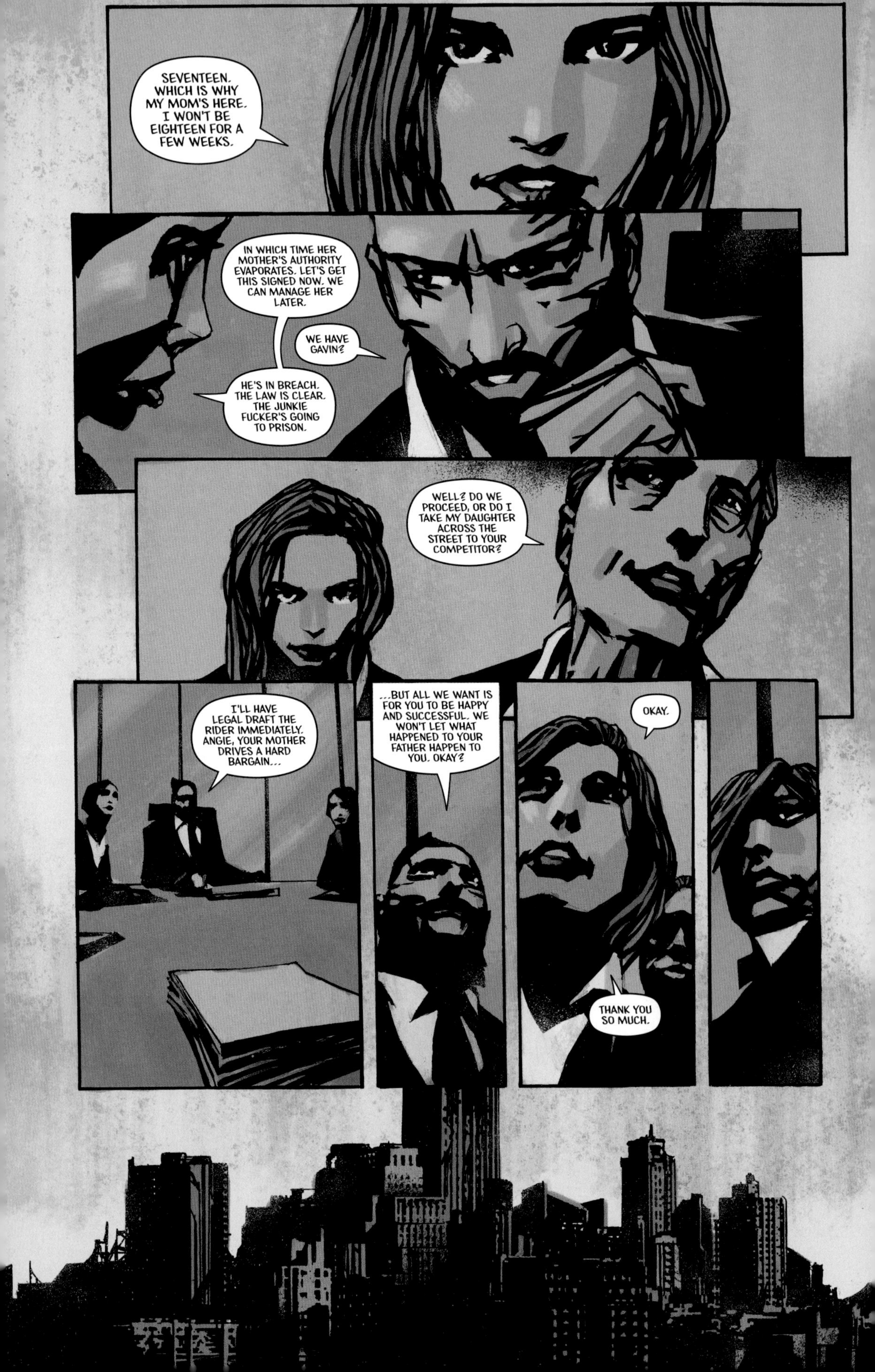
SEVENTEEN. WHICH IS WHY MY MOM'S HERE. I WON'T BE EIGHTEEN FOR A FEW WEEKS.
IN WHICH TIME HER MOTHER'S AUTHORITY EVAPORATES. LET'S GET THIS SIGNED NOW. WE CAN MANAGE HER LATER.
WE HAVE GAVIN?
HE'S IN BREACH. THE LAW IS CLEAR. THE JUNKIE FUCKER'S GOING TO PRISON.
WELL? DO WE PROCEED, OR DO I TAKE MY DAUGHTER ACROSS THE STREET TO YOUR COMPETITOR?
I'LL HAVE LEGAL DRAFT THE RIDER IMMEDIATELY. ANGIE, YOUR MOTHER DRIVES A HARD BARGAIN...
...BUT ALL WE WANT IS FOR YOU TO BE HAPPY AND SUCCESSFUL. WE WON'T LET WHAT HAPPENED TO YOUR FATHER HAPPEN TO YOU. OKAY?
OKAY.
THANK YOU SO MUCH.

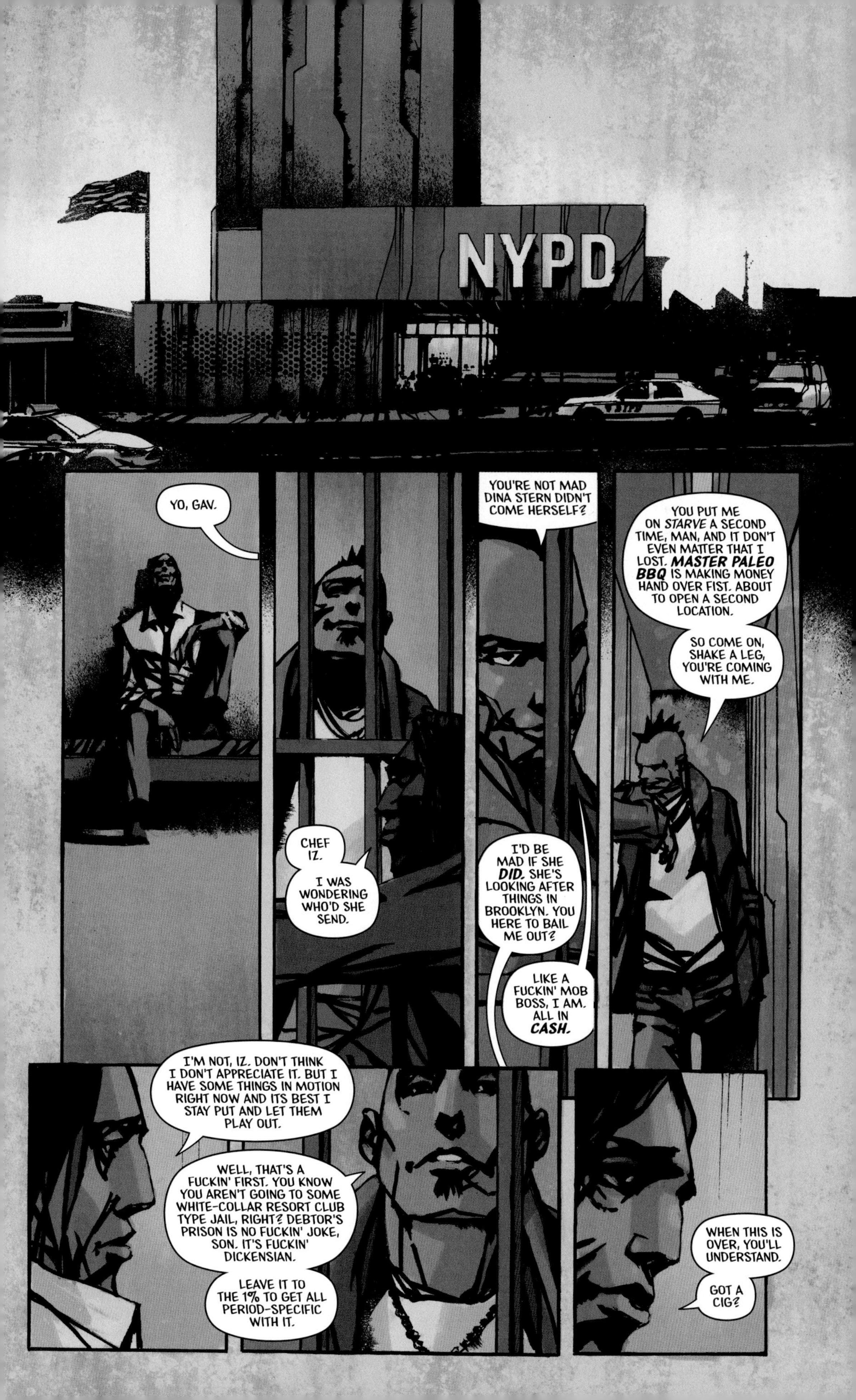
NYPD
YO, GAV.
CHEF IZ.
I WAS WONDERING WHO'D SHE SEND.
YOU'RE NOT MAD DINA STERN DIDN'T COME HERSELF?
I'D BE MAD IF SHE DID. SHE'S LOOKING AFTER THINGS IN BROOKLYN. YOU HERE TO BAIL ME OUT?
LIKE A FUCKIN' MOB BOSS, I AM. ALL IN CASH.
YOU PUT ME ON STARVE A SECOND TIME, MAN, AND IT DON'T EVEN MATTER THAT I LOST. MASTER PALEO BBQ IS MAKING MONEY HAND OVER FIST. ABOUT TO OPEN A SECOND LOCATION.
SO COME ON, SHAKE A LEG, YOU'RE COMING WITH ME.
I'M NOT, IZ. DON'T THINK I DON'T APPRECIATE IT. BUT I HAVE SOME THINGS IN MOTION RIGHT NOW AND ITS BEST I STAY PUT AND LET THEM PLAY OUT.
WELL, THAT'S A FUCKIN' FIRST. YOU KNOW YOU AREN'T GOING TO SOME WHITE-COLLAR RESORT CLUB TYPE JAIL, RIGHT? DEBTOR'S PRISON IS NO FUCKIN' JOKE, SON. IT'S FUCKIN' DICKENSIAN.
LEAVE IT TO THE 1% TO GET ALL PERIOD-SPECIFIC WITH IT.
WHEN THIS IS OVER, YOU'LL UNDERSTAND.
GOT A CIG?

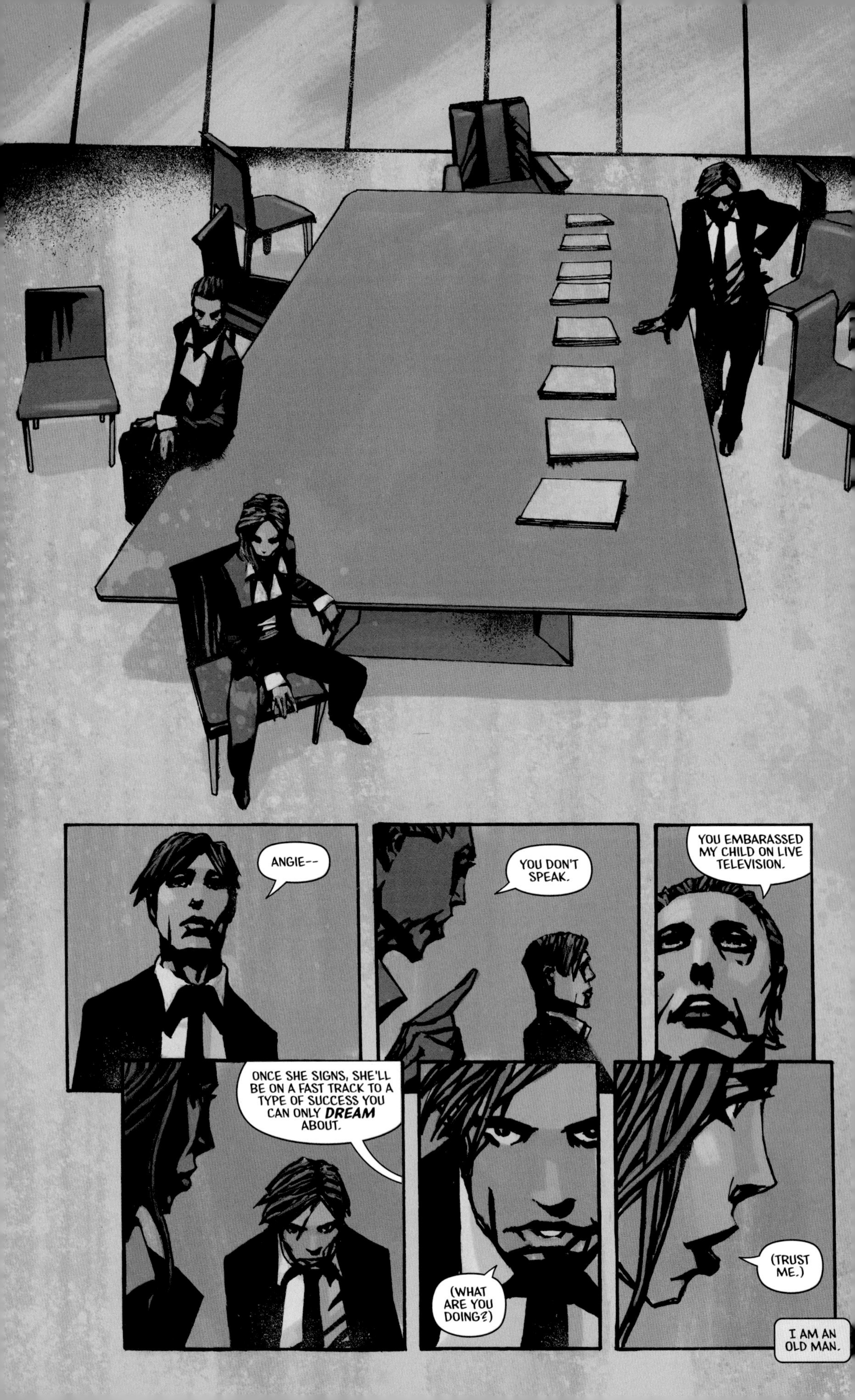
ANGIE--
YOU DON'T SPEAK.
YOU EMBARASSED MY CHILD ON LIVE TELEVISION.
ONCE SHE SIGNS, SHE'LL BE ON A FAST TRACK TO A TYPE OF SUCCESS YOU CAN ONLY DREAM ABOUT.
(WHAT ARE YOU DOING?)
(TRUST ME.)
I AM AN OLD MAN.

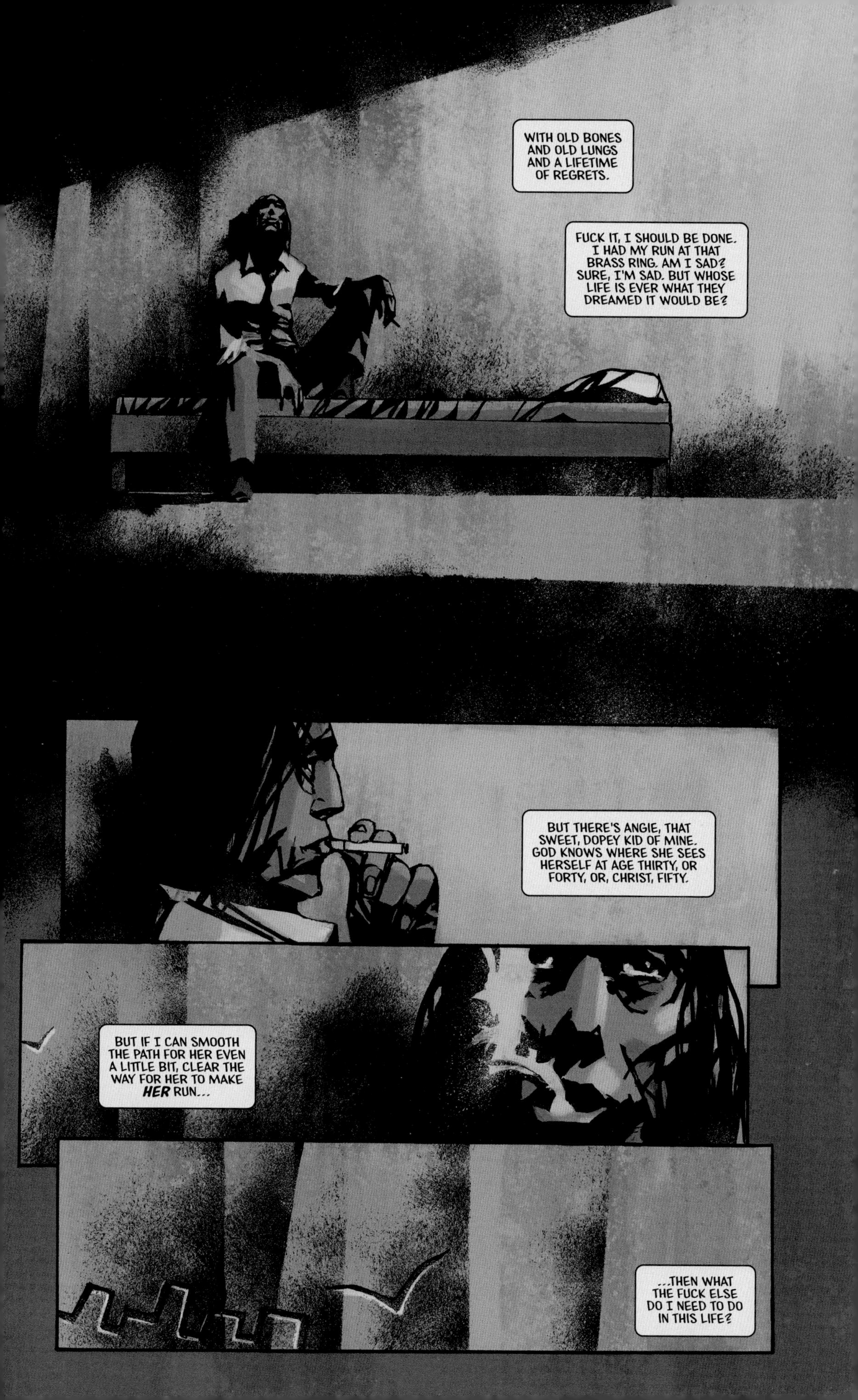
WITH OLD BONES AND OLD LUNGS AND A LIFETIME OF REGRETS.
FUCK IT, I SHOULD BE DONE. I HAD MY RUN AT THAT BRASS RING. AM I SAD? SURE, I'M SAD. BUT WHOSE LIFE IS EVER WHAT THEY DREAMED IT WOULD BE?
BUT THERE'S ANGIE, THAT SWEET, DOPEY KID OF MINE. GOD KNOWS WHERE SHE SEES HERSELF AT AGE THIRTY, OR FORTY, OR, CHRIST, FIFTY.
BUT IF I CAN SMOOTH THE PATH FOR HER EVEN A LITTLE BIT, CLEAR THE WAY FOR HER TO MAKE HER RUN...
...THEN WHAT THE FUCK ELSE DO I NEED TO DO IN THIS LIFE?

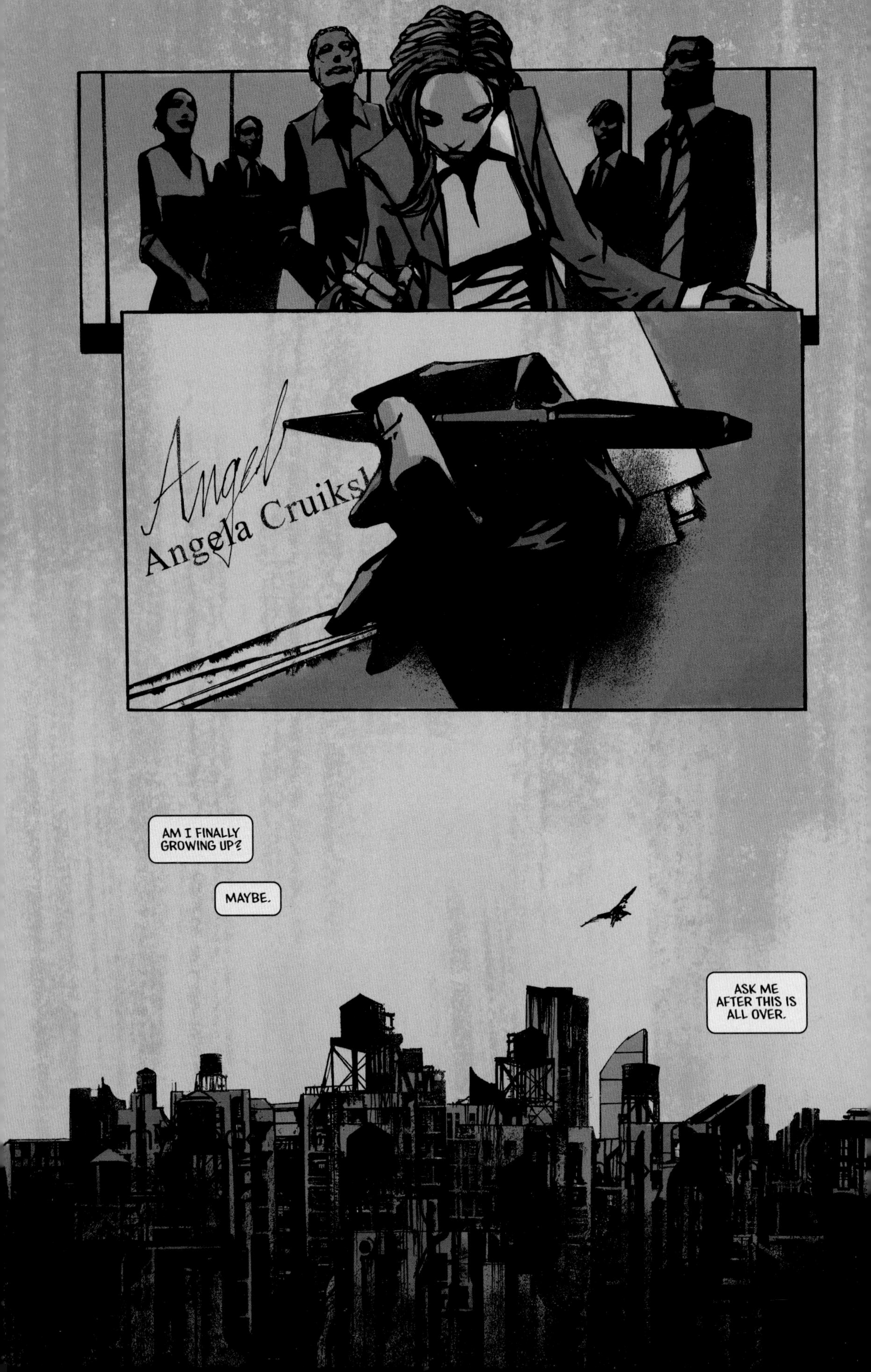
AM I FINALLY GROWING UP?
MAYBE.
ASK ME AFTER THIS IS ALL OVER.

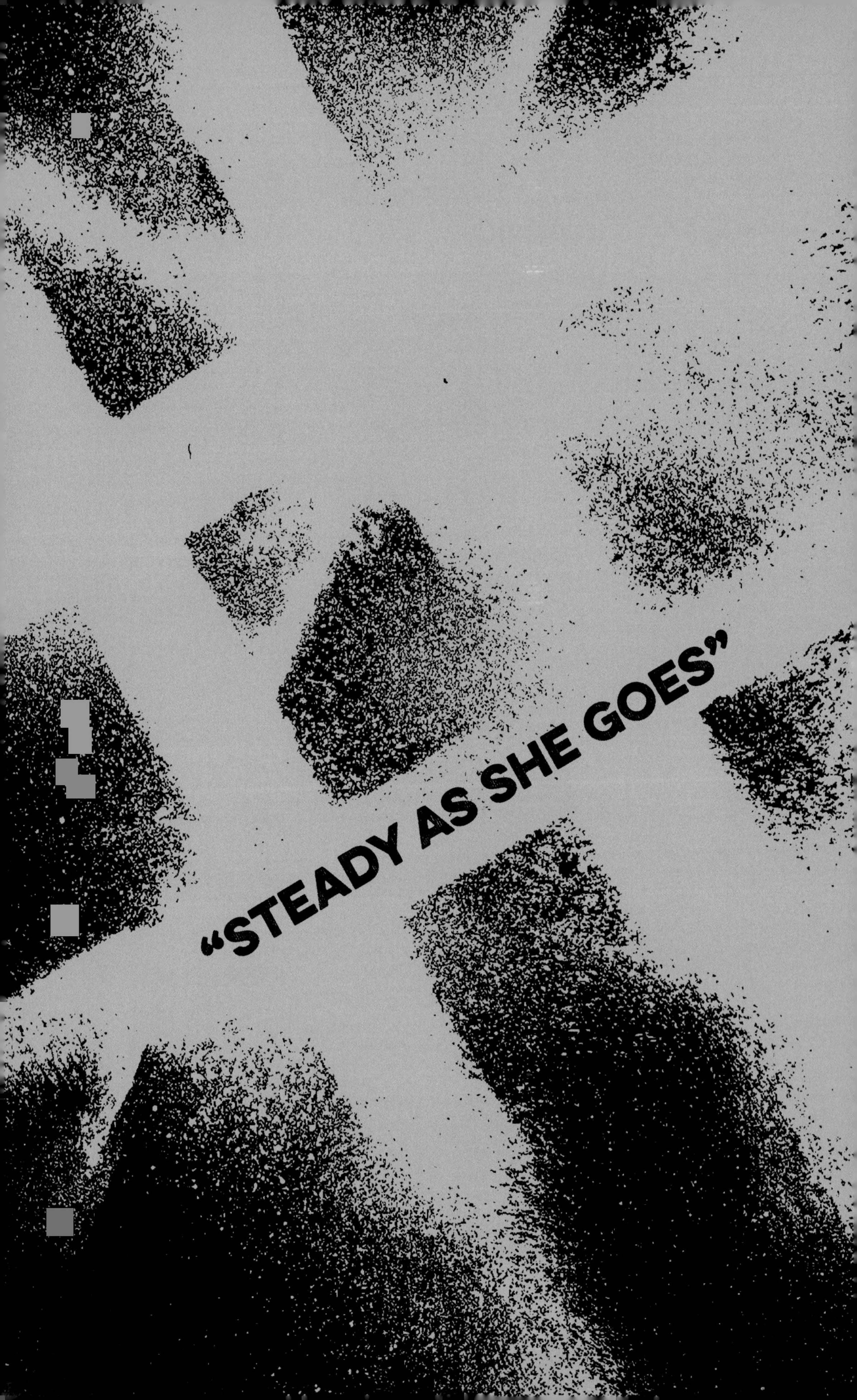
"STEADY AS SHE GOES"

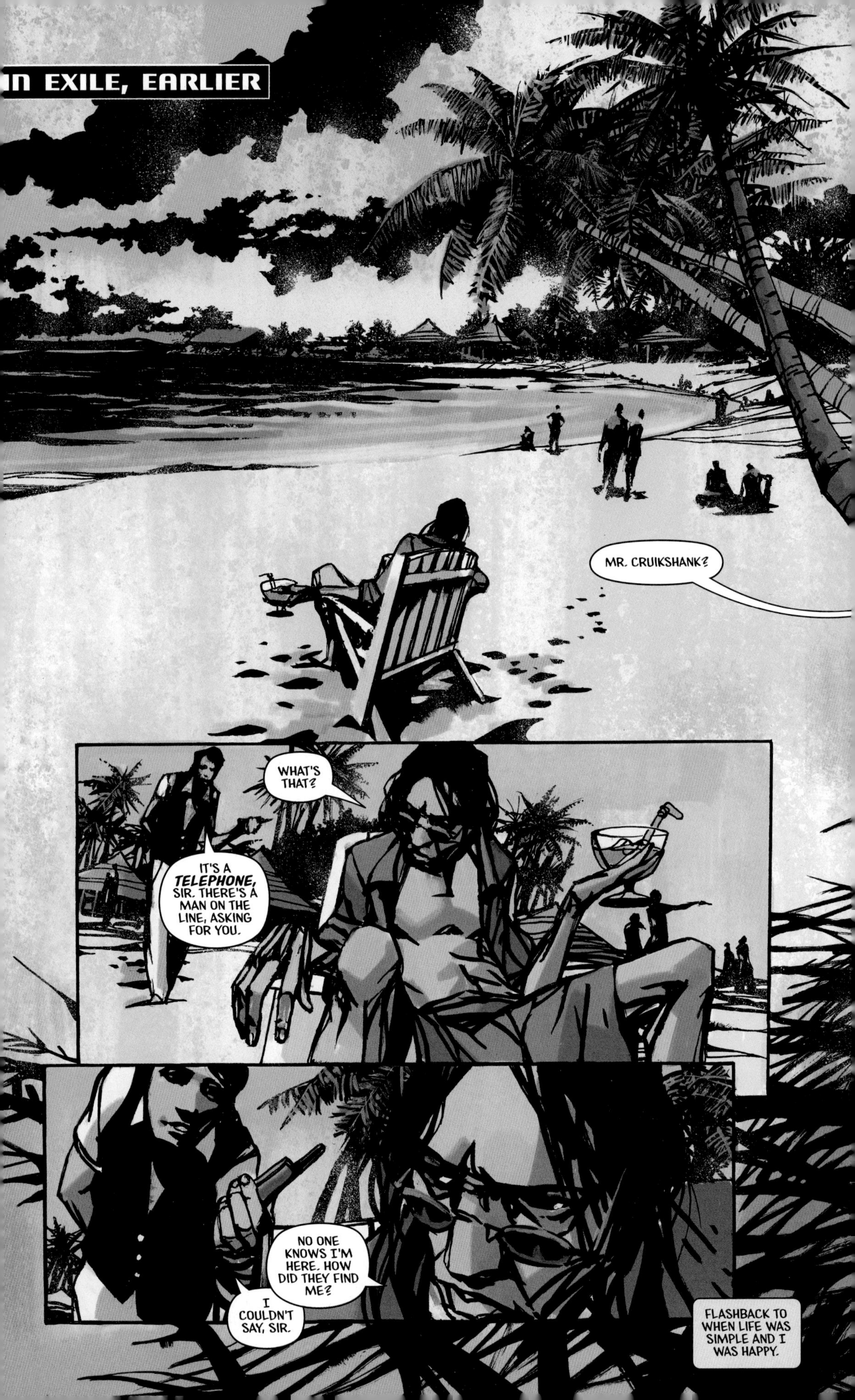
IN EXILE, EARLIER
MR. CRUIKSHANK?
WHAT'S THAT?
IT'S A TELEPHONE, SIR. THERE'S A MAN ON THE LINE, ASKING FOR YOU.
NO ONE KNOWS I'M HERE. HOW DID THEY FIND ME?
I COULDN'T SAY, SIR.
FLASHBACK TO WHEN LIFE WAS SIMPLE AND I WAS HAPPY.

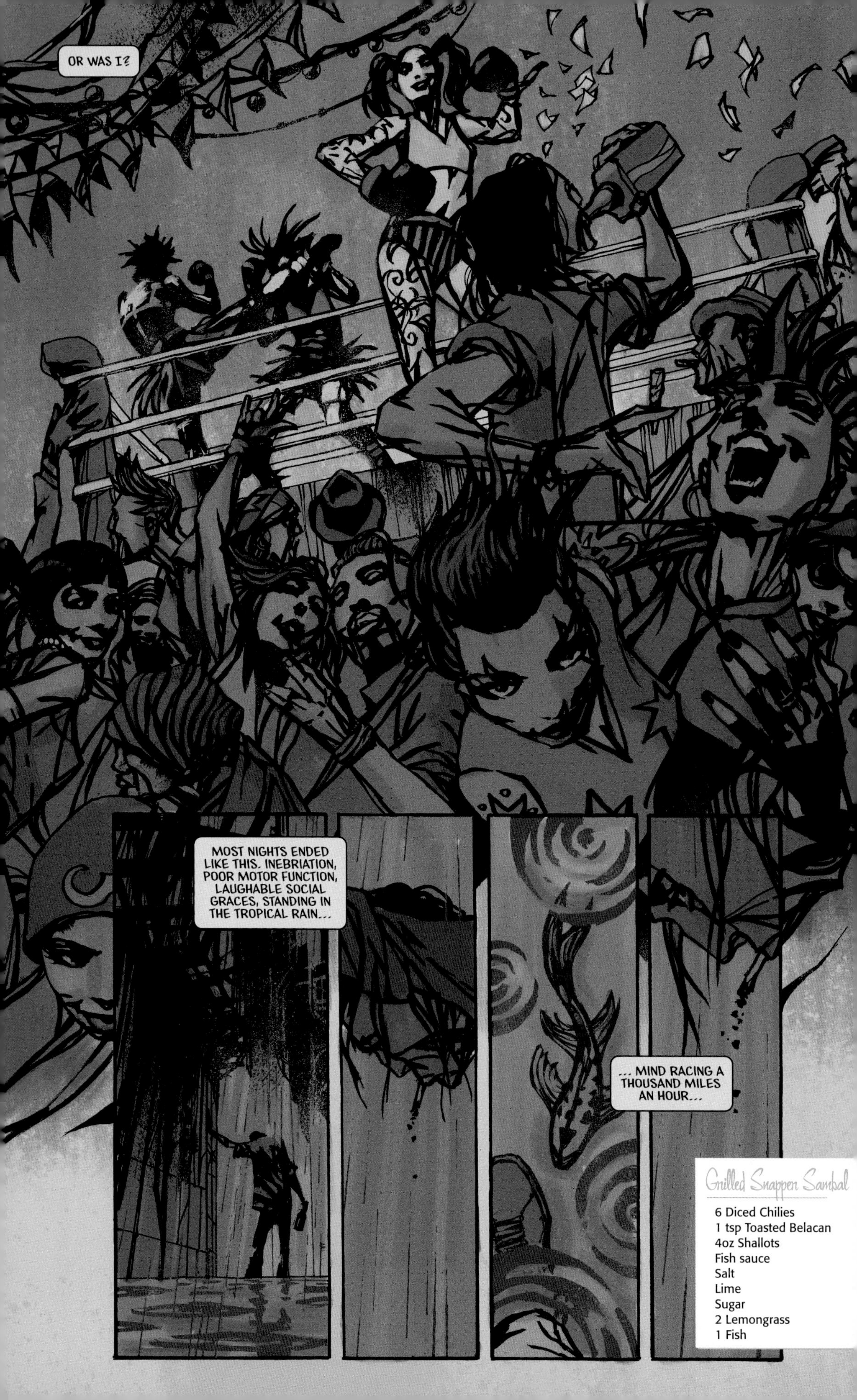
OR WAS I?
MOST NIGHTS ENDED LIKE THIS. INEBRIATION, POOR MOTOR FUNCTION, LAUGHABLE SOCIAL GRACES, STANDING IN THE TROPICAL RAIN...
... MIND RACING A THOUSAND MILES AN HOUR...
Grilled Snapper Sambal
6 Diced Chilies
1 tsp Toasted Belacan
4oz Shallots
Fish sauce
Salt
Lime
Sugar
2 Lemongrass
1 Fish

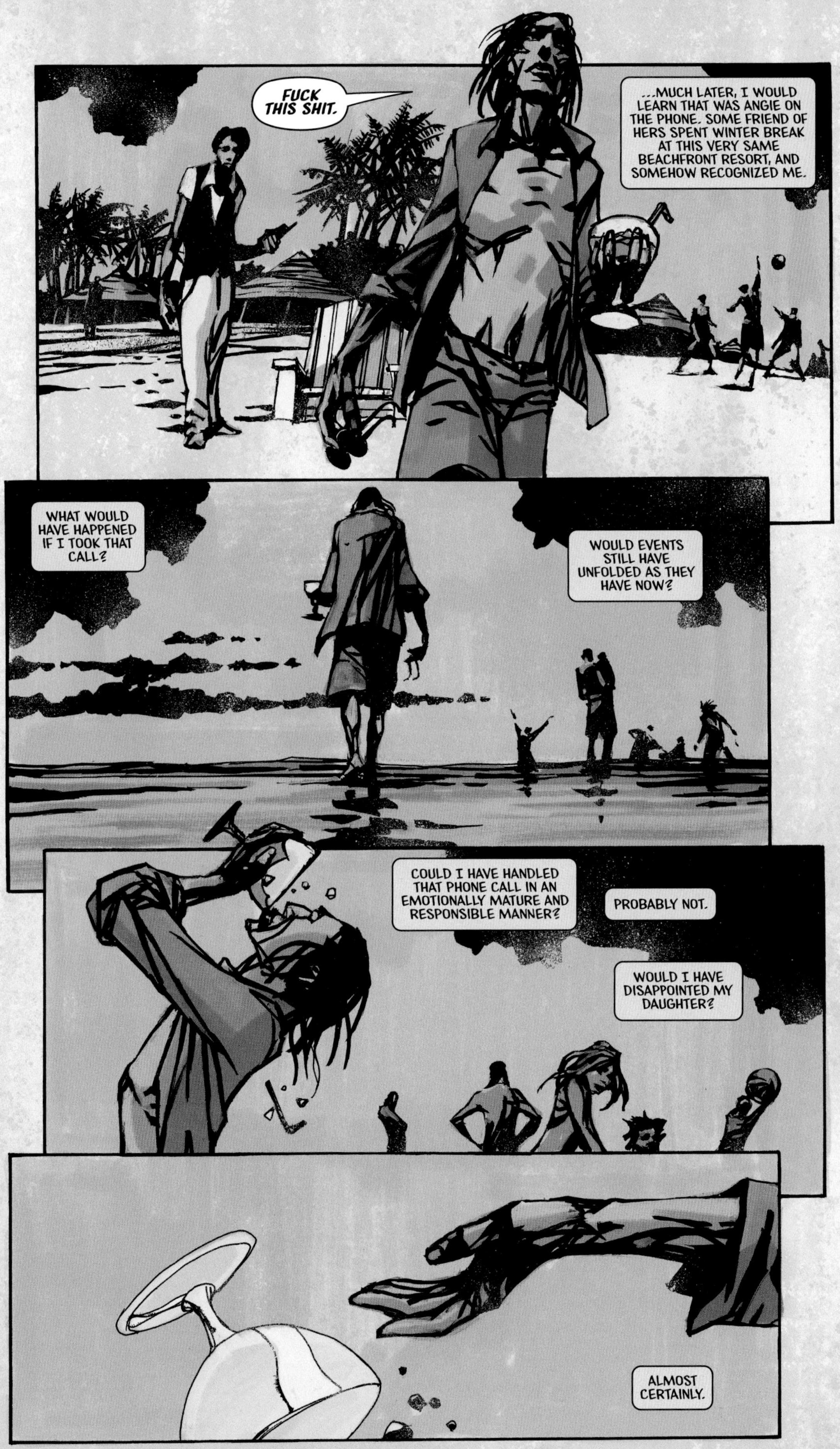
FUCK THIS SHIT.
...MUCH LATER, I WOULD LEARN THAT WAS ANGIE ON THE PHONE. SOME FRIEND OF HERS SPENT WINTER BREAK AT THIS VERY SAME BEACHFRONT RESORT, AND SOMEHOW RECOGNIZED ME.
WHAT WOULD HAVE HAPPENED IF I TOOK THAT CALL?
WOULD EVENTS STILL HAVE UNFOLDED AS THEY HAVE NOW?
COULD I HAVE HANDLED THAT PHONE CALL IN AN EMOTIONALLY MATURE AND RESPONSIBLE MANNER?
PROBABLY NOT.
WOULD I HAVE DISAPPOINTED MY DAUGHTER?
ALMOST CERTAINLY.

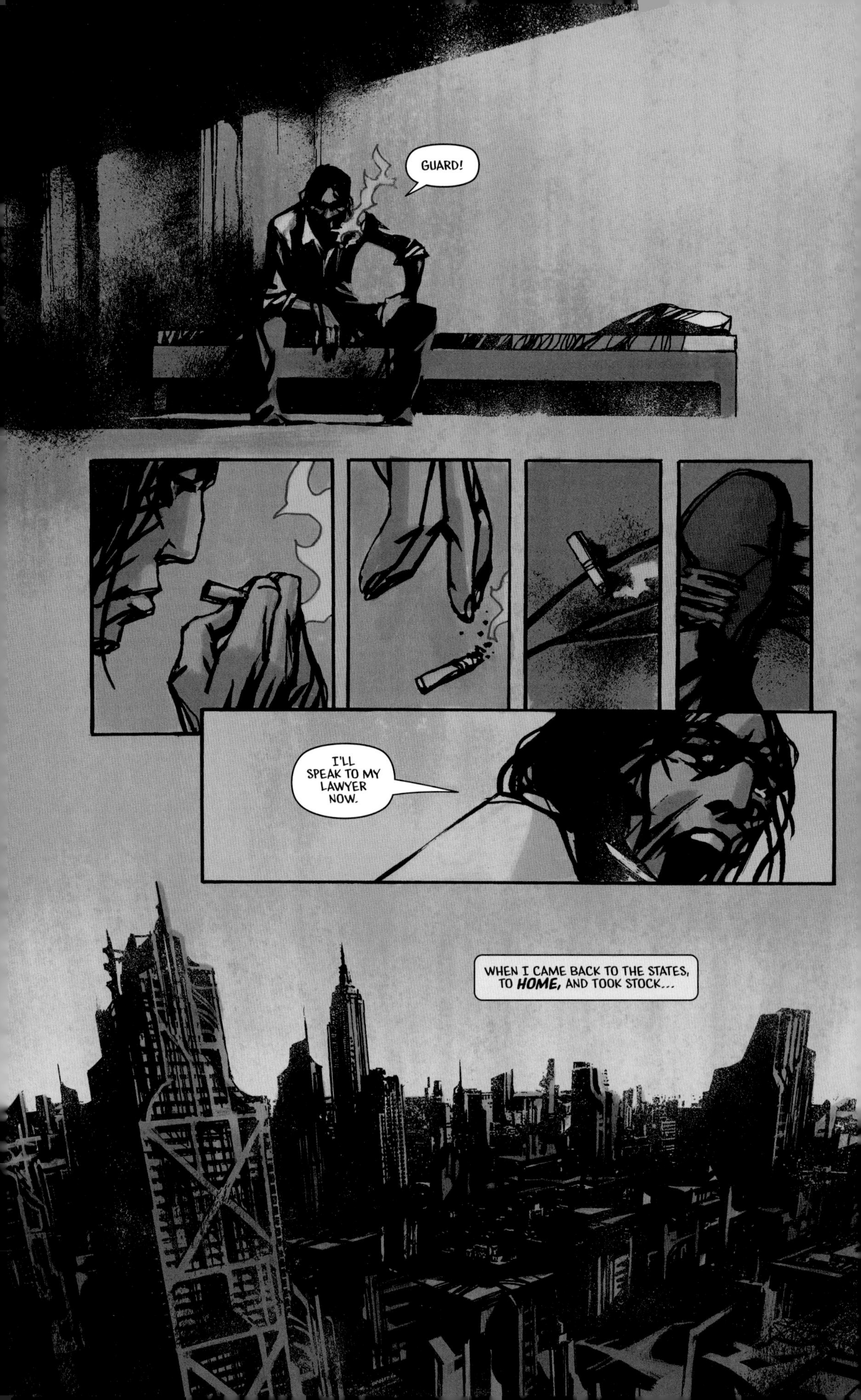
GUARD!
I'LL SPEAK TO MY LAWYER NOW.
WHEN I CAME BACK TO THE STATES, TO *HOME,* AND TOOK STOCK...

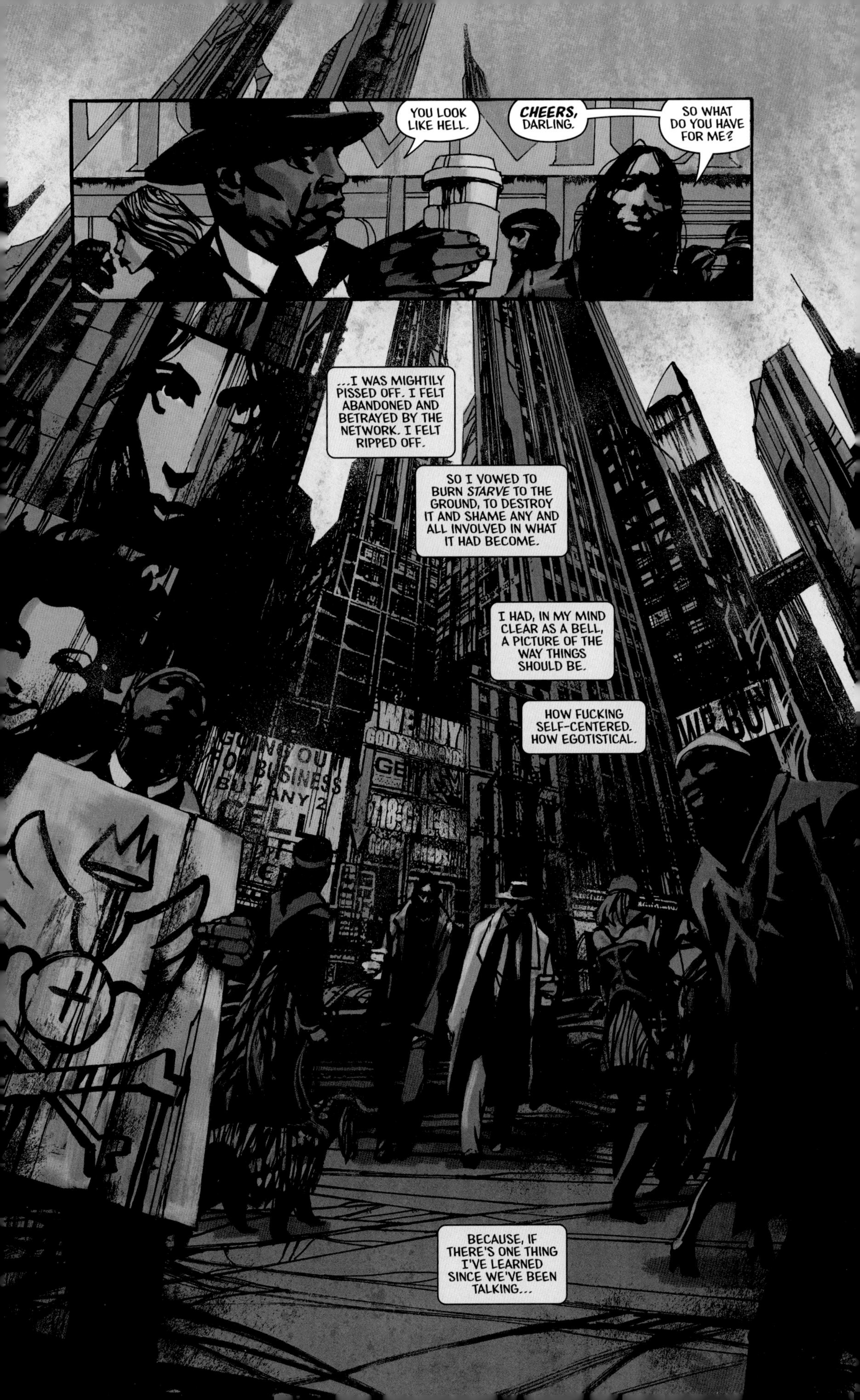
YOU LOOK LIKE HELL.
CHEERS, DARLING.
SO WHAT DO YOU HAVE FOR ME?
...I WAS MIGHTILY PISSED OFF. I FELT ABANDONED AND BETRAYED BY THE NETWORK. I FELT RIPPED OFF.
SO I VOWED TO BURN STARVE TO THE GROUND, TO DESTROY IT AND SHAME ANY AND ALL INVOLVED IN WHAT IT HAD BECOME.
I HAD, IN MY MIND CLEAR AS A BELL, A PICTURE OF THE WAY THINGS SHOULD BE.
HOW FUCKING SELF-CENTERED. HOW EGOTISTICAL.
BECAUSE, IF THERE'S ONE THING I'VE LEARNED SINCE WE'VE BEEN TALKING...

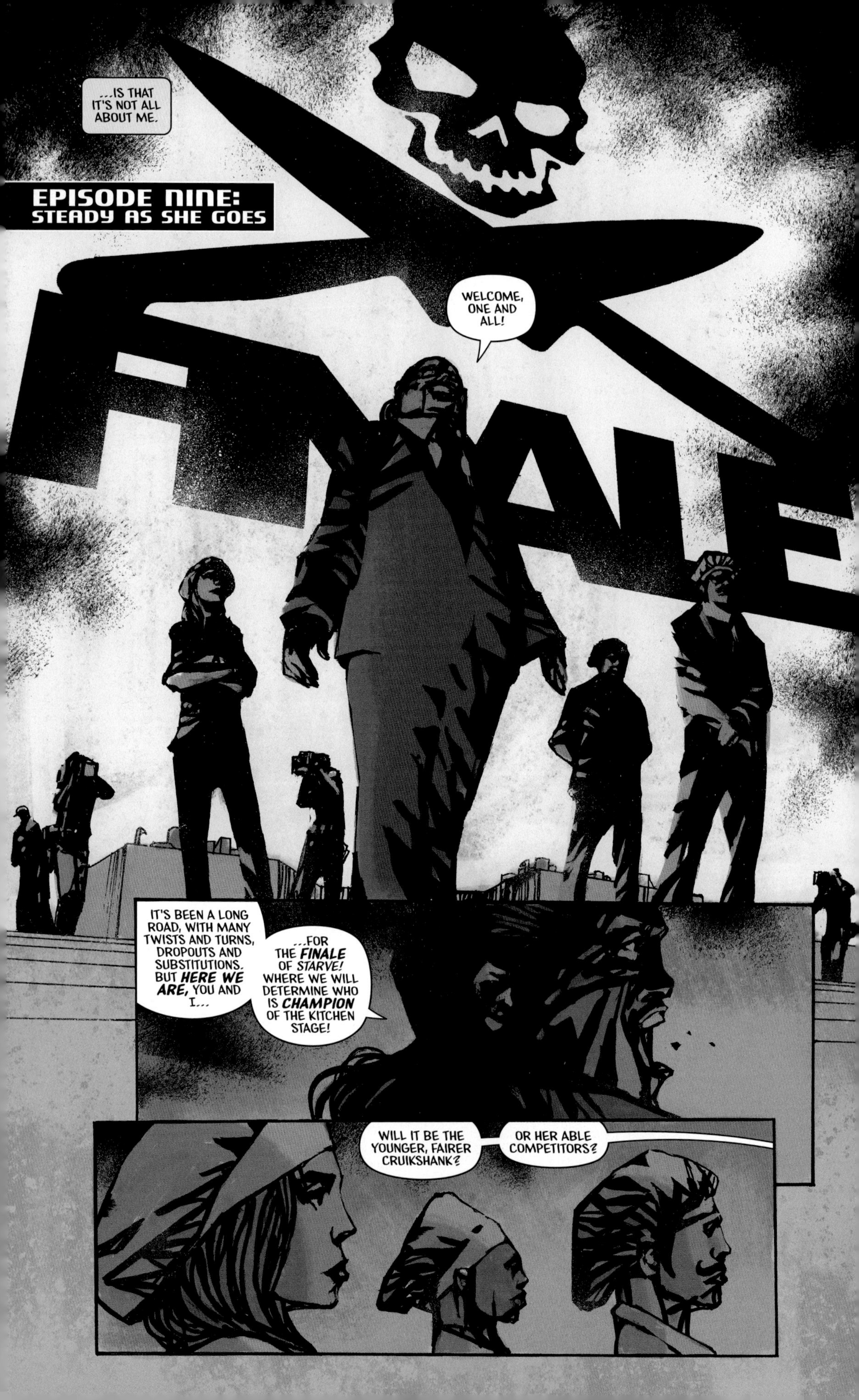
...IS THAT IT'S NOT ALL ABOUT ME.
EPISODE NINE: STEADY AS SHE GOES
WELCOME, ONE AND ALL!
FINALE
IT'S BEEN A LONG ROAD, WITH MANY TWISTS AND TURNS, DROPOUTS AND SUBSTITUTIONS. BUT HERE WE ARE, YOU AND I...
...FOR THE FINALE OF STARVE! WHERE WE WILL DETERMINE WHO IS CHAMPION OF THE KITCHEN STAGE!
WILL IT BE THE YOUNGER, FAIRER CRUIKSHANK?
OR HER ABLE COMPETITORS?

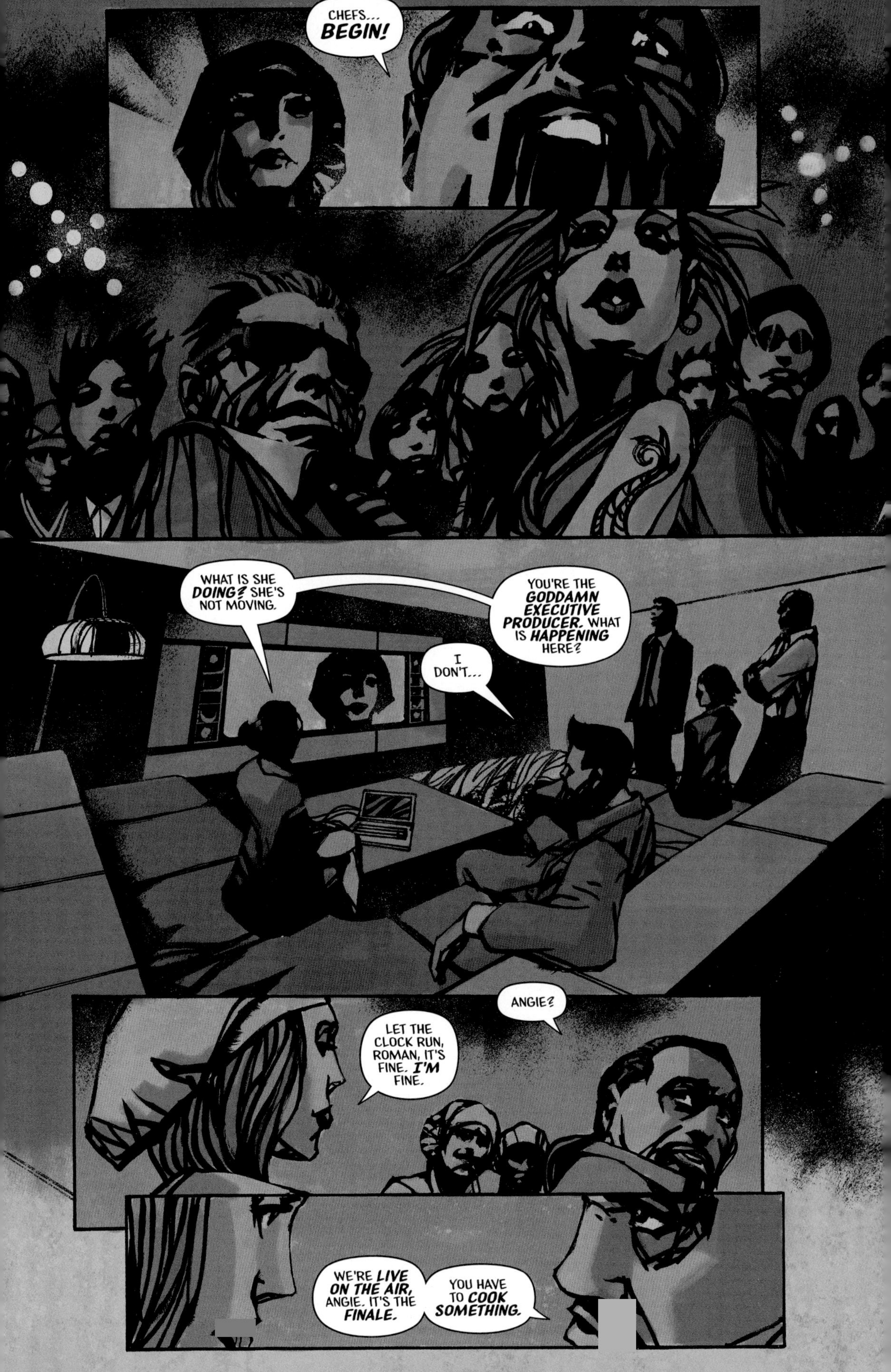
CHEFS... BEGIN!
WHAT IS SHE DOING? SHE'S NOT MOVING.
YOU'RE THE GODDAMN EXECUTIVE PRODUCER. WHAT IS HAPPENING HERE?
I DON'T...
ANGIE?
LET THE CLOCK RUN, ROMAN, IT'S FINE. I'M FINE.
WE'RE LIVE ON THE AIR, ANGIE. IT'S THE FINALE.
YOU HAVE TO COOK SOMETHING.

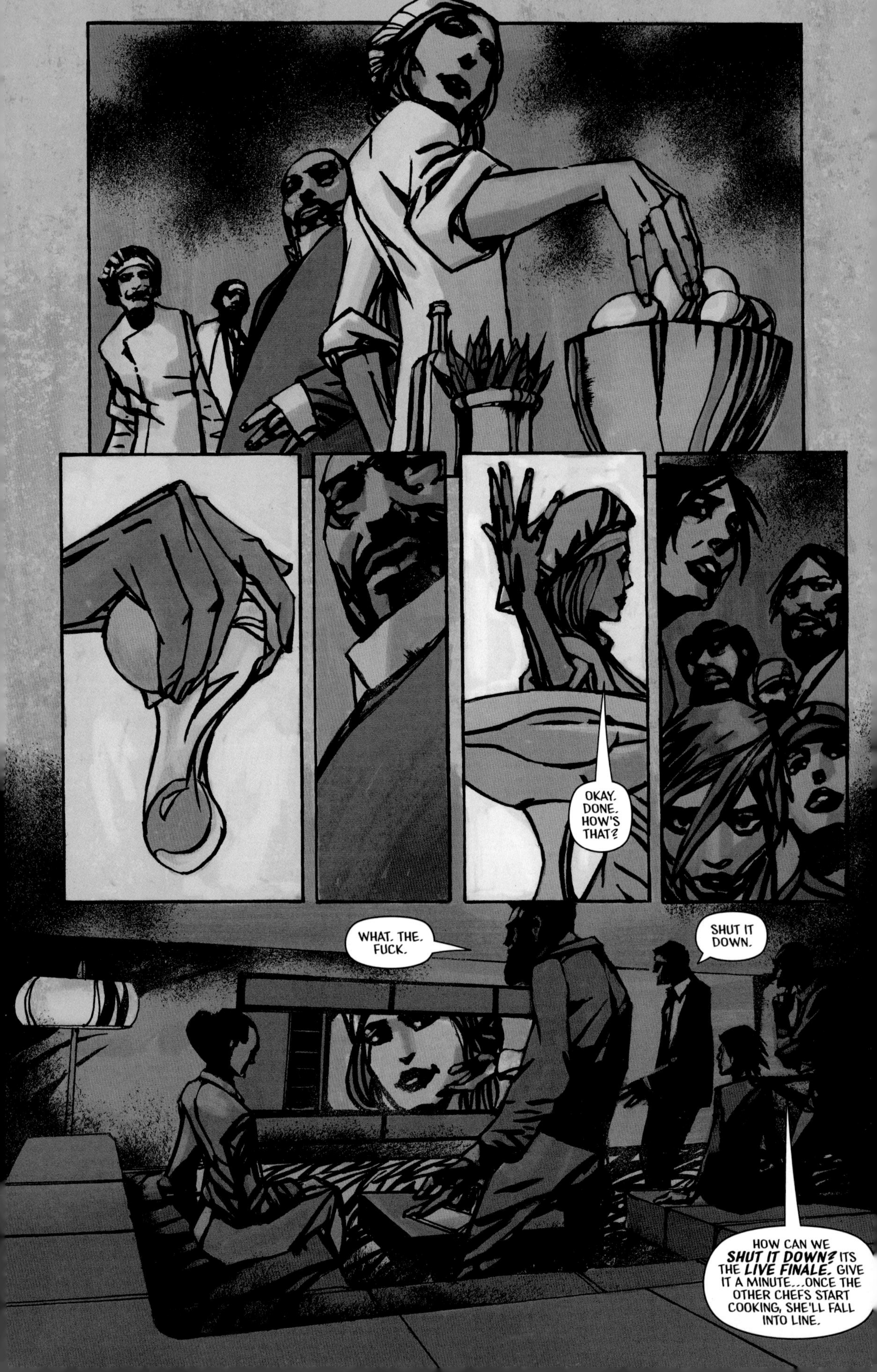
OKAY. DONE. HOW'S THAT?
WHAT. THE. FUCK.
SHUT IT DOWN.
HOW CAN WE SHUT IT DOWN? ITS THE LIVE FINALE. GIVE IT A MINUTE...ONCE THE OTHER CHEFS START COOKING, SHE'LL FALL INTO LINE.

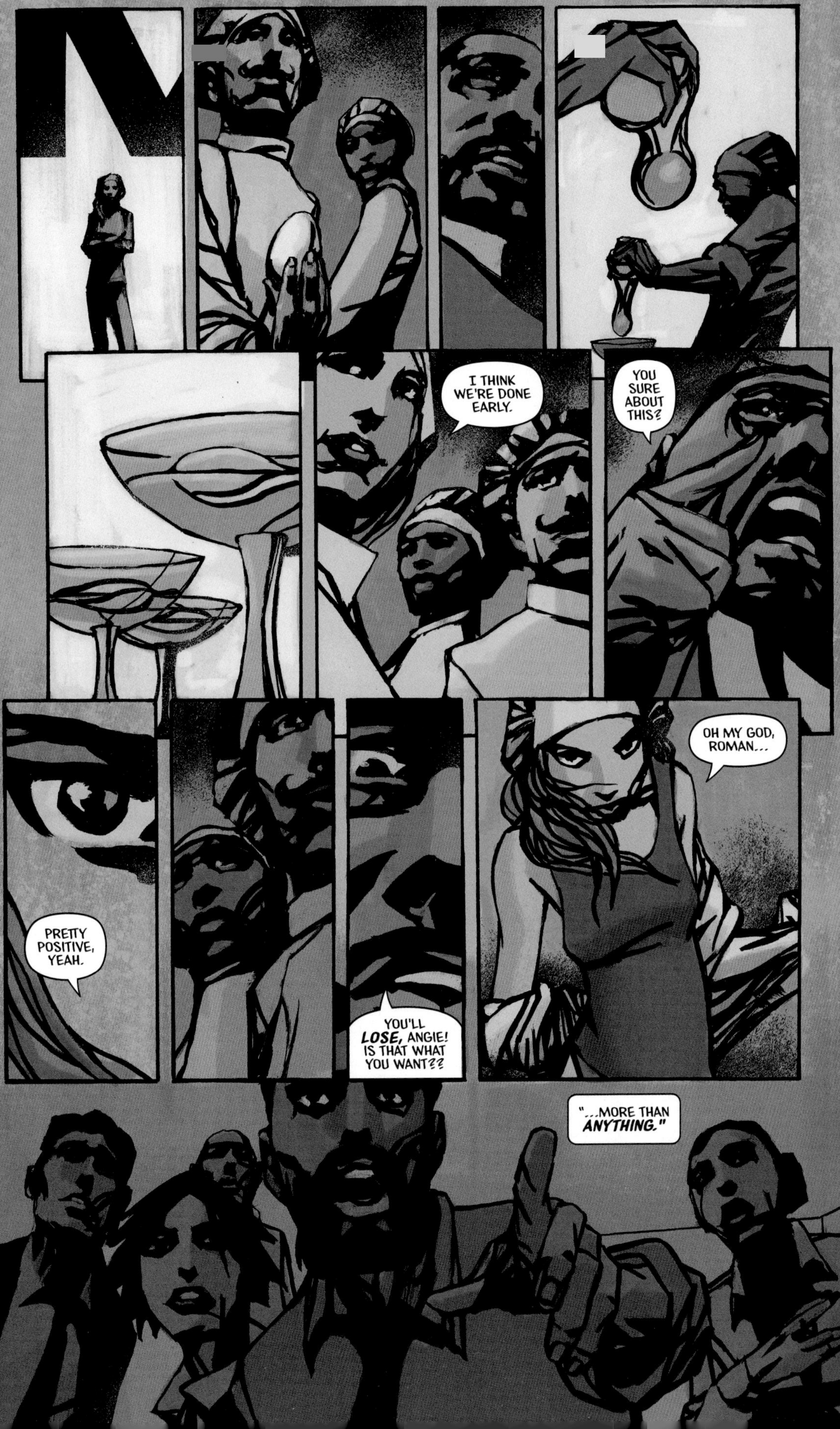

I THINK WE'RE DONE EARLY.
YOU SURE ABOUT THIS?
PRETTY POSITIVE, YEAH.
YOU'LL LOSE, ANGIE! IS THAT WHAT YOU WANT??
OH MY GOD, ROMAN...
"...MORE THAN ANYTHING."

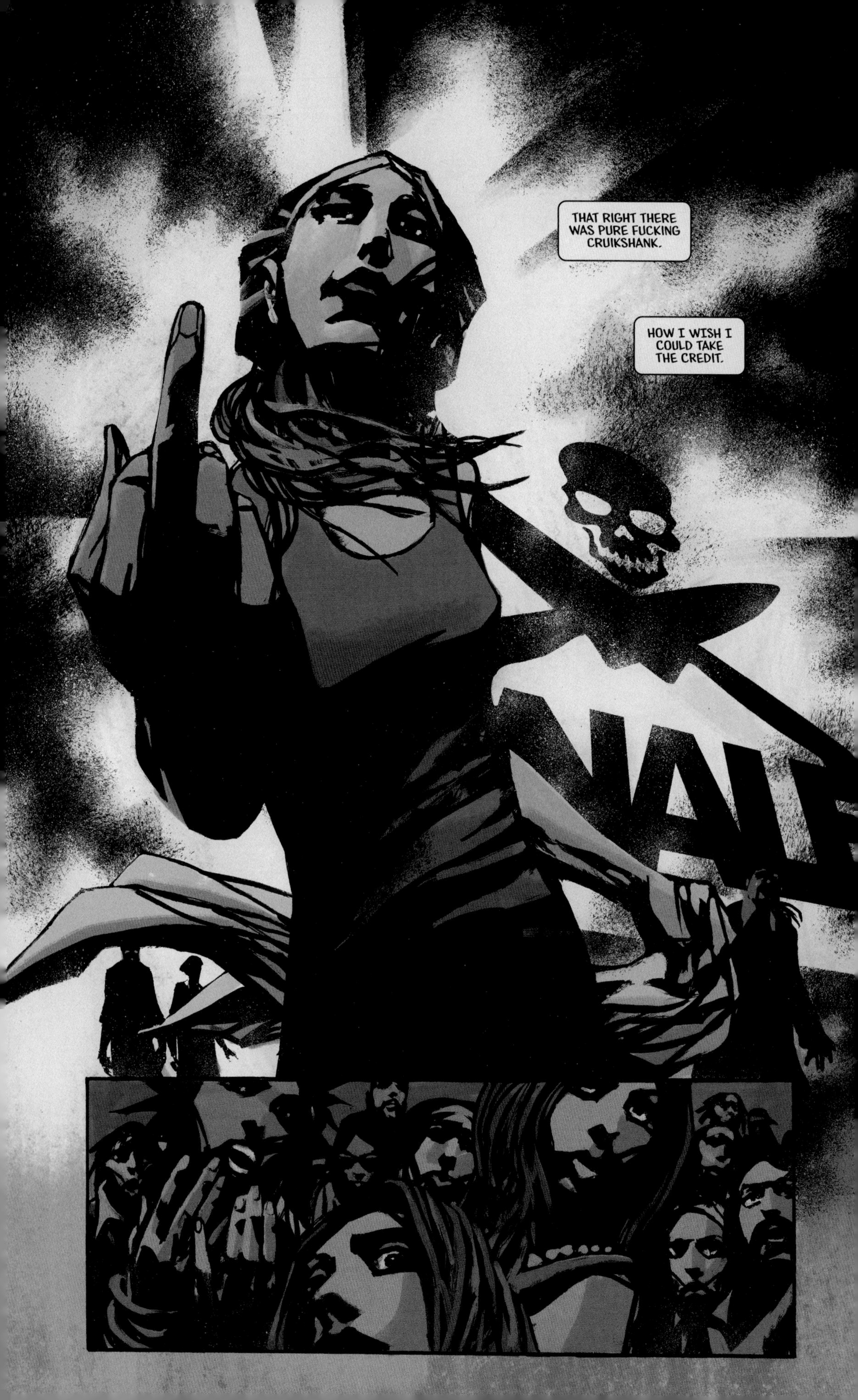
THAT RIGHT THERE WAS PURE FUCKING CRUIKSHANK.
HOW I WISH I COULD TAKE THE CREDIT.

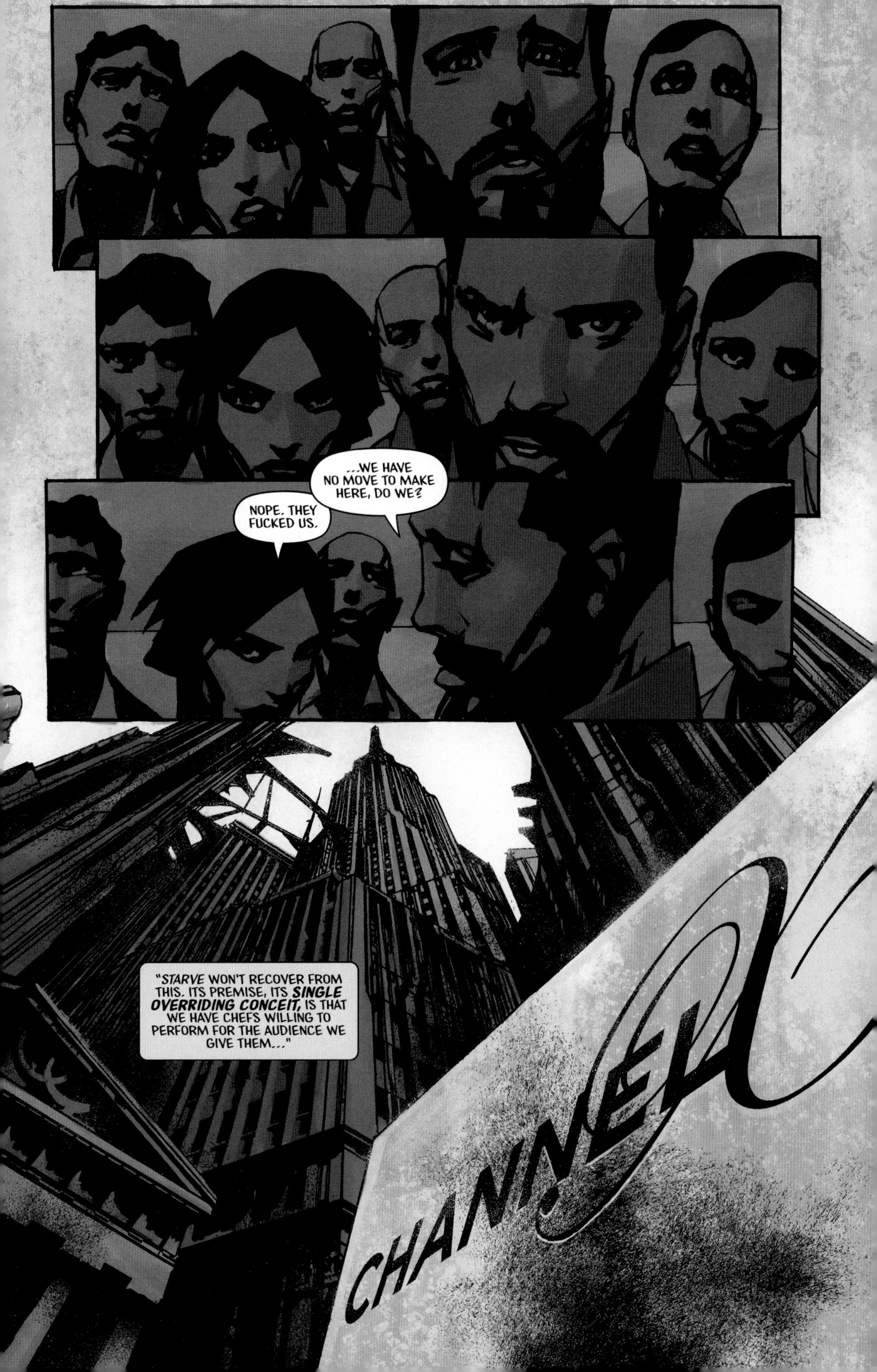
...WE HAVE NO MOVE TO MAKE HERE, DO WE?
NOPE. THEY FUCKED US.
"STARVE WON'T RECOVER FROM THIS. ITS PREMISE, ITS SINGLE OVERRIDING CONCEIT, IS THAT WE HAVE CHEFS WILLING TO PERFORM FOR THE AUDIENCE WE GIVE THEM..."
CHANNEL

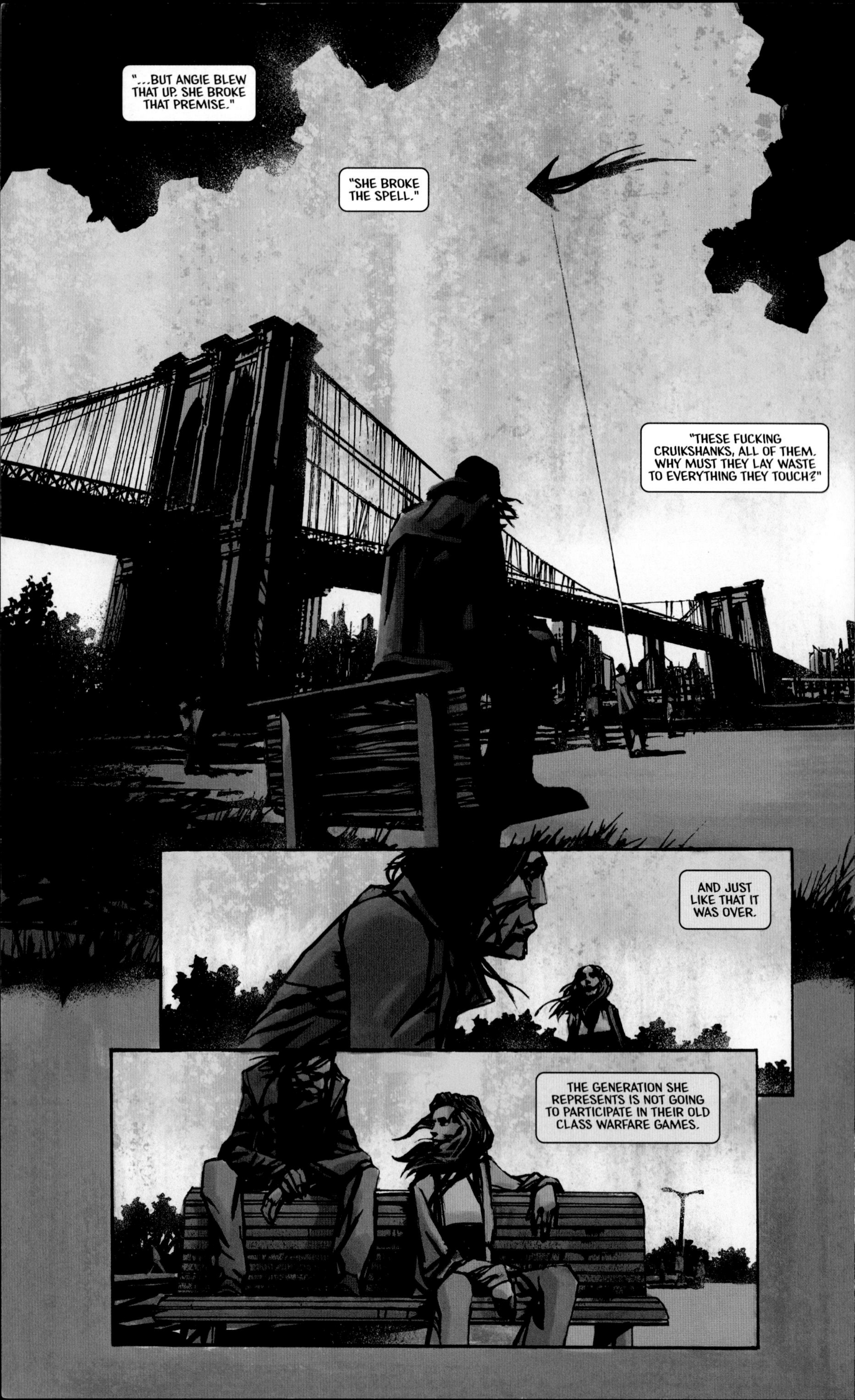
"...BUT ANGIE BLEW THAT UP. SHE BROKE THAT PREMISE."
"SHE BROKE THE SPELL."
"THESE FUCKING CRUIKSHANKS, ALL OF THEM. WHY MUST THEY LAY WASTE TO EVERYTHING THEY TOUCH?"
AND JUST LIKE THAT IT WAS OVER.
THE GENERATION SHE REPRESENTS IS NOT GOING TO PARTICIPATE IN THEIR OLD CLASS WARFARE GAMES.

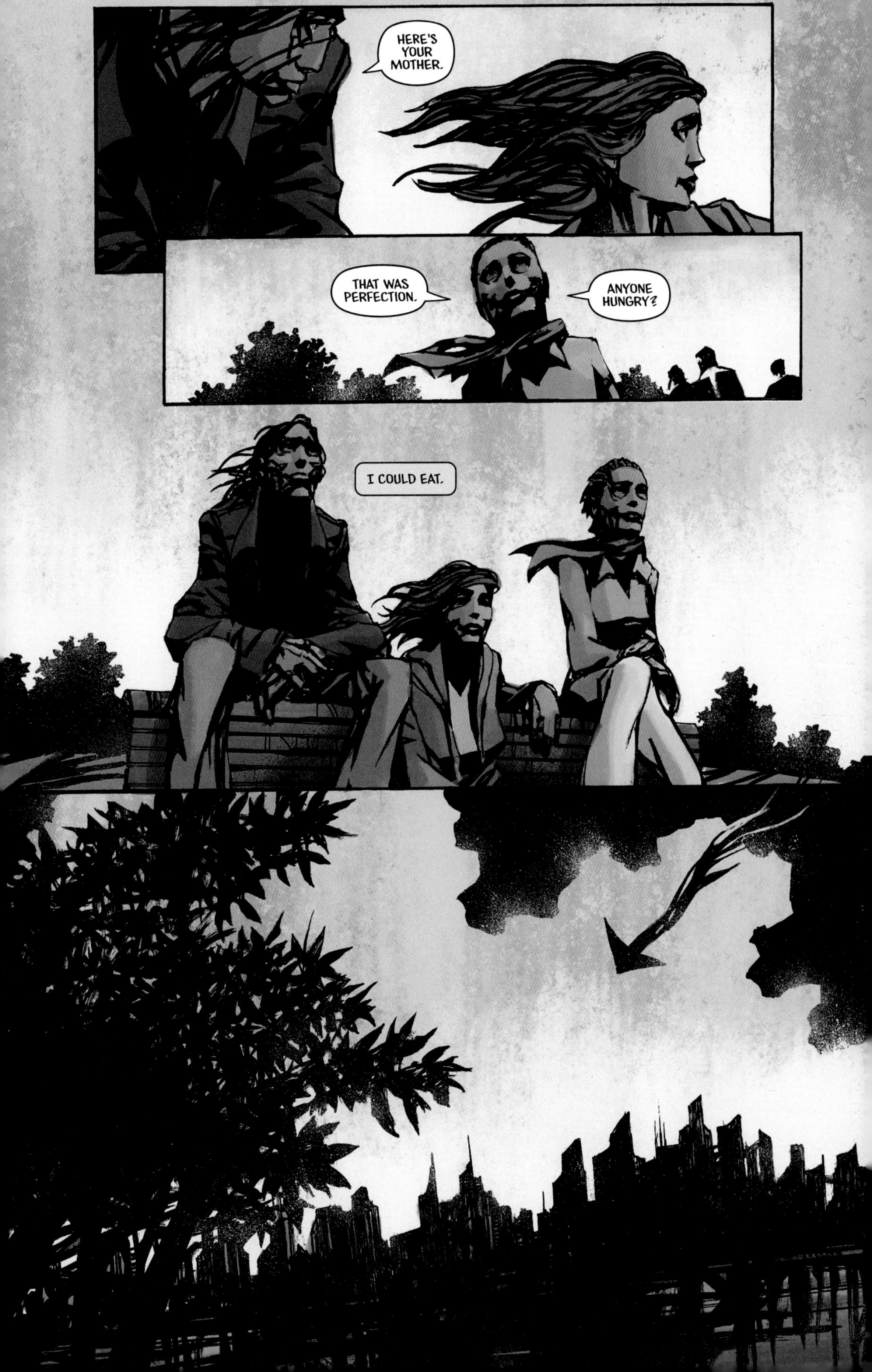
HERE'S YOUR MOTHER.
THAT WAS PERFECTION.
ANYONE HUNGRY?
I COULD EAT.

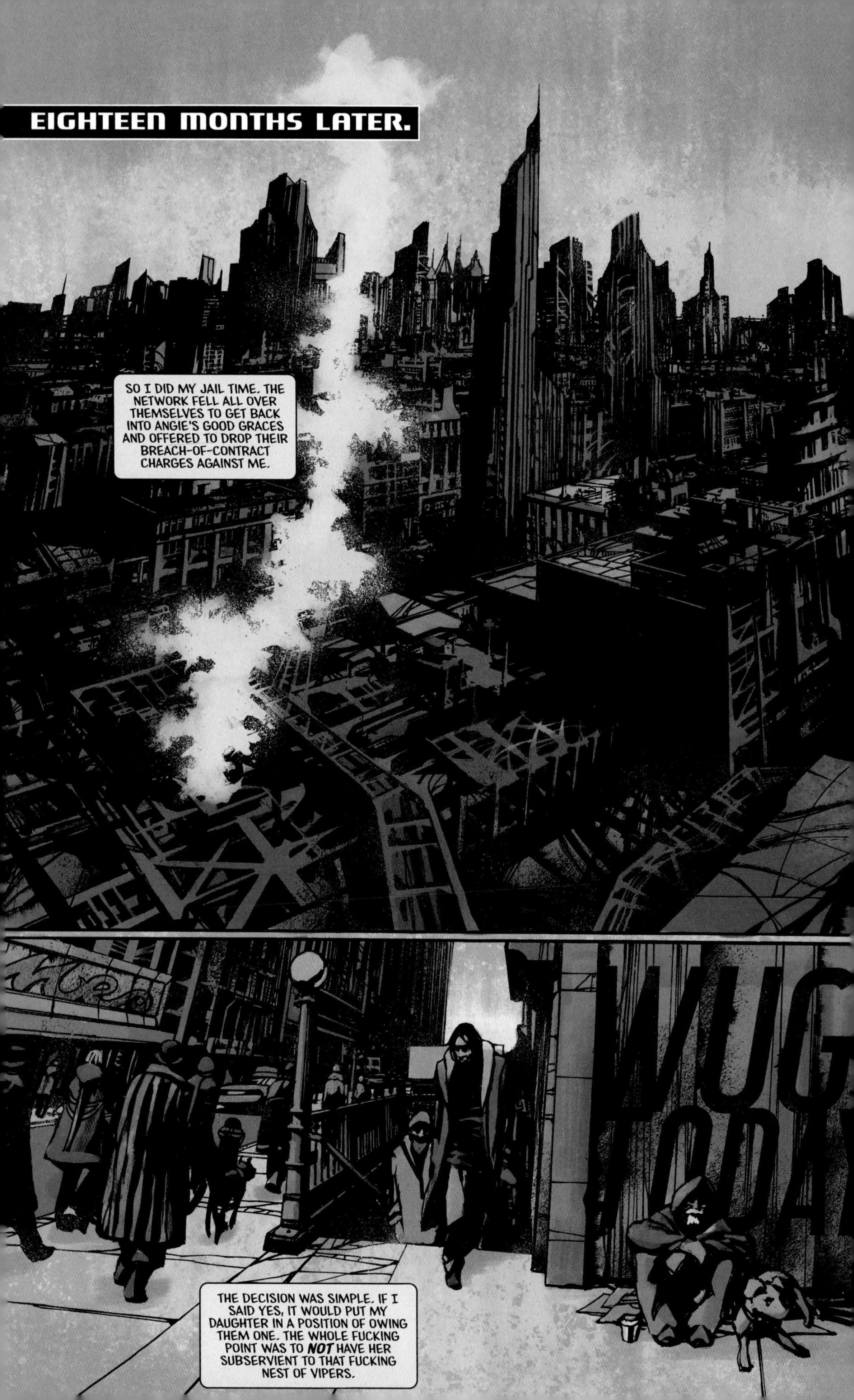
EIGHTEEN MONTHS LATER.
SO I DID MY JAIL TIME. THE NETWORK FELL ALL OVER THEMSELVES TO GET BACK INTO ANGIE'S GOOD GRACES AND OFFERED TO DROP THEIR BREACH-OF-CONTRACT CHARGES AGAINST ME.
THE DECISION WAS SIMPLE. IF I SAID YES, IT WOULD PUT MY DAUGHTER IN A POSITION OF OWING THEM ONE. THE WHOLE FUCKING POINT WAS TO NOT HAVE HER SUBSERVIENT TO THAT FUCKING NEST OF VIPERS.

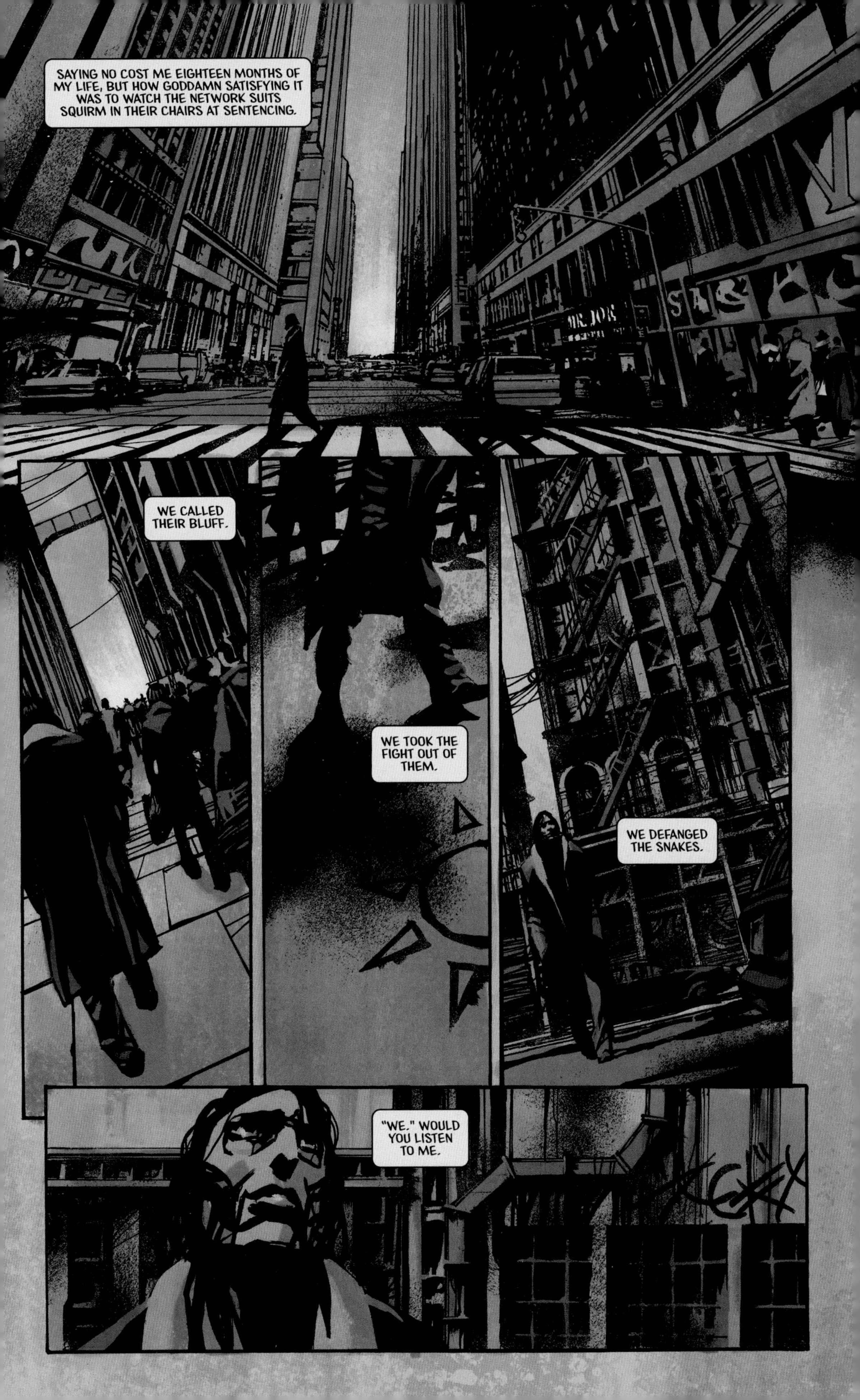
SAYING NO COST ME EIGHTEEN MONTHS OF MY LIFE, BUT HOW GODDAMN SATISFYING IT WAS TO WATCH THE NETWORK SUITS SQUIRM IN THEIR CHAIRS AT SENTENCING.
WE CALLED THEIR BLUFF.
WE TOOK THE FIGHT OUT OF THEM.
WE DEFANGED THE SNAKES.
"WE." WOULD YOU LISTEN TO ME.

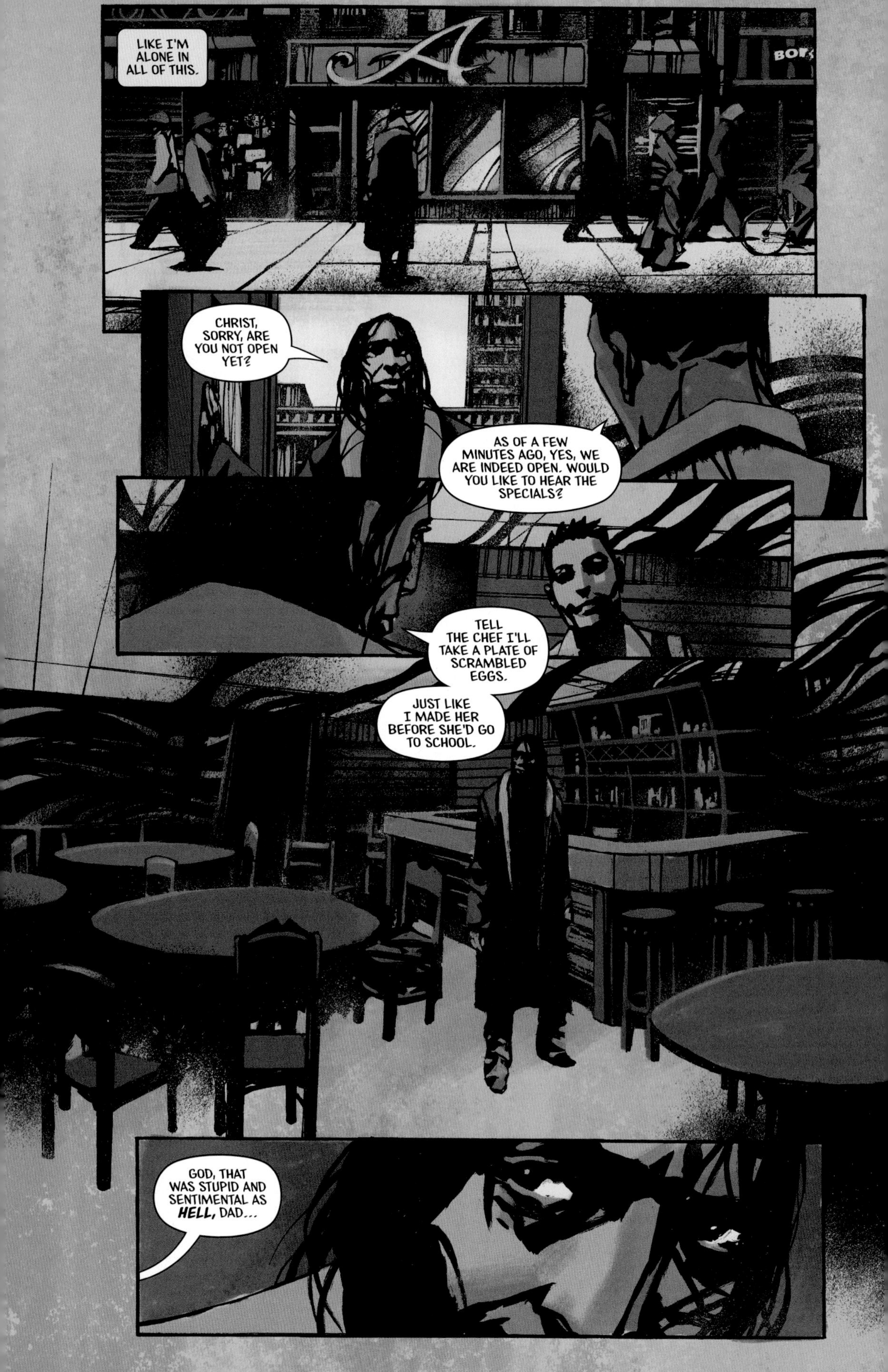
LIKE I'M ALONE IN ALL OF THIS.
BOR
CHRIST, SORRY, ARE YOU NOT OPEN YET?
AS OF A FEW MINUTES AGO, YES, WE ARE INDEED OPEN. WOULD YOU LIKE TO HEAR THE SPECIALS?
TELL THE CHEF I'LL TAKE A PLATE OF SCRAMBLED EGGS.
JUST LIKE I MADE HER BEFORE SHE'D GO TO SCHOOL.
GOD, THAT WAS STUPID AND SENTIMENTAL AS **HELL,** DAD...

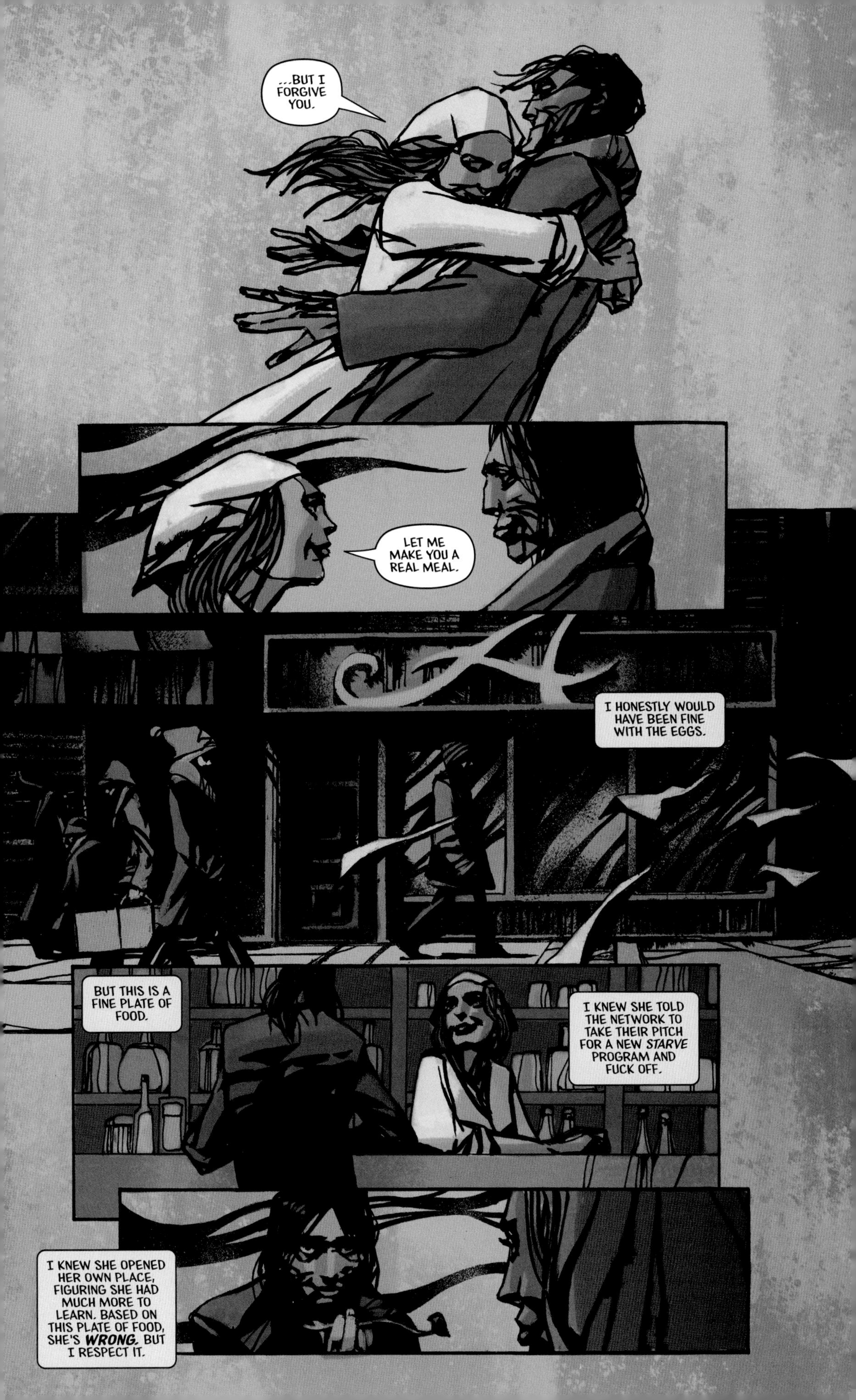

...BUT I FORGIVE YOU.
LET ME MAKE YOU A REAL MEAL.
I HONESTLY WOULD HAVE BEEN FINE WITH THE EGGS.
BUT THIS IS A FINE PLATE OF FOOD.
I KNEW SHE TOLD THE NETWORK TO TAKE THEIR PITCH FOR A NEW *STARVE* PROGRAM AND FUCK OFF.
I KNEW SHE OPENED HER OWN PLACE, FIGURING SHE HAD MUCH MORE TO LEARN. BASED ON THIS PLATE OF FOOD, SHE'S ***WRONG.*** BUT I RESPECT IT.

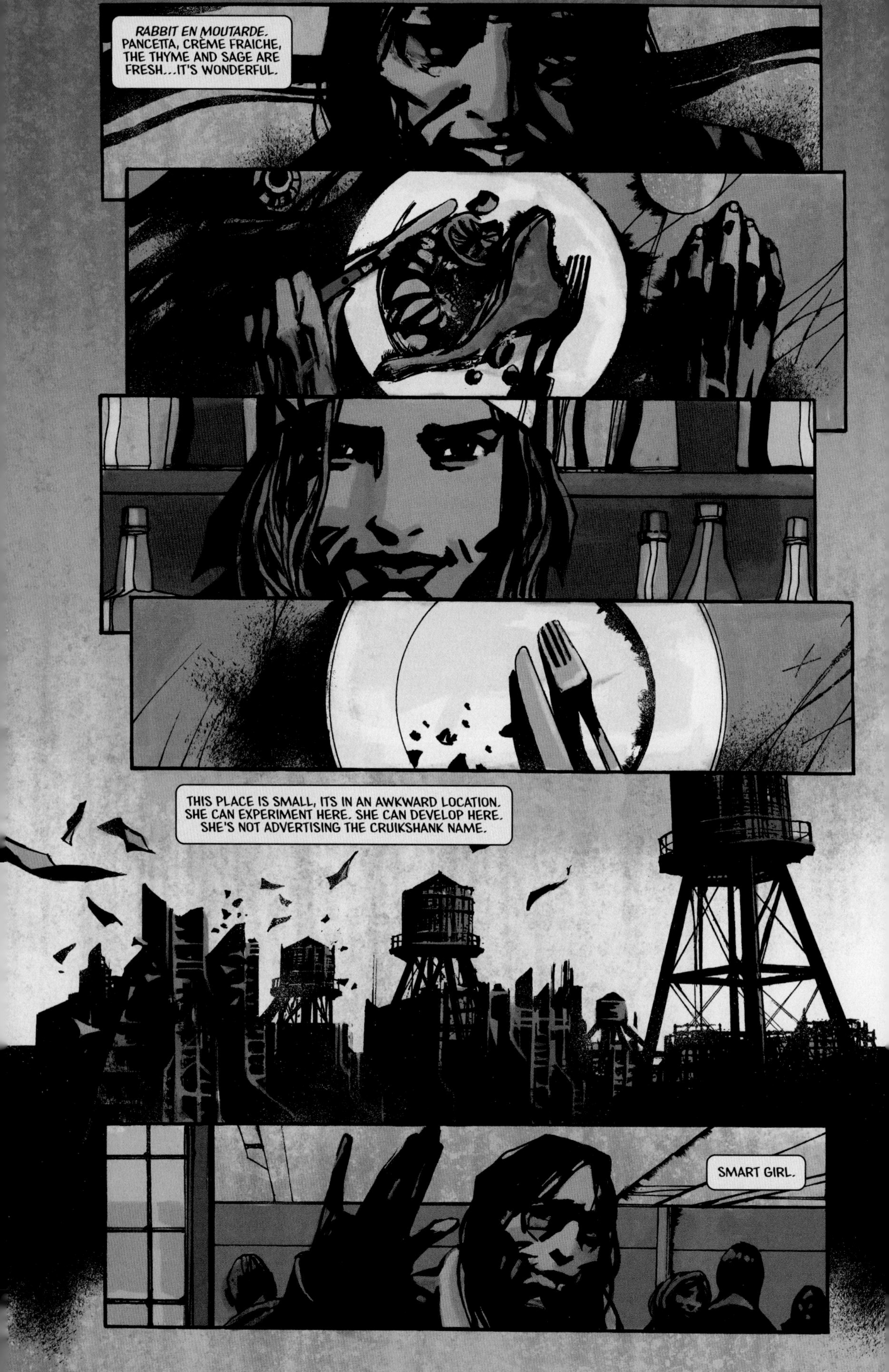
RABBIT EN MOUTARDE. PANCETTA, CRÈME FRAICHE, THE THYME AND SAGE ARE FRESH...IT'S WONDERFUL.
THIS PLACE IS SMALL, ITS IN AN AWKWARD LOCATION. SHE CAN EXPERIMENT HERE. SHE CAN DEVELOP HERE. SHE'S NOT ADVERTISING THE CRUIKSHANK NAME.
SMART GIRL.

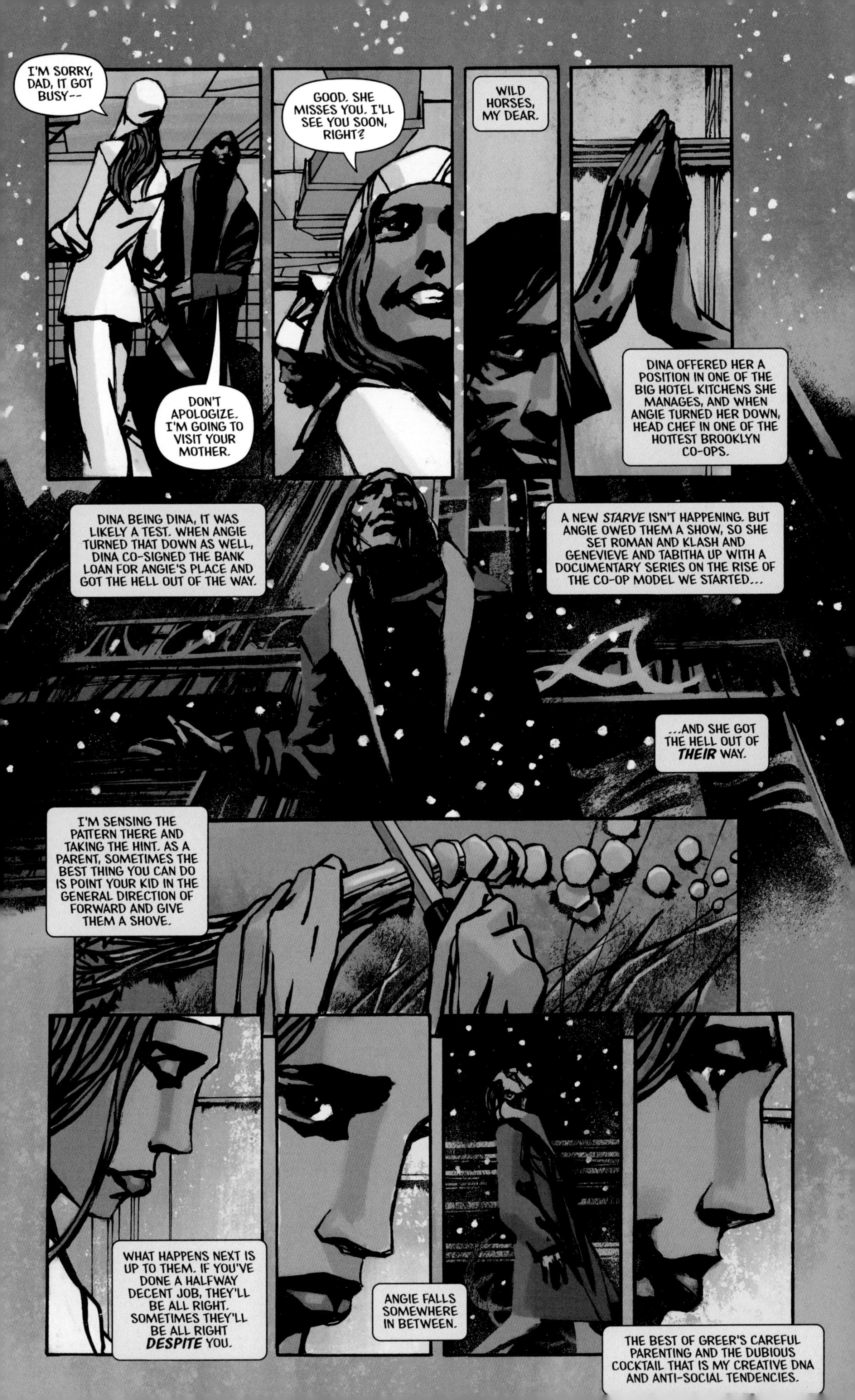
I'M SORRY, DAD, IT GOT BUSY--
DON'T APOLOGIZE. I'M GOING TO VISIT YOUR MOTHER.
GOOD. SHE MISSES YOU. I'LL SEE YOU SOON, RIGHT?
WILD HORSES, MY DEAR.
DINA OFFERED HER A POSITION IN ONE OF THE BIG HOTEL KITCHENS SHE MANAGES, AND WHEN ANGIE TURNED HER DOWN, HEAD CHEF IN ONE OF THE HOTTEST BROOKLYN CO-OPS.
DINA BEING DINA, IT WAS LIKELY A TEST. WHEN ANGIE TURNED THAT DOWN AS WELL, DINA CO-SIGNED THE BANK LOAN FOR ANGIE'S PLACE AND GOT THE HELL OUT OF THE WAY.
A NEW *STARVE* ISN'T HAPPENING. BUT ANGIE OWED THEM A SHOW, SO SHE SET ROMAN AND KLASH AND GENEVIEVE AND TABITHA UP WITH A DOCUMENTARY SERIES ON THE RISE OF THE CO-OP MODEL WE STARTED...
...AND SHE GOT THE HELL OUT OF ***THEIR*** WAY.
I'M SENSING THE PATTERN THERE AND TAKING THE HINT. AS A PARENT, SOMETIMES THE BEST THING YOU CAN DO IS POINT YOUR KID IN THE GENERAL DIRECTION OF FORWARD AND GIVE THEM A SHOVE.
WHAT HAPPENS NEXT IS UP TO THEM. IF YOU'VE DONE A HALFWAY DECENT JOB, THEY'LL BE ALL RIGHT. SOMETIMES THEY'LL BE ALL RIGHT ***DESPITE*** YOU.
ANGIE FALLS SOMEWHERE IN BETWEEN.
THE BEST OF GREER'S CAREFUL PARENTING AND THE DUBIOUS COCKTAIL THAT IS MY CREATIVE DNA AND ANTI-SOCIAL TENDENCIES.

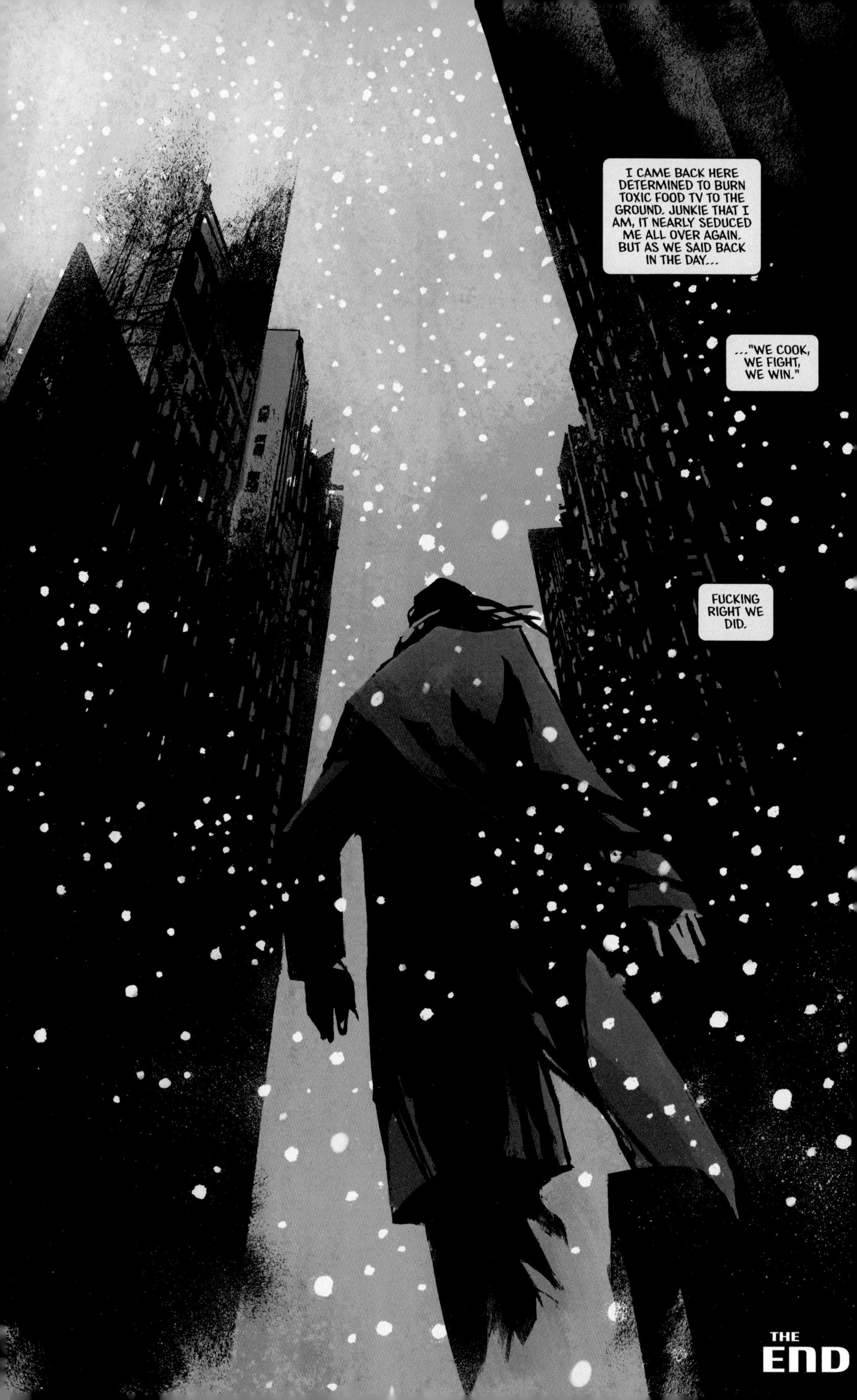
I CAME BACK HERE DETERMINED TO BURN TOXIC FOOD TV TO THE GROUND. JUNKIE THAT I AM, IT NEARLY SEDUCED ME ALL OVER AGAIN. BUT AS WE SAID BACK IN THE DAY...
..."WE COOK, WE FIGHT, WE WIN."
FUCKING RIGHT WE DID.
THE END

COVER GALLERY

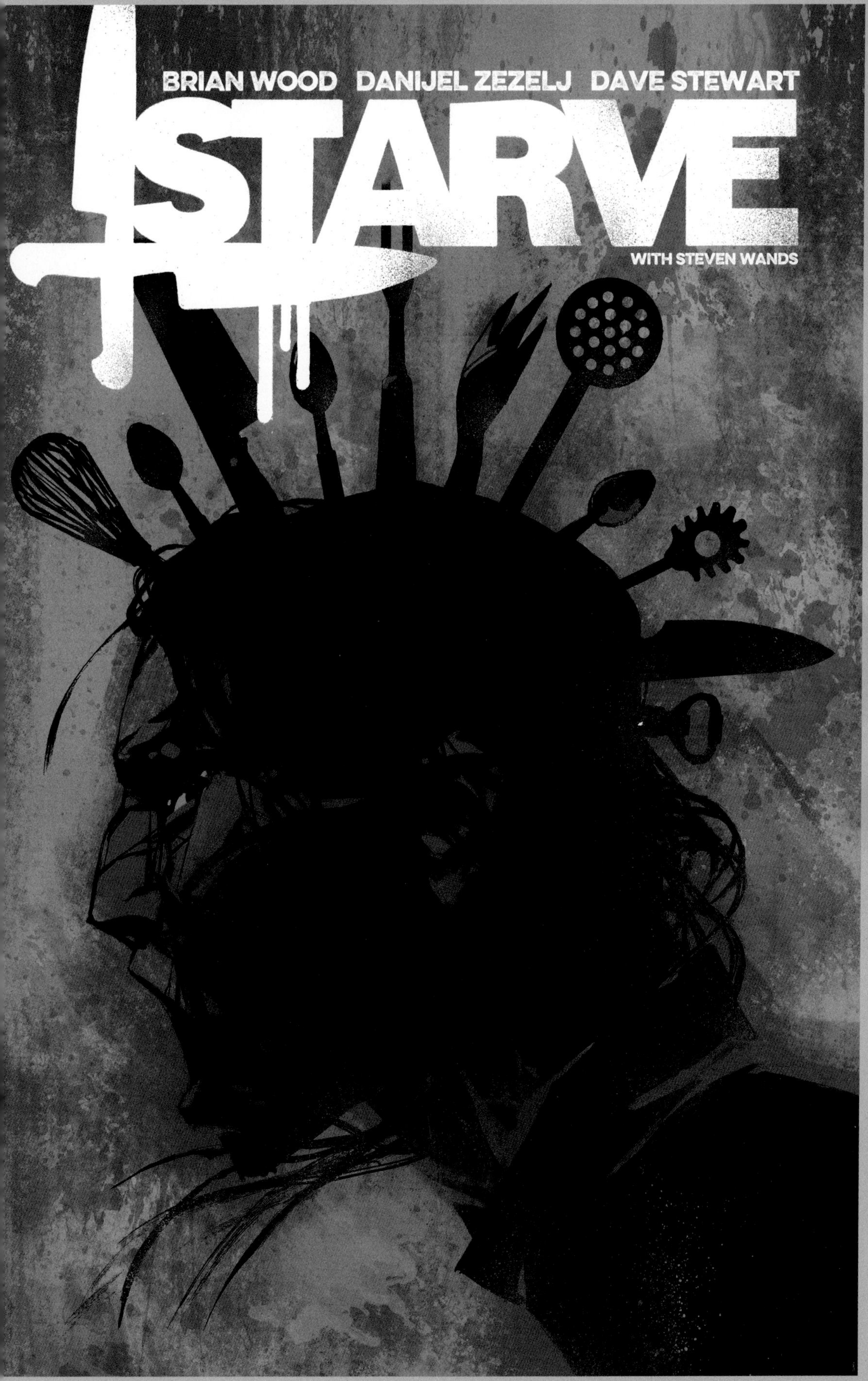
BRIAN WOOD DANIJEL ZEZELJ DAVE STEWART
STARVE
WITH STEVEN WANDS

ISSUE #6

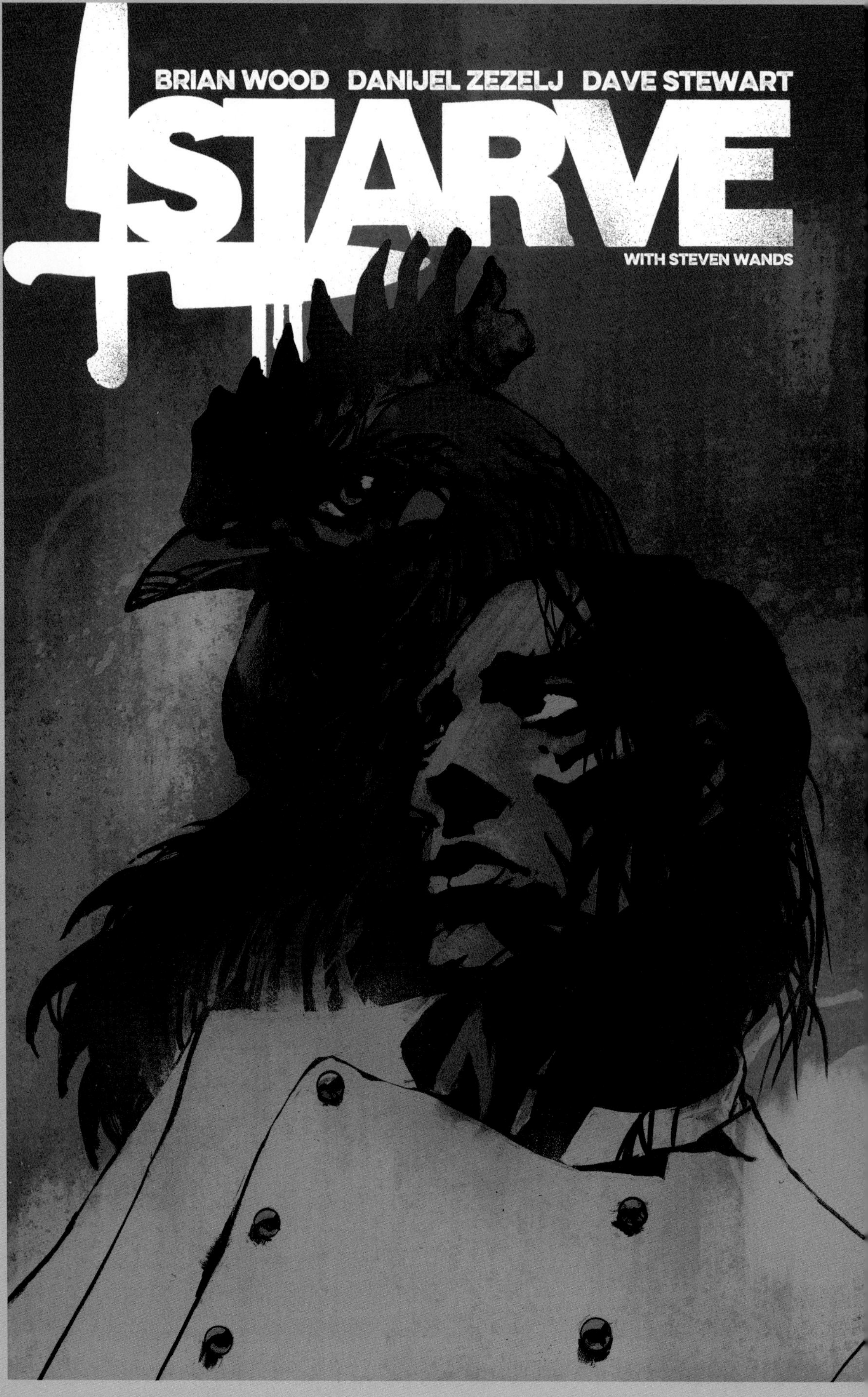
BRIAN WOOD DANIJEL ZEZELJ DAVE STEWART
STARVE
WITH STEVEN WANDS

ISSUE #

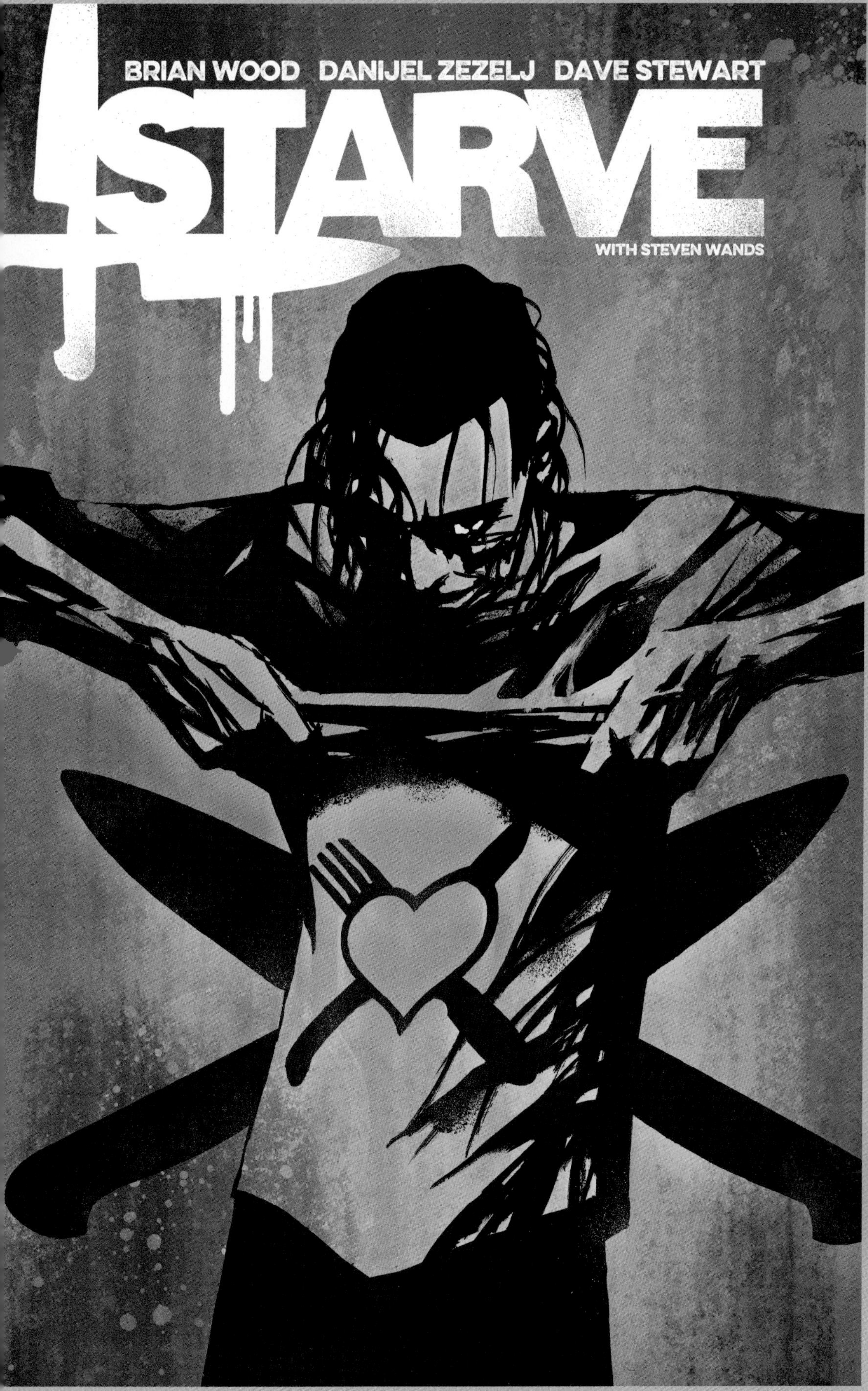
BRIAN WOOD DANIJEL ZEZELJ DAVE STEWART
STARVE
WITH STEVEN WANDS

ISSUE #8

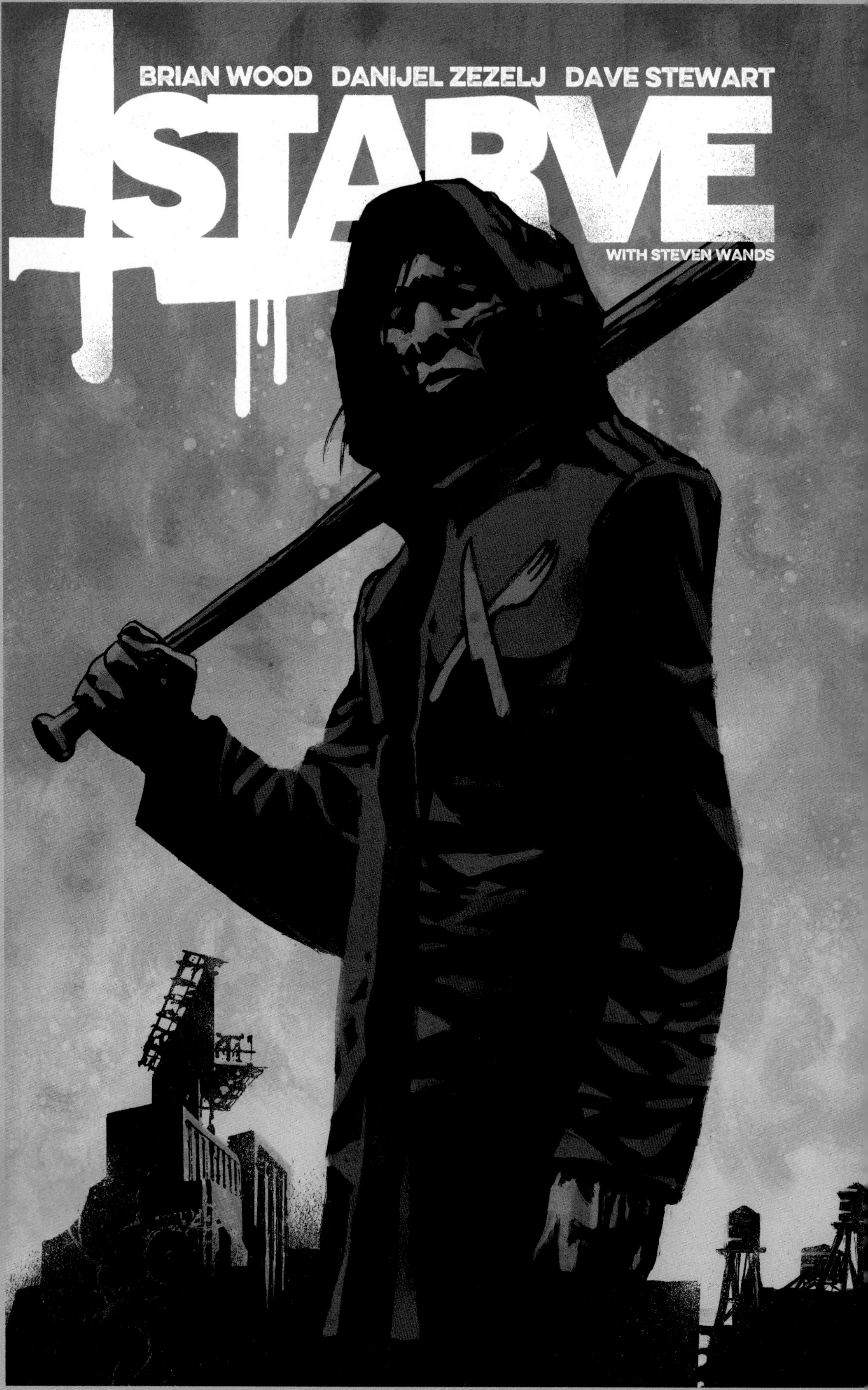

BRIAN WOOD DANIJEL ZEZELJ DAVE STEWART
STARVE
WITH STEVEN WANDS

ISSUE #

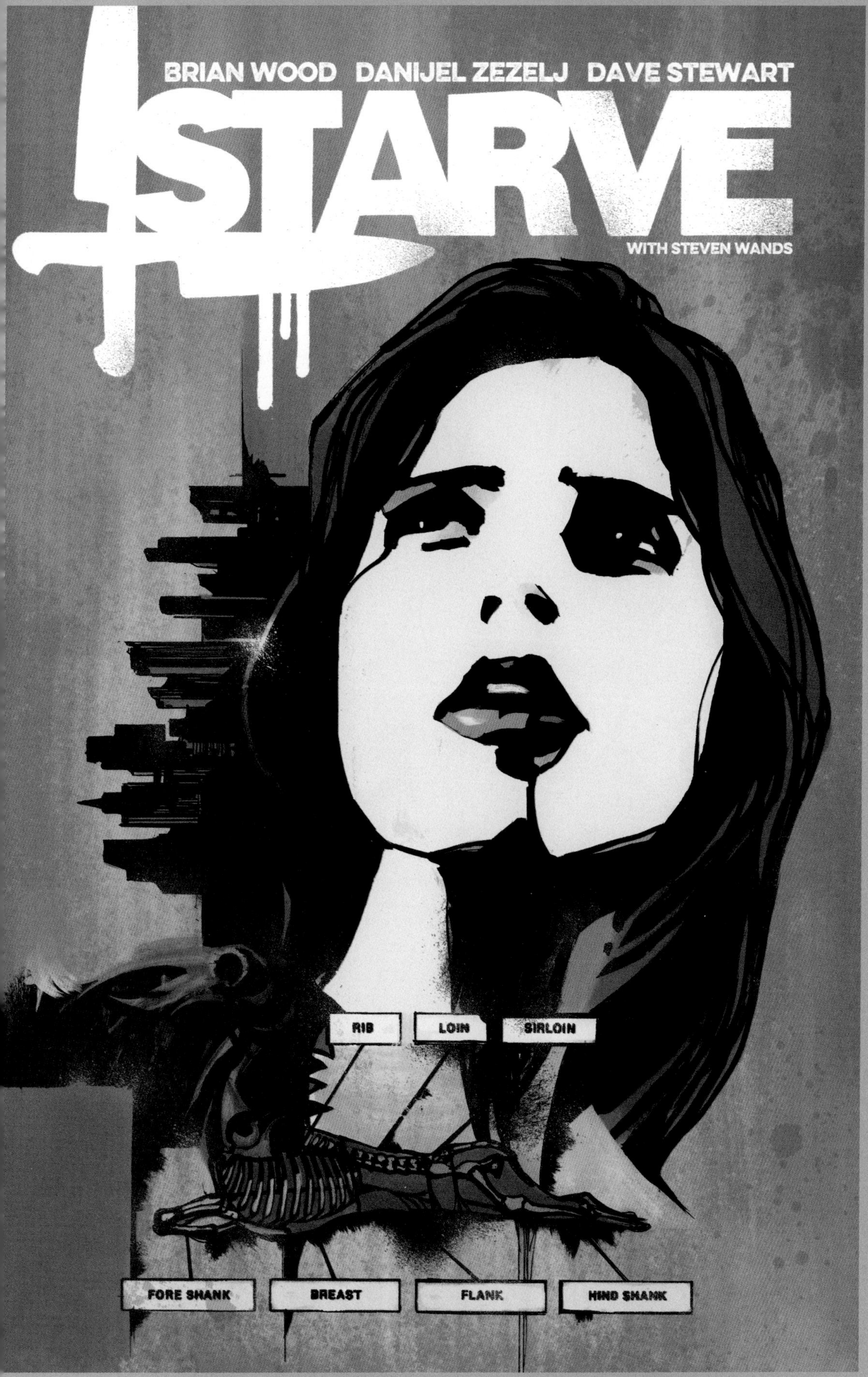
BRIAN WOOD DANIJEL ZEZELJ DAVE STEWART
STARVE
WITH STEVEN WANDS
RIB
LOIN
SIRLOIN
FORE SHANK
BREAST
FLANK
HIND SHANK

ISSUE #10

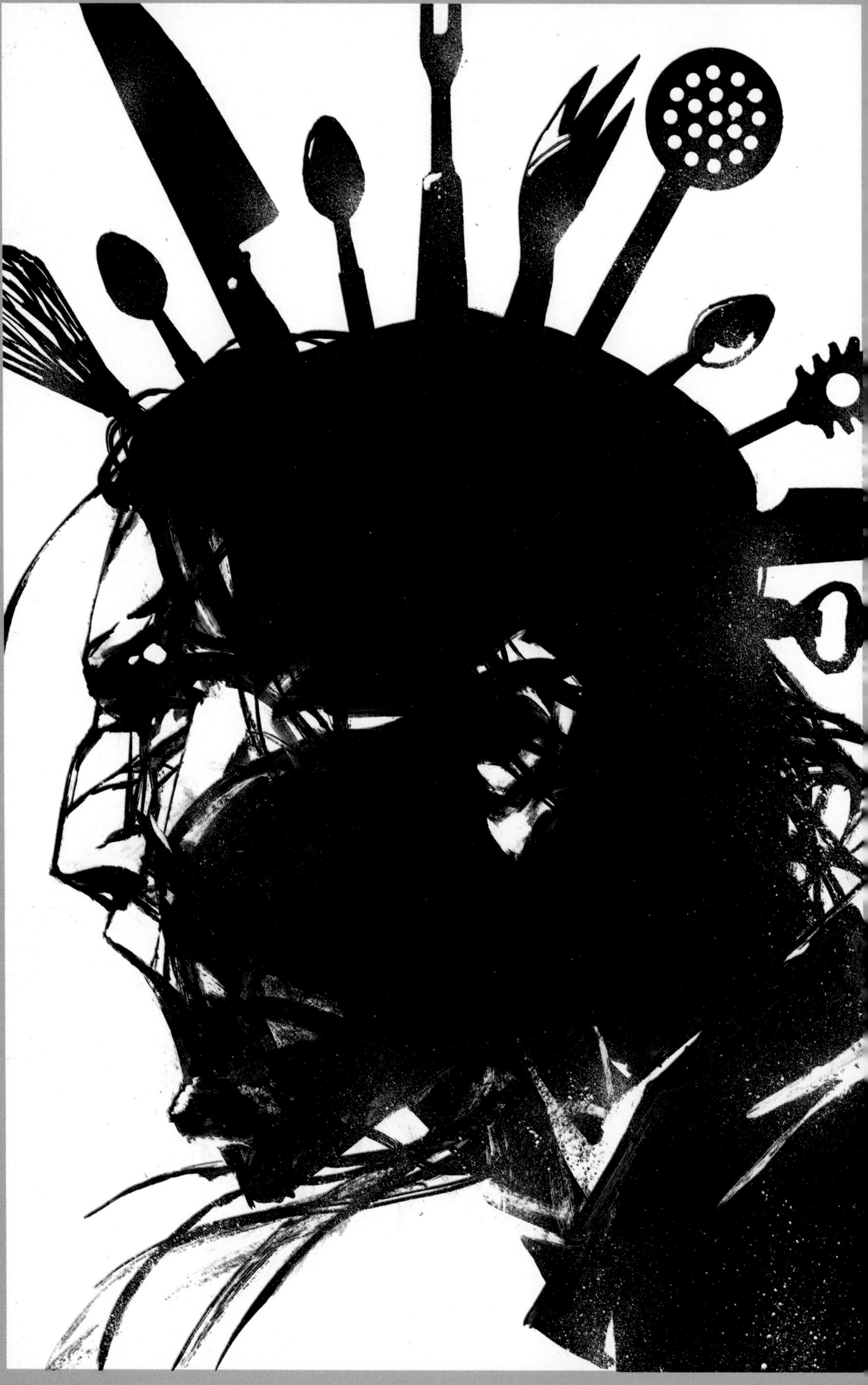

ISSUE #1 ORIGINAL PAINTED ART

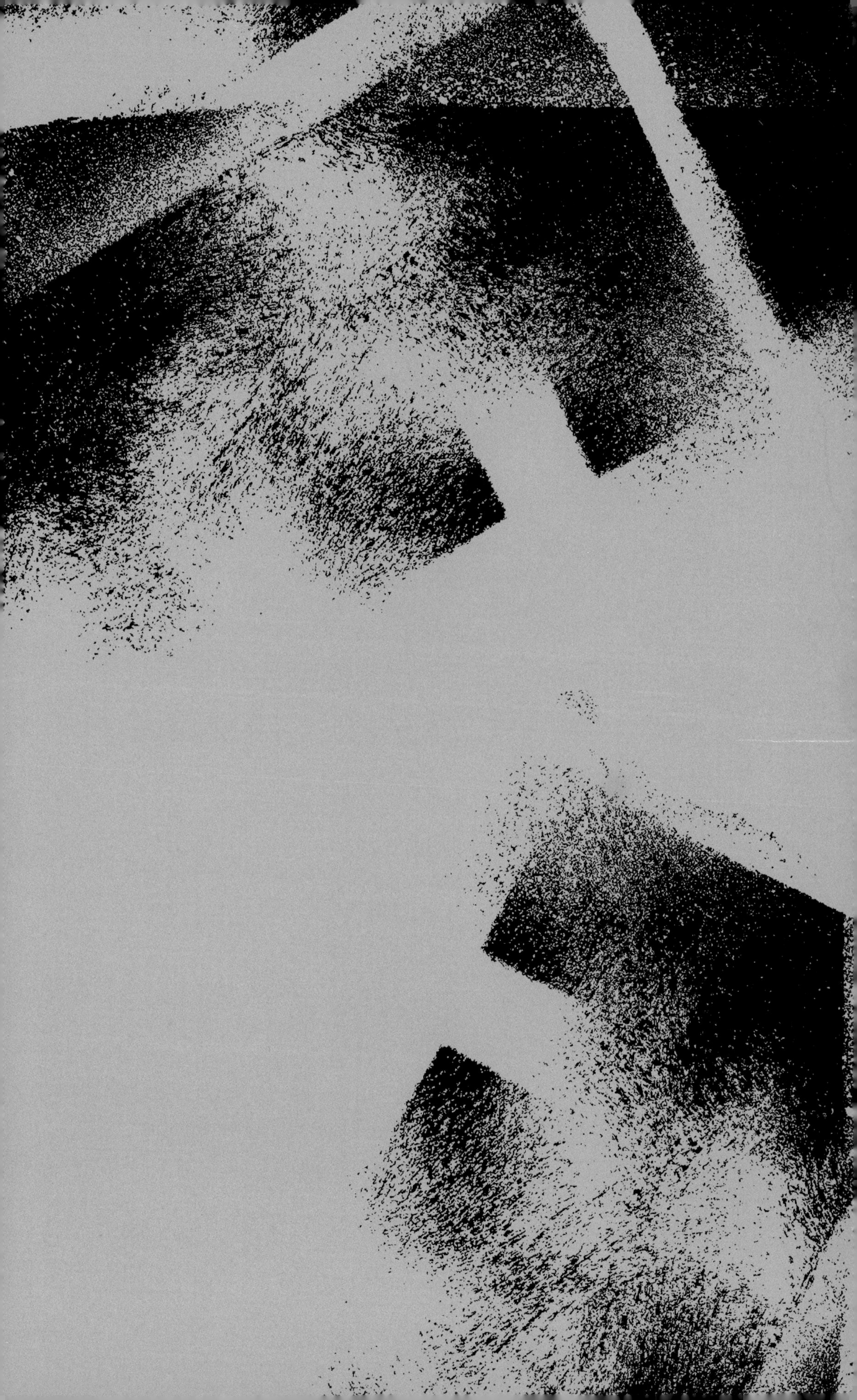

STARVE

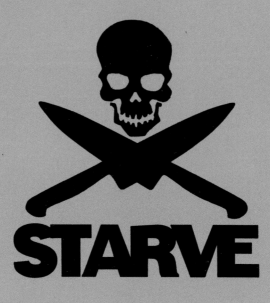